Henry James and the Art of Dress

Also by Clair Hughes

A LONG WAY TO GO: A Pictorial and Literary Collage of 19th Century Women

ENGLISH PORTRAITS

THE ENGLISH FAMILY PORTRAIT

Henry James and the Art of Dress

Clair Hughes
Professor of English and American Literature
International Christian University
Tokyo
Japan

palgrave

First published 2001 by
PALGRAVE
Houndmills, Basingstoke, Hampshire RG21 6XS and
175 Fifth Avenue, New York, N.Y. 10010
Companies and representatives throughout the world

PALGRAVE is the new global academic imprint of
St. Martin's Press LLC Scholarly and Reference Division and
Palgrave Publishers Ltd (formerly Macmillan Press Ltd).

ISBN 0–333–91430–9

This book is printed on paper suitable for recycling and made from fully managed and sustained forest sources.

A catalogue record for this book is available from the British Library.

Library of Congress Cataloging-in-Publication Data
Hughes, Clair, 1941–
    Henry James and the art of dress / Clair Hughes.
        p. cm.
    Includes bibliographical references and index.
    ISBN 0–333–91430–9
        1. James, Henry, 1843–1916—Knowledge—Clothing and dress. 2.
    Costume in literature. 3. Women in literature. I. Title.
    PS2117.C58 H84 2000
    813'.4—dc21
                                                              00–055709

10   9   8   7   6   5   4   3   2   1
10   09 08 07 06 05 04 03 02 01

Printed and bound in Great Britain by
Antony Rowe Ltd, Chippenham, Wiltshire

For George

Contents

List of Plates

The plates and line illustrations are not intended to illustrate James's texts but to serve as background references to dress of the period. James himself only allowed unpeopled photographs as accompaniments to his texts and I have tried as far as possible to honour the spirit of his preference by choosing black and white contemporary photographs as my main illustrations. The photographs are not necessarily tied to a single text, but can operate across several. This is particularly true of the chapters dealing with *The Wings of the Dove*, *The Ambassadors* and *The Golden Bowl*.

List of Figures

Acknowledgements

This study has been many years in the conception and making, and I have incurred many debts on the way. Dr Anita Brookner and the late Michael Kitson were initial and enduring influences. I am grateful to the International Christian University, Tokyo, for the six months' research leave which enabled me to lay the foundations of my study. Professor Joseph Wiesenfarth of the University of Wisconsin, Madison, gave me early and helpful encouragement. Correspondence with Adeline Tintner and many years of letters from Judith Funston provided kindly support from fellow Jamesians.

I wish to acknowledge the central importance to this study of C. Willett Cunnington's unsurpassed work on nineteenth-century dress. Both Anne Hollander's theoretical and interdisciplinary work on the history of dress and Aileen Ribeiro's rigorously historical approach have provided role models.

Robin Hamlyn and Richard Ormond generously answered art historical queries, and The Fashion Research Centre, Bath, was helpful and efficient about providing photographs, and my colleague Professor Richard Wilson helped with technical questions over the line illustrations. But above all I wish to acknowledge how much I owe to George Hughes without whose selfless and unfailing encouragement, guidance and belief in my project, nothing would have happened.

Portions of Chapter 4 first appeared in the *Henry James Review* 18 (1997); a version of Chapter 5 in *Corresponding Powers*, ed. George Hughes (Cambridge: Boydell and Brewer, 1997); a version of Chapter 9 in the *Australasian Victorian Studies Journal*, 3 (1998). All are reproduced here by kind permission of the publishers.

1
Costume and James

On the subject of dress, Elizabeth Bowen says, almost no one is truly indifferent; as topics 'love, food, politics, art or money are all very much safer'. Love, art and money are central themes in the work of Henry James and have naturally received much critical attention. Food (despite his own habits of frequent dining-out) and politics, seeem not greatly to have interested James as a novelist. But what of dress? If this apparently frivolous but dangerous topic inspires, as Bowen says, so much 'subterranean interest and complex feeling',[1] we might expect him to be aware of the latent power and subterranean complexities of dress in his exploration of the passions. Can we, then, develop a reading of James on the basis of such an awareness, and suggest that dress performs important functions in his fictional world? It is the argument of this book to suggest we can.

In a recent, posthumously published study of *The Ambassadors*, Dorothea Krook complains that James's treatment of dress in his fiction generally is 'masculine in its vagueness and paucity'[2] – a sexist enough comment. Krook, however, does at least bring up the question of dress, unlike most literary critics. Michael Irwin gave a general chapter to the topic in his study of the role of description in the nineteenth-century novel, but we have happily come a little further than remarks about historical dress in fiction that characterise it as 'pretty, picturesque, quaint'.[3] Kimberley Reynolds and Nicola Humble, for example, in their 1993 study of Victorian heroines, have a brief but perceptive chapter on dress codes in relation to Victorian attitudes to gender and class relations.[4] Dress historians, in contrast, have been more perceptive because more focused on the topic, and Anne Hollander in her influential study of clothes and art, *Seeing Through Clothes*, draws particular attention to James's deployment of dress in his fiction. Not, as she admits, that James makes more than the occasional reference to dress, but his reticent consideration of clothing may come from his own 'very deep acknowledgement of the power of clothing, of its much greater importance than that of other inanimate objects'.[5] It is not surprising that James's fiction should demonstrate the power of clothes: Honoré de Balzac, James's acknowledged master, declared dress to be 'the most powerful of symbols': the French Revolution, for example, was, he believed, as much 'a question of fashion, a debate between silk and cloth',[6] as it was a question of politics. Franco Moretti, commenting on the central role of dress in Balzac's *Lost Illusions*, writes that 'if one wants to see in capitalism an immense and fascinating narrative system, there is no better way to observe it than from the viewpoint of fashion'.[7] On the other hand, if, as the modern French historian, Philippe Perrot, suggests 'nothing appears less serious than a pair of underpants or more laughable than a necktie or sock'[8] – and we must agree that James was nothing if not serious – then there might be some difficulty in arguing that James considered dress a significant aspect of his art.

Dress is, of course, only one of the many possible approaches to the rich complexity of James's work. It is not the point of this book to argue that it excludes others. There has long been a recognition of James's special and educated interest in the visual arts; in photography and the early cinema as well as in more traditional areas of painting and sculpture. Viola Hopkins Winner, Adeline Tintner, Charles Anderson and David Lubin have written of James's work in relation to the figurative arts, Jean-Christophe Agnew has placed these concerns within late nineteenth-century consumerism, Jonathan Freedman against the background of aestheticism and Peter Rawlings has described the 'Kodak' factor in James. An essay by Martha Banta makes an elegant analogy between 'the aesthetic of absent things practiced by [the designers] Madame Paquin, Paul Poiret and Elsie de Woolf'[9] in the early 1900s and the exclusions and refinements that shaped James's revisions of his novels for the New York edition; but apart from some brief remarks by Adeline Tintner and Lyall Powers, dress has not figured much in Jamesian criticism. Given James's acute visual sensibility, there is no reason to believe that he was unmindful of the quotidian but none the less significant art of dress. In our contemporary visual climate, it seems time to give substantial attention to the topic. It is by no means insignificant that James has gained a new and wider audience through recent film and television versions of his work, and that costume design (as the newspaper reviews widely indicate) plays an important part in the current enjoyment of films of *The Portrait of a Lady* and *The Wings of the Dove*.

One of the important points of this book is to draw on the material evidence of contemporary dress to try to approximate the clothes James was likely to have in mind. I am not content with the vague images of the generalized modern memory-bank, and I aim to place costume in a clearly stated cultural and historical context. Noting the references to dress in a literary text, and relating them to sources, is however a more slippery business than, for example, tracing allusions to paintings or places. Dress is almost subliminally woven into the fabric of our lives and images of its appearance in a text may surface from other texts, from the visual or representational arts, from daily life, history or memory. The textualisation of dress is not simply a matter of description, and at best one can only speculate intelligently. The final imprecision of such cultural history does not, however, impede my project, since my chief concern is to use a reading of costume to illuminate Jamesian texts. The reading opens up the texts, and, in my contention, the texts justify the reading.

Dress was, in fact, in James's own life, the occasion of an early 'terrible experience'; an experience which, as he recalled in later years, he could never forget, 'for in that moment I experienced my first sense of disillusionment'.[10] It was a matter of a quantity of brass buttons on the jacket of the seven-year old James which attracted the attention of William Thackeray, on a visit to the James family. Thackeray laughed, James remembered, and remarked 'that in England, were I to go there, I should be addressed as Buttons. It had been revealed to me in a flash that we were somehow *queer*.'[11] The significance of personal appearance, to others, to one's sense of self and even to one's nationhood, is acutely felt and recorded. The consciousness of looking, in all innocence, somehow all *wrong* was to surface in his fiction: comically, as with Mitchy's clown-like appearance in *The Awkward Age*; embarrassingly and sadly in Catherine Sloper's overdone red dress of *Washington Square*; Milly Theale's costume in *The Wings of the Dove* is so badly wrong as to be a question of life and death. There is, of course, in James's recollection of the jacket incident, also an amused, self-deprecatory note, as though acknowledging some comic disproportion between the painfulness of the memory and the triviality of its cause. But that embarrassing jacket wove itself into the narrative of James's own life, re-emerging in his *Notes of a Son and Brother* to convey the disquiet of his 'small uneasy mind, bulging and tightening in the wrong . . . places, like a little jacket ill cut or ill sewn'.[12] No one, as Bowen says, feels truly indifferent about dress.

Dress, it must be admitted, rarely qualifies for serious attention for its own sake. Too great an interest in the shifting ephemera of fashion suggests to most of us a trivial turn of mind, and fashion's urgent imperatives towards novelty and hedonistic consumerism can inspire anything from unease to the moral outrage of the Old Testament prophet, Isaiah, threatening the daughters of Zion with scabs, sackcloth, baldness and burning for their indulgence in a long and splendid list of 'tinkling ornaments'.[13] But, as Aileen Ribeiro has pointed out, it is 'the only art that relates so closely to the narrative of our lives, both as individuals and in relation to the wider world; for clothing is simultaneously personal (a reflection of our self-image), and as fashion, it is in the words of Louis XIV, "the mirror of history"'.[14]

It was in the context of James's art and theatre journalism – dress as a 'mirror of history' – that I first noticed his particularly pointed and informed references to dress. Reconsidering James's fictive world in the light of this observation, it seems to me that while James's use of dress-imagery is always economical (in the context of the realist novel), it has an increasing part to play in the thematic and symbolic patterning and development of his fiction: a development that shifts from the pictorial to a more compressed and dramatic symbolism. As a 'commodified symbol'[15] – to use Jean-Christophe Agnew's term – dress is certainly polyvalent. On the whole, the function of dress in James's fiction is weighted towards symbolism rather than realism, but dress references also place characters in a precise social and historical framework to an extent that would have been obvious to early readers, but is now easily underestimated. It is this double pattern I hope to trace in the course of what follows. As James's deployment of dress not only develops across his work but also operates in distinct ways in each novel or tale, I propose to address the topic in terms appropriate to each text: these terms may be symbolist, sociological, historical, semiotic, feminist, theatrical or painterly. It should be possible, therefore, to take the argument of each chapter independently, though linked to others by the thread of James's developing narrative technique.

I begin by looking at manners, morals and extravagance in dress, in the European/American contexts of some of James's early fiction, particularly *Daisy Miller*, 'The Pension Beaurepas' and *Washington Square*. The two subsequent chapters, on *The Portrait of a Lady* and *The Wings of the Dove*, while shedding some new light on the international theme in James, are linked by their focus on the black and white dresses of their central characters and the way in which these apparently simple contrasts shift and are coloured by changing meanings. Hats punctuate the narrative of the next novel to be considered, *The Princess Casamassima* – appropriately, when one considers its themes of class-mobility, conspiracy and disguise. As three of the novel's characters are involved in the fashion business, the text contains more dress references than any other of James's novels. *The Princess Casamassima* is, in fact, something of an anomaly among the works of James's middle years where dress-references actually decrease. Although *The Spoils of Poynton* (1896), for example, focuses on a struggle over objects of material beauty it is oddly lacking in dress references – apart from Mona Brigstock's boots, which trample all over those objects. Fred Kaplan's biography of James notes that in the last three completed novels, James returns to his interest in the international theme, transforming it 'from the satirical comedy of misperception into a drama of the search for self-knowledge';[16] and, interestingly, references to dress increase concurrently. Dorothea Krook, who, as we have seen, complains of the paucity of dress references in James's work, exempts *The Ambassadors* on the basis of the careful realisation in dress of the figure of Marie de Vionnet. My chapter on this novel focuses on Strether's 'process of vision' which, like Winterbourne's mystification over Daisy, registers the ambivalence of Madame de Vionnet's image, an image finally defined by a *lack* of clothing. The two final chapters deal first with *The Golden Bowl*, and then with a selection of James's ghost stories. In the first of these, Maggie Verver has first to uncover the meanings under appearances and then, with the power that knowledge confers, change what lies below and restore appearances, undisturbed, to maintain her 'necessary lie'. Finally and unnervingly it is with James's ghosts that we arrive at the most material of his representations of dress.These images of ghostly dress are bound up with the disturbance and usurpation by the ghost of the identity of the narrator or the 'reflecting consciousness' – a conclusion that illustrates the way attention to dress illuminates James's narrative method and development.

* * *

Before considering the function of costume in Jamesian texts, it is as well to note the biographical contexts that support such a reading. In the narrative of James's own life, the bad 'Buttons' experience is relived in the autobiographical *A Small Boy and Others*; one of the volume's many childhood memories evoked in terms of dress. One of these – of the ancient Mrs L. in a headdress 'consisting in equally striking parts of a brown wig, a plume of some sort waving over it and a band or fillet' – is conveyed from a small child's viewpoint: 'I see its wearer at this day bend that burdened brow upon me in a manner sufficiently awful, while her knuckly white gloves toyed with a large fan and a vinaigrette attached to her thumb by a chain.'[17] James records here only those details that would meet the child's eye, or loom into his field of vision. Dress is always going to be described in a novel by naming certain things or effects, and by leaving out many other details: written descriptions are not full pictures. James's ability to re-enter the child's viewpoint demonstrates his focus on detail, and the way in which he makes detail functional. It is a technique that, for instance, shapes the narrative of *What Maisie Knew*, when Maisie feels herself being caught up and smashed against the glitter of her mother's over-garnished bosom, as though against a plate-glass window. We sense in both the memory and this fictional echo the undertow of a child's alarm at the unpredictability of adults and the mystery of their outward aspects.

Reflecting on the relation between his writing and his personal life, James wrote that '[w]e seize our property by an avid instinct wherever we find it.' It was some years after the 'button' incident when the now adolescent James experienced 'an hour that has never ceased to recur to me all my life as crucial, as supremely determinant'.[18] After some heady summer days in Paris, the family set off by coach for Switzerland across the Jura mountains. James was suffering from malarial fever at the time (obviously the elder Jameses operated on rather loose principles of child care), and so they paused for a rest at a village inn, where the street opened out onto a view of a ruined castle among the mountains:

> At a point in the interval, at any rate below the slope on which this memento stood, was a woman in a black bodice, a white shirt and a red petticoat, engaged in some field labour, the effect of whose inter-vention just then is almost beyond my notation.... She had in the whole aspect an enormous value, emphasising with her petticoat's tonic strength the truth that sank in as I lay – the truth of one's embracing there, in all the presented character of the scene, an amount of character I had felt no scene present.... Supremely, in that ecstatic vision, was 'Europe', sublime synthesis, expressed and guaranteed to me – as if by a mystic gage.... It made a bridge over to more things than I then knew.[19]

The 'property' James seized upon contains both aesthetic and symbolic implications for his future work. With precocious insight he has grasped the landscape pictorially, recognising in the petticoat a sharp colour-note crucial to the composition; he has also perceived that this black, red and white figure – just 'a sordid old woman scraping a mean living'[20]

– carried a dramatic symbolism, a mythic quality for the story-teller, of infinite potential. Looking ahead almost fifty years to James's favourite novel, *The Ambassadors*, we might see such an epiphanic moment re-enacted in the movement of the narrative from Lambert Strether's intoxication with Paris, to the instant when the pink colour note of a parasol in a landscape completes a picture for him; but which, when he recognises the parasol's owner, suddenly reassembles itself into a dramatic tableau portentous with meaning.

Dress plays a significant part in James's reminiscences of his early life, but we might wonder whether James's own personal appearance was memorable to others. Portraits show him carefully, if conventionally, dressed. (There is an early photograph of him in the embarrassing jacket.) There are hints that he may even have occasionally been over-dressed, giving C. C. H. Millar the impression, in 1890, of having just come from a particularly smart wedding. Some ten years later Edith Wharton remembers him as only spasmodically fastidious about his dress, James having by then become rather portly. Catching him in what must have been one of his unfastidious moments, Henry Sidgwick, around the same date, recalls 'a figure of vaudeville ... tight check trousers, waistcoat of a violent pattern, coat with short tails ... none matching; cravat in a magnificent flowery bow',[21] an outfit matched by that worn by Mitchy in *The Awkward Age* of 1900: 'There was comedy ... in the form of his pot-hat and the colour of his spotted shirt, in the systematic disagreement, above all, of his coat, waistcoat and trousers'[22] – a likeness which can only have been coincidental, unless James was blessed with a preternatural sense of the personally ridiculous. But perhaps he always had a sartorially subversive side, since, on a hot day in 1889, Joseph Pennell caught James, at work on an article, sitting in the garden in red underwear.[23]

In the recollections of his contemporaries, James's hats figure largely and often eccentrically. H. G. Wells remembered a range of hats in the hall of Lamb House lined up to meet all social contingencies. These were not proof against every embarrassment, however. A. C. Benson, on a childhood visit, recalled James coming down into the street to say good-bye in a black velvet smoking-jacket with red trimmings and reaching for a tall white hat: then, suddenly aware of the oddity of his appear-ance, hurriedly retreating into the porch. This was probably simple absent-mindedness, but Hugh Walpole's late Jamesian adventure of the 'High Hat' suggests that hats came to have a quite arcane Beckettian significance for James. After searching his rooms at the Reform Club, he produced for Walpole 'an extraordinary hat': something between a top hat and a bowler, it was glossy with a curly brim and a red silk lining. It was too small for him, James explained, but was meant for 'a wise and elegant head, had in it every kind of suggestion of glory and promise and summer weather and success, was miserable and ashamed by its long imprisonment in the wardrobe... was gifted no doubt with some especial power of conveying brilliance to the head that it crowned... there was no hat like it and I – I alone – must wear it!'[24] Although the hat was manifestly unfashionable, Walpole was unable to refuse and had to proceed down Pall Mall, watched benevolently by James until, turning the corner, he flung himself into a cab. But he kept the hat, seeing it in later years as marking an important though enigmatic moment in their relationship.

Hats and James also surface in the narrative of Edith Wharton's autobiographical *A Backward Glance*. Having failed to attract his attention with a carefully chosen pink Doucet frock at her first meeting, in the 1880s, Wharton had a second opportunity to catch James's eye, a year or two later, with 'a new hat: *a beautiful new hat*!... But he noticed neither the hat nor the wearer.' There is just a hint of revenge in her anecdote of many years later, when, on one of their motor tours of France together, James has a sudden urgent need for a hat in Poitiers: 'almost insuperable difficulties attended its selection'. James seems to have become entangled in one of his late-style sentences with the shopkeeper, until Wharton rescued him with a joke in French, and a hat was found and bought, 'to the rich accompaniment of chuckles'.[25] Hats punctuate the entire range of James's fiction – they almost deserve a book to themselves – but cluster most significantly in *The Princess Casamassima*.

*   *   *

Dress was important to James, and it is, within the restrictions of his technique, important in both his fictional and critical *oeuvre*. Art, theatre and book reviewing constituted, from first to last, a minor but vital part of his work, and, as might be expected, it is here that we find his most directly expressed views on the topic. These writings also form an important context to an informed reading of the novels. In 1897, for example, he rounds off an enthusiastic article on two art exhibitions with the moral, whose levity, he says, we may find surprising: 'simply the glory of costume, the gospel of clothes.... If you are to be represented, if you are to be perpetuated, in short it is nothing that you be great or good, – it is everything that you be dressed.'[26] There is an element of jesting exaggeration here, and if he felt dress to be important in the representational arts, he also saw that pedantic over-attention to it could diminish and trivialise. His views on the use and misuse of costume in painting and the theatre are indicative of how he himself saw dress functioning in his fictional world and how best its sign-systems could be employed without falling into traps of over-determination.

James's defence of the novel as an autonomous form rests, according to Viola Hopkins Winner, 'on the resemblances he notes between it and painting.'[27] As James's narrative technique was a continuing process of development and experiment, so also he remained open to and interested in developments in art throughout his life. While he was never wholly in sympathy with French Impressionism, his preferences moved in that direction away from what he saw as the banal narrative realism of the work of James Tissot, Winslow Homer or the French artist, J. L. Meissonier. Of a painting by Meissonier he wrote in 1876 that the best thing in it was a certain cuirassier, 'and in the cuirassier the best thing is his clothes, and in his clothes the best thing is his leather straps, and in his leather straps the best thing is the buckles'. The spectator, James says, 'resents the attempt to interest him so closely in costume and type, and he privately clamours for an idea.'[28]

James, one can see, has an acute sensitivity to surface appearances, but the recordings of those appearances, whether in words or paint, were not, for James, to be ends in themselves, they were to be seen as instruments towards the revelation of moral meaning. 'Imitation,' he wrote of Velásquez's portraits, 'is not the limit of his power...his men and women have a style which belongs to his conception of them quite as much as their real appearance';[29] in other words, the clamour for 'an idea' is met. Towards the end of the century he developed an appreciation of the elliptical style of his compatriot J. M. Whistler, but reserved his greatest enthusiasm for the work of John Singer Sargent, writing admiringly of 'the quality in the light of which the artist sees deep into his subject, undergoes it, absorbs it, discovers in it new things that were not on the surface'. This quality is embodied for James in the portrait of the four Boit children: 'it is a scene, a comprehensive impression; yet none the less do the little figures in their white pinafores (when was the pinafore ever painted with that power and made so poetic?) detach themselves and live with a personal life.' It gave, he said, the sense 'of assimilated secrets and of instinct and knowledge playing together'.[30] Anne Hollander rightly sees in James's verbal allusions to dress a parallel to Sargent's pictorial ones: 'well-chosen and well-placed fitful gleams with a very precise personal flavor, thrown up against a more generally suggestive background.'[31]

James's lively contempt for the leaden pedantry of archaeologically correct costume, expressed in his criticism of Meissonier, similarly informs his critical attacks on Henry Irving's productions at London's Lyceum Theatre. The 1882 production of *Romeo and Juliet*, he complained, 'is not acted, it is costumed; the immortal lovers of Verona become subordinate and ineffectual figures.' Costume has been substituted for content and imagination: 'the more it is painted and dressed... the less it corresponds with our imaginative habits.'[32] James always found the French theatre more enlivening than the London one, and it was at a performance of a comedy by Octave Feuillet in Paris in 1877 that he identified a costume 'moment' whose suggestiveness illuminated the rest of the piece for him, and perhaps provided an early version of the 'dramatic analogy' for his fiction. He was charmed by the dress of an old lady – 'the Comédie Française was in every fold of it' – but it was the bonnet, which 'with its handsome, decent, virtuous bows was worth coming to see. It expressed all the rest.... Such matters are trifles, but they are representative trifles.'[33] James's focus here on theatrically significant headgear is fascinatingly reworked in the terms of a cinematic 'zoom' onto a hat in his story of 1909, 'Crapy Cornelia'. He finds a significance in these two images of hats that anticipates Roland Barthes' account of the semiotics of dress; he is focusing on and detailing a 'fragment' – the hat – because that described fragment carries more symbolic weight than the whole dress – it is exactly a 'representative trifle'.

One might summarise James's comments on costume in his autobiography, and in his reviews on art and the theatre, by saying that while he wanted to make plain the absurd and even damaging effects of burdening a work of art with redundant detail, he understood the powers of suggestion latent in dress signs, their ability to evoke powerful emotions, to permeate their immediate circumstances as well as to remain keenly in the memory. When we turn to James's early literary journalism we find such opinions already being caustically formulated in his review of the American novelist, Harriet Prescott, who, he wrote, treated her readers to gorgeous dolls, given to 'repeated posing, attitudinizing, and changing of costume'. Not, he went on to say, that such details invariably lacked importance – far from it. Balzac, in *Eugénie Grandet* – with whom James witheringly compares Miss Prescott – informs us exactly 'as to the young girl's stature, features and dress' and the information is both interesting and crucial. Why? 'It is because these things are all described *only in so far as they bear upon the action*, and not in the least for themselves. If you resolve to describe a thing, you cannot describe it too carefully. But as the soul of a novel is its action, you should only

describe those things which are accessory to action.'[34] With Miss Prescott James was perhaps breaking a butterfly on a wheel, but he could be
similarly devastating when dealing, in 1865, with the British and for-
midably popular Mary Braddon. Lady Audley, eponymous heroine of
Braddon's best-seller, is, of course, James declares, a nonentity – no
heart, no soul, no reason; but 'what we may call the small change for
these facts – her eyes, her hair, her mouth, her dresses, her bedroom
furniture...are so lavishly bestowed that she successfully maintains a
kind of half-illusion...[w]ith a telling subject and a knowing style she
[Braddon] proceeds to get up her photograph.'[35] It is as though Miss
Braddon has grasped the importance of naturalist attention to detail,
but has failed to see what the point of all this detail finally is. When
James later dismissed the contemporary English novel as '"padded" to
within an inch of its life,'[36] it was surely such luridly detailed descriptions he had in mind.

James took the critical hatchet to Miss Prescott and Mary Braddon
with youthful relish; but judicious admiration of one's immediate predecessor, on home ground, was perhaps a more demanding exercise.
James's pioneering study of Nathaniel Hawthorne was published in
1879, and he returned to the topic throughout his life with increasing
appreciation. Athough James, in the early essay, famously deplored the
lack of a background of castles, cottages and country gentry for
Hawthorne to draw upon, he nevertheless admired his ability, in *The
Scarlet Letter*, to convey the 'old Puritan consciousness of life'. Not,
however, James adds, because the story happens to be an historical
one, 'to be told of the early days of Massachusetts and of people in
steeple-crowned hats and sad-coloured garments. The historical colouring is rather weak than otherwise; there is little elaboration of detail, of
the modern realism of research.' What James finds and admires is the
moral presence of the New England Puritans 'in the very quality of his
own vision, in the tone of the picture.'[37] Hawthorne's introduction of
supernatural pyrotechnics to illuminate the symbolism of the embroidery of Hester Prynne's dress, at the climax of the novel, drew James's
strongest criticism in this early study; but interestingly, two years later
in his own novel, *The Portrait of a Lady*, we find an echo of that glittering
emblem of adultery in the silver ornament on Madame Merle's breast,
first recorded as a necklace and later, when exposure of her adulterous
past threatens, expanded into a silver corselet. In his later essays on
Hawthorne, in 1896 and 1904, James not only was no longer offended
by the scene in question, but actually declared that 'no page of Hawthorne's shows more intensity of imagination...the author has read the

romantic effect into the most usual and contemporary things.'[38] His changing views on Hawthorne's romanticism paralleled his own increasing preference for metaphor over metonymy, and his use of the creative tensions between dramatic symbolism and pictorial realism which was to be so much a part of his later style.

From James's critical journalism as a whole we might reasonably conclude that, in relation to the function of dress in the novel and the representational arts, he favoured an economical and discriminating treatment, preferring the symbolic and fragmentary to a realistic density of detail. This conclusion, however, collapses in the face of the 'all-devouring love of reality'[39] of James's greatest literary hero, Honoré de Balzac. James's writings on Balzac span nearly forty years and in the best of them, 'The Lesson of Balzac', James frankly acknowledges that he has learned more of the art of fiction from Balzac than from anyone else. In his earlier comments on Balzac, however, we find James repeatedly wrestling with, on the one hand, his conviction that photographic realism was aesthetically and intellectually trite, and on the other, his absolute admiration of Balzac's ability to make us conscious of 'the machinery of life, of its furniture and fittings, of all that, right and left, he causes to assail us, sometimes almost to suffocation, under the general rubric of *things*'. Baffled by the problem, he admits that '[t]hings, in this sense with him, are at once our delight and our despair'.[40] But by 1905, in 'The Lesson of Balzac', James has arrived at an understanding of Balzac's poetic realism that recalls his comments on Sargent's portraits: 'It is a question, you see, of *penetrating* into a subject... to handle, primarily, not a world of ideas, animated by figures representing these ideas; but the packed and constituted, the palpable, proveable world... by the study of which ideas would inevitably find themselves thrown up.'[41] In what was to be the final work published in his lifetime, *Notes on Novelists*, James develops this argument in his comments on Balzac's use of dress to embody the theme of money in *César Birotteau*:

> This prompt and earnest evocation of the shell and its lining is but another way of testifying with due emphasis to economic conditions. The most personal shell of all, the significant dress of the individual, whether man or woman, is subject to as sharp and as deep a notation. ... *César Birotteau*... besides being a money-drama of the closest texture, the very epic of retail bankruptcy, is at the same time the all-vividest exhibition of the habited and figured, the representatively stamped and countenanced, buttoned and buckled state of the persons moving through it.[42]

Habits, buttons and buckles thus retain their significant function to the end. James's narrative technique from *The Portrait of a Lady* onwards is, of course, increasingly occupied with 'placing the subject' in the consciousness of his characters; to this end we, and the characters, have to live within and experience the material, 'personal shell' of that character in a way that, we might say, prefigures Virginia Woolf's Clarissa Dalloway and suggests she is Isabel Archer's direct descendant. Dress is a significant part of that personal shell; such characters do not walk naked through the streets, and we find that James's dress references increase as he develops his *oeuvre*; as for example, in the revised version of *The Portrait of a Lady*. In the 1909 preface to *The Golden Bowl*, James looks back on his revisions in general for the New York edition, in the person of a nursemaid fussing over a brood of elderly infants, 'twitching' their 'superannuated garments', that might 'let one in, as the phrase is, for expensive renovations'. *The American*, in particular, he feels had suffered from prolonged exposure 'in a garment mis-fitted, a garment cheaply embroidered and unworthy of it'.[43] Not only the characters but the novels themselves need to be kept up to sartorial scratch, their habits, buttons and buckles kept in good order.

Dress and fashion are, of course, deeply imbued in modern society with problems of money, with consumption and economic exchange, but it is an important part of this book that, for James, they are never simply reducible to such terms. The language of dress always means more, has deeper social and textual meanings, often excessively confusing ones. James paradoxically achieves an effect that is both intensely symbolic – Hawthornean, in fact – and yet also socially and historically specific; very much the effect he describes Balzac achieving in *César Birotteau*. The essence of the power of the dressed image was that of imprinting itself on the consciousness, but of being an imprint that because of its very ordinariness and the rightness of its placing is often – and, indeed, at its best perhaps – unacknowledged and overlooked, particularly by readers bound up in plot. It has a subterranean and complex power.

2
Daisy Miller and 'The Pension Beaurepas'

Dress is by definition a surface show, a cover of nakedness, but James uses dress as a covert underlayer to the action – what Peter Brooks calls 'the moral occult'[1] – to suggest a wealth of meaning, beautiful as well as sinister, expressive as well as deceptive. From one of the earliest of his short stories, 'A Romance of Certain Old Clothes', where a set of haunted clothes avenges their dead owner, to the unfinished novel, *The Sense of the Past*, in which the mystery of the hero's unresolved fate may hang on the colour of a coat in a portrait, dress threads itself insidiously through James's *oeuvre*. Dress can be a sign of what we are, what we would like to be and even what we are not. The question of costume, Balzac writes in *Lost Illusions*, 'is one of enormous importance for those who wish to appear to have what they do not have, because that is often the best way of getting it later on'.[2]

To dress beyond one's means in order to achieve those means is an extravagant gamble. Balzac, in *Lost Illusions*, is referring, of course, to male dress and in particular to the refurbishment of Lucien Rubempré's wardrobe as an expression of his ambitions in Paris. Dress in modern society is always involved with economics. It represents economic power; it consumes money. It was particularly female extravagance in dress that fired the invective of the writers of nineteenth-century British and American advice manuals; an extravagance, that, being uncon- nected to any career plans, was unproductive consumption, mere world- liness and vanity, a sin against both housewifely thrift and maiden modesty. Thomas Carlyle's satire of 1834 on nineteenth-century materi- alism, *Sartor Resartus*, in which clothes not only *are* the man, but actu- ally replace him, provides an extreme but popular expression of such hostility. James's views were altogether more liberal and imaginative, but his use of dress in the early stories anticipates by some twenty years another satirist, Thorstein Veblen, who, in the guise of an economic thesis, argued that conspicuous consumption and conspicuous leisure had become the reputable forms in American society of the demonstration of pecuniary success. It was the responsibility of the American female, in particular, Veblen argued, to function as visual testimony to her male's financial standing; but at the same time, by virtue of her 'purity' (and her ignorance), she remained cut off from the sources and processes of money-making.

The critique of consumer capitalism as a form of entrapment for women has become something of a cliché. In starting my discussion in this book of two stories where consumption is certainly important, *Daisy Miller* and 'Pension Beaurepas', I hope to indicate how James goes beyond the simplicities of the usual accounts. In the first place he is responsive to the transatlantic dimension of nineteenth-century attacks on American consumerism: Charles Dickens, visiting America in 1842, exclaimed 'How the ladies dress, ... what rainbow silks and satins!'[3] Another English commentator of 1859 used the American example as a warning to Englishwomen: 'We used to point to America as the country in which excessive dress was a reproach: the rich silks, the black satin shoes, and the décollée evening dresses of the fair inhabitants of New York, even in Broadway, are themes of comment to us all.'[4] The American Mrs Louisa Tuthill, in her advice manual of 1848, *The Young Lady's Home*, bewails her countrywomen's 'passion for display. Are we falsely accused of it by foreigners, as the ruling passion?'[5] This 'passion' might well be seen as flying in the face of the tenets of American republicanism, but as Lois Banner points out in *American Beauty*, 'the growth of fashion consciousness was in keeping with the rampant individualism, materialism, and search for status and success that were as much a part of basic American values as the egalitarianism traditionally associated with the rise of 19th century democracy.' Women were as much a part of American 'Go-Aheadism' as men; 'they sought ways to carve out roles that would fulfil their own strivings and yet not violate cultural conventions about women's role. In their quest they expanded domesticity...and made the pursuit of fashion into a career.'[6] American women are not, therefore, simply passive in their consumption or display of wealth. Their role is complex and, in European eyes, often extremely confusing. James's *Daisy Miller* and 'Pension Beaurepas' are deeply involved in the confusions of this transatlantic discourse. *Daisy Miller* is, for many readers, the most attractive and representative portrayal of American innocence in James's *oeuvre*. 'Pension Beaurepas', a lesser known story, is more crudely critical of American women shopping their way across Europe. Both stories, however, shape much of their meaning through clothes, their choice or purchase. And both stories, as we shall see, rely on a play of narrative technique to add nuance to their descriptions. If excessive consumption is vulgar, so also, James suggests, is the snobbery that rushes to judge the taste of others.

*   *   *

Europe criticised Americans' use of their money, and the free-spending habits and modish extravagance of Daisy Miller and Sophy Ruck can thus be read as aspects of the international theme in James's early fiction. While the American male immersed himself in business, the American girl (often with her mother) roamed Europe, free in a way that no European woman was, but qualified to do only what she had been brought up to do – shop, and shop very often for clothes. 'An American woman who respects herself,' remarks Mrs Westgate in 'An International Episode', 'must buy something every day of her life. If she can't do it for herself she must send out some member of her family for the purpose.'[7] A reviewer in *Woman's World*, of 1889, comments on the extreme frivolity of the atmosphere of these tales, the 'aimless flittings' about Europe, the feeble mothers, apathetic and helpless in the face of their daughters' pursuit 'of a real good time'.[8] Daisy Miller, launched upon Europe with a poor excuse of a mother, and the target of most of this reviewer's comments, may be James's American 'heiress of all the ages', but her freedom, bounded by naivety and ignorance, is a chimera in the class-conscious and convention-bound expatriate American society in which she finds herself. Mrs Miller, who in Veblen's terms is the natural representative of Mr Miller's wealth, is, as Ian Bell points out, 'ill-equipped for such display, and the mantle falls on her daughter',[9] adding to the national icon of wealth, beauty, restless energy and freshness – but also, unfortunately, shockingly bad manners.

Dress is the conspicuous outward aspect of Daisy's moral code. Winterbourne, observing the exuberant comings and goings of the stylish American girls in the Swiss resort town of Vevey, is struck by Daisy's prettiness when he first sees her 'dressed in white muslin, with a hundred frills and flounces, and knots of pale coloured ribbon. She was bareheaded; but she balanced in her hand a large parasol with a deep border of embroidery.'[10] The similarity between the wording of this description of Daisy and that of James's review of James Tissot's painting of 1877, 'The Deck of the H.M.S. Calcutta', has already been noted by earlier commentators,[11] although it could be said that here Daisy's appearance more nearly resembles Tissot's portrait of Miss Lloyd of 1876, which features the same dress as the later work, with the addition of a parasol balanced in the model's hand. The dress in question actually belonged to Tissot and figured several times in his work of the late 1870s. James, whilst admiring Tissot's skill in rendering high fashion with 'perception and taste', in fact clearly disliked 'The Deck of the H.M.S. Calcutta', finding its realism 'vulgar and banal', its sentiment 'sterile and disagreeable' and was convinced that a longer acquaintance with the lady's 'stylish back and yellow ribbons' would be 'intolerably wearisome'.[12] Why, then, did he choose to reproduce such an image in this early scene in *Daisy Miller* and indeed return to it, when he later describes Winterbourne's eye as lingering on Daisy's 'stylish' rear-view: 'as she moved away, drawing her muslin furbelows over the gravel, [he] said to himself that she had the *tournure* of a princess' (29)? We might wonder whether the reader's delight in Daisy, mediated by Winterbourne, has been a mistake all this long while. A similar view of Sophy Ruck's costume in 'The Pension Beaurepas' affords the narrator little pleasure.

James called Tissot's picture hard and trivial, though he quickly added that this was not because the clothes were in the current fashion; what he discerns is the hard finish that denied any imaginative response and which so closely rivalled a fashion-plate that its figures become mannequins, drained of potential life. It is tempting to suggest that James wanted to show what could be done with such material in more talented hands. He was aware of clothes as economic markers, but in *Daisy Miller* he wants to foreground Daisy's innate taste and grace, rather than her father's wealth. When she dresses for her expedition to Chillon with Winterbourne she appears 'in the perfection of a soberly elegant travelling costume' (53): any vulgarity here is Winterbourne's in that the costume excites him to thoughts of elopement with her.

Daisy's dress is not *all* extravagance. Moreover, the description of the earlier Tissot-like dress shows James drawing attention to the ribbons and flounces rather than to a clearly identifiable fashion garment. It is the witholding of such readily recognisable information that can mislead a recent commentator on Bogdanovich's film of the novel, for example, into declaring that 'James gives virtually no information about costume'.[13] James reveals what Anne Hollander describes as a traditional novelistic preoccupation with extraneous detail in costume, taking the basic garment as 'read', but using 'ribbons, ruffles, patterns – unfocused finery to convey the notion of frivolity',[14] The reviewer in *Woman's World*, though deploring much about Daisy, is finally seduced by that Tissot back-view: 'It is with a pang that we see the pretty girlish figure, decked out in its dainty furbelows and laces, walk down into the grim Valley of the Shadow.'[15] Daisy has indeed a succession of lavishly decorated frocks, the by-product of her father's capital, amassed in Schenectady, but James makes it clear that if Daisy's dresses are frivolous, they are not vulgar. Mrs Costello, Winterbourne's aunt and arbiter of Vevey society, declares that Daisy 'dresses in perfection – no, you don't know how well she dresses. I can't think where they get their taste' (31). It is here in the conjunction between taste and money that the problem lies.

The mantle that falls on Daisy from her mother, we might say, is an excessively frivolous object. Her frivolity, together with her impropriety, is, according to Bell, an expression of American freedoms being developed contemporaneously – especially in relation to women – freedoms little understood and simplistically misinterpreted by Europeans. 'They [Europeans] waste no time in hair-splitting,' James wrote, in an essay on Americans abroad, in 1868, 'they set it down once for all as very vulgar'.[16] The restrictive etiquette that an older generation of New York ladies had tried to introduce into *post-bellum* society never quite established itself, since the social status quo was constantly being challenged and altered by the changing fortunes of those profiting from the financial boom of those years. Post-Civil War fiction 'had produced a new heroine – the Girl of the Golden West . . . independent in mind and body, [she] combined the Western influence with the tradition of the soubrette.'[17] Daisy Miller was sometimes compared to Charles Dana Gibson's 'Gibson girl', but in fact, as a product of provincial society, she has more in common with the Western girl. Whatever her origins, such was the novel's success, or notoriety, that Daisy quickly became a byword for parvenu behaviour. Mrs John Sherwood's guide to *Manners and Social Usages*, published in New York in 1884, refers several times to the novel, declaring that '[e]veryone laughed at the mistakes of Daisy Miller, and saw wherein she and her mother were wrong'.[18] Mrs Lynn Linton wrote gushingly to James, hinting at a kinship between Daisy and her own notorious, if English, 'Girl of the Period', a notion James politely quashed.[19] The novella, indeed, turns on more complex moral problems than either Mrs Sherwood or Mrs Linton addressed: the question that the young expatriate American, Winterbourne asks himself of Daisy: 'Was she simply a pretty girl from New York State . . . or was she also a designing, an audacious, an unscrupulous young person?' (23). For an answer we must test not only Daisy but Winterbourne on the relation between their outward aspects – Lionel Trilling's 'hum and buzz of implication'[20] – and their moral code.

In so brief a tale, James's use of detail is more than simply descriptive of Daisy's loveliness – though it is that, too. Daisy's problem is that, despite her intuitive aesthetic sense, she is comprehensively uncultivated and socially unaware. She is the victim (or beneficiary) of that American indulgence of young women, described later by James as 'that universal non-existence of any criticism worthy of the name...to which we mainly owe...the unlighted chaos of our manners'.[21] She is, therefore, generally unable to assess her own conduct in relation to others or to control any social situation in which she finds herself. When things get awkward, when she knows she is blundering, she starts to fiddle with her dress and accessories. When she first meets Winterbourne she smoothes her frills and plays with her parasol. But more startling is her behaviour in Rome when asking Mrs Walker's permission to bring the egregious Giovanelli to that lady's party. On this occasion it is actually with Mrs Walker's dress that she busies herself: '"Just hear him say that!" said Daisy to her hostess, giving a twist to a bow on this lady's dress' (71–2); she compounds the social solecism of her request with a quite unwarranted familiarity with her hostess's person. This fussing with dress is a sign of her unease, but it is also a need to touch familiar objects. Dresses and accessories are things that Daisy *does* understand and *can* control, and her concern for such objects is almost talismanic: 'Whenever she put on a Paris dress she felt as if she were in Europe. "It was a kind of wishing-cap"'(21) (See Plate I). Fans and parasols, on the other hand, she deploys partly as instruments of flirtation, but also partly as defences against unpleasantness and awkward truths. Both these functions are in play when, after she has defied Mrs Walker by continuing to parade with Giovanelli in the Pincian Gardens, she comes up closer to him, 'and he held the parasol over her; then still holding it, he let it rest upon her shoulder, so that both of their heads were hidden from Winterbourne' (92).

Daisy's instinct for dress ought to alert those around her to an aesthetic discrimination which, despite her farouche ways, only requires a little encouragement to develop further. Her insistence on seeing the Colosseum by moonlight and her real delight in it suggest an openness to those 'conquests of learning and taste' that are later to enchant Hyacinth Robinson in *The Princess Casamassima*, and Lambert Strether in *The Ambassadors*. Winterbourne at times perceives this, but for the others her taste in dress deludes them into expecting more appropriate manners and conduct. Money has, in fact, put within her reach attributes and a way of life that raise expectations of which she has only the dimmest perceptions and not the least ability to fulfil. James was later to point out, in an article for *Harper's Bazaar*, 'that a consistent care for the civilities has to contend with . . . our immense general prosperity';[22] that is, the general air of confidence lent these American 'princesses' by sheer weight of money, together with an absence of parental guidance, deludes both them and those around them as to the extent of their 'civilization'. In dress Daisy has the instincts of an aristocrat, 'the *tournure* of a princess' in Winterbourne's words, and it is his awareness of this 'singularly delicate grace' that constantly frustrates his attempts to stereotype her simply as a flirt.

James uses the term *tournure* here with subtle ambivalence, a usage he repeats in 'The Pension Beaurepas'. To Winterbourne, resident in Geneva, the French word *tournure* would mean 'bearing' or 'demeanour', but by 1869 *The Englishwoman's Domestic Magazine* was using the term to describe horsehair padding at the back of skirts, and by 1874, according to the O.E.D., it had become a synonym for the newly fashionable bustle. The word usefully particularises a rather absurd fashion item as well as suggesting a more general but inherent personal dignity, nicely pinpointing Winterbourne's dilemma. In order to behave appropriately himself, he has to take into account both his perception of a finer sensibility in Daisy, *and* the unacceptable and repeated crudity of her conduct. If she is a cheap little American flirt, he can either snub her or exploit her as a holiday amusement. If she is *not* a cheap little flirt, then she merits his kindness and respect.

Daisy's violation of etiquette can initially be put down to sheer ignorance, but as her social awareness grows, it can only be described as wilful and self-destructive blindness; she has no code to substitute for the one she rejects. Winterbourne, on the other hand, prides himself on his savoir-faire in matters of European social usages – he has, for example, an older 'lady friend' in Geneva. Therefore, when he not only suggests an excursion, *à deux*, to Chillon but also happily goes along with Daisy's request for a midnight boat-ride in Vevey, he must be fully conscious of the improprieties involved. Despite his endless agonisings about assigning so much 'that was pretty and undefended and natural' to a vulgar place among 'the categories of disorder' (113), his interpretation of her appearance and behaviour is weighted towards categorising her as 'a little American flirt' from the first, since it conveniently licenses him to play the role of Lothario without incurring the threat of matrimony. If Daisy knows how to dress, he believes, then she should know how to behave and he need not bother his handsome head over the possibility that what he dismisses as vulgar flirtation may be no more than a rather indiscriminate and democratic flow of friendliness. But the puzzle of the novella is that Daisy's taste in clothes may reflect a genuine aesthetic sensibility as much as it does the despised New Money of *post-bellum* America. In James's recasting of Tissot's 'stylish back' and 'yellow ribbons' Daisy Miller becomes a figure impossible to classify firmly, of inexhaustible interest. The consequences of Winterbourne's refusal to acknowledge the more complex implications of her appearance, thus transform the fictional appropriation of Tissot's 'hard' realism into gentle even tragic suggestiveness.

* * *

Daisy's outfits are the refined trophies of conspicuous consumption; in 'The Pension Beaurepas' we see the less discriminating processes of a consumer urge, as Mrs Ruck and her daughter Sophy loot and pillage Europe of clothes and jewellery with single-minded ferocity. It is finally impossible to sentimentalise Daisy Miller as wholly blameless or laugh at her as culpably vulgar, but to be excessively concerned with fashion, according to Balzac's theory of dress, his 'vestignomie', is 'to become a caricature'.[23] Sophy Ruck and her mother appear as caricatures, unambiguous embodiments of a monstrous shopping urge – they would now be recognised as shopaholics, bad credit risks. Other than a fascinated horror, the sympathies of the narrator are not really engaged with either of them, in fact, but with their effect on the pathetic figure of the physically and financially-collapsing Mr Ruck.

The unnamed narrator, an expatriate American like Winterbourne, encounters Mr Ruck as he is wearily but good-naturedly accompanying his women-folk around Switzerland. Ruck's sole function as far as they are concerned is to provide the means for their unceasing expenditure; he scans the financial pages of such American newspapers as he can find while they shop: 'Well, they wanted to pick up something. . . . That's the principal interest for ladies.'[24] Glued to business for 23 years, he has now neither the will nor the heart left to communicate with his family or oppose their wishes. He sees his duty as an American husband and father to keep them 'going'; and as all the sights of Europe they want to see are the shops, their only communication with him is of money or acquisitions. If the extreme separation of spheres between the American male and female reduced women to commodified symbols, then there was also a concomitant cost to the male – Christopher Newman, in *The American*, might have expanded to become a tycoon in the Adam Verver mould (at another kind of cost) or be reduced to an emasculated

Mr Ruck: for if success as a *post-bellum* American male is defined by success on Wall Street, then financial failure is also sexual failure. Mr Ruck is a recognisable American archetype, a forerunner of Arthur Miller's Willie Loman, and his tall, sickly appearance crowned by a high black hat, 'pushed back from his forehead and more suspended than poised' (399), lends him an air of an exhausted and *dépaysé* Uncle Sam.

We can assume that in terms of gross expenditure on frocks there is little to choose between Daisy Miller and Sophy Ruck, but in contrast to his several vivid and seductive impressions of Daisy's appearance, James limits information about the Rucks' style of dress to the narrator's one cutting comment: 'Both of these ladies were arrayed in black silk dresses, but ruffled and flounced, and if elegance were *all* a matter of trimming they would have been elegant' (406–7). Accessories, ruffles and flounces typified the costume of Daisy, but this is even more true of the Rucks – the pursuit of accessories is what we see them at for most of the story: in this they are of their age. Willett Cunnington records that a general complaint of the 1870s was that a woman's wardrobe was becoming more and more expensive; '[i]t was not the materials so much as the trimmings and accessories which raised the cost. This decade was the great age of trimmings.'[25] By the early 1880s the day dress 'suggested a solid block of masonry draped with flags . . . and there is a feeling that the wrappings are not an integral part of the costume, but have been hung on it to give it a festive touch'.[26]

In Europe, however, the *black* silk dresses of the Rucks would, by 1879, have been considered oddly outdated and formal for day-wear. After mid-century, black was worn only by servants, the elderly or those in straitened circumstances, except, of course, for mourning-wear. And black silk was not considered to be mourning in either England or America. One of the Dryfoos sisters, Mela, in W. D. Howells' *A Hazard of New Fortunes*, is wearing 'solid sable' for her dead brother, but Christine 'was not in mourning. He [the artist, Beaton] fancied that she wore the lustrous black silk, with breadths of white Venetian lace about the neck . . . because he praised it.'[27] The Dryfoos family are 'natural gas' millionaires, who, at the end of the novel are about to follow in the Rucks' footsteps to Europe. Christine's dramatically trimmed black silk, like that of the Rucks, would be seen as a species of especially American conspicuous consumption, for Americans in the second half of the century continued customarily to wear black. Paul Poiret – who was to launch the new Empire-style in Paris in the early 1900s – remembered the American woman as 'dressed in black satin, with a black velvet hat.

This extreme sobriety in dress betrays the influence of the clergy.'[28] In her memories of an Albany girlhood, Huybertie Pruyn Hamlin recalls her Uncle Abe, in 1889, 'who liked pretty clothes',[29] asking his wife to dress a little more smartly, to which she responded by buying a length of black silk. Worn as a travelling costume, black silk might well be described as going beyond conspicuous consumption into the realms of conspicuous waste. The anonymous author of *Woman, her Dignity and Sphere*, berates her countrywomen for their 'inappropriateness of dress [which] belongs especially to us as a people than to any other nation. The English woman, in travelling, provides herself with coarse, strong garments, and discards jewellery.'[30] Miss Oakey's *Beauty in Dress*, published in New York in 1881, has a chapter devoted to 'The Trying Effect of Black Silk', which, in her opinion, has an unjustified reputation for 'a universal becoming- ness. . . . It appears to us to possess a certain hardening effect.'[31] Unsur- prisingly, she recommends relieving it with trimmings.

James's choice of black silk for the Rucks may thus first of all be an indication of their blind nationalism. The scenery of Switzerland, after all, leaves the Rucks unmoved – there are plenty of mountains back home – and they may be similarly impervious to the magic Daisy finds in her light-coloured Paris frocks, viewing Paris fashions simply as necessary items on the self-respecting American shopping-list. Black silk appears here as a superfluous gesture towards American middle-class gentility, but pictorially it provides a hard, shiny setting against which to display the lace and jewellery amassed by the Rucks. When Sophy contemplates the purchase of a diamond bracelet, she demands a satin, not a velvet, box to set it off. Miss Oakey again has some apposite remarks on Amer- icans and jewellery, which she says they do not really understand: 'One sees few handsome jewels worn in America, with the exception of dia- monds.' This, she says, is to be regretted, since the diamond 'from its excessive brilliancy and hardness of light, is not becoming to many women: and most of them admire it only for its costliness'.[32] Taste is what redeems Daisy's consumerism, not because it provides evidence of a cultivated and educated moral sensibility in the traditional eighteenth- century sense, but because it both indicates an educability in such mat- ters and is, aesthetically, a delight. The Rucks, however, have no taste at all; values are exclusively financial in their world, all is metallic shine in which culture and civility play no part. In this rebarbative climate, the narrator's good manners desert him: Sophy, in the closing pages, demands his approval of the glittering bracelet she proposes to buy – ' "Don't you think that's sweet?" I looked at it a moment. "No, I think it's ugly" ' (474). In his choice of adjective, the narrator implies as much moral as aesthetic disapproval, for the purchase will be the last financial and physical straw for the visibly failing Mr Ruck.

By this time the narrator thoroughly detests the female Rucks. Initially comic figures,[33] they become repellant and unfunny, finally exposing poor Mr Ruck to public humiliation and disrespect: 'To get something in a "store" they can put on their backs – that's their one idea...,' hisses the narrator, '[b]etween them they are bleeding him to death' (460). This is an aside made to Mrs Church, the mother in another, contrasting American mother/daughter pair, over whom the narrator confusedly blows hot and cold. Interestingly, the two Europeans, Madame Beaurepas and Monsieur Pigeonneau, are much more relaxed about the Rucks than is their compatriot, who feels some personal stake – as James did himself – in the behaviour of Americans abroad. (James, in a letter of 1873, groans at '[t]hese shoals of American fellow-residents with their endless requisitions and unremunerative contact.'[34]) Madame Beaurepas, as their landlady, likes their undemanding acceptance of what comes their way, in contrast to the cheeseparing and exacting Mrs Church. Monsieur Pigeonneau declares himself frankly delighted by the Rucks' style and their physical charms: 'They have a tournure de princesse – a distinction supreme' (414) and particularly recommends the Rubensian qualities of the mother. Mrs Church he characterises as an austere Quakeress; more of an American, in fact, than Mrs Ruck with her Flemish opulence. As Mme Beaurepas and M. Pigeonneau are presented as sensible, if quietly amused spectators, we need perhaps to take a step back from the narrator's viewpoint, which, while damning the Rucks, leaves the question of the Churches, as a comparison, wide open. It is not so much a question of Old Money versus New, as Ian Bell explains, but rather an antagonism between 'the new and the recently new',[35] between those who have become recent and zealous converts to the conventions of Europe – like Mrs Walker in *Daisy Miller* – and those, like the Rucks, to whom such things are either of no interest or simply baffling. Howells's Dryfoos girls are examples of this latter type, though set on their native soil. There was a third and genuinely older class, to which James himself belonged, interested neither in 'endless requisitions' nor spurious concerns about decorum, but representing earlier Republican values. The narrator of 'Pension Beaurepas, who is something of a snob, sees himself and the Churches as belonging to this third group.

By the side of the elaborately garnished and glossy embonpoint of the Rucks, Mrs Church and Aurora are 'very simply and frugally dressed' (418), habitués of Europe's cheapest pensions, eking out whatever is left of the late (we assume, for we are not told) Mr Church's money, rather than return to America. Making a virtue out of necessity, Mrs Church presents herself as in pursuit of the cultural and intellectual life of Europe rather than the material; art galleries, museums and small volumes of German literature rather than frocks, lace and jewellery. The narrator, with his horror of vulgarity, naturally finds Mrs Church's air 'of quiet distinction' (418) sympathetic. What he misses is the fact that Mrs Church's wares are in a sense as much on display as those of the Rucks. Her volumes of German literature are deployed as accessories to her frugal attire, as are her tireless references to the latest intellectual fads or to old European families. In order to draw attention to the contrast between her own unworldliness and the unedifying showiness of the Rucks, Mrs Church refers to herself and her quest for culture in coyly diminutive terms – 'my little quiet persistent way...my devoted little errand' (457). This 'errand' not only includes Aurora, but is apparently carried out solely for her benefit, though what her ultimate purpose can be in marching the reluctant Aurora through the galleries, museums and cathedrals of Europe is not quite so clear.

In her proscriptive interpretation of the parental role Mrs Church often seems to look forward to Gilbert Osmond's terrorization of his daughter; but Aurora has elements of rebellion in her make-up that distinguish her from the unhappy Pansy. She is, for example, less simply dressed than her mother, and openly expresses her dislike of her present way of life as well as her wish to return to America. Simultaneously, she maintains so elaborate and so public an obedience to her mother that one might well suspect her of irony. Sophy, who is at her best with Aurora, encourages her rebellious dreams of America: '"Well, any one can see that you're an American girl... You've got the natural American style." "I'm afraid I haven't the natural American clothes," said Aurora in tribute to the other's splendour. "Well, your dress was cut in France; anyone can see that." "Yes," our young lady laughed, "my dress was cut in France – at Avranches"' (425–6). As Avranches is a small Breton seaside town, far from Paris, Aurora's laughter is wry, a fact underlined by her glance at the more knowledgeable narrator. Spectator of her own performance and of its effect on the narrator, Aurora confides in him her sense of the falsity of her position, and, in a kind of defensive game, frequently accuses herself of hitting false notes before he can. She tells him what her mother's snobbery and tyranny have brought her to – 'I've to pretend to be a jeune fille. I'm not a jeune fille; no American girl's a jeune fille' (449). Her self-conscious attempt to redefine herself as 'the American girl' in fact only achieves the effect of deferring her meaning for the narrator even further; 'she had by no means caught . . . what Miss Ruck called the natural American style' (426). Ironically, she has instead become enough of a European to see that her mother's 'little' errand is a fool's errand: 'Mamma thinks so much of them simply because they're foreigners. If I could tell you all the ugly stupid tenth-rate people I've had to talk to . . .' (453). Aurora's regimen of European culture and cultivation of *soi-disant* aristocracy are as close to the real thing as Avranches' fashions are to Paris, but they are close enough to make her despise her mother and deprive herself of the freshness and freedom of 'natural' American girlhood she so admires in Sophy. Both her personae are inauthentic.

Is the Churches' Grand Tour, then, simply a disinterested, if misdirected, quest for enlightenment, and their modest attire an expression of their sacrifices to that end? Mme Beaurepas places the question of Mrs Church's pursuit of the Higher Life in a rather more realistic light for the narrator; 'c'est une de ces mamans, comme vous en avez, qui promènent leur fille.' The mother, she says, is after a 'gros bonnet of some kind' (436–7) for Aurora, and, continues the landlady – either warning the narrator or reassuring him – Americans need not apply. However, she believes that one fine day Aurora will up and off with some young American, who will be all the America she needs. The narrator protests at this cynical view of mother and daughter, but later, when he finds himself alone, at night, in the garden with Aurora, he remembers Mme Beaurepas' warning: 'perhaps this unfortunately situated, this insidiously mutinous young creature was in quest of an effective preserver' (468). He declines, however, to act the hero and rescue Aurora, although he has given her every indication of an interest in her welfare. He stupidly suggests she is free to leave, when he must know for a young woman in her situation there is no such freedom.

With the Rucks, what you get is what you see: a kindly but collapsing Uncle Sam figure and two overdressed, florid women whose 'vision of fine clothes rides them like a fury' (460). As with *Daisy Miller*, however, we must not jump to assumptions about people and clothes. James does not, like the narrator, subscribe to the view that female extravagance in dress is profoundly wicked: 'A young girl of fashion dressed to suit her own taste is undeniably a very artificial and composite creature, and doubtless not a very edifying spectacle'[36] – but nothing worse. In an article of 1868 on Mrs Lynn Linton's reactionary essays in *The Saturday Review*, James rejects her attack on luxurious dress as 'wanton exaggeration in the interest of sensationalism', and denies that such indulgence is the monopoly of women – 'we are all of us extravagant, superficial, and luxurious together.'[37] The Rucks are insanely acquisitive, certainly, but they are just as capable of random kindness as they are of gratuitous rudeness, neither of which goes very deep.

It is too simple, then, to isolate the Rucks and their shopping problems in this story. They must be seen in contrast to Aurora Church, and in relation to the filter of a hostile narrator. Aurora Church, with her pinched wardrobe, has been 'finished' to such a degree that she has lost sight of any authentic identity. The Rucks' swank has no design beyond self-gratification, but Mrs Church's perambulation about Europe with Aurora is in fact a trawl for a husband with sufficient wealth and class to keep Mrs Church in a manner to which she is very anxious to become accustomed. The frugality of their dress is a kind of double-bluff: if their clothes were identified as reflecting the real exigencies of their budget, the desirable 'gros bonnet' might spot them as fortune-hunters and take flight. By representing their scrimped attire as deliberately chosen to reflect traditional female modesties and rejection of material values in favour of cultural ones, European males – who were increasingly taking American heiresses to wife in this period – might be fooled both as to the extent of Aurora's finances and her accomplishments. Aurora, as Mrs Church's 'principal interest', is actually more elaborately, if metaphorically, 'got up', draped and garnished than the Rucks in their flounces and jewellery. And Mrs Church's materialism is finally more deeply, if covertly, ingrained than is their noisy recreational shopping. James could enter into the Rucks' state of mind to some extent as in 1888 he described his own 'consuming vision of life'[38] on his first adult visit to London: the feeling that it was 'desirable and even indispensable that I should purchase most of the articles in most of the shops'.[39] What he did find unforgivable, however, was the exploitation of one human creature for the benefit of another. It is not the awful taste of the overtrimmed Rucks that is odious; it is their exploitation of and insolent indifference to one who stands in a close and vulnerable relation to them. We are, therefore, left with ominous shadows gathering around the future of two victims of greed, Mr Ruck and Aurora Church – and a question about one notably absent figure: Whatever happened to Mr Church?

The narrator pretends not to understand Aurora's eleventh-hour plea for help and leaves her to her own devices. Furthermore, he packs his bags and is off before the Rucks and their catastrophes can return to the Pension Beaurepas: indeed, his stance as a representative of civilised values and as a knowledgeable, amused spectator of contrasting American styles no longer seems either honourable or tenable. The questions that will remain unanswered for him are whether Aurora will go spinning on across Europe, playing the *jeune fille* in her simple frocks. Will she finally get her Prince Casamassima? And will that improve her situation? Will the Rucks, *mère et fille*, rally Mr Ruck and light out for the territories to try the American Dream once more?[40] This would be the optimistic American thing to do. Or will they take the loot and leave him? This returns us to the question of the possible fate of the shadowy Mr Church, fading away in some other *pension*, perhaps, in some other time? 'Everything has happened chez moi,' says Mme Beaurepas *à propos* of Aurora's predicted rebellion, 'But nothing has happened more than once. Therefore it won't happen here. It will be at the next place they go to, or the next' (437–8). The Churches and the Rucks, despite the apparent radical opposition of their dress signs, may have more in common than either they or the narrator would care to acknowledge.

Ian Bell draws attention to the 'variousness'[41] of Daisy, to the fact that her dressed performances are expressions of her American freedom to explore possibilities, to create a self untrammelled by the restrictions of etiquette or the imperatives of the marriage market. She resists categorisations of her behaviour and her single moment of anger is when Winterbourne accuses her of being in love with Giovanelli: she neither wishes to appropriate nor be appropriated. She is more 'various' than he thinks. Although Sophy Ruck lacks Daisy's complexity, like Daisy, flirtation, not marriage, is on her mind; Aurora's closely monitored appearance, however, *is* stage-managed towards that matrimonial end, and against her own wishes. Mrs Church sentimentally describes herself as of 'the old, old world' and she does indeed seem to belong to some dark, feudal past in her repressive definition of the social role of young women, especially when seen against the late nineteenth-century, consumer capitalist world of increasing female freedoms.

3
The Ironic Dresses of *Washington Square*

It is not clear whether it is the values of *ante-bellum* America or those of an even older Europe that Mrs Church claims to subscribe to – her allegiance is sentimental and bogus in either case. But in *Washington Square* and *The Europeans* James chose a pre-Civil War period in which to place his heroines, and marriage, as the potential and logical outcome of events, is foregrounded. James's two historical novels are set in a period when the consumer values of the latter part of the century were just beginning to emerge; and as such, details, like those of dress, take on a particular importance, since they chart and colour the historical background to those changes. Referring back to Aileen Ribeiro's words quoted in my introduction, clothes in *Washington Square*, in particular, can be seen simultaneously as reflections of a self-image and – as fashion garments – the mirrors of history.

If it is 'old world' to define a young woman in terms of her adventures in the marriage market, then *Washington Square* certainly starts off in a recognisably traditional mode with a quite un-Jamesian exegesis on Catherine Sloper's antecedents, bringing her – like Jane Austen's earlier Catherine of *Northanger Abbey* – to the stage in her life when the entry of a marriageable hero is to be expected. This exegesis simultaneously leads up to one of the most startling colour notes in James's fiction – Catherine's awful red dress. The plot is set in motion at the moment we encounter the dress, which is placed on the traditional stage for gorgeous gowns and romantic encounters, a dance party. It is the crimson centre of the novel, the soft heart of Catherine's love, or the bleeding heart of her betrayals. Romantically, it should be the target for Cupid's arrows, but it attracts instead the shafts of her father's sarcasm and the cash-register eyes of a fortune-hunter – for the dance party is also a time-honoured marriage market, with what George Moore called its 'muslin martyrs'.

The dress is startling, but Catherine herself, as the narrator explains, has developed into adulthood in an entirely unremarkable fashion, much to her father's disappointment. She has, however, developed a lively sense of dress which she has the means to indulge, and for this first important party – her début in effect – at the age of twenty-one, she treats herself 'to a red satin gown trimmed with a gold fringe'.[1] We are in a different fashion world from that of the late 1870s, the world of Daisy Miller and Sophy Ruck, with its burgeoning department store culture filled with clothing mass-produced by the rapidly developing sewing-machine. The sewing-machine was not in general commercial use until the 1850s so Catherine would have had her dress sewn by a dressmaker, and would have chosen the colour, style and trimmings and have seen it take shape. For her this has been a most deliberate process, and indeed we are told she has been secretly coveting the garment for years. Catherine, as we are often reminded, is a big healthy girl and in the fashions of 1847 (I calculate that she was born *circa* 1826) she would have appeared even bigger. The light cage-crinoline was not invented until the mid-1850s but skirts were already expanding unstoppably by the mid-1840s, supported by layer upon layer of horsehair-stiffened petticoats, also known as crinolines. In England, in 1842, Lady Aylesbury is recorded in a diary as wearing '48 yards of material in each of her gowns, and instead of crinoline she wears a petticoat made of down or feathers which swells out this enormous expanse and floats like a vast cloud when she sits down or rises up.'[2] On the first page of *The Europeans*, set in 1848, we see Eugenia Münster – a lady of uncertain years and a shaky marriage – pacing before a mirror in 'much-trimmed skirts [which] were voluminous'.[3] No wonder, then, that such a dress makes Catherine look 'when she sported it, like a woman of thirty' (38).[4]

Setting aside questions of fashion, there was a code to be followed for unmarried girls, one that Daisy's light-coloured, frilly dresses and Aurora's contrived simplicities conformed to in their different ways. Although the New York social scene had not yet formulated its social mores into those obscure but inviolable 'hieroglyphics' that Edith Wharton was later to satirise in *The Age of Innocence*, none the less, the visual code for the first public appearance of a young girl, from the eighteenth century onwards, demanded virginal white – 'White tulle over white silk (or white lace), and bouquets of flowers . . . are the favourite dress of the young lady.'[5] Pansy Osmond's unvarying little white dresses of around 1876 suggest an almost hysterical vigilance over her wardrobe, in excess of that practised by Mrs Church. Daisy's and Catherine's unsupervised dresses, however, are somehow dislocated from the persons beneath them. Daisy's instinctive taste in pale-coloured, girlish dresses makes her *look* socially competent – much of her tragedy lies in the mismatch between the apparent knowledgeability displayed by her elegant appearance and her ignorance of the rules by which she is assumed to be playing. The effect of Catherine's dress is equally if differently misleading: more of a child than most at twenty-one, she seems to all the young men, as Mrs Almond says, 'to be older than themselves. She is so large, and she dresses so richly. They are rather afraid of her. She looks as if she had been married already' (60).

Mrs Almond is discussing her niece, Catherine, with Di Sloper, whose dismayed response to the sight of Catherine's party dress has been one of the 'woeful strokes', described by Elizabeth Hardwick, 'in the merciless comedy of the "red satin gown"'.[6] His internalised reaction is at first reported in reasonable terms: 'he had a dread of vulgarity. . . . It simply appeared to him proper and reasonable that a well-bred young woman should not carry half her fortune on her back' (38). Balzac's *Eugénie Grandet* was to a large extent James's model for *Washington Square*, and in my earlier discussion of his literary journalism we have already seen how James referred to Balzac's employment of dress signs in this novel as exemplary. In his essay, 'Traité de la Vie Elégante', Balzac maintains that a central tenet of those who have acquired power or money is the avoidance of vulgarity: it follows that 'the elegant life lies therefore essentially in a knowledge of manners'.[7] When Sloper actually addresses Catherine on the topic of her dress, however, it could be said that it is *he*, for all his horror of vulgarity, that is the more unmannerly of the two: '"Is it possible that this magnificent person is my child?" . . . "You are sumptuous, opulent, expensive, . . . You look as if you had eighty thousand a year."' In part what lies behind this heavy sarcasm is Sloper's American Puritan heritage. We find a cruder variety of this kind of Old Testament fulmination voiced in an American advice book of 1860 (translated from French and therefore presumably originally Roman Catholic). Extravagance in dress is morally vicious, this author declares; 'women who lose their virtue may . . . trace the beginning of their disorders and ruin to a love of dress.'[8] Sloper, while not going this far, exhibits a somewhat overheated distaste for Catherine's appearance; but more unforgivable is the way he bludgeons Catherine with his brutal employment of 'the ironical form', to which his adoring and simple-hearted daughter has no answer. She has wanted to please him, and from his pseudo-compliment she (reinscribing dress-making into her thought processes) has to 'cut her pleasure out of the piece.... There were portions left over, light remnants, snippets of irony, which she never knew what to do with', for Sloper's oblique references to the shady world of the *demi-mondaine* can mean nothing to Catherine. As she has pored over the creation of her gown, she now tries to fashion something positive from the sarcasms of her father, but fails and ends by 'wishing that she had put on another dress' (46). Clearly, the red dress means one thing to Catherine and another to her father.

Worse than the inappropriateness and suggestive crudity of Catherine's choice of red and gold is the *nouveau-riche* vulgarity, as Sloper reads it, of its frank and public statement of her financial expectations from him. (James, in fact, follows up the comments on Catherine's taste in dress with details of Sloper's income.) As Ian Bell, in his study of the novel's 'styles of money', points out, we are moving here from a period in which 'the value of an object was determined by its inherent properties'[9] to a period of paper money, speculation and banking – and bank statements are apt to be confidential. How Republican and old-fashioned, or how 'New Money' is Sloper's reaction to Catherine and her dress? Karen Halttunen has documented the change in the social manners of this period from a sentimental demand in the 1830s and early 1840s for candour and sincerity, to a requirement, reflected in the proliferation of guides on etiquette from the 1850s onwards, for the more theatrical skills of the kind of smooth social performance put on by Morris Townsend or Eugenia Münster – Jamesian exemplars of Halttunen's Confidence Man and Painted Woman.[10] As a self-made man of the previous generation, Dr Sloper likes to think of himself as subscribing to the values of sincerity and the austerities of demeanour of the earlier Republican world; but in the same way that Mrs Church stage-managed Aurora's social performance of modest unworldliness, so he wishes Catherine to manage hers to give the stereotyped *appearance* of simplicity, to be *less* candid than she in fact is. The impression that Sloper would like Catherine to produce is that produced on Felix Young, in *The Europeans*, by his young New England cousins, Charlotte and Gertrude Wentworth: a 'physical delicacy which seemed to make it proper that they should always dress in thin materials and clear colours' (81). Catherine's indelicate dress signs, so incongruous in relation to her age and situation, would suggest that she is without a self-image, unaware of her effect on others and ignorant, in her motherlessness, of the language of dress. The dress is chosen and worn neither to advertise her wealth (about which she is indifferent and possibly ignorant) or her charms to potential suitors, nor to defer to the dictates of fashion and etiquette, but simply to win her father's approval. Catherine's character conforms to the model held up by Mrs Tuthill in her advice manual: 'A young lady who is not an affectionately docile daughter...cannot make a good wife.'[11] She is the Child-Woman described by Coventry Patmore as 'all mildness and young trust', and, logically, why should such a one not wear red and gold, a child's favourite colours?

Catherine, at the age of twenty-one,[12] however, needs to move beyond the stasis of childish naivety. Discriminations in dress and behaviour are a part of a necessary negotiation and communication with the social, adult world, but one in which sympathetic help is needed. Derelictions in this respect are rarely as fatal as they were in the case of Daisy Miller, but they can cause lasting damage. In a late story, 'The Two Faces', James shows how a young wife's début into society is destroyed in the eyes of an English country-house gathering, by being 'dressed' – or more precisely *over*-dressed – by her husband's former mistress. Aunt Penniman is Catherine's obvious mentor here, but as her guides to behaviour are drawn from penny novelettes and cheap melodramas, Catherine can expect no real help: she is on her own.

How would Catherine's appearance have been generally judged and how would this have influenced her fortunes on the marriage market? By the 1840s, according to Lois Banner, '[s]implicity in dress seemed a style of the past, and fashionable display had triumphed over republican frugality.'[13] But even so, this was the 'Sentimental Gothic' period in dress, a period which, if it favoured elaborate decorative effects, also preferred muted shades such as lilac and pale green: Willett Cunnington records that in the 1840s '[p]rimary colours were no longer considered good taste; indeed they were thought to be almost vulgar.'[14] Miss Oakey, in her handbook on dress, not only warns against 'all violent effects of color', but also declares that '[n]o young girl looks as young or as lovely in heavy velvets and loaded trimmings as in simple muslins'.[15] It was not simply a matter of aesthetics, either, for a particular working-class type was emerging in the New York of the 1840s, the 'Bowery Gal', who, '[d]isdaining the muted colors of respectable middle-class women... delighted in startling contrasts, "a light pink contrasting with a deep blue, a bright yellow with a brighter red."'[16] These young women operated on the raffish edges of city life (the location of Mrs Penniman's assignation with Morris) and they were certainly the very last type of young female expected in the drawing-rooms of Washington Square. Dr Sloper's move to this address has, after all, been to achieve a 'quiet and genteel retirement' (39).

Figure 1   White evening gowns. *Godey's Lady's Book*, 1849.

Poor Catherine's robustness would also have told against her as 'an appearance of rude health was regarded as scarcely ladylike'.[17] Miss Oakey describes Catherine's type as one frequently to be found in America: 'An Unappreciated Type', she calls it. 'Women belonging to it,' she writes, 'are ordinarily set down as plain ... they have dull, light brown hair, and no brilliancy of complexion; the eyes are often grey or blue. We find them making one of two mistakes in the color of their dress, in hopes of mitigating this ineffectiveness: one is to wear reds.'[18] Mrs Sherwood, about the same date but more concerned with manners, takes a similar, if more sympathetic line with shy women: they feel 'the effect of handsome clothes as a reinforcement, but somehow miss the mark: 'Some women, otherwise good and true, have a sort of moral want of taste and wear too bright colors, too many glass beads... [they] are either wanting in good taste or their minds are confused with shyness.'[19] Miss Oakey and Mrs Sherwood are united, however, in deploring the American taste for costly show: 'Let us emancipate ourselves from the idea that beauty and costliness are synonymous.'[20] Catherine's appearance, then, by her father's standards and by any standard of mid-nineteenth century fashion, etiquette and morals, is a disaster.

Poor taste is frequently the result of indifference to questions of dress, but not for Catherine, who loves clothes. Her indulgence in dress, James tells us, 'was really the desire of a rather inarticulate nature to manifest itself; she sought to be eloquent in her garments, and to make up for her diffidence of speech by a fine frankness of costume' (37). What is it that Catherine wishes to articulate? Critical comment on the novel has frequently focused on this scene with the dress, but there is a critical silence as to just what it is that Catherine wants to say with her dreadful get-up. The dress, in this case, is clearly not the woman; it is what Catherine, in all humility, believes to be an improved alternative to her dull, colourless and silent self. We have established that she has no notion of attracting young men or conforming to fashion; her wish is for her father's approval. Why should she imagine that this dress will do the trick? She looks mature, magnificent, married and rather large: consequently, young men of her own generation find her unapproachable. Their unease may be compounded by the garment's undertones of the *femme du monde*. The lustrous icons of femininity created by Ingres for mature women such as the Baronne de Rothschild, in his portraits of the late 1840s, for example, are gorgeous, but in relation to a young girl, would seem louche. Cut off as she has been from all sensible female guidance Catherine can be aware of none of the effects she produces. Richard Poirier has pointed to the strong fairy-tale element in the structure and characterisation of the novel,[21] an element which accords with Catherine's child-like nature, her taste for Romantic operas and her choice of dress. But Catherine does not see herself as the fairy-tale princess here. She is the queen in regal red and gold; she is trying to be her own lost mother, who had 'dazzled' her kingly father, and was the model of feminine loveliness, accomplishment and taste that she has always had before her to underscore her own inadequacies.[22] It is the small girl's story-book vision of the ultimate in gorgeousness, queenliness and beauty that she seeks in the dress. James, indeed, calls it her 'royal raiment'. Her concern is with the beautiful effect the *dress* will have, not the effect that *she* will have in the dress, for 'her anxiety when she put them [the clothes] on was as to whether they, and not she, would look well' (38). Catherine knows she is not 'brilliant' like her mother, so she chooses a 'brilliant' dress.

As we know, she fails; it is her exchange-value, the 'brilliance' of money, that first Sloper and then Morris instantly recognise in her appearance. Sloper's hostility to Morris could be said to spring from the fact that it takes one to know one. Sloper, to do him justice, acknowledges Catherine's moral worth and he wants her marriage to be founded on a recognition of that worth. But his habitual under-estimation of her 'goodness' and his immediate reading of her as a commodity make his objection to Morris illogical, in one sense. Why should he require true love for her from others when he has none to give himself? Catherine realises her dress has been a failure at the party. But surprisingly this is not the first and last appearance of the red dress. Some weeks later Morris is asked to dine in Washington Square, and '[a]fter dinner Morris Townsend went and stood before Catherine, who was standing before the fire in her red satin gown' (64). Catherine has already surprised her father by making a little joke about Morris's atten-tiveness; he will again be surprised by the persistence of her loyalty to Morris, and we may imagine that in the wake of his masterly ironic attack on her toilette, the persistence of the dress on his own hearth will be profoundly unsettling. He believes that there is nothing more to the docile Catherine than meets his narrowed eye, and, as it is the essence of the ironic form *never* to be surprised, he chooses not to examine the causes of these surprises. Richard Poirier, sharing Sloper's view, contends that 'the novel does nothing to convince us until after the trip to Europe that Catherine is not stolid, tedious and dully sweet'.[23] This is a mistake, I believe, for in deciding to wear the dress for the second time Catherine records an important emotional shift. She cannot hope to please her father, but the dress does seem to have miraculously pleased the eye of beautiful Morris Townsend – Aunt Penniman had said so – and so, naturally, she wears it again, *despite* her father and *for* Morris. Dr Sloper, if he were as acute as he claims to be at reading surfaces, would realise that he has already begun to lose the battle.

From this point until the trip to Europe we hear nothing of Cather-ine's appearance other than her own dim impressions of it: 'Poor Cath-erine was conscious of her freshness.... It seemed proof that she was strong and solid and dense, and would live to a great age' (130). The trip to Europe is no more successful as an introduction of Catherine to the world than the party was, although Sloper's action in taking her on this trip is as much – or even ahead – of its time, as his view of Catherine as a commodity has been. Some twenty years later Mr Miller of Schenectady launches Daisy onto Europe, and poor Mr Ruck lives (or dies) to regret the decision to accompany Sophy on her triumphal shopping trip. Dr Sloper gives Catherine the Mrs Church Cultural Tour, about which, he grumbles, 'she is about as intelligent as a bundle of shawls', though he concedes that while the shawls 'tumble' about, Catherine is 'always at her post and had a firm and ample seat' (152). A cashmere shawl, however, is what Catherine brings back from Europe as a present for her aunt, who is genuinely delighted.

Willett Cunnington traces the career of the shawl from its start, around 1840, as the 'pelerine', 'the first of an immense series of such veiling garments . . . serving to disguise the outlines of the figure', to the shawl, which, increased in size, 'was even more satisfactory and was destined to outlive many of its rivals'.[24] An English visitor to New York in 1849 noted that 'the women were all wearing white shawls',[25] and by 1851 a fashion commentator judged that '[w]e scarcely knew a truer test of a gentlewoman's taste in dress than her selection of a shawl, and her manner of wearing it'.[26] If Catherine is not intelligent about art and architecture she does know that the ultimate genteel fashion accessory around 1850 is the shawl, especially in cashmere; and shawls, moreover, help the ampler figure. Catherine's travels will have reinforced the message of the shawl: Ingres' female portraits of the mid-century are a testimony not only to the popularity of shawls amongst elegant French-women, but also 'to the sculptural qualities of fine cashmere as it draped on and around the body'.[27] We are not shown Catherine in a shawl, but Dr Sloper is caustic over Catherine's indulgence in finery in Europe, and Mrs Penniman remarks on her expanded wardrobe which one imagines must include a shawl or two. The lesson of the red dress has encouraged in her the beginnings of a self-image, and, indeed, on her return, Mrs Penniman notes that Catherine's appearance has improved, she has become 'embellished' (164), although Catherine unnerves her aunt by also being a good deal more critical and authoritative. Articulation of the self in dress is clearly an aid to articulacy in general.

Eugenia Münster, in *The Europeans*, is an accomplished conversation-alist, one, indeed, who never allows strict truthfulness to stand in the way of her narrative flow. She wears the fashionably voluminous skirts that were so unbecoming to Catherine, but for the rest of the novel her dress style is characterised by shawls and scarves. Catherine's gift to Mrs Penniman, another 'not absolutely veracious' lady, may be a symbolic tribute to her obliquity as well as being a desirable fashion item.

Baroness Münster not only drapes her person in shawls but she discon-
certs her cousins by distributing shawls, cloaks and strips of velvet and
lace all over the Quakerish house they have lent her. Gertrude, the less
austerely New England of the two girls, is finally enchanted by the
effect: ' "What is life, indeed, without curtains?" she secretly asked
herself; and she appeared to herself to have been leading hitherto an
existence singularly garish and totally devoid of festoons' (79). When
Eugenia's 'festoons' prove to be embellishments of fact as well as of her
person and her décor, these vagaries prove too much for the New
England conscience and they wreck her matrimonial schemes.

The shawl's long life obviously owes much to its infinite varieties of
concealment and embellishment, whether of undesirable truths,
unwanted bulk, or frugality of décor; moreover, as Gertrude points out
to her more pious but less stylish sister, Charlotte, the shawl can prettify
the unguarded rear aspects of one's appearance. Charlotte finally marries the dull Mr Brand – a man above the seductions of shawls – but
Gertrude is joyously carried off by the more picturesque Felix to further
opportunities, one hopes, in the artistic distribution of drapery. This
deployment of shawls is one of the more subtle effects in *The Europeans*,
and Gertrude's expertise in their arrangement is a proleptic sign of the
novel's unusually happy ending.

Felix, it has to be said, acquires a nice income along with Gertrude: his
requirements, however, are quite modest in this respect and his love and
admiration for Gertrude have never seemed contingent upon her prospects. Morris Townsend, in *Washington Square*, is however impervious to
any improvements in Catherine's appearance. The only improvement
that could fire his ardour is an improvement in her financial expectations, and these, alas, have decreased on her return from Europe. Without her father's substantial fortune, Catherine's substantial self lacks
charm. When the dress ceases to correlate with a secure bank account,
Morris loses interest and, despite her European trousseau – 'quantities of
clothing and ten pairs of shoes' (173) – he unceremoniously dumps her.
Ironically, perhaps the worst moment of this betrayal is Dr Sloper's
mockery of one of those ceremonial gestures, expressed in dress, of
male respect to women: as Catherine stands at the window looking
out into the gathering dark, by now almost certain that Morris has left
her, Sloper, returning, spots her 'and gravely, with an air of exaggerated
courtesy, lifted his hat to her' (185). The exaggeration of the gesture is an
echo of his earlier, elaborately ironic demolition of her red dress – the
moment which set the train of events into motion which has now
almost arrived at its conclusion. Unlike that first occasion, Sloper can-

not now know the full cruelty of this gesture. Like that first occasion, however, Catherine has no answer for him, with the important difference that now her silence is calculated and eloquent: when he seeks to know the truth behind her break with Morris 'it was his punishment that he never knew – his punishment, I mean, for the abuse of sarcasm in his relations with his daughter' (199). Catherine has learnt the power of the arts of concealment. In admiring the reticences of an earlier age, Sloper has fashioned a rod for his own back.

Catherine does, however, finally get to wear the virginal white frock she so signally failed to wear at her début: 'One of those warm evenings in July... Catherine was within the room, in a low rocking-chair, dressed in white, and slowly using a large palmetto fan' (210). Her dress, appropriate to summer fashions and in accord with the rules of etiquette for an unmarried woman, also signals the final stages of mourning for her father's death a year before. (Isabel Archer wears a similar dress, a year after her father's death.) Sloper himself might even have appreciated the irony. We are told that by the age of forty Catherine has become an authority 'on all moral and social matters' (204): the social humiliation Sloper inflicted on her twenty years before over the incongruity of a dress is therefore not to be repeated. In a replay of that first encounter at the dance-party, Morris enters to try his luck again with Catherine, now correctly and chastely attired; and, having found her voice in dress, she is equally precise in her usages of etiquette and language. She does not allow him to sit or to put down his hat, both of which would have signalled a willingness to go beyond the bare ceremonials of greeting. By the 1860s the circumference of the crinoline skirt (Plate II) had reached its furthest extremities, usefully serving to keep Morris at a decorous distance. Catherine expresses her displeasure at his coming, her unequivocal condemnation of his conduct to her in the past and her wish never to see him again – an exemplary demonstration of Republican candour.

To paraphrase James's own words (quoted in Chapter 1) on the differences between Balzac's employment of realistic details and that of lesser writers, the dressed images of Daisy Miller, Sophy Ruck and Aurora Church can to *some* extent be said to be figures animating ideas. This is true in so far as they contribute to contemporary discourses about American consumerism, or about contrasting European and American versions of young womanhood. But if Daisy Miller's figure resists reduction to the tabloid press caricature suggested by Mrs Lynn Linton, and if her dress transcends that of Tissot's fashion mannequin from which it was taken, then the evolution of Catherine Sloper's dress sense, its relation to her character and to the action of the novel, resists even more strongly reductions to questions of either nationality or finance. As Eugénie Grandet finally becomes her father's daughter, using money as an instrument of power, so, I believe, does Catherine become something of an ironist, a process reflected mainly in her choice of costume, for, as always, she is more eloquent in her garments than in her speech.

At the conclusion of the 1949 film version of the novel, *The Heiress*, Catherine carries out an almost sadistic revenge on Morris – promising to marry him and then closing the door on him – to which Mary McCarthy rightly objected, because she believed, wrongly, that nothing can really happen to Catherine: she is 'an unbudging entity' whose middle age 'knows no grudges or regrets but smiles placidly back on its memories like a blue and empty day'.[28] Catherine is not 'unbudging'; her restrained appearance and her mannerly, undramatic dismissal of Morris at the end of James's novel are the articulation of a self-image that has been forged out of disillusionment and betrayal, but has also been driven by her ruling passion for goodness. James himself felt that evil, essentially, lay at the heart of man, agreeing with W. D. Howells that effective goodness has to be learned and nurtured: 'natural goodness doesn't count . . . what really makes for harmony in society is "the implanted goodness" . . . what we call civilization'.[29] Catherine's nurtured goodness has made her self-aware; aware of her duties to herself as well as to others. The wording of her dismissal of Morris is clear, considered and without rancour, as her white dress is a measure of her final realisation of herself – a symbol of virtue, freedom and mourning. In terms of the etiquette of her situation, it reflects correctly, if ironically, her virginal forty-year-old state and her decision to remain in it. For her there can be no substitute for Morris – she may even still love him – but he is none the less, in justice to herself, impossible.

Eugénie Grandet, too, having cleared the way for Charles's social-climbing marriage by paying his debts, looks down the final, empty prospect of the years with dry-eyed clarity. The description of her personal appearance in Balzac's novel, in contrast to Catherine's two-colour notes of red and white, is, however, oddly monochrome and unspecific for Balzac. In contrast, the clothes of her parents are concretely noted, and the costume of the beautiful Charles on his first appearance in the dingy Grandet household, as well as the contents of his luggage, occupy several pages of description. But as James pointed out to Miss Prescott, nothing in Balzac is described that is without bearing upon the action. Charles's splendour signals family wealth, it points up the contrasts between provincial Saumur and fashionable Paris, and it warns us of the self-indulgent nature of the young man. But it also sets into motion the action of the novel, as Catherine's dress precipitates events in *Washington Square*. Charles's beauty dazzles the young girl, whose naturally passionate nature in these miserly surroundings has been starved of any emotional or aesthetic outlets other than those of religion. He seems to Eugénie a young god, as Morris will seem to Catherine, and as such no sacrifice will be too great. Of Eugénie's own appearance we are, however, given scant details. Why? and – given its paucity – in what ways did James find the depiction of Eugénie fruitful for the creation of Catherine?

It might be surmised that James saw in Balzac's insistence on Eugénie's goodness and purity the central dynamic for Catherine's character: virtue, consciously maintained, shapes the image and the fate of both heroines. In the shifting, increasingly material and secular world of mid-century New York, with its supposed democratic absence of class distinctions, James's 'vestignomie' of virtue had to draw, however, on a far less clear semiotic system than that available to Balzac. There is a great clarity about Eugénie's image, the Grandet house and family, and provincial Saumur. 'He set down things in black and white,' James points out to Miss Prescott, 'not . . . vaguely . . . in red, blue, and green.'[30] Both Grandet's gold and his avarice are publicly known and discussed – evidenced, on the one hand, in his spectacular business deals and, on the other, in the material deprivations of the Grandet household. The Grandets' status in provincial Saumur is also clear – no one mistakes the poverty of their outward aspects as a sign of membership of the labouring class. The piety and goodness of Eugénie and her mother are also publicly displayed in their church-going, charitable works and their austere dress. Balzac, although no supporter of the established Church, draws on a wealth of generally understood Catholic symbolism and imagery in the creation of Eugénie.

Eugénie first becomes aware of her own appearance shortly after Charles's arrival in the house. Her immediate response had been to attempt to ornament his dreary bedroom, but the following morning she turns her attention to herself. The description of her early morning toilet emphasises aspects of character as much as appearance: 'shy candour', 'purity of line' and 'prim tidiness'. She washes in 'cold spring water', puts on 'new stockings and her prettiest shoes'. M. A. Crawford's English translation then speaks of her pleasure in 'a new, well-made dress that suited her',[31] translating the original French 'fraîche' as 'new', though Balzac has already used 'neufs'[32] in relation to her stockings. Although 'frais' can mean new, here 'freshness' would seem the more probable connotation. Balzac develops Eugénie's image with comparisons to a christianised Venus de Milo and to the Madonnas of Raphael. Her capacity for love is awakened by Charles's beauty, and appropriately it is her gold she gives him in all innocence in his bedroom, for she concludes that this is what he needs above all: 'I am not good-looking enough for him!' (94) she says to herself in the mirror. The gift of her gold, together with her growing passion for Charles, changes her looks from the Virgin of the Annunciation to that of the Virgin Mother; the only dress reference here is to an all-enveloping cloak. Balzac retains the purity of her image until the end of the novel by leaving that first, single description of her intact, while paradoxically developing it by drawing on the recognised double icon of the Virgin as both Maiden and Mother.

In his 'Traité de la Vie Elégante', Balzac compares his new science of 'vestignomie' to Lavater's science of physiognomy. He argues that although in the post-revolutionary society of nineteenth-century France almost all are dressed alike, it is in fact easy for the careful observer to make distinctions in dress among the various city types, between classes and between professions. These distinctions are almost invariably distortions or faults in costume, such as the misshapen pockets of the *flâneur*, stretched by his hands, or the soiled jacket of the miser, too mean to pay for laundering. If, as Balzac says, 'a tear is a catastrophe and a stain a vice',[33] then the discriminations of 'vestignomie' cannot be applied to Eugénie, for she is without stain, without experience or knowledge of the world. Nothing can mark her appearance. All that she learns is that her mother was right: 'One can only suffer and die' (236); consequently, by what is in effect the end of her life, '[s]he dresses as her mother did', and like Catherine keeps to the rules and regulations of her girlhood, remaining 'unspotted by contact with the world' (247) in her father's house. Balzac comments in his closing passages that she has found – as Catherine was to find – that in the eyes of others she can only be defined by money, and that '[t]he pale cold glitter of gold was destined to take the place of all warmth and colour in her innocent and blameless life' (248). That first pure image of Eugénie in the bright morning of her love (most scenes in the novel are set in the gloomy parlour in the evening) must therefore remain for the reader in its unspotted, colourless, detail-less state: the only colour note associated with her is the carefully enumerated hoard of gold coins she counts before giving them to Charles. Gold is materially and obsessively present at the dark heart of the Grandet house, replacing paternal affections. It is the dominant colour note of the novel, but, because it is a study in avarice, it is locked away and rarely used. The irony of the novel is that, finally, despite Eugénie's intrinsic and inviolate goodness, she has to operate according to the rules of her father's cash-centred world after his death; it is the only *modus operandi* available to her, for no one else – not even the Church – offers an alternative. Through a tightly controlled, almost negative, use of his 'vestignomie', Balzac provides a commentary on the corruptions of provincial society, from which only Eugénie remains free.

In the Sloper household gold is banked and thus materially absent, not discussed, nor its processes and powers acknowledged. Catherine is therefore both ignorant of the meaning money has for others and of the social markers of wealth, such as those of dress. Her red dress   which both *is* a symbol of gold (it was expensive) and *isn't* (Catherine doesn't know it as such) – is like the gift of a red rose, a value-free expression of love towards those for whom she wears it, and an attempt to replicate the loved and lovely mother she has never seen. It is the loveliest thing she can imagine; but its cost is a matter outside her female sphere, therefore not a part of her language or her meaning. And because she, like Eugénie, is as yet without knowledge of the world and lacks all awareness of a self-image, she, like Eugénie, cannot control the way she is seen.

For Catherine, in her transitional, secular New York world, language, in both words and dress, must connect with the reality of her feelings; she cannot advertise her *jeune fille* status in empty, formulaic terms at the party because she is not aware of language as a manipulable aspect of herself. That long period of suspense, from her engagement to Morris to the break with him, when Sloper watches Catherine, and Catherine watches Morris, is when Catherine's suffering makes her self-aware: aware of her need to be 'good', and also aware of the need to conceal. Her father's death frees her into a clear expression of herself and what she has learnt. The rejected scarlet dress had signalled the abundance of the love she had to give, and, in an ironic reversal of the understood norms of the language of dress, it had also represented her candour and purity. It may be crimson, but it is the moral equivalent of Eugénie's pure whiteness. At the end with Catherine's knowledge of the past, her clear-sightedness about her present circumstances and future prospects, she dresses her good, chaste and wiser self in white, and knows that it is all too late. This is also ironic, in the sense that it is an *antiphrase* representing the innocence she no longer possesses. The ironies of Catherine's dresses will be ones only she can appreciate, as the real uses – and uselessness – of gold was something that only Eugénie came to learn. Their knowledge is as solitary as Isabel Archer's and Lambert Strether's will be. The dress of the dead past of Eugénie's mother, symbol of Christian suffering and resignation, replaces that of Eugénie's fresh and hopeful girlhood; for Catherine the fairy-tale red and gold dress, imagined for a brilliant mother to dazzle a kingly father, is replaced by the now sterile white icon of girlhood; but ironically, without hope. It is after all also a mourning garment.

4
The 'Colour of Life' in *The Portrait of a Lady*

By the time Catherine Sloper gets to wear her proper white dress, around 1866, it has become more of an ironic reflection on her forty-year-old maidenhood than a celebration of it. Daisy Miller's pale-coloured frivolities of the 1870s, while fashionable and appropriate to her youth, mark a shift into a fussier, more fiercely polychromatic period of dress than that of the mid-century, following the introduction of the sewing machine and the development of aniline dyes. Tissot's images of lemon and white dresses from the 1870s may have provided the inspiration for Daisy's appearance, but they are fairly restrained when compared to the riot of colour and trimmings in his other works. Bright colours of chemical intensity and complicated flounces might indeed be taken as much more typical of the 1870s. Hyppolite Taine, in a book reviewed by James, talks of 'violet dresses, of a really ferocious violet'; 'purple or poppy-red silks, grass-green dresses decorated with flowers, azure blue scarves'.[1] These seem to lie behind the model of dress taken for the first filmed version of *The Portrait of a Lady*, made by BBC television in 1968, and set in the 1870s.

Isabel Archer appeared in this film in a dazzling succession of highly wrought frocks, flounced, bustled and beribboned in sky-blues and sugar-pinks.[2] In view of the relative novelty of colour television in Britain at the time this garishness was almost, if not quite, forgivable; if the designer had consulted James's novel, however, rather than costume histories or contemporary paintings, she would have found the colours hopelessly unrepresentative of the text: Isabel Archer dresses throughout the novel largely in black, occasionally in white. This Quakerish wardrobe is shared by Pansy Osmond, in reverse – she is seen mainly in white, once in blue and once in black. James own assertion that 'every touch must count',[3] suggests deliberate aesthetic choices in a novel that calls itself a portrait. He was, after all, also a distinguished art critic: he was careful over visual detail. Colour, or the absence of it, matters.

Colour – or the absence of it – was likewise the subject of remark in the reviews of Jane Campion's 1996 movie version of the novel. Commentators found the movie 'ominously dark',[4] for example; and, indeed, as well as using a gloomy overall palette, Campion actually introduces black-and-white footage at the start and during the course of the film. In a discussion of Campion's film, Diane Sadoff felt there was a modishly sadomasochistic gothicism in the colouring of some of its scenes: 'Shot in the film's pervasive cold blue light, with a virtually chiaroscuro palette, the scene's style is gothic.' She goes on to point to the insistent shots of the black-and-white floor, 'the giant black candelabrum' and the focus on black-gloved hands.[5] The film's final wintry night-time image of Isabel, dressed in black, backed up against the closed door of Gardencourt, contributes a further slant to the controversial ending of the novel for another commentator, who felt that 'the colorless tone of the shots deny the possibility of vividness or fruitfulness'.[6] If Jamesian commentators seem divided over the film's success as an interpretation of the novel, it has to be said that this director paid close and effective attention to James's dress references, using their colour and style to underscore the film's themes of suffocation, negation and entrapment.

James's employment of black and white is central to Campion's filmic interpretation of the novel, and in comparison to the sugar-plum silliness of the 1968 telecast, there is a sense of intellectual engagement with James, to which the austerity of the film's colouring contributes. James's aesthetic decisions in relation to dress were taken seriously by Campion and do seem to justify further enquiry. Why black? The most obvious answer is that Isabel is at first in mourning for her father, then her uncle and finally her cousin. Isabel significantly shares her black and white wardrobe with one other of James's heroines, Milly Theale, who arrives in Europe even more comprehensively bereaved than Isabel. The simple association with mourning might seem to bring further speculation to a dampeningly premature conclusion; but in fact the association of darkness and death with a young woman opens rather than closes avenues for exploration. The image was considered by Edgar Allan Poe, for example, as the most poetically beautiful he could imagine; the courting of death rather the mourning of it was a part of the Romantic tradition in literature – a 'delicious forbidden practice'[7] – and in this respect James could be placed within an American 'romance' tradition that contains both Poe and Hawthorne. Black also recalls the bright but dead figure of Minny Temple, whose memory provided James with inspiration for *The Portrait of a Lady* and *The Wings of the Dove*. Minny Temple died in 1870, at the age of twenty-four, before she could make her longed-for trip to Europe. She, like Isabel and Milly, was orphaned, much bereaved, and because of the requirements of mourning in the 1860s – the years when James knew her best – would have worn a good deal of black. White, on the other hand, as we have seen in relation to Catherine Sloper, was the appropriate formal wear for unmarried girls and Minny's youth, independent spirit and fair colouring makes her memory radiant to James. Extremes of light and dark are therefore, for James, inescapably woven into Minny Temple's figure.

These oppositional contrasts recall the sharp chiaroscuro of Eugénie Grandet's image, and to some extent these oppositions point up the melodramatic aspects of James's novel – melodrama's logic of 'the excluded middle',[8] in Peter Brooks' phrase. But unlike contemporaries working at the sensationalist end of the melodramatic genre, such as Mary Braddon, who are specific at length and to a fault, James employed dress sparingly, as an intrinsic part of the novel's pattern of symbols. As Adeline Tintner remarks, clothes in the iconography of *The Portrait of a Lady* are '[f]ar from surface decorations, they are integral to the novel'.[9] In this novel James uses images of dress which are inseparable from and essential to his themes of the blighting of hope, the denial of youth and the crushing of the spirit. The flights and drops between black and white are a reminder of, but also a dissent from, the melodramatic trope to which the novel partially conforms.[10]

The close relation of James's fiction to the world of galleries and painting has already been established by Viola Hopkins Winner, Adeline Tintner and David Lubin. Lyall Powers too, in the Coda to his study of the novel, not only notes Isabel's black dresses, but also associates this colour note with the portrait, or the 'framing', of Isabel. Visual arts seem to provide an inescapable context for this novel: the recent movie was seen as an 'art' film and Campion certainly made full use of shots of paintings and statuary, as well lingering on the sensuous surfaces of velvets and silks. And within the portrait, or portraits, of the novel we have a figure of a woman in a dress.

Although there are comparatively few scenes in *The Portrait of a Lady* in which dress is dealt with at any length, their frequency is not an index of their importance. James in fact enhanced his references to dress, in tandem with his increased emphasis on Isabel's consciousness, in the revised 1908 edition of the novel.[11] Isabel's first appearance, seen from a distance, is simply as 'a tall girl in a black dress... bare-headed, as if she were staying in the house'.[12] She emerges from the shadows of the doorway of Gardencourt into a sunlit garden and into the view of three men to whom she is still a stranger. The description is distant and economical, registering simply the dramatic colour note against grass and sunshine, and the social implication of her hatlessness.

The next dressed image of Isabel is in the garden itself, in high summer, where 'in a white dress ornamented with black ribbons she formed among the flickering shadows a graceful and harmonious image' (1.139–40). Mourning for a parent in the 1870s required nine months in black, three months in half-mourning, and Isabel's dresses conform to these demands; the ribbons are characteristic of the highly decorated fashions of the time. James believed that it was only as an historian that the novelist had the smallest *locus standi*, and he is precise in such matters. However, the second image of Isabel is not merely historically and socially accurate. It also moves the novel into a different emotional and visual climate; not one of mourning but one close in atmosphere to that of the early Impressionists – Monet's *Women in the Garden* of 1867, for example, where figures in white touched with black, drift in a dazzle of heat and shadow, beneath trees. This is an authorial narrative voice describing Isabel and therefore a 'painterly' one: as Anne Hollander remarks, '[b]lack and white used together have a dramatic beauty without the need of symbolism'.[13] We have a sense that Isabel has stepped from the airless gloom of her past in the Albany house, into a Europe full of bright promise, of widening garden vistas, in a white dress appropriate to her age and hopes at this new stage in her life, one which is touched with only the lightest memories of mourning.

Anne Hollander, in her discussion of the usages of black in the history of dress, usefully discriminates between 'the conventionally sober, self-denying black and the dramatic, isolating and distinguishing black'[14] – what she calls 'sober' black and 'emotional' black: a discrimination which becomes particularly necessary in relation to the latter part of the nineteenth century, where the colour black seemed ubiquitous not only in male fashions and in the excesses of mourning-dress, but where it had also become the standard colour for the work-wear of the new clerical classes. The satanic, erotic connotations of black, however, inherited from early Romantic traditions in art and literature were still an optional reading for women's black dresses in the second half of the century; the furore caused by Sargent's portrait of Mme Gautreau, *Madame X*, in an off-the-shoulder black dress, shows how close such meanings lay to the surface. Mme Gautreau's mother threw a noisy scene in Sargent's studio, declaring her daughter to be the mockery of Paris and a lost woman as a consequence of the portrait.

James played on the ambiguities contained in black dress from the start of his career as a writer and Isabel's version was not the first to have appeared in his fictional world. In 'The Story of a Masterpiece' (1868), a young woman, having her portrait painted, is asked by the artist to wear black. The permission of her fiancé, who has commissioned the portrait, is sought in case he objects to the colour. But he is 'enthusiastic for the black dress, which, in truth, seemed only to confirm and enrich ... the young girl's look of undiminished youth'.[15] It seems, however, that black has other meanings for the artist, which begin to be evident to the fiancé as the portrait progresses. The painter has known the girl himself in the past but found her shallow and heartless. The finished work, though a masterpiece, so horrifies the fiancé that he destroys it. What he first saw was the girl's youthful fairness enhanced and dramatised by black; what he finally sees is fairness besmirched by a moral darkness that is intrinsic to the way the portrait is painted. The negative properties of black clothing, 'its connotations of fatal sexuality', thus gradually emerge from the portrait for the fiancé: 'A lady in black,' according to Hollander, 'is not only dramatic and dignified but also dangerous.'[16]

This is 'emotional' black, quite different from the 'sober' variety to be found in the black dress worn by the deaf-mute Miss Gifford in 'Professor Fargo', a story of 1874, where the colour of the dress has a positive value, representing the last shred of her father's respectability and integrity. He is a failed inventor turned travelling showman, the partner of a mountebank spiritualist he despises. The girl's shabby dress, her disability and her pale prettiness, paradoxically represent for him the only bright spot in this tawdry world. Her black dress is the black of self-denial, respectability and straitened means, typified for the whole of the second half of the century by Richard Redgrave's hugely popular painting, *The Poor Teacher*. The dull garment separates Miss Gifford off from the blowsy theatricality of her setting, as Redgrave's painting isolates the teacher from the brighter and more hopeful outside world. Any mitigation of Miss Gifford's dull black is a step into the world from which her father still desperately holds himself aloof. Indeed, he declares that were he to see her in a pink dress and artificial flowers he would quit the partnership. The narrator later notices that her dress has acquired a coloured sash and a suggestion of flounce, but this change does not signal an attempt to titillate flagging audiences, as we might expect; more sadly it denotes the transfer of the girl's affections from her father to the fraudulent Professor Fargo. In both these stories we see James experimenting with the positive/negative implications of young women in black: by the time he comes to Isabel Archer's wardrobe he has found in these apparently simple contrasts promisingly complex possibilities.

The death of Mr Touchett in Chapter 19 of *The Portrait of a Lady* closes the idyllic, 'garden' stage of Isabel's career; she leaves off white and resumes black for her uncle, but emerges from this mourning with prospects made even more brilliant, for in fairy-tale fashion she has inherited a fortune. The question of how she *now* sees herself, and therefore how she expresses herself to others, becomes critical. Just before Mr Touchett's death Isabel has her famous conversation with Madame Merle on the subject of personal appearances: how the 'self' is related to its 'shell' and 'cluster of appurtenances'. Echoing one of Balzac's theories of 'vestignomie' – that we impress ourselves on our surroundings and on everything we own[17] – Madame Merle believes 'that a large part of myself is in the clothes I choose to wear. I've a great respect for *things*. One's self – for other people – is one's expression of oneself.' Isabel, the idealist, begins reasonably enough by rejecting the notion that things can express her adequately: 'Nothing that belongs to me is any measure of me .... Certainly the clothes which as you say, I choose to wear, don't express me .... My clothes may express the dressmaker, but they don't express me. To begin with it's not my own choice that I wear them; they're imposed upon me by society' (1. 287–8). Madame Merle exposes Isabel's jejune line of reasoning by asking her if she would prefer to go without clothes: and James arranges that the novel should largely underwrite Madame Merle's dissent from Isabel's view. Taken to its logical conclusion, Isabel's argument would lead to a rejection of all social forms; but she does not see this. In the story of Cinderella, the first sign of the transformation from rags to riches is the momentous ballgown in which she finds her prince and becomes a princess. Isabel too, with her American freedoms and now her American money, has become one of James's princesses, but she enters, in Dorothea Krook's words, 'this infinitely encumbered and encrusted condition of life'[18] in a black dress, which effaces her identity. James, as an accurate social historian, puts her in mourning for her uncle, and as this is the last description we have of her appearance until we see her three years after her marriage – again in black – the image must linger.

In the revised 1908 edition of the novel, with its greater emphasis on Isabel's consciousness, James expands Isabel's impression of her first brief stay in Rome to contain 'the figure of some small princess of the ages of dress overmuffled in a mantle of state and dragging a train that it took pages or historians to hold up' (2: 16). Tintner sees this revision as an extension of Isabel's 'capacity for poetic flights to make it more credible that Osmond has caught her imagination'.[19] While this may be so, it seems more specifically to prefigure Isabel's own reappearance, after marriage, in a dress whose long train weighs portentously upon her, and which James took the trouble to describe twice. It is also one of those moments in the novel, outside the famous chapter 42, when we share Isabel's consciousness of herself, how it feels to inhabit her 'personal shell'. Significantly, Isabel's odd description of her Roman sojourn occurs only moments before Osmond's proposal of marriage. The suggestions of suffocating convention that underlie this imagined impression are to be fully realised in Isabel's later physical appearance as witnessed by Ned Rosier and Ralph. Otherwise, the great events in the traditional heroine's career, courtship and marriage, classic opportunities for a display of finery, pass without any notation of Isabel's appearance. Her wedding indeed disappears into a three-year gap between chapters. How then has she appeared to her 'prince', Gilbert Osmond, in the crucial years between the two black dresses?

Having denied that any material object can be an expression of her 'self', Isabel fatally fails to take into account how the wealth she has inherited – invisible but certainly material – might define her image for others. Eugénie Grandet's gold is known to be physically there, in the same house, occupying a room, as Eugénie does. In Henry James's world of paper money, material gold is absent and represented by signs of analogies and connotations only – the thing itself is banked and shrouded, spoken of confidentially, in moments of almost sexual intimacy, as when Madame Merle and Osmond are discussing Isabel's inheritance. The change in Isabel's financial status is publicly, if silently signalled by her embarkation for Italy with her aunt. The inheritance is the means by which she is launched into international society, and despite her negative dress, her wealth is what Madame Merle and Osmond have seen before anything. But Osmond's fastidiousness demands more than mere money. His ideal of womanhood, something of which he must have seen in Isabel, is expressed in the image of his daughter, Pansy, presented to us during Osmond's courtship of Isabel as the ultimate *jeune fille*.

Pansy is seen from her sixteenth through to her twentieth year, and is therefore only a few years younger than Isabel, but this 'little girl from the convent' (1. 367) hardly seems to advance beyond childhood. Almost every reference to Pansy in the text is qualified by 'small', 'little' and 'diminutive'. We first see her in 'a scant white dress' with 'her small shoes tied sandal fashion about her ankles' (1. 365). Her subsequent dresses are 'prim' and 'white', 'scanty' and 'too short', and, to enhance the infantile effect, worn with coats that are long and hats that are too big. Since the late eighteenth century white had been considered the appropriate colour for the 'best' dresses of children and unmarried girls; in France in particular, 'no ornaments, with the exception perhaps, of a single bracelet, are allowed to the *jeune fille*; her dress must be white; the flowers in her hair white also . . . the appearance of a French ball is that of spotless white.'[20] Pansy has been sent to the convent to learn French, among other things, and the convent sister with whom Pansy is most closely associated is French, but even so, Pansy's wardrobe seems quite excessively and eerily white. The dazzling warmth and freshness we had associated with Isabel's earlier white dress is here turned into a caricature of youthfulness, and the smallness and scantiness of Pansy's clothes seem designed to impede the growth and movement appropriate to her youth. Pansy breaks the rule of white on only two occasions. One is at the evening party where she declares her love for Rosier and where Warburton first sees her – 'that young lady in the blue dress. She has a charming face' (2. 131). (The attentive reader might remember an early description of Madame Merle's appearance, at a Gardencourt dinner, dressed in dark blue.) For once there is nothing diminutive about her; she is seen by Warburton as a young lady, and she speaks her mind to Rosier independently of her father. But this is Pansy's only moment of self-expression; retribution follows and Osmond bundles her back, aged nearly twenty, to her convent-prison, from where we have our sad last glimpse of her, described by Madame Merle as 'a little dismal . . . . of course, she has no occasion to dress. She wears a little black frock' (2. 376/7). She dwindles, not into childhood white, but more ominously, into black.

Unlike the paired heroines of the nineteenth-century sensation-novel, Isabel and Pansy, despite their black and white colouring, are not contrasted. Each serves the other as a mirror, reflecting warningly into both the past and the future. Pansy is Osmond's creation, an artificially conserved *tabula rasa*: denied normal development, she is 'the white flower of cultivated sweetness . . . a pure white surface, successfully kept so' (2. 26). Her role first as daughter and then putative wife of a chosen husband, will be entirely in the service of male requirements – a warning that Isabel ignores. Isabel's early history, as the motherless youngest daughter of an eccentric father, may also remind us of Pansy. Perhaps not coincidentally, Pansy's appearance conforms to John Ruskin's late, mad taste for Kate Greenaway nymphets; her demure girlishness is very different from Isabel's earlier unguarded but intelligent spontaneity. In Judith Woolf's memorable phrase, Pansy's state is 'achieved by a kind of bonsai technique, a trimming of the roots of the spirit'.[21] Unconsciously, Isabel reads the semiotics of Pansy's appearance, and trims the roots of her own spirit to please Osmond. Pansy's whiteness signals uncritical ignorance as well as bland innocence, and so Isabel has to negate and suppress the complexity of her spirited and questioning self to achieve the desired effect on Osmond. We are therefore given no description of Isabel's appearance during Osmond's courtship of her – neither black nor white – for we never go 'behind' him to see what he sees; we have instead Isabel's registering of Pansy's appearance and her romantic misreading of Osmond.

Isabel sees in Osmond what she believes she wants – 'a person whose own identity has been and continues to be defined by lack'.[22] Her belief that the self is capable of expression without material means is a deadly mistake in more than one sense. It is, in the first place, as we have seen, a kind of anti-physical death-wish more characteristic of Albigensian heresies than late nineteenth-century consumer capitalism. It also blinds her to the way others may see her, and worst of all leads her to read positive qualities into the mere absence of 'things' in others. 'He was dressed,' James says of Osmond, 'as a man dresses who takes little other trouble about it than to have no vulgar things' (1. 329). Such an absence of signs has to be as carefully worked at as the appearance of a dandy – is in fact a version of dandyism. The chief aim of George Brummell, the *beau idéal* of dandyism, was, after all, 'to avoid anything marked. . . . Long hours of concentration and preparation, of finicky attention to detail, were required to produce its [effect of] dignified simplicity.'[23] One might imagine that the dandy would be the hero of Balzac's 'Treatise on the Elegant Life'. But Balzac sees him as a heretic in the religion of elegance. The Elegant Life is 'the manifestation of thoughts in outward appearances' . . . it makes 'poetry out of the material life', and dandyism is simply 'an affectation of fashion . . . in becoming a dandy a man becomes a piece of boudoir furniture, an ingenious doll to be put on a horse or a sofa – but a thinking being – never!'[24] The dandy sees only the fashion in fashions, not the thought or the feeling. Osmond's ceaseless search for superiority should betray him, for in the Elegant Life, according to Balzac, there is no superiority; equals treat with equals. Isabel fails to read Osmond's appearance correctly; instead her devotion to 'romantic effects' supplies 'the human element which she was sure had not been wanting' (1. 383). His meagreness and constriction, the result of modest means as well as artful arrangement, are seen by Isabel as distinguished and intriguing, marks of some imagined suffering which make him so much more serious and mysterious than either Warburton or Goodwood. What she does not see is the snobbery and greed which drive him. His offer of marriage is disarmingly negative – no vulgar 'things': 'I've neither fortune, nor fame, nor extrinsic advantages of any kind. So I offer nothing' (2. 18) – which cleverly makes Isabel feel better about being rich. He offers her an aesthetic of negation which she mistakes for unconventionality, sensitivity and intellectual freedom. One should be clear that Osmond does not deceive Isabel; he persuasively presents himself, while she deceives herself by misreading him, and deceives him into misreading her: 'if she had not deceived him in intention she understood how completely she must have done so in fact. She had effaced herself when he first knew her; she had made herself small, pretending there was less of her than there really was' (2. 191). She has made herself into a version of Pansy, misleading Osmond into seeing her as another blank surface. Black and white are both colours that deny colour; Isabel and Pansy are the two sides of Osmond's valueless coin.

Isabel does get her ball-gown, but unlike Cinderella's dress it comes as a consequence of her marriage, not a prelude to it. Gilbert Osmond has married her for money, so the novel in effect poses a question: is Isabel's 'cluster of appurtenances' – her dress – now an expression of herself or her circumstances? Is she creating a self-portrait, or is her portrait in the hands of others? Isabel's ball-gown is seen twice; once by Ned Rosier and once by Ralph Touchett. As we saw in *Washington Square*, the symbolism of dress is at its most telling on ceremonial occasions, such as balls and evening-parties, so James arranges that we should see Isabel's appearance as it registers itself on two very different consciousnesses: each reads into her image meanings appropriate to his relation towards her. Rosier and Isabel have known one another as children, but now as an admirer of Pansy, Rosier sees her as Pansy's stepmother and potential mother-in-law: roles with a generational distance as well as latent darker shades. He registers the changes to Isabel's appearance, in the doorway of her Roman Palazzo Roccanera: 'She was dressed in black velvet; she looked high and splendid . . . framed in the gilded doorway, she struck our young man as the picture of a gracious lady' (2. 105). As a collector of fine china, Rosier's eye for surfaces notes the contrast of black velvet against gilt. Velvet is a rich fabric appropriate for a mature 'gracious lady', and indeed her radiance has gone, transferred to her frame, for velvet absorbs rather than reflects light. She pauses in the doorway, attracting Rosier's attention: this is 'emotional' black, black as 'a brilliant *coup de théâtre* in the ballroom', described by Hollander as a usage of the colour in the 'anti-fashion, rebellious tradition, which seeks to isolate and distinguish the wearer'.[25] Rosier focuses on the 'lady-like' quality of the effect she creates. By the latter half of the century the choice of black for evening wear signalled a class distinction, which was no less fierce because – being American – it had to be unspoken. Lois Banner notes that developments in the textile industry had made cheap versions of bright, showy evening-fabrics available to working-women.[26] If aspirants to 'La Vie Elégante', according to Balzac's theory of 'vestignomie', wished to distinguish themselves from the vulgar as clearly as possible – the dynamic that drives Osmond's whole existence – then to wear rich black velvet (and cotton-velvet is easily distinguished from the silk variety) was to be a 'Lady'. There is a cost: instead of the spontaneity of her movement out of the doorway into the garden, in the first black dress at Gardencourt, Isabel now stands framed in artificial light, at an evening party, in a palace of black stone, decorated by Caravaggio, master of night-scenes and violent dramas. The bright day of promising vistas has narrowed into a shadowy interior, already envisaged for us by Rosier as a dungeon with a dark past.

A shadow that has fallen across her life is the death of her child: 'but it was a sorrow she scarcely spoke of . . . it belonged to the past moreover, it had occurred six months before and she had already laid aside the tokens of mourning' (2. 143). The significance of the black velvet dress, therefore, is not mourning for her child. James is careful to make this point, because what immediately follows is Ralph's first view of her since marriage. Ralph, the novel's central intelligence, has wanted to see what Isabel has made of the world that has lain all before her, freed as she has been from the limitations of poverty or family ties, with all the advantages of health, intelligence and beauty. He is horrified by what he sees: 'Poor human-hearted Isabel, what perversity had bitten her? Her light step drew a mass of drapery behind it; her intelligent head sustained a majesty of ornament . . . what he saw was a fine lady who was supposed to represent something. . . . What did Isabel represent? . . . Gilbert Osmond' (2. 143–4). Rosier's rather awed image of Isabel is here reinterpreted by Ralph's more perceptive glance, which focuses on the dragging mass of her clothing (Plate III), the heavy burden on her head and the sacrifice of identity that this implies. She has become the 'overmuffled princess' of her own earlier imagining. Appropriately it is Ralph, the source of her wealth, who measures its weight upon her. These gorgeous ornaments speak of Osmond's good fortune not Isabel's, for the appearance of the nineteenth-century wife, as Veblen was soon to point out, was the attestation of her husband's bank account.

Isabel's choice of black is her single idiosyncracy – an isolating gesture, as we have seen, with elements of rebellion, as well as distinction, attaching to it. Miss Oakey's advice book on dress has a chapter headed 'The Danger of Black Velvet'[27] and in Mrs Oliphant's novel of 1876, *Phoebe Junior*, the eponymous heroine rejects her mother's suggestion of white tarlatan for a ball – '[w]hite shows no invention,' she says: 'What I incline to, if you won't be shocked, is black.' Her mother *is* shocked – 'Black!...As if you were fifty! Why, I don't consider myself old enough for black.' Phoebe puts herself into black silk and her mother in black velvet, explaining that black will 'tone us down' (in terms of their blonde colouring) as well as 'throw us up'[28] – that is, dramatise and distinguish them. Phoebe is, of course, a success at the ball. This gesture, at the beginning of the book establishes her as independent, self-aware and in control of her image, as well as something of a rebel. She outrages everyone, then organizes them into successful solutions of their various problems, and finally marries a self-confessedly feeble-minded, but rich young man whom she intends to organise into Parliament. The final pages record Phoebe's mild irritation at seeing her mother at the wedding, back into her favourite, conventionally cheery tints. The hints of sedition contained in Isabel Osmond's dress are not as openly declared as in Mrs Oliphant's description of Phoebe, who is the heroine, after all, of a comedy. The note of dissent from convention, however, is there at the heart of Isabel's appearance at her evening party; moreover, the tradition of dressing Tragedy Queens in black velvet adds a darker undertone to the note of rebellion, given the theatrical nature of this occasion.

Isabel's style otherwise conforms to that of the Perfect Lady of the mid-1870s, described by Willett Cunnington, as 'swathed in a maze of polychromatics, festooned with trimmings, beads, jewels, feathers, ribbons, lace'.[29] The skirts of this period were so constricting that they were 'frightful scabbards', all the weight of the material being in the immense train at the back. The standard dress length was 12 yards, but an evening gown such as Isabel's needed some 20 yards. From 1873 to about 1878 hats and headdresses expanded upwards, and hair extended both up and down (with the addition of false hair) in heavy braids, sausage curls and loose chignons (see Figure 2). Cunnington describes an evening hairstyle for a married woman in 1876 (the year in which this chapter of *The Portrait of a Lady* is set, though it is, of course, written in 1880) featuring several piled-up coronets of plaits, with a couple of ringlets falling on to the shoulders; gold braid crosses the top tier of plaits, with a gilt dagger on one side: a spray of leaves with gold fruit falls down the back.[30]

While James's image is authentic, then, because it is based on a recognisable moment in fashion, its function in the novel is symbolic. He
focuses on those elements of fashion that will contribute to the image
of Isabel's dress as a carapace of class, wealth and magnificence, but which
will also foreground the meaning of its dragging, pitiful weight. The
vulnerable orphan in white has become a tragic queen in black velvet;
the lightness of Isabel's step and the intelligence of her head have suc-
cumbed to the heavy restrictions of a tyrant. Later, she looks back and
tries to chart the journey of her marriage from hope to nightmare, and
'[w]hen she saw this rigid system close about her... that sense of darkness
and suffocation... took possession of her' (2. 199). Jane Campion's film
reinterprets James's words in one of the movie's most violent and powerful images: as Isabel moves across Osmond's room to the door, after he has
accused her of preventing Pansy's marriage to Warburton, Osmond follows her and deliberately steps on the heavy train of her dress, bringing
Isabel crashing to the ground. He does not, in conventionally gothic
terms, threaten to imprison her, but his action warns her of her essentially subordinate position and of her committment to him, however
painful, in her marriage vows. Unless she proposes to follow in the
vulgarly adulterous footsteps of the Countess Gemini – all frills and
feathers – she is trapped, and bound to him. The straitjacket of dress has
spread to her psychological and emotional environment; the one

Figure 2 Ladies' coiffures. *Harper's Bazaar*, 1876.

independent gesture she can freely make is to represent her new-found sorrow in black – the colour, as John Harvey says, 'that is without colour, without light, the colour of grief, of loss, of humility, of guilt, of shame'.[31]

Osmond requires that Isabel shall become his Angel in the House to match Pansy, his little Convent Flower. She will become part of a decorative scheme with 'nothing of her own but her pretty appearance' (2. 195). Isabel *does* become an Angel – for Pansy, for Ralph and also for Osmond, though not the one he had planned. The evening dress of black velvet leads in to Isabel's nocturnal vigil of Chapter 42, where she starts to piece together the ominous meanings of her marriage relationship and refashion her identity within the means at her disposal. Her second appearance in white follows this and takes place at night, when, on their return from an evening party, Osmond accuses Isabel of intercepting Warburton's letter requesting Pansy's hand. As she witnesses Osmond's descent into heartless greed, and as he ascribes to Isabel the squalid scheming into which he himself has sunk, she rises to her feet, like an Archangel over Satan: 'in her white cloak which covered her to her feet, she might have represented the Angel of Disdain, first cousin to that of pity. "Oh Gilbert, for a man who was so fine – !"' (2. 276). With her arms concealed by the cloak, this one resumption of white gives Isabel the appearance of having great wings; it is also a moment of clarity as to the nature of the man she has married. Like a flash of lightning in the night it seems to signal impending divine retribution but, we might add, melodramatically, it also illumines the horror.

Osmond has in this same scene indicated that Pansy's feelings for Rosier (or indeed for anyone other than himself) are of no consequence to him, and thus Isabel's position as guardian angel to Pansy is reinforced. Pansy herself has already assigned such a function to Isabel, and in her final scene with Isabel, reminds her of it, when in a sudden moment of terror she clutches at Isabel's dress and begs her not to leave. With new maturity she has noticed Isabel's unhappiness – an echo, and harbinger perhaps, of her own. Isabel's demonstrated contempt for Osmond's ambitions gives her the balance of power in their relationship, which, if it will not make for marital harmony, will at least give her a negotiating position and a role in relation to Pansy. The white cloak, though far from the sunlit hopes of the Gardencourt scene, represents, one might say, a glimmer of independence, a way out of the deadly 'mold and decay' of the Palazzo Roccanera.

Isabel has appeared as a white angel of disdain to Osmond and as a mother's sheltering skirt for Pansy, now to complete this stage she must become Ralph's black angel of death. Positive and negative associations of black and white, life and death, are subverted, for this is a positive role which combines her love for Ralph with a hard-won sense of freedom. She has had to defy Osmond and assert her moral and physical independence of him in order to be at Ralph's bedside. Ralph and Isabel are now for each other the ghosts of suffering they spoke of six years before: 'they talk about the angel of death', Ralph says to Isabel, 'It's the most beautiful of all. You've been like that' (2. 412–13). She is all in black again, and as Mrs Touchett remarks, it is ' "a very odd dress to travel in." Isabel glanced at her garment. "I left Rome at an hour's notice; I took the first that came." "Your sisters, in America, wished to know how you dress... they seemed to have the right idea: that you never wear anything less than black brocade" '(2. 406). Unreconstructed Americans, like the Rucks of 'The Pension Beaurepas', held elaborate black silk to be a secure sign of both wealth and respectability, a sentiment shared, one imagines by Isabel's un-Europeanised sisters. Such meanings have long since ceased to concern Isabel, but neither is it that Isabel has been too preoccupied to give the matter thought; black so dominates her wardrobe that it comes most naturally to hand.

Isabel's choice of black is out of her unhappiness but equally it is a positive expression of herself by material means, independent of what others have tried to make of her, with their 'genius for upholstery.' If Osmond has wished to grind Isabel in the mill of conventional dress, her choice of black is a denial of his princely ambitions. Black fashions, according to Harvey 'have tended... to be anti-fashion fashions'.[32] As Mrs Oliphant's Phoebe saw, black paradoxically both effaces itself and is conspicuous; for Isabel it is thus a clear denial of showiness as well as an isolating and distinguishing sign. She chooses to dress like this when fashion, as we have seen, favours the crudely bright. Perrot, tracing the career of the black dress in Europe after 1860, notes that 'from a classic it declined to the most common of the commons. To wear a black taffeta dress on social calls or for promenades is to advertise a precarious budget or imposed thrift.'[33] The anxious, sisterly enquiries from America about Isabel's wardrobe represent the way in which European fashion has been, for America, high fashion. Depending on how *au fait* Isabel's sisters are with transatlantic fashions, Isabel may have thoroughly confused them by choosing fashionably rich fabrics in an unfashionable colour, or reassured them, with her costly black, of her unchanging and respectable Americanness.[34]

Isabel's final appearance is a disappearance, into the darkness, through the doorway which framed her original entrance across the sunlit lawns of Gardencourt – a negative of the original positive. As in that first image, she wears mourning black. The dress may seem the same but its meaning has changed: 'Her attitude had a singular absence of purpose; her hands, hanging at her sides, lost themselves in the folds of her black dress' (2. 429). Her energetic optimism has been smothered in demoralising grief, not only for Ralph, but for herself and her marriage. Goodwood comes upon her, sitting in the garden at night, and it takes his kiss, an act of attempted possession, and his offer of a false notion of individual liberty, to crystallise Isabel's view of her situation and what she needs to do about it: the black dress is a reinforcement of her negative answers to both Goodwood and Osmond. J. C. Agnew sees Isabel here as freeing herself from her role as a commodity: 'she casts off her mask and recovers a serenity that has become hers by virtue of an act of self-conscious renunciation, an act that raises her above the sorts of exchange to which she is, in form, submitting by her marriage to Osmond.'[35] The measure of herself, achieved through suffering, and given material expression in her dress, sends her back through the doorway, in her own version of freedom, to Rome, Osmond and Pansy.

The black and white definition of Isabel's clothes can be contrasted with Isabel's own perceptions of the images presented by Mrs Touchett and Madame Merle. *The Portrait of a Lady* is concerned with suggesting the truths and realities that hide beneath surface appearances; both of these women are identified by the resistant surfaces they have developed to baffle disclosure. Mrs Touchett's appearance is characterised by her 'comprehensive waterproof mantle' (1. 31), a garment that Isabel refers to three times in connection with her aunt. It is again worth noting James as historian here: weatherproofing of outer clothing began in the late 1840s, and in 1879 Thomas Burberry took out a patent for his waterproof cloth – a much improved version of the stiff, evil-smelling Mackintosh fabric. Obviously, the waterproof has other meanings within the scheme of the novel, but independent lady travellers such as Mrs Touchett would no doubt have taken enthusiastically to a Burberry.

After Mr Touchett's death, Isabel begins to reflect pityingly on the apparent impermeability of Mrs Touchett's nature which has 'so little surface' and offers 'so limited a face to the accretions of human contact' (1. 317). Mrs Touchett's approach to human relationships is dry and distancing, as if she fears the vulnerability that emotional contact entails. But her defences finally crumble at the death of her son, Ralph. Isabel, at his bedside, not only notices that now her aunt is wearing 'a little grey dress of the most undecorated fashion' (2. 404), but that she is no longer so 'dry' (2. 406). Mrs Touchett accepts Isabel's embrace and allows herself one stark expression of her grief and loneliness. James does not, of course, suggest that she has spent most of the novel's six years in a raincoat; but for Isabel this garment becomes symptomatic of her aunt's difficulties with the life of the emotions. Isabel's own developing awareness and maturity – about herself and others – enable her to read beneath Mrs Touchett's resistant and indeterminate surface.

Madame Merle has quite other secrets to hide beneath a surface that is thick with 'accretions'. Isabel and Ralph refer frequently to the finish and elegance of Madame Merle's social persona – Isabel, at first with admiration and envy; Ralph, with a warning undertone of mockery. There appears to be no irregularity or weakness on this perfectly spherical, polished surface, no place where insight might find some purchase. We have only one description, however, of her dress, which is when she rustles into dinner, shortly before Mr Touchett's death, 'fastening a bracelet, dressed in dark blue satin, which exposed a white bosom that was ineffectually covered by a curious silver necklace' (1. 252–3) – an image that rests somewhere between a Madonna and a Magdalen. References to Madame Merle later in the novel synthesise the image of her polished exterior with that of the silver ornament, giving Isabel the impression of an oddly military figure, 'completely equipped for the social battle' her necklace now 'a sort of corselet of silver' (2. 154–5).[36] While Isabel at first admires Madame Merle's presentation of herself, the very image of the accomplished 'Lady', she has also uneasy intimations that it is rather overdone. Lois Banner, commenting on the American 'woman of fashion' in the nineteenth-century novel, notes that the late-century version is 'even more dangerous' than the *ante-bellum* adventuress, for 'they are not usually unattached women, but rather wives and mothers with direct power over husbands and children'. They are not only representative of the worst in American consumerism and materialism, but their grasping ambition threatens the lives of women of 'heroic qualities and happy lives'.[37] After her marriage, when she glimpses Osmond and Madame Merle together in a scene suggestive of unwarranted intimacy, Isabel begins the process of uncovering the layers of the older woman's protective glaze. Madame Merle has earlier warned Isabel that she herself has been 'shockingly chipped and cracked' and when seen in a strong light she is 'a horror' (1. 27). She is, indeed, finally exposed to the searching light of Isabel's accumulated perceptions. The horror that the corselet of silver has concealed is not only adultery and an illegitimate child, but also the more recent sale and betrayal of Isabel's affections. Madame Merle's one described dress is thus in effect a sinister version of an adulteress's garment, like Hester Prynne's embroidered dress in Hawthorne's *The Scarlet Letter*. Serena Merle also conceals beneath her emblem the deeper shame of her co-conspirator, Osmond.

If Isabel, in her black and white dresses, is clear and transparent, vulnerable to interpretation and manipulation by others, Mrs Touchett (who is colourless and resistant to contact) and Madame Merle (who is polished and ungraspable) seem invulnerable and in control of the effects they produce. Finally, of course, Isabel's clarity proves a stronger defence against the betrayals of the heart than either impermeability or surface gloss. Faced with Osmond's hatred of her revealed self, she is able to reject strategies of concealment: 'there was no use pretending, wearing a mask or dress' (2. 190). Her deepening understanding of the other two women, the giving or withholding of sympathy towards them, are crucial elements in the fashioning of Isabel's projected new self. That she pities their self-imposed, loveless isolation, is a measure of the strength of her mature identity.

Isabel, then, has begun by denying that appearance can reflect identity, although she herself has judged the men in her life in just this way, often mistakenly: 'You judge only from outside – you don't care' (1. 112), Warburton complains. But as a consequence of her judgements she falls into the hands of those who seek to make her in their own image. Her growing, conscious resistance to exploitation, her attempt to take her portrait into her own hands, is signalled by her choice of black, a denial of show. The portrait, as James suggests in his Preface to the novel, is one that aspires to self-portraiture: the key was to '[p]lace the centre of the subject in the young woman's own consciousness' (1. xv). The Preface, however, is part of the 1908 revision and could be said to emphasise the role of Isabel's consciousness in the novel rather more than is justified. The strategy of the 'reflecting consciousness', arrived at *through* writing this novel, is one which James is to explore further in his later work. Isabel's portrait is thus not quite a self-portrait; as Lyall Powers suggests, the three framed images of Isabel's black-dressed figure are three superimposed images, not separate and sequential ones. Furthermore, they suggest that the portrait is not necessarily a finished one and that James was working, in a prefiguring of the novel of 'spatial form', towards something akin to what he admired in the painted portrait.

Placed within the cultural context of dress and the representation of dress in the actual painted portraits of the period, James's treatment of

dress in the novel takes on a new weight. In a review of the picture
season in London of 1877, James singles out G. F. Watts's portrait of Mrs
Percy Wyndham 'for the art of combining the imagination and ideal
element in portraiture with extreme solidity and separating great elegance from small elegance':[38] that is, the portrait is solidly but not
laboriously specific. Its surface, and treatment of dress, are impression-
istic in their broad, loose effects, a contrast to the glossy photographic
realism of painters such as James Tissot, whom James compared unfa-
vourably with Watts. Watts's composition has depth and suggestiveness
and the bold, asymmetric sunflower pattern of the dress is the focus of
interest, rather than material detail and finish. As we have seen, James's
only concessions to fashion details are when the touch counts – the
heaviness of the train of Isabel's evening dress, for example, or the white
cloak that reaches to the ground. Otherwise there is an economy about
what he chooses to record: Concord black-and-white, one might say, in
preference to European elaborations. James's later enthusiasm for the
work of Sargent indicates his continuing taste for the suggestive qualities he had discerned in Watts. 'An American,' James said of Hawthorne,
'can read between the lines – he completes the suggestions – he con-
structs a picture.'[39]

A notable feature of early comments on *The Portrait of a Lady* were
complaints such as Mrs Oliphant's, that it was no portrait at all. It was
not what readers had been used to. What was it that James failed to
supply? Mrs Oliphant herself, as we have seen, was aware of the significance of dress in the construction of a character – she actually wrote a
book on dress herself – but for profusion of realistic costume detail she
pales beside the indefatigable and best-selling Mary Braddon who, in
1884, published another of her sensation-novels, *Phantom Fortune*. The
novel's dénouement, in which the anti-heroine, Lesbia, *nearly* runs off
with a handsome cad in preference to her rich, elderly fiancé, is pre-
ceded by a description of the outfit in which she proposes to do this:

> Lesbia's Chaumont costume was a success.... the dark-blue silken
> jersey, sparkling with closely studded indigo beads, fitted the slim
> graceful figure as a serpent's scales fit the serpent. The coquettish
> little blue silk toque, the careless cluster of gold-coloured poppies,
> against the glossy brown hair, the large sunshade of old gold satin
> lined with indigo, the flounced petticoat of softest Indian silk, the
> dainty little tan-coloured boots with high heels and pointed toes
> were all perfect in their fashion.[40]

This is only the last in a long succession of descriptions of dress, encrusta-
tions slapped gratuitously onto the fabric of the narrative, causing it to
sag somewhat. In order to distinguish her prose from that of magazine
fashion-pages Braddon here drags in a clumsy 'serpent' simile, but the
image is given without viewpoint, sense of distance or context.
Although this is in a way a 'vivid' description, it is the literary equivalent
of a Tissot painting, leaving no room for the workings of the imagination.

James had read half a dozen or so of Mary Braddon's works and
reviewed them for *The Nation* during the late 1860s, making occasional
but invariably derisive references to her work thereafter. In an appreci-
ative article of 1875, on William Dean Howells's short story, 'A Foregone
Conclusion', James compares the original and poetical qualities of
Howells's heroine with the polarised simplicities of the type peddled
by Miss Braddon and her like, 'where the only escape from the bread-
and-butter and the commonplace is into golden hair and promiscuous
felony'[41] – an obvious reference to the eponymous Lady Audley. It is
interesting, then, that in order to *avoid* such simplicities James should
choose to dress so many of his early heroines (girls who often confuse
the hero) in black or white. Faithless Lizzie Crowe in 'The Story of a Year'
wears white; Charlotte Evans of 'The Travelling Companions', a sensible
if rather chilly girl who finally succumbs to romance, begins crisply in
white piqué, but ends in black – in love but suffering. Black, as we have
seen, underwent radical changes of meaning in the girl's portrait central
to 'The Story of a Masterpiece'. The value of the black dress in the eyes of
the young man depended on himself, and on his developing perception
of the portrait, which changed from positive to negative. The more
sophisticated *Portrait of a Lady* contains dress which seems positive
and negative simultaneously, as well as all shades between. Black, as
J. M. Whistler's teacher, Charles Gleyre, said, was the basis of all tone.

Each window of the 'house of fiction' in James's Preface to the novel,
is described as having an observer in it. They are all watching the same
show, 'but one seeing more where the other sees less, one seeing black
where the others see white, one seeing big where the other sees small' (1.
xi). In the sensation novels of Mary Braddon we see highly coloured
images, but a black and white moral scheme. Conversely, in *The Portrait
of a Lady*, we have two central figures in black and white, but each
accumulates shades and nuances, overlapping, blurring and shifting.
These images are not simply sequential, as in the early short stories,
but they build up a picture that has depths and shadows behind and
beyond itself: what J. C. Agnew has described as 'the sedimentation of

cumulative effects: a mask or shell or collaborative manufacture that solidifies with every representation'.[42] We ask what Isabel has *become*, rather than what will happen to her next, and her clothes, since they are so directly concerned with her self-representation in society, are a part of her self-fashioning. She becomes an almost tragic figure, rather than a melodramatic one; for, 'the tragic effect', according to Dorothea Krook, 'depends upon our recognising that the hero shall be in some way responsible for the fate that overtakes him'.[43] Isabel acknowledges that she is in part responsible for what has happened to her, and at the end she embraces responsibility for her actions in a way that gives her tragic stature.

Isabel's measure of herself has wider implications, it seems to me, than the purely personal: she has taken account of what it meant, in late nineteenth-century terms, to become 'a lady', an aspect of her story which Jane Campion foregrounds in her filmed version. From the 'tall girl in a black dress' of the Gardencourt opening, Isabel becomes Rosier's 'picture of a gracious lady' in a dark palace, and then 'a fine lady' who, for Ralph, represents Gilbert Osmond: the Osmond who, in Campion's film, picks her up and plumps her – like a buttoned-up, helpless Barbie Doll – onto a pile of cushions. Addressing her as 'Mrs Osmond', he reminds Isabel of the nature of their commitment to one another – a reminder that weighs at least as heavily as Pansy's plea does on her decision to return to the marriage.

The canonical text which defined the role of a lady for Victorian England, Ruskin's 'Of Queens' Gardens' maintained that the 'rights' and 'missions' of women were inseparable from those of men, and that women were to regard themselves as neither inferior nor submissive in that partnership. Drawing on examples from literature, Ruskin declared woman's mission to be redemptive in relation to the male, and protective, in relation to the less fortunate outside her walls. Ladies were to be queens, within their own spheres of influence, symbolised above all by the garden. Isabel, we should recall, is seen in a garden setting at the start of the novel. But that promisingly fertile image is transformed, in Chapter 42, into one that reflects her horrified consciousness of the sterile prison which Osmond has made for her. There are, of course, escape routes, but to fulfil her mission as a lady, in Ruskinian terms, she must be 'incapable of error...enduringly, incorruptibly good...not for self-development, but for self-renunciation'.[44] To be a lady is to take on those freely chosen bonds and responsibilities and operate within them; without servility but also, as Lambert Strether was to say in *The Ambassadors*, without having got anything for herself.

And if Isabel chooses to be Osmond's angel of disdain, in white, the full measure of her tragedy is in her mourning – which like Chekhov's Masha – she finally wears for her own life.

The function of dress in this novel has then been weighted towards symbolism rather than realism. Every touch counts towards the creation of James's symbolic and thematic pattern, though that is not in conflict with the way these touches also place character in a precise social and historical framework to an extent that one might easily underestimate. James's notations of dress are modest; they suffice for that singleness of effect recommended by Poe; but they are not so conventional as to allow the reader the comfort of unquestioning familiarity – there is a defamiliarising element, for instance, in the insistent white of Pansy's dress. We have seen how Isabel's dresses, while scarcely differentiated in a realistic, 'Miss Braddon' sense, are endlessly suggestive and can operate, I believe, on our reading of the novel in a powerful if not always obvious way. If every touch must count morally as well as aesthetically then it must also have specificity, 'felt life', as James says in the Preface to the novel. Part of that 'felt life' lies in 'the significant dress of the individual', and James's enhanced references to dress in the 1908 revision underline the importance he assigns to this aspect of the socially presented personality. Isabel's choice of dresses are resonant with the movements of her consciousness and of her moral life, and, while James has not yet fully worked out his technique of inhabiting the personae of his characters as the hand fits the glove, the careful specificity given where it counts allows us to place Isabel as a 'Lady' in her time, as well as to sense her resistance to the violence that underlies Osmond's demand for conformity. Her wardrobe finally is a grim comment on the ruin of her marriage, a flag of independence planted in its ashes: clothes are her 'magical, life-giving ornaments'.[45]

5
Milly Theale in *The Wings of the Dove*

We speculate as to how Isabel Archer feels in her persistent black dresses, since James has only just begun to see the possibilities in his narrative strategy of the 'reflecting consciousness'. But Milly Theale's evolving awareness of how she is seen, and how she she sees others, is crucial to the unfolding of the plot of *The Wings of the Dove*. Half-way through Book 1, Milly, as a New Yorker on a visit to Europe, is launched onto the London social scene. She sits at a dinner table trying to make sense of what she sees and hears, and reflects that 'the smallest things . . . were all touches in a picture and denotements in a play'. One of the touches Milly has noted is 'the special strong beauty' of her hostess's niece, Kate Croy, 'which particularly showed in evening dress'.[1] *The Wings of the Dove* is a novel balanced between these two characters: Milly and Kate. And an important way in which the balance has been built into the narrative is through contrasts between colours, styles and images of dress.

Throughout most of the work Milly is in black, Kate is in light but indistinct colours. The way they dress has much to do with painting and with the theatre: Milly's figure is generally pictorial and fixed; Kate is seen in terms of the dramatic *effect* of her dress and her movements in it. But the novel is also framed by contrasting images. It starts with a detailed picture of *Kate* in black, looking at herself; while Milly's final appearance is in *white*, and this time it is an image of Milly performing – again it is the *effect* of her appearance that counts. But the contrast between the two women, between their black and white, is never straightforward. One might say that the novel presents one figure dressed in elegant contemporary European style (Kate) and one who is timeless and yet often ungainly and out of place (Milly). Yet this also is too simple: dresses and colours pass between the two women, they reflect one another, not as mirror-images are usually understood, but as reflections of absence as well as presence. Each has what the other lacks and each hides a secret. In one of the novel's key *symboliste* moments James describes Kate and Milly as 'figures so associated and yet so opposed, so mutually watchful' (2.139). I propose therefore, in this chapter, to look at James's descriptions of their appearance in association with each other, as they watch each other, and to examine the meaning that the dress of one lends to the other, and to the novel's metaphoric pattern.

Although the design of the novel is, in a sense, clear – even symmetrical – James confessed in the Preface that because of Milly's late entry into the novel, Book 2 of *The Wings of the Dove* was somewhat lopsided. However, the need to build up the preliminary presentation of Kate Croy 'absolutely declined to enact itself save in terms of amplitude'. James describes his technique here as one of 'close-packed bricks' (1. xii), and indeed, compared to later impressions of Kate, and the first distant sight of Isabel Archer at the opening of *The Portrait of a Lady*, the reader's first view of Kate through the author's eye *is* distinct and close. Kate, waiting for her deplorable father, is looking at herself irritably in a small mirror in a 'vulgar little room' in London: 'She stared into the tarnished glass too hard indeed to be staring at her beauty alone. She adjusted the poise of her black closely-feathered hat; retouched beneath it, the thick fall of her dusky hair. . . . She was dressed altogether in black, which gave an even tone, by contrast to her clear face and made her hair more harmoniously dark.' The mirror reflects not only Kate but also her growing distaste for the place; it starts simply as a 'glass', then it is 'tarnished' and finally a 'poor little glass'. Kate's sharp black note of elegance stands out in the grubby room, but her jangling feelings are themselves out of key with the harmony of her ensemble. James then stands back and notes the general effect she produces: 'More "dressed" often, with fewer accessories, than other women, or less dressed, should the occasion require, with more, she probably couldn't have given a key to these felicities' (1. 5).

Our initial impression of Kate is thus of a young figure in black, as it was of Isabel Archer, and will be of Milly Theale. Kate is in mourning for her mother; though we hear also of a late brother-in-law. The account of Kate's mourning black, however, seems less concerned with bereavement than with its enhancement of her powers of attraction: in the long paragraph dealing with her first appearance there are no less than seven synonyms for 'beauty' and 'grace'. This is Hollander's 'emotional' and distinguishing black, rather than the sober, self-effacing variety. An English advice manual of 1892, *Manners and Rules of Good Society*, proposes that the extent and depth of mourning should now be left to the individual's judgement as 'periods of mourning for relatives have within the last few years been materially shortened and the change generally accepted'.[2] Societies for the reform of mourning dress had been started in Britain in the 1870s, and in 1889 Lady Harberton, the dress reformer, in an article in *Woman's World*, deplored the strains that mourning expenses imposed on the lower classes.[3] By 1897 *The Tailor and Cutter* acknowledged: 'it is a custom that is on the wane, and we think this is well, for there is no disputing the fact that this custom has often developed into strange absurdities.'[4]

In America, on the other hand, mourning actually seems to have become more and not less stringent at the end of the century: *The Ladies' Home Journal*, in 1891, recommended that widows be shrouded in a floor-length veil for three months; 'after that it is thrown back, and at the end of another three months, a single veil, reaching to the waist is worn. This may be worn for six months, and crape then be laid aside.' Joan Severa, commenting on the passage in her study of nineteenth-century American fashion, suggests that '[p]erhaps deep mourning...had its apogee on the very eve of its dismissal'.[5] A quasi-Islamic shrouding of the female form in this way would certainly have struck a bizarre note in the Europe of 1900.

In James's short story of 1893, 'The Chaperon', the incongruous effect of deep mourning in London's fashionable world marks the heroine's first meeting with her charming but delinquent mother after many years apart. Mrs Tramore exclaims at the girl's mourning outfit for her father (her own unlamented husband) – 'Heavens, dear, where did you get your mourning?'[6] In the New York edition of 1908, James revised the sentence to 'where did you get your impossible mourning?' enhancing both the frivolity of Mrs Tramore and the un-chic effect of excessive black. Interestingly, on the next page James puts his heroine – after several months under her mother's roof – in an opera dress of 'the softest black':[7] clearly a very different and fashionable black. Black was always a dramatic option for evening wear, but while heavy mourning became unfashionable, black for daytime wear did have a brief revival at the end of the century, according to Hollander, before disappearing in around 1900. Kate's outfit seems to share in something of this *fin-de-siècle* chic, while Milly's American version of mourning, when it appears in the novel, might be deemed 'impossible'.

The comprehensive and almost unvarying black that characterises Milly's costume from the start of *The Wings of the Dove* looks, therefore, disproportionate and alien when compared to Kate's. Black for daily wear, as I pointed out in Chapter 2 in relation to the costume of the Rucks, was more widely worn in nineteenth-century America than in Britain, but even to her American companion, Susan Stringham, Milly's clothes, when we first see her, 'were remarkably black even for robes of mourning, which was the meaning they expressed. It was New York mourning, it was New York hair, it was a New York history... of the loss of parents, brothers, sisters, almost every human appendage' (1. 105–6). The number of dead family members that Milly has left behind her in New York certainly defeats the niceties of mourning etiquette. Death, one might say, encompasses Milly, for she is first seen on an Alpine peak, on the edge of a precipice. In contrast to the restless Kate she is a still, enigmatic note in her sublime but dangerous landscape setting.

Kate's mourning is primarily stylish and she remains well-dressed throughout the novel. Her taste is instinctive, as we see when, taking in the luxuries of Aunt Maud's house on her return from her father's, she reflects on her own 'dire accessibility to pleasure from such sources' (1. 28) – from lace, ribbons, silk and velvet, as well as upholstery. Milly, on the other hand, despite her 'helplessly expensive little black frock', gives the impression of 'a sort of noble inelegance'; her 'curious and splendid' red hair is done 'with no eye whatever to the *mode du jour*' seen 'from under the corresponding indifference of her hat' (1. 121). Milly – even to Mrs Stringham's affectionate gaze – looks hopelessly and carelessly unfashionable.

Susan Stringham is from Boston and she accounts for Milly's inept appearance by the fact that her mourning is New York mourning; it was not 'the mourning of Boston, but at once more rebellious in its gloom and more frivolous in its frills' (1. 109). We have here, some twenty years on, a less brutal version of the Old/New Money snobberies of *Daisy Miller*. By the 1890s the fabulous riches of certain New Yorkers had, according to Lois Banner, become a source of fascinated awe to Americans in general. It was not, however, just the producers of these fortunes who were interesting, it was their consuming wives and daughters: Caroline Astor, Irene Langhorne, Consuelo Vanderbilt – rich New York beauties who became as great a focus of public interest as figures in politics or the arts.[8] We never learn the sources of Milly's vast wealth from James, but, coming from the New York of circa 1900, one might see her as the last and refined relict of a newly rich, millionaire family like the Dryfoos of W. D. Howells's *A Hazard of New Fortunes* – a much younger sister, for example, of the saintly Conrad Dryfoos. The high-colouring and sartorial excesses of Conrad's two sisters in Howells's novel are the subject of comment, especially by the Bostonian Basil March, Howells's narrator. Howells himself had in fact moved from Boston to New York in 1888 and wrote to James about using 'some of its vast, gay, shapeless life in my fiction'. Tony Tanner sees this move as heralding the shift of 'the literary centre of America . . . out of Brahmin New England . . . [to] the mixed turbulence of New York'.[9]

The excesses, the restlessness, the ignorance or disregard for civilities that characterised New-Money New Yorkers for both Howells and James are mirrored, for Susan Stringham, in the messy contradictions of Milly's ensemble – too frilly for bereavement, too insistently black for the changing conventions of the time. Boston was also the home of the American Woman's Movement – and, of course, the setting for James's novel on that topic, *The Bostonians*: for an independent, spirited Boston-ian like Susan Stringham, in her sensible Tyrolean hat, Milly's appear-ance is thus both drearily conventional and too insistently feminine. English Kate, in her jacket-and-skirt ensembles is almost more of a 'Bostonian'. Milly, unlike Kate, never looks in a mirror and consequently seems unable to control the meaning of her clothes; her dual New York inheritance of wealth and death have taken her over: 'she couldn't dress it away, nor walk it away . . . that was what it was to be rich' (1. 121). Everyone who sees Milly 'sees' money, though what she actually wears is a black dress.

An effect of which she is certainly unaware, but which may none the less operate on a male view of her, is the new modishness of red hair around 1895. After centuries as an emblem of 'deviance and evil', red hair now symbolised 'the new sensuality of the end-of-the-century era',[10] a *fin de siècle* note which James will strike again in relation to Milly. Furthermore – as Anne Hollander points out – '[t]he blacker and heavier the mourning, the sexier the effect, worn with grave pallor and shining hair.'[11] These are erotic aspects of her appearance of which Milly is oblivious and are thus as inadvertent as the element of rebellion that Susan detects in Milly's pervasive gloom. Ironically, it is not until she is told of her potentially fatal illness that she becomes aware of the inap-propriateness of her voluminous black clothes against her summery surroundings and realises the need to take control of her image. Until then, mourning fills Milly's past, permeates her present and shadows her future, removing her from real time and creating barriers between appearance and identity that blind her, and allow others to sentimental-ise her. Iain Softley's recent film version of the novel also sentimentalises

James's image of Milly by dressing her in up-to-the-minute, flatteringly gorgeous 'Ballets Russes' outfits from the start, thus losing any sense of her development, or of the contrast between the two women in the story. Most damagingly, this failure to register James's picture of Milly's clothes nullifies her omnipresent tragic inheritance of death.

For Kate Croy, on the other hand, mourning is a becoming if temporary sign of regret; one that is apparently over by the time she meets Milly at the dinner-party. A latent element in Milly's appreciation of Kate's looks throughout the novel is the contrast Kate's elegance presents to Milly's own oddity. Neither she nor Kate ever articulates this contrast, but as their friendship grows 'each thought the other more remarkable than herself... or assured the other she did.' Milly wonders 'if Kate were sincere in finding her the most extraordinary... person she had come across' (1.173–4). Milly, lacking personal vanity, admires Kate without envy; but Kate's 'dire accessibility' to material pleasures, her vigil before the glass in the opening chapter, suggest a hedonistic nature, which if unsatisfied, might well be accessible to envy. Kate's reflections on Milly do not really confirm Milly's doubts, but they are open to interpretation: 'this record of used-up relatives... that had left this exquisite being her black dress, her white face and her vivid hair as the mere last broken link: such a picture quite threw into the shade the brief biography... of a mere middle-class nobody in Bayswater' (1. 174). Kate's view of Milly is thus not lacking in admiration and sympathy, but it has at its core the contrast between the dramatic excesses of cash and death of a strange American 'princess' – 'the girl with the crown of old gold' (1. 109) – and the dingy compromises of a member of a downwardly-mobile, English, shabby-genteel class.

There is a good deal of the New Woman in Kate, although she chooses to work through a man – Merton Densher – to gain her ends. As she paces before the glass in the opening scene she 'thought of the way she might still pull things round had she only been a man' (1. 6); and as Milly's intimacy with Kate grows, she begins to see Kate as 'the wondrous London girl in person... the heroine of a strong story... [with] her umbrellas and jackets and shoes' (1. 171–2). Milly's concept of a 'London girl' is based on *Punch* cartoons and popular literature, both of which were having considerable fun in the 1890s with the New Woman – a tall, pushy character they associated in a muddled way with bicycles, Votes for Women and university education. In du Maurier's cartoons of the 1880s and 1890s the New Woman is recognisable by her 'tailor-made' – a skirt and jacket in plain material, free of the trailing drapes of conventional fashions; this was a style associated with the London

tailor, Redfern, and popularised by the Princess of Wales, later Queen
Alexandra. 'The universal adoption of a coat and skirt bespeak the fin de
siècle woman, energetic, spirited and sensible.'[12] This was an outdoor
costume, and an active way of life was further encouraged by the introduction in 1897 (ironically, in view of Milly's image of Kate as the
London girl) of the long pointed shoe from America. Du Maurier's
own novel of 1894, *Trilby*, introduced a boyish heroine with large feet

Figure 3   American girls in London. Charles Dana Gibson, *The Eduction of Mr. Pip*,
1899.

and substantial shoes who became a fashion icon of the period: there were, for example, Trilby hair-styles, hats, coats and slippers. Kate, in her clandestine dashes across London or Venice in the rain to meet Densher, would certainly have needed umbrella, jacket and stout shoes.

But as we have seen, Milly's dress bears no relation to any recognisable fashion: she is 'the awfully rich young American who was so queer to behold' (1. 219) in the eyes of the weekend guests at Matcham, the country house rented by Lord Mark. It is here that she encounters one of the images that is to define her. For Susan Stringham and Kate she is a princess or a dove; for Lord Mark she is the Bronzino portrait in the Matcham collection. None of these metaphors locates Milly in a contemporary world; she is either of the past or beyond time. At Matcham, Milly herself feels that she is in an 'extravagantly grand Watteau-composition' (1. 208); in an Arcadian fantasy – beautiful but melancholy. James colours the whole Matcham episode in Watteauesque blue, pink, lavender and old gold – Lady Aldershaw, bejewelled and in 'the palest pinks and blues' is an embodiment of the scene. But to move from such a *fête champêtre* to the Bronzino portrait, 'deep within' the house, is also to encounter significantly darker tones and colours.

Viola Hopkins Winner has identified Bronzino's portrait of Lucrezia Panciatichi, in the Uffizi in Florence, as the Matcham Bronzino.[13] There is now no escaping the image. But if James, according to Tony Tanner, increasingly resisted 'any pressure . . . to engage in "excesses of specification"',[14] we may be in danger of allowing the Panciatichi portrait and the blandishments of Lord Mark to over-define our image of Milly. Lord Mark's compliment as he leads her to the picture – 'the beautiful one that's so like you' – may not be disinterested, as, after all, he hopes to marry her. Milly is certainly charming, but we are often told she looks odd, and she knows it. Milly's comment on the portrait, 'I shall never be better than this', rejects as well as recognises it as a likeness. Milly's idyll is ended by Lord Mark, who confronts her with the dark reflection of the portrait. Milly sees a kind of princess certainly, 'only unaccompanied by a joy. And she was dead, dead, dead' (1. 220–1).

The Panciatichi portrait rearranges Milly's colouring, with its red dress and white face. Milly's mourning black, its meanings reaching both into the past and future, is, one might say, transformed into the darkness of the portrait's background, that quality of mortality which so disturbs her impression of the painting. Milly does not detail the sitter's appearance, but fastens rather on the 'pastness' of certain aspects – before the fading of the hair it must 'have had' a family resemblance to her; it has 'eyes of other days', 'recorded jewels' and 'wasted reds'. It is from this moment that Milly begins to recede into a time and place that is increasingly distant from the contemporary world. The encounter with the portrait is less with a double than with a ghost. As Judith Woolf points out, it is a version of the scene in *The Portrait of a Lady* when Isabel, in the picture gallery, asks Ralph to show her the ghost.[15] Isabel eventually sees the ghost at Ralph's death, but what Milly sees is her own 'pale sister'. To want to become the girl in the portrait, to see a reflection of the self, is to desire entry to a dead world, to deny the future. Death, in Cocteau's *Orphée*, comes through a mirror.

In a sense, Isabel Archer fashions her self-portrait according to the romantic Ruskinian paradigm of a Lady. Milly, in front of the Bronzino 'princess', not only recognises herself but experiences a piercing recognition of vivid life that, because it is of the past, is simultaneously a reminder of mortality. Edith Wharton admired *The Portrait of a Lady* (though not *The Wings of the Dove*), and the scene in Wharton's *House of Mirth* of 1905, where Lily Bart 'becomes' Mrs Lloyd, the aristocratic subject of a portrait by Joshua Reynolds, is surely a reference to James's novel, the title of which may itself be taken from another Reynolds portrait. One might also detect echoes of *Wings of the Dove* here, in that the invocation of the portrait foreshadows Lily's death; though unlike Milly's inward and darkly painful recognition of herself in the Bronzino portrait, Lily Bart's identification with Mrs Lloyd is a very public and, to her, an unqualified triumph.

Lily has dressed herself in an approximation of Reynolds's generalised 'classical' draperies, and poses as an English 'Lady', in a tableau at an evening party, much as Isabel, in her black evening dress, framed her European 'fine lady' persona in the doorway of the Palazzo Roccanera. The crucial difference is that while Lily's assumption of this persona is a temporary and factitious disguise, in a dress that is doubly of the past in being both eighteenth century and 'classical', Isabel's is the contemporary, real right ladylike thing. Lily has, as Wharton says, banished 'the phantom of [Reynolds's] dead beauty'[16] by her living grace, but the moment of triumph has been deceptive: like Milly she has appropriated the past from a portrait, a ghost which is a forewarning of her own mortality – a theme which James was to develop, but never resolve, in *The Sense of the Past*. The male eyes that devour Lily do not see her as a 'Lady', for her appearance, unlike Isabel's, is removed from a recognisable reality and, furthermore, lacks the background male guarantor needed for respectability. It is this progressive erosion of character that will finally kill her. Lily, just for a moment, brings the dead to life, but what she cannot know is that her pose is read by her male audience as an advertisement of sexual availability, adding another nail to the coffin of her reputation. For Milly the image of the dead princess is both a recognition of her own living identity and also a private and frightening intimation of mortality.

But Milly does see a way of 'being' in the Bronzino; she sees how she is seen and therefore what she might *become*. The Bronzino is thus a mirror for Milly in awakening her self-awareness – in this she has grown more like Kate. But as a reflection of herself it is problematic. Art, as James said in an essay on Daumier, is an embalmer.[17] At this point in the novel Milly looks at Kate and wonders, 'Is this the way she looks to *him*?' (1. 225). How does energetic, elegant Kate look to Densher, compared to eccentric, ailing Milly, embalmed in black?

We have been reading *The Wings of the Dove* in terms of dress, in terms of appearances. But the complexity of James's art is only grasped when we acknowledge that dress is also a form of disguise. Dressing is also dressing-up. There is thus a distance between Milly and what she now chooses to wear. After her second visit to Sir Luke Strett, Milly's new self-awareness makes her conscious of her vulnerability: 'It was as if she had to pluck off her breast, to throw away some friendly ornament... that was part of her daily dress; and to take up... some queer defensive weapon... conducive in a higher degree to a striking appearance' (1. 248). In order to protect herself – from what she isn't sure – she must consciously refashion her appearance, find an identity and live. As she wanders through anonymous London streets trying to lose herself, she sees 'in people's eyes the reflexion of her appearance.... She found herself moving at times in regions visibly not haunted by odd-looking girls from New York, duskily draped, sable-plumed, all but incongruously shod' (1. 249). Her voluminous black clothes, big, black-feathered hat and heavy shoes look out of place, she realises, in the August light and heat, in a London of working women and of spirited girls like Kate (see Figure 4). Black, according to John Harvey, was 'the colour with which one buried one's self – the colour that, having no colour, effaced and took one's self away'.[18] 'Losing' herself for the moment, in Regent's Park, she decides she must 'find' herself, take charge of her image and, as Sir Luke has advised, live all she can. She concludes, after her long London walk, that if, then, she is to be a princess, she needs a court and a setting: 'If one *could* only be Byzantine!' (1. 255) she concludes. 'Acting' for the first time, she invites Kate, Mrs Lowder and Susan Stringham to her hotel to prepare for the journey from modern London, where she looks all wrong, to Venice, city of the past – where she hopes to reinvent a Byzantine self.

Figure 4   Full mourning attire. *Harper's Bazaar*, 1898.

If Milly has wondered how Kate looks to Densher, in comparison to herself, Kate's appearance at the hotel in a light, floating dress provides a pointed and demoralising contrast to Milly's own cumbersome garments. Kate acts the part of the modern woman to perfection: American as well as English – the du Maurier girl as well as the Gibson girl. Although the tailor-made costume – which characterised both types – was 'becoming more and more, and the evening confection less and less, the true symbol of the time,[19] Kate somehow manages, at different times, to

accommodate both images, since we now see her also in the softly feminine answer to the 'tailor-made' (Plate IV). Milly, in her hotel room, fossilised by her unchanging black, has been speculating with Mrs Lowder
about Densher's return from America, when their talk is halted by Kate's
return to the open window, 'the outer dark framing in a highly favourable
way her summery simplicities and lightnesses of dress' (1. 272).

James's treatment of Kate's dress is intentionally indistinct, for we are
seeing her through Milly's consciousness and Milly is becoming aware of
things that are not clear, that are being held back. Milly has met Densher
in New York and knows something of his friendship with Kate; she
therefore puzzles over Kate's evasion of the topic: 'What was behind
showed but in gleams and glimpses; what was in front never at all
confessed to not holding the stage' (1. 274). Evasiveness might also be
said to characterise the style of dress Kate is wearing. Cunnington notes
that by 1897 the Perfect Lady was 'up to her knees in froth'; and while
'the day-bodice preserved a swathed obscurity...the evening cors-
age...bowdlerized by falling lace and chiffon, was almost equally evasive.'[20] The two girls are left to talk. 'Kate moved as much as she
talked...taking slowly, to and fro, in the trailing folds of her light
dress, the length of the room – almost avowedly performing for the
pleasure of her hostess...the occasion...had the quality of a rough
rehearsal of the possible big drama' (1. 275–6). It is here that Milly,
searching for an identity, is told she is a 'dove' by Kate. Kate is prowling
to and fro, speaking while Milly sits, and Milly later recalls the scene as a
violent, frightening moment 'alone with a creature who paced as a
panther' (1. 282). James's imagination of disaster saw a world where
creatures of prey sink their claws into the 'children of light', a place
where black felines stalk white doves. Though Kate is here actually in
light colours, the underlying suggestion from the start of this scene,
with her change of style, is that she has been acting a part, and that
something important is being obscured.

The role-playing of the two women, the reflection and interaction of
their appearances is made more striking in so far as it takes place around,
and is perceived by Merton Densher. Only Densher, back from America,
places Milly within a normal time-and-place perspective: he recalls
meeting Milly in her New York setting: 'the princess, the angel, the
star were muffled over...with the little American girl who had been
kind to him in New York' (2. 173). Densher thus listens uneasily to Milly
being discussed as 'weird' and unknowable at another of Mrs Lowder's
parties – an occasion later referred to as Milly's 'failure'. Milly fails at the
dinner because she is ill, but this same occasion becomes Kate's success.

At the first of the dinner parties we were drawn into Milly's admiration of Kate's beauty; we now see, through Densher's gaze, Kate's 'beautiful' entrance which precedes her faultless act before guests: she was to 'dress the part, to walk, to look, to speak, in every way to express, the part' (2. 34). Densher's admiration, however, is qualified by a recognition of the tawdriness of Kate's role, and the extent to which she is subject to Aunt Maud's fiercely watchful eye: 'But she *passed*, the poor performer... [with] her wig, her paint, her jewels' (2. 35).

We have seen Kate playing the boyish New Woman role in her tailor-made, and the Eternal Feminine in an evening 'confection' for the benefit of Milly: in the more public setting of the dinner party we are not given details of her appearance, simply told of its faultless effect: she is the professional 'Beauty'. But in Densher's evolving consciousness of the scene she appears bedizened in stage paint and props. The dramatic development of her character takes place within what Peter Brooks terms the 'moral occult'[21] – she wears an imaginary *and* real dress, though which is which would be difficult to say. Although Milly is absent from the feast, she is a spectre at it, the victim of speculation, and therefore in a sense present, if immaterial.

While Kate and Densher debate the nature of Milly's illness, and while it is obviously a vital engine in the plot, it remains unspecified. Milly herself is 'fiercely shy' about the illness, never allowing the smell of the sickroom to reach the world outside. She does not want her sickness to become the thing that defines her, for if Densher is to love her she must seem capable of a future. When Densher realises that Kate wants him 'to make up to a sick girl', he visualises Milly 'on a pile of cushions and in a perpetual tea-gown' (2. 56). In obedience to Kate he visits Milly, but she quickly makes him understand that '[s]he was never, never... to be one of the afflicted for him' (2. 74). The Invalid Woman in nineteenth-century iconography is, of course, a familiar figure. Densher's tea-gowned stereotype is found in Mrs Lynn Linton's essay 'In Sickness', which rather unpleasantly suggests that a 'real woman... is never more charming than as an invalid... the long, loose folds of falling drapery, with their antique grace, perhaps suit her better.'[22] Milly's own unsentimental view of her condition is closer to that of Mrs Panton, who produced out of her experience of illness *Within Four Walls: a Handbook for Invalids*. Mrs Panton advised the invalid never 'to sink into the mere wearer of a dressing-gown or tea-gown. Stick to your ordinary costume... one feels hopelessly "gone" in a loose gown, and unfit for polite society.'[23] Black, blue or heliotrope she felt, were colours for the invalid. One might add that tea-gowns also had rather risqué connotations:

some considered the tea-gown 'as a sign of the indolence and degeneracy of the times'.[24]

It is revealing that Densher visualises Milly specifically in a tea-gown; a garment often pale in colour and smothered in lace. Milly, in fact, avoids tea-gowns, but when she dresses for an outing with Densher, she appears in 'her big black hat, so little superstitiously in the fashion, her fine black garments throughout, the swathing of her throat, which Densher vaguely took for an infinite number of yards of priceless lace, and which, its folded fabric kept in place by heavy rows of pearls, hung down to her feet like the stole of a priestess' (2. 96). Milly is thus still in exorbitant mourning. She could indeed be trapped indefinitely in her cerements and with no perceivable reason for calling the whole morbid business to a halt, if we take into account an unforeseen by-product of America's supposedly classless and therefore etiquette-free society: '[i]n America, with no fixity of rule, ladies have been known to go into deepest mourning for their relatives... or for people, perhaps, whom they have never seen, and have remained as gloomy monuments of bereavement for seven or ten years.'[25] Milly is, however, finally making some attempt to palliate her gloom. Densher's attention is caught by the yards of lace, which together with the pearls constitute a dramatic change to Milly's uniform black. Typically, she is wearing an excessive amount of excessively expensive lace. She wants to find an identity which is not that of death and sickness, but which suggests the expectations of an eligible young woman. Unfortunately, she has contrived here to remove all modishness and softness from her lace by wearing it wrongly – the contrast of pale lace hanging down straight against her black dress is sacerdotal rather than feminine. Furthermore, she has muddled the conventions of mourning dress by wearing lace; for 'lace', according the etiquette books, 'is never mourning'.[26] She has overdone and confused the effect of her costume, not because she is extravagant and ignorant, but simply and sadly because she is so walled in by the 'mere money' of her situation that she doesn't know how otherwise to dress. She has only Susan to help, and Susan thinks Milly is a princess. The effect on Densher – even with his more realistic view of Milly – is to increase the sense that she belongs to other worlds and other times.

Milly's move to Venice is, therefore, a move in search of a setting where she will no longer be incongruous, or where her incongruity will seem perhaps merely a part of a general picturesqueness. Taking her cue from Kate, Milly has decided to 'act' in order to live. She rents a palace which is, as Frederick Crews says, 'a symbol of her unreal world and a stage for her battle to survive'.[27] Milly's self-esteem is now so low that she feels not even her compatriots can make her out, for she is 'too plain and too ill-clothed for a thorough good time, and yet too rich and too befriended ... for a thorough bad one' (2. 137). How is she, then, to find the confidence to transform herself – an odd-looking American – into a beautiful princess who will win the love of a hero and live? Her solution is to retreat into her palace and stay within the make-believe scenery that lends conviction to the part she intends to play. Lord Mark repeats his ploy of flattering her with glamorous art-historical analogies to the paintings of Veronese, but Milly is no longer the passive replica of a portrait; she has arranged, as James says in the Preface, 'for Drama essentially to take possession [of] the whole bright house of her exposure' (1. xx).

Kate, we have seen, is a consummate actress in the fashionable world and now Milly joins her, if on a different stage – to play a role that is not fashionable, but her own creation. The question we may ask is: for whom are the women acting? Their friendship would suggest that for one another their masks will be laid aside. But Milly is conscious that '[i]t was when they called each other's attention to their ceasing to pretend ... that what they were keeping back was most in the air' (2. 138–89). James here creates a metaphor to dramatise their mutual watchfulness. It is one of the few images in the novel created outside the consciousness of a character, and is based loosely on a Maeterlinck play, *La Princesse Maleine*. In this image Milly's strange Byzantine appearance is marvellously 'right': not passively pictorial but full of dramatic power – even, in its own way, fashionable:

> Certain aspects of the connexion of these young women show for us ... in the likeness of some dim scene in a Maeterlinck play ... the angular pale princess, ostrich-plumed, black-robed, hung about with amulets, reminders, relics, mainly seated, mainly still, and that of the upright restless slow-circling lady of her court who exchanges with her, across the black water streaked with evening gleams, fitful questions and answers. The upright lady, with thick dark braids down her back, drawing over the grass a more embroidered train, makes the whole circuit, and makes it again, and the broken talk, brief and sparingly allusive, seems more to cover than to free their sense. (2. 139)

In Maeterlinck's play Maleine, princess of a European country in a remote fairy-tale time, has lost everyone but her nurse. Placed in the seeming affectionate care of the evil Queen Anne, Maleine puts on a black velvet robe. Maleine grows weaker, and is finally isolated and murdered in her tower room. At her death the swans desert the castle; and lifting her, a servant exclaims 'Elle ne pèse pas plus qu'un oiseau.'[28] The play and novel plots have only glancing points of similarity, but bird imagery and black and white are common to both.

In this imaginary realm created by James, of palatial Venice suffused with the medieval colouring of Maeterlinck, Milly's costume can also be related to another kind of dressing-up – the anachronisms of Aesthetic Dress, fashionable in the London world of the 1890s. The connection is not entirely surprising, since there were cross-currents of influence between the fashions of the drawing room, those of the stage and the dresses reproduced in the works of artists such as Burne-Jones. Indeed, Adeline Tintner points out that Milly with her red hair and sickly pallor resembles the much discussed Fatal Woman of Decadent Art.[29] Sargent's portrait of Ellen Terry as Lady Macbeth, admiringly reviewed by James in 1897, is almost an amalgam of Kate and Milly in the Maeterlinck scene. Sargent shows the actress in a flowing, medieval costume glittering with embroidery; Terry's dark red hair hangs in long braids against her bronze-green dress. The Aesthetic style favoured soft dresses, such as this one, in natural colours rather than aniline dyes. It used embroidery, reflecting an interest in the crafts of earlier periods: 'Antique and exotic effects were frequently sought after and the ideal colours were described as "old-looking", "strange" or "indescribable tints".'[30] James's strategy in the Maeterlinck image is not, however, directly to suggest that Milly and Kate wear Aesthetic dress: he gives them an authentic physical presence by suggesting such dress, but finally leaves the reader with a visionary image of the two women.

Milly tells Densher that in her Venetian palace she is 'freed from time'. In a city uniquely outside time she can play a princess of the past without incongruity. Venice is also a city of carnival and theatre, and Milly as her own stage-manager is in control of her effects. But although she has now found an active role, she is weakening physically. Venice is a city of death too. When Milly, at her great party, makes an entrance, she casts a spell on her guests: part of her magic is her 'wonderful white dress [which] brought them somehow into relation with something that made them more finely genial' (2. 213). Here then is one of the central contrasts of the novel. Milly's white dress not only transforms her guests but also herself. Densher realises it is the first time he has seen her in white and it makes her 'different, younger, fairer.... Much as the change did for the value of her presence, she had never yet ... made it for *him*.' If she is not doing it for him, he none the less tries to understand it: 'She was acquitting herself tonight as hostess . . . under some supreme idea. . . . She was the American girl as he had originally found her' (2. 214–15). Milly's voice disappears from the novel after her rejection of Lord Mark, so we cannot know from her what her 'supreme idea' is. Her white dress would suit the role both of dove and princess, but Densher's association of Americanness with her appearance here is a reiteration of the way he has always seen her. As Milly's exaggerated mourning had recalled her New York origins to Susan Stringham, so does her white dress to Densher, and, interestingly, a reference back to 'An International Episode', of 1879, finds James using repeated accents of white dress to convey the dazzling first impact of America on two young Englishmen landing on her shores.[31] As Fred Kaplan has pointed out, James's last three completed novels are a return to and 'a culmination of his concern with the international theme . . . . transformed from the satirical comedy of misperception into a drama of the search for self-knowledge'.[32]

Milly, 'let loose' among them, is now acting out her view of herself. She is clear, in white, but unclear in intention. Milly is acting, one guesses, for *herself* – to escape others' definitions of her. The white dress, which had been traditional formal wear for the *jeune fille* for a century or more, is an assertion of her will to live, an escape from her grave-clothes, a belief in herself as marriageable, and therefore in the possibility of Densher's love for her. These beliefs are interdependent – in order to live she needs Densher's belief and love, and to love her he must see her unobscured by the signs of wealth and death which in London had effaced her identity. At this moment Milly is acutely aware of life and of how much she wants it. Faced with the Bronzino portrait she had seen death; looking now at her own reflection in the eyes of Densher and Kate she wills them to believe her act.

If we think the meaning of her white dress is now clear, however, and that it means life and hope, and American spontaneity, we should remember that white was acceptable as mourning on formal occasions. Pansy Osmond's white is crushingly negative, and one might also recall the unvarying white garments of the terrible Mrs Ambient in 'The Author of *Beltraffio*', whose obsession with innocence causes the death of her child. White can be deadly, and if her spell on her guests is beatific, for Kate, author of the dove-image, it will prove baleful. The shifting meanings in Milly's white image thus flicker between past and future, as if caught between two facing mirrors.[33] 'What James with his incredibly imaginative and sensitive antennae, likes to pick up,' writes Tony Tanner of James's fondness for ghosts, 'are the invisible after-traces.'[34] Milly's image leaves after-traces that destroy Densher's love for Kate, for ghosts pursue the living who have wronged them.

This dramatic about-turn in *The Wings of the Dove* occurs in Densher's mind as he watches Kate watching Milly: 'he noted that Kate was somehow – for Kate – wanting in lustre. As a striking young presence she was practically superseded...she might fairly have been dressed tonight in the little black frock...that Milly had laid aside' (2. 216). Ironically, then, the great shift of Densher's feelings in the novel is explained through the unlikely image of a single 'little black frock' passed between the two women. His feeling moves one way: the dress, in effect, moves the other way entirely. Densher reads the moment as the 'opposite pole' of Kate's success at Mrs Lowder's dinner-party, which had then also been Milly's failure. Now their roles are reversed: negative turns positive, black turns white; although it is important to note that Kate's *actual* appearance remains unstated. It is Densher's imagination, his 'moral occult', that puts her in black, effaces her and replaces her with Milly – and if we draw melodramatic conclusions from this, maybe we are intended to.

Kate insists that Densher look at Milly's pearls: 'Kate's face, as she considered them, struck him: the long priceless chain wound twice round the neck, hung, heavy and pure, down the front of the wearer's breast' (2. 217). Densher realises that her vision is filled with the pearls as symbols of the power of Milly's wealth. Kate is in effect in front of a mirror again: ' "Oh yes," ' she says, ' "I see myself" ' .... Milly's royal ornament had... taken on the character of a symbol of differences, differences of which the vision was actually in Kate's face...pearls were exactly what Merton Densher would never be able to give her' (2. 219). We have, once more, two mirrors: Kate looks at Milly and sees herself, and Densher looks at the reflection of that glance in Kate's face. Mirror images are reverse-images, so it is Kate's real desire for the pearls, not her ostensible admiration of Milly, that is visible in the second, 'corrected' mirror-image.

Pearls against a white dress are key symbols of Milly's goodness and riches. Here they appear as a chain of improbable length, hanging to the floor – a sign of the burden of wealth, since pearls after all usually come in strings and do not sweep the floor. Pearls were fashionable at the turn of the century, and we also find that James's floor-length pearls are not all that improbable. James had been writing approvingly of Sargent's work for some time and about the portrait of Mrs Carl Meyer (1897) he was especially enthusiastic: 'The subject of Mr. Sargent's principal picture wears a pale pink satin dress.... She has round her neck a string of pearls, ineffably painted, that hangs down to her shoes.'[35] Mrs Meyer's pearls are indeed wound twice round her neck and come to rest by a pink shoe. With pearls on this scale Mrs Meyer is very rich. When Milly then sends across the room to Kate and Merton 'the candour of her smile, the lustre of her pearls, the value of her life, the essence of her wealth' (2. 229), the cash 'value' they choose to see in her image determines their own fate. As a result of their venality, the after-trace of Milly's glance will rout, dismay and turn the tables on them.

Kate returns to London, leaving Densher in Venice to propose to Milly. But Densher, the reflecting consciousness of the final chapters, is unaccountably turned away from Milly's door. Her withdrawal into her palace and into silence is inherent in the novel's discourse. We learn, piecemeal, that Lord Mark has again destroyed an illusion by hinting at Kate and Densher's secret engagement. She had hoped that by recasting her image she might counteract the growing loneliness of her role as sign and symbol for others, and come down into the real sociable world: but Lord Mark's news makes it clear there is no escape. It seems her 'act' has failed, and that even to Densher she has meant only wealth and death. 'She received me just as usual,' Densher tells Kate, weeks later, of his last meeting with Milly, 'in the dress she always wears, from her inveterate corner of the sofa' (2. 328). Her usual dress on the 'inveterate' sofa reinforces a sense of return and resignation to the meanings of her old image. Densher's account of Milly thus emphasises her unchanging-ness, although when we unravel the chronology of the novel's final chapters, doubling and redoubling back on itself, we find that his description of her is relayed close to the moment of ultimate change, her death. However, this last sight of Milly, as Kate later perceives, has also changed Densher.

What seems in retrospect to be a clear closure to the narrative – the heroine's death – turns out to be inconclusive and occluded. It is Milly's act of living, in white, that remains in the mind, not her dying. '[T]he dress she always wears', we may assume, is mourning black, but this is not spelt out. It is perhaps here we should recall Milly's prototype, Minny Temple, whose photograph James kept by him always. The final pages of the autobiographical *Notes of a Son and Brother* (1914), are devoted to Minny and although he conveys the persistence of her light and vivid figure in his memory, it is inescapably coloured by her death: 'the image of this, which was long to remain with me, appeared so of the essence of tragedy that I was in the far-off aftertime to seek to lay the ghost by wrapping it . . . in the beauty and dignity of art.'[36] For the reader Milly's final described appearance is in white, but that radiance

is undercut in Densher's report of his final meeting with her, by the
return to and persistence of her mourning. Her figure is to haunt
Densher, as Minny's had haunted James; and we might add to this a
second and more recent ghost for James – that of Constance Fenimore
Woolson, who threw herself to her death from a window in Venice in
1894.

Lyndall Gordon's biography of James, which focuses on Minny
Temple and Fenimore Woolson, opens with an arresting, tragi-comic
picture of James, later in 1894:

> a middle-aged gentleman, bearing a load of dresses, was rowed to the
> deepest part of the Venetian lagoon. ... [H]e began to drown the
> dresses, one by one. There were a good many, well-made, tasteful
> and all dark, suggesting a lady of quiet habits and some reserve....
> But the dresses refused to drown. One by one they rose to the surface,
> their busts and sleeves swelling like black balloons. Purposefully, the
> gentleman pushed them under, but silent, reproachful, they rose
> before his eyes.[37]

Gordon returns to this scene at the conclusion of her biography, seeing
in it a metaphor for James's continuing attempts to keep at bay the two
female presences that had come closest to him and most threatened his
emotional privacy. It is tempting to see Fenimore Woolson's unsinkable
wardrobe, as well as Minny's remembered radiance, resurfacing in the
haunting 'after-traces' of Milly's image on Densher, in the novel written
only a few years after this bizarre scene on the lagoon in Venice.

The news of Milly's death in *The Wings of the Dove* reaches Densher in a
confused flurry of mistaken assumptions, unexpected news and unex-
plained presences and absences, which take place outside another closed
door. It isn't until he is left to recreate Milly in his imagination and
reflect on the still unopened letter written from her death-bed that 'in
the light of how exquisite the dead girl was he sees how little exquisite is
the living'.[38] It is not that Kate is less beautiful, but that her person is
overlaid by Milly's now changeless lustre. Kate's talent has lain in her
consciously controlled performances, symbolised, as we have seen, by a
chameleon ability to suit her costume to the moment. Changes to her
image now take place in Densher's imagination, outside her control and
coloured by his vision of Milly. Milly's had been the clear, still picture;
Kate's the impression of energy and movement. But Kate's vitality no
longer counts; what now provides the dynamic for the final dramatic
dénouement is Milly's imperishable after-image operating on Densher:

'since I have lived all these years as if I were dead, I shall die, no doubt, as if I were alive' (1. 199), Milly says presciently to Mrs Stringham. Only in her absence can her 'presence' act on events. Evasive Kate, now back in London with Densher, is victim of her own uncertainty over the terms of Milly's bequest and she demands clarification of Densher. But Densher's insight at Milly's party reflects back on Kate and defines her for him, immobilises her and loosens her hold on him.

Kate burns Milly's death-bed letter to Densher before he has read it. However, like Milly's absent self, the absence of the letter simply works on Densher's imagination to Kate's detriment. It is not the content he imagines but '[t]he part of it missed for ever was the turn she would have given her act . . . the loss of which was like the sight of a precious pearl cast before his eyes . . . into the fathomless sea' (2. 396). The pearls which in the material world had signified Milly's wealth now resume their older erotic (as well as spiritual) association with Venus and love. Because Densher has seen Milly with imagination he knows the letter contains Milly's final act of loving generosity. In dying and in spending she has shed the signs of wealth and death that obscured her image and left to Densher the memory with which, as Kate rightly perceives, he falls in love.

I have been talking a good deal of the metaphorical mirrors and reflections used in the novel: how Kate sees herself in Milly, how Milly sees herself in the Bronzino portrait, and how Densher sees Kate's greed reflected in her face. But the novel also begins and ends with real mirrors, in front of which Kate Croy stands, adjusting her hat. Milly, in front of the Bronzino portrait, begins to be a 'surveyor' of herself,[39] but Kate's survival in her Aunt Maud's circle in London has always depended on the public performance she so constantly monitors. We have now lost the language of hat etiquette, but James (with his own range of headgear in the hall of Lamb House) knew all the nuances. Despite Kate's busy fussing with her hat in front of the mirror in her father's rooms at the opening of *The Wings of the Dove*, she does not finally remove it: she will therefore not stay. The scene that follows hangs on her offer to reject her aunt's world and throw in her lot with her father. When he impatiently flings the offer back in her face, locating her use to him as out there in 'the world of grab', she again adjusts the poise of her hat before the mirror. Seeing the gesture, Lionel Croy cries 'Oh you're all right!' (1. 16), affirming his belief in the social and financial value of her looks.

There is, of course, an increasing structural symmetry in James's later work, like the geometry of French classical drama – or like mirror-images. Kate's hat, now veiled, reappears, along with the memory of an earlier moment, in the final pages. We are back in Densher's modest London rooms with Kate before a glass adjusting her hat, and, watching her, he is reminded of their sexual encounter in his Venetian lodging. On that occasion as on this one, 'after she had failed a little to push up her veil symmetrically and he had said she had better take it off altogether, she had acceded to his suggestion before the glass' (2. 397). On both occasions too, Kate is veiled – presumably because their plot depends on keeping their relationship hidden, but also, quite simply, because she would not wish to be recognised visiting a bachelor's rooms – she is no radical. As in the opening chapter, Kate's adjustments to her hat indicate her uneasiness about what is to follow; in the Venetian encounter she removes rather more than her hat for Densher, in exchange for his agreement to woo Milly; in the final London scene, she has broken the seal of a lawyer's letter to him, containing news of the success of their enterprise – the gift of Milly's money. Kate's 'flight', launched in the first chapter, has landed the prize on which her father was counting. James, in the Preface, refers to Kate's father, Lionel Croy, as 'poor beautiful dazzling, damning apparition ... cocking again that fine form of a hat which has yielded him for so long his one effective cover' (1. xiv). Unseen, but reported in the novel's final pages as abject and weeping, he and his hat may now function as Kate's *memento mori*.[40]

Kate's recourse to mirrors to check the effect she is producing is flawed, for she can never see what the world sees. A mirror-image, as Anne Hollander reminds us, is a private fiction, 'a self-delusion ... arranged for gratification instead of seeking for truth'.[41] Kate's constricted vision within this pinched setting reflects the unchanged meanness of her world. Her redemption, and her punishment, is that she does finally see the implications: turning from the mirror and facing Densher, Kate realises that Milly's memory is Densher's love, and although he says he will marry Kate, and that they will be '[a]s we were', she recognises their irreversible loss: 'We shall never be again as we were' (2. 405). The conclusion of the novel has not really been Milly's death, but an inconclusion, where Milly's image persists in returning to the surface, paradoxically changed and unchanging. Kate, one might say, has lost the game, returns to her dingy start and collects nothing. It is her future that has changed; all that her beauty and vitality promised has been extinguished by Milly's image, and she is left with reflections in the mirror, the 'fine form' of her hat and an empty auditorium.

Dress is, then, a consistently recurring but unobtrusive element in *The Wings of the Dove*, allowing the reader to 'guess the unseen from the seen, to trace the implication of things, to judge the whole piece by the pattern'.[42] Dress establishes the oddity of Milly, her dislocation and dis-ease within the European world. One of her mistakes has been to look in the wrong mirrors for her identity: at a long-dead girl, at a spiritual symbol, and finally at Kate, the London girl, performing in her variously elegant outfits. But nevertheless, it is when she chooses, like Kate, to perform in her 'wonderful white dress' that she springs into vivid and lovable life for Densher, while the 'lustre' of her pearls illuminates Kate's inhumanity and greed. Her image, which has achieved its meaning through all these subtle shifts and contrasts, not only transcends her own death but gains in power, to return and haunt Densher and eclipse Kate, as the novel concludes.

6
Hats and *The Princess Casamassima*

James concluded his preface to *The Princess Casamassima* by claiming that the effect he most wished to produce in the novel was that 'of our not knowing, of society's not knowing, but only guessing and suspecting and trying to ignore, what goes on irreconcilably, subversively, beneath the vast smug surface.'[1] One of the things the Prince Casamassima does not know is whether the young men who process in and out of his estranged wife's London house are her lovers or her tradesmen. When Madame Grandoni, his wife's companion, explains that the current young man, Hyacinth Robinson, is a bookbinder, he protests '[w]hy, then does she have him in her drawing-room – announced like an ambassador, carrying a hat in his hand like mine?' (1. 305). Confused by a tradesman in the wrong part of the house, by Hyacinth's style of dress – and by the fact that, seemingly *au fait* with the requirements of etiquette, he has removed his hat in the drawing-room and is waiting to greet his hostess before relinquishing it – the Prince, a straightforward if limited man, understandably wonders whether this bookbinder has designs on his status, his silver, or his wife.

The Princess Casamassima, written in 1886, is about the continuities between secrecy and spectatorship,[2] the performance of class distinctions and aspirations, in a London whose 'smug surface' is troubled by an undertow of social unrest. This is the closest James gets to writing a novel of social realism; a reflection of his own unease – expressed mainly in letters – at the evidence of social deprivation and unrest in the London of the 1880s. It is a 'notebook' novel and although it is not weighted with information about its society in Zolaesque style, it still carefully presents certain important details as social markers and social codes. Interestingly, among these details, hats and headgear are of key importance – odd but insistent grace-notes, punctuating the narrative: signals rising to the social surface from below, more significant than we might at first think, for hats, according to F. M. Robinson's history of the bowler hat, are 'stressed words in the grammar of costume'.[3] Hats, as we have seen, figure prominently in recollections about James himself, and – fifteen years after *The Princess Casamassima* – he chose to begin and end *The Wings of the Dove* with a hat that operates as an indication of Kate's submission to the narrow imperatives of her London upper-class world. If, as James says, *The Princess Casamassima* is a novel about undercurrents that herald social change, then hats are one indication of an individual's position in relation to those changes – is this or that individual 'old hat' or ahead of the times? A commentator on politics in dress in *Woman's World* of 1889, notes that 'to have the head covered and the feet shod has been from very early times a sign of freedom', and '[b]eing the most conspicuous feature in a man's dress, the hat has naturally been used as a political flag'.[4] Kate *appears* to be something of a New Woman, but in fact, despite her stylishness and intelligence, she subscribes to increasingly outmoded ideas about women, and the hat in which she exits seems little different in either meaning or style to the one in which she entered the novel.

James's attention to hats in *The Princess Casamassima* may seem less remarkable if we consider the ubiquity of hats at the time, as well as the astonishing size of female headgear from the 1870s onward: 'at all the canonic sites of modernity – the street, the café, the brothel and the race-track – there they are soaring above the assembled throng...ubiquitous witness to the birth of European modernity.'[5] Because we have largely ceased to wear hats, we have lost the 'hum and buzz' of their implication, but until the mid-twentieth century hats were a mandatory item of one's outward appearance.[6] In two of James's novellas, *The Turn of the Screw* and *The Other House*, a character seen out of doors without one is so alarming that it is rightly felt to herald disaster. 'Males and females alike,' Gwen Raverat remembers of the 1890s, 'we had always to wear something on our heads out of doors.'[7] As symbols of deference, self-respect and identity hats were only abandoned *in extremis* – the first hat we see in *The Princess Casamassima* is the torn straw of Millicent Henning, the child of a family about to be evicted from their slum. The dramatic change in her fortunes is signalled by a change of hat. From the slum the narrative moves to the theatre, a place where headgear is a guide to identity and character but also a disguise convention. The theatre operates as a central metaphor in the novel and Hyacinth, Captain Sholto and Paul Muniment variously play the conspiratorial role, a stage character typically seen under a slouched hat. Central to my argument, however, is the fact that for both male and female (though in different ways), in the rapidly changing social and economic climate of the late nineteenth century, a hat was a relatively cheap and readily available fashion sign: a sign in the Barthesian sense in that it was evolutionary rather than static, adding to and modifying its meanings while retaining older associations. Princess Casamassima herself is a fashion icon, and three other women in Hyacinth Robinson's life live by the fashion industry, which by the 1880s, with the advent of mass production and the department store, had taken on a central role in social and economic life. Balzac contended that as social distinctions in the nineteenth century blurred, and status and occupation were no longer clearly visible in increasingly mass-produced clothing, nuances of dress became revelatory: the large pockets of the shopkeeper 'always gaping as though to complain of being deprived of packages...collars, more or less clean, powdery or pomaded; buttonholes more or less frayed'.[8] Although Balzac's remarks mainly apply to male dress, they are equally applicable to female, and James, one might say, discreetly operated a version of Balzac's 'vestignomie' throughout his *oeuvre*. In *The Princess Casamassima* it is especially the hat, often seen together with gloves, which becomes the site for multiple meanings – social, theatrical or modish. A certain hat in the novel may be a stable, a transitory or an ambiguous sign of the status of the wearer, and of the wearer's relation to his or her time. Some hats may be performances or deceptions, others imaginary, others out-of-date. Who wears the hat of deference, or of poverty? Who, on the other hand, deserves the crown of the successful usurper of privilege?

Both Hyacinth's real mother, the French Florentine Vivier, and his adoptive mother, the Londoner Amanda Pynsent, are dress and bonnet makers. The traditional English comedic association of 'the little French milliner'[9] with sexual adventure had in Florentine's case ended badly with the murder of the English peer who betrayed her, and who is Hyacinth's putative father. The question of Hyacinth's paternity is never settled and he is not told until he is almost an adult of the identity of the woman to whose prison deathbed he was taken as a child. On this nightmare visit to Millbank prison with Miss Pynsent the child sees 'dreadful figures, scarcely female' in 'perfect frights of hoods' (I, 46), muffled, faceless creatures who add to the horror and incomprehensibility of the whole incident. Hoods are timeless and concealing; Hyacinth's origins are for him and for us, therefore, a matter of guessing and suspecting, an incalculable element in his life's outcome.

Amanda Pynsent tells untruths 'as freely as she invented trimmings' (1. 11), scattering romantic innuendoes about his 'noble' birth throughout Hyacinth's childhood and dreaming of the day when he will come in to his own. But Pinnie's romancing fails, as does her dress-making, based as they both are on sentimental outdated notions. In the 1908 version of the novel, James added a sentence which underscores the connection between fashion and the fashioning of Hyacinth's story: once Hyacinth learns the facts behind his childhood visit to the prison, he sees that Pinnie's fabrications have been 'so much cutting and trimming and shaping and embroidery, so much turning and altering and doing up' (1. 176). His recovery of Florentine's story marks the end of Pinnie's interest in dressmaking; her 'play of invention' deserts her and 'she ceased to notice or care how sleeves were worn'. (1. 70). But Pinnie's education of Hyacinth, under the ruling idea of his aristocratic lineage, her concern for style and appearance, colour the effect he has on others, as we see when Millicent Henning revisits Lomax Place, the slum in which both she and Hyacinth grew up.

'Do you want to know what you look like?' Millicent exclaims when she sees him again, 'You look for all the world like a little plastered-up Frenchman!', and she notes the way 'his little soft circular hat' (1. 75, 79) displays his curly front hair to advantage. It is the way Hyacinth wears these things, what James described as 'the hint of an "arrangement" in his dress', which makes him exotic and theatrical in Millicent's eyes. Hyacinth is therefore distanced in some way from what he wears, and when Millicent tells him that he 'would look very nice in a fancy costume', he is about to reply that 'he wished to go through life in his own character; but he checked himself, with the reflexion that this was exactly what he was apparently destined not to do... he was to go through life in a mask, in a borrowed mantle; he was to be every day and every hour, an actor' (1. 86). Hyacinth recognises the contradictions and uncertainties of his origins, but he does not, as has been suggested, wish to hide that past.[10] Hyacinth is not hiding under his hat; on the contrary, he is seeking an identity, a way of playing the hero in his own drama. He longs for a role, as Philip Sicker says, that will integrate 'some private ideal of self with a social image'.[11] Who is he to himself? Anything or everything he wears might be a disguise.

Hyacinth's hat, and his brown velveteen jacket, however, are typical of the leisure-wear of the upwardly-mobile, British working man of the period: an engraving in *The Graphic* of 1884 of the crowds at the Whitechapel Exhibition of Pictures[12] shows a predominance of soft circular hats and velveteen jackets. The hat is a predecessor of the Homburg of the twentieth century, it marked a move towards classlessness in male dress, since it was favoured by the Prince of Wales and had become widely worn by all classes by the late 1880s.[13] Hyacinth's first described hat is thus one that could be appropriate to his rank, but is also a high fashion item, promoted by royalty, crossing class-boundaries in a downward egalitarian direction. His hat might be plebeian, princely or French, depending on how he wears it and who sees it. Removing it can be a gesture of deference or simply a gentlemanly act on entering a house. The hat's ambiguities, which would defeat Balzac's system of 'vestignomie', and are complicated by Hyacinth's innate stylishness and *savoir-faire*, create uncertainties as to whether he belongs to his proper artisan class or is anticipating the future by usurping the privileges of a gentleman.

It is Millicent's hat, however, that is the star turn of her visit to her old home, an emblem of her elevation to fashion model and salesgirl in one of the new department stores; 'a more exciting, a more dramatic department of the great drapery interest' than the 'dismal little room' in

THE ESPAGNOL.   THE NEVA.   THE LAUSANNE.

Figure 5   Ladies' hats. *Woman's World,* 1888

Lomax Place 'where nothing had been changed for ages'. Millicent is scornful of Miss Pynsent's claim in her shop window to be a purveyor of fashionable bonnets; 'as if the poor little dressmaker had the slightest acquaintance with that style of headdress'. Pinnie herself is all too aware of the contrast as she looks at Millicent's hat, 'a wonderful composition of flowers and ribbons; her eyes had travelled up and down Millicent's whole person, but they rested in fascination on that grandest ornament' (1. 62, 57–8). Millicent's own gaze takes in the fact that Pinnie is 'bald and white and pinched . . . her hideous cap didn't disguise the way every-thing had gone' (1. 62) – trade, one guesses, as well as hair. The indoor cap had been the traditional wear of married and mature women, but by the mid-1880s dress caps had been discarded by all but the elderly Worse still for Pinnie's professional standing, the hat was displacing the bonnet:[14] '"Young women regard the hat almost as a symbol of emancipation" and the bonnet was becoming the token of advancing age.'[15] Millicent's own hat is an example of the vertiginous millinery fashionable in 1885, 'a singular high-crowned hat, popularly known as "three storeys and a basement "'' (see Figure 5).[16] Unlike male hats, which earlier in the century had lost their ornamental functions to those of social convention and simple protection, the excess of pointless ornament on female heads of the 1880s had become surreal, dizzy confections of flora and fauna.

How did she come by her 'grand ornament', this girl we first saw in an old straw hat? Millicent's position now is at 'a great haberdasher's in the neighbourhood of Buckingham Palace'. This was almost certainly Gor-ringe's in Buckingham Palace Road, which opened in 1858 as a small draper's and expanded rapidly to become one of the most prestigious of the London stores: at its seventieth anniversary celebrations what its customers chiefly remembered about it was its wonderful hats.[17] Milli-cent presumably both models hats and buys them, for as she says, 'I like to look nice' (1. 66, 67), and the new department stores had established that clerks 'could behave and dress like gentlefolk'.[18] Bill Lancaster, in his history of the department store, identifies the store as one of the three institutions of display in the late nineteenth century; the one which in fact offered the supreme visual experience.[19] Unlike Hyacinth's socially ambiguous headgear, the meaning of Millicent's exuberant hat – the crown on her social surface – is like Millicent's personality, dramat-ically clear: she is successfully staging her own class revolt. These gar-gantuan confections can be seen as the last ornament of the nineteenth century: 'the modernist new, before it encased itself in the ideology and style of functionalism, poured itself into that which was about

to disappear.'[20] Millicent's hat thus at once echoes and usurps the ornamental privileges of the past, and lays claim to the future. Poor Pinnie in
her *démodé* cap ends by gazing at her 'as if she had been a public
performer of some kind, a ballad-singer or a conjurer' (1. 69).

The relationship between the world of fashion and the stage was to
become even closer in the next decade; William Archer caustically wrote
of 'the fashion-play' as '*the* art-form of the late 19th century'.[21] Millicent, instinctively – and ahead – of her time, demands to be taken to the
theatre by Hyacinth. Her interest in the theatre is as an occasion for
display, rather than a wish to see the play itself, for like the department
store, the theatre was a platform for marketable commodities – for
people as well as clothes.

For James, each occasion had its hat. H. G. Wells recalls the selection
of headgear lying on the hall table of Lamb House: 'a tweed cap and a
stout stick for the marsh, a soft comfortable deerstalker if he were to turn
aside to the golf club, a light brown felt hat and a cane for a morning
walk down to the harbour, a grey felt with a black band and a gold-
headed cane of greater importance if afternoon calling in the town were
afoot.'[22] James's hats signalled the social nature of each occasion. An
event in Europe, such as the opera, James observed, 'produces the tiara',
whereas in America 'this symbol has ... to produce the occasion'.[23]
Appropriately, it is the half-American Christina Light – now the Princess
Casamassima – in her diamond-starred headdress, who creates the dramatic occasion for Hyacinth, the great turning-point of his life 'when
the creative self finds its necessary image[s]'.[24] The play to which Hyacinth escorts Millicent is a banal melodrama; the real drama, however,
happens in a box in the darkened auditorium, to which Hyacinth is
mysteriously summoned by the Princess.

James builds up towards this meeting over two chapters in an almost
cinematic way, starting with a distant glimpse of the Princess's bare,
braceleted arm, then focusing more closely on her female companion,
Madame Grandoni, a grotesque, pantomime figure 'with a fair, nodding,
wiggy head', round which, 'as if to keep her wig in place, she wore a
narrow band of tinsel decorated in the middle of the forehead by a jewel
which the rest of her appearance would lead the spectator to suppose
false' (1. 194). The first image is erotically disturbing, like the glimpse of
Madame Bovary's naked arm behind the blinds of her cab; the second is
a parody of female charm and an echo of the tinsel artificiality of the
stage. Such contradictions and confusions are to characterise Hyacinth's
relations with the Princess, when, led up winding staircases and cor-
ridors by Captain Sholto, he finally sees her.

The Princess in her curtained box is in darkness, her back to Hyacinth, but her effect, as she turns towards him, is dazzling: 'The vision had been only of a moment, but it hung before him, threw a vague white mist over the proceedings on the stage.' When finally he makes out her figure, the effect is again of darkness and dazzle; her dress is dark and rich, worn with pearls, but it is her brilliant head upon which he fixes: 'That head, where two or three diamond stars glittered in the thick, delicate hair which defined its shape, suggested to Hyacinth something antique and celebrated, something he had admired of old . . . in a statue, in a picture, in a museum' (1. 206, 207). The Keatsian echoes in the novel have already been noted,[25] and are located mainly in the country house episode, where Christina plays La Belle Dame to Hyacinth's pale Knight. But if Hyacinth is a soul awakening to beauty, then he is surely also Keats's Endymion gazing at Cynthia:

> Methought I lay
> Watching the zenith, where the milky way
> Among the stars in virgin splendour pours;
>   . . . yet she had,
> Indeed, locks bright enough to make me mad;
> And they were simply gordian'd up and braided,
> Leaving, in naked comeliness, unshaded,
> Her pearl round ears, white neck and orbed brow.[26]

The story of Cynthia (or Diana) and Endymion has frequently figured in paintings and sculpted reliefs; several examples would have been available to Hyacinth at the time, notably a version by Rubens in the National Gallery. Ian Jack, in his book on Keats and art, records an eighteenth-century engraving of the scene, in which Cynthia descends in an aureole of stars on Endymion, who shields his eyes against her brilliance.[27] The reality of Cynthia for Endymion, in Keats's poem, is uncertain, as she appears to him only in dreams. He seeks her as a poet seeks inspiration, as a Knight pursuing the unattainable Lady, a quest that can only end badly.

The Princess's appearance, however poetic and mythic, does also have a material reality in the fashion images of the day. In 1888 and 1889, respectively, the Marquise d'Hervey Saint Denis and Madame Stern had themselves painted as the goddess Diana, each with a diamond crescent in her hair;[28] the political hostess, Lady Randolph Churchill, in a photograph of *c*.1888 (Plate V) wears diamond stars in her hair as well as on her dress;[29] and Willett Cunnington notes that by 1885 hair styles for the evening were 'very high with combs, fancy-headed pins, jewelled butterflies or a tuft of flowers'.[30] Christina, like Millicent, has on her head that odd, late nineteenth-century fusion of the artificial and the natural, the reworking of old forms of ornament (diamonds) in a futuristic fantasy of natural forms (stars, insects or flowers). James's description of the Princess is rooted in a fashionable reality, but what counts is the dramatic *effect* she has on Hyacinth, which is derived from the aesthetic associations of her image, drawn from the past. She turns and blinds him with the 'spotlight' in which she always seems to be held. Does she represent an authentic icon of beauty, a goddess or a princess? Or is she an actress in costume, like Madame Grandoni whose wig is secured by tinsel and paste? Hyacinth is too dazzled to question his vision, but both women are play-acting in some sense. Neither is Italian, despite their names, and if Hyacinth only knew it, Christina Light's origins are as dubious as his own. She is only Princess by a marriage that has long since foundered, and as guardian of Christina's virtue, Madame Grandoni's position is barely tenable. Her unease in the role is embodied in the 'rather soiled white gloves [which] were too large for her' (1. 194).

As a result of the encounter in the theatre, Hyacinth is invited to the Princess's London house, where, as we have seen, his appearance so unnerves the Prince. James intervenes to remark that Hyacinth 'dressed more carefully than he had ever been in his life before, stamped with that extraordinary transformation which the British Sunday often operates in the person of the wage-earning cockney, with his handsome head uncovered... might have passed for anything rather than a carrier of parcels' (1. 280). The average working man of the late 1880s might have had an everyday suit, a Sunday suit and an overcoat. The Sunday suit was likely to have been a short-jacketed, navy blue serge garment which by the 1890s became 'the Sunday wear of every British working man who could afford one, and the daily wear of those of the middle-classes whose employers were liberal enough to allow them to discard the dying frock-coat and silk hat'.[31] Not only Hyacinth's hat but his entire appearance is one in which class boundaries have become confused – no wonder the Prince is bewildered. We might note, however, that his head is deferentially uncovered. Paradoxically, Hyacinth's innate gentility means that the Prince has nothing to fear from him – Hyacinth is already halfway committed to the Prince's values.

The Princess, however, is not pleased: 'you've nothing of the people about you today – not even the dress... I wish you had come in the clothes you wear to work.' Christina, in effect, is still in the theatre,

wanting Hyacinth to dress the part she has in mind for him. Had she
considered him realistically she would realise that a young man invited
to a princess's house in Mayfair, as her *guest* would not be wearing
working clothes; indeed, to suggest that he might is an insult, since no
member of the working class – a class with the highly developed sense of
decorum seen in both Pinnie and Millicent – would make a social call in
working clothes. Hyacinth is not so besotted that he does not see this –
'you do regard me as a curious animal' (1. 292), he replies. Despite her
egalitarian posturing, she wants Hyacinth to *look* plebeian to gratify her
self-image as a class-rebel; in particular she wishes to 'épater le bourgeois' in the person of her husband.[32]

Hyacinth also visits Medley, the Princess's country house; a preparation, aesthetically, for the conversion he undergoes in Paris and Venice.
Christina's appearance in the theatre was not itemised, and, similarly,
the house is not described in concrete detail; but as Philip Grover points
out, 'we are given solidity of specification … in the responses and eva-
luation of the characters to the house[33] – and Hyacinth's response is one
of intoxication expressed in Keatsian terms. This episode is in truth just
another theatrical show, since the house with its antiques and art is
rented, and apart from Christina and Madame Grandoni, it is empty.
Christina's socialism does not stretch to asking her own circle to rub
shoulders with a bookbinder for the weekend. One could say that Christina's occupation of Medley is at odds with her commitment to revolution; but then so is her devotion to her personal appearance. The
Princess dresses for her rural idyll 'in fair colours, as simply as a young
girl', but she becomes a lady of fashion, a Belle Dame, for her Sunday
drive together with Hyacinth, when she appears 'with a dark hat and
clear parasol, drawing on fresh loose gloves' (2. 14,16). As he sits in the
carriage Hyacinth reflects that '[the Princess's] performance of the part
she had undertaken to play was certainly *complete*, and everything lay
before him but the reason she might have for playing it' (2. 19). He
might also wonder, as Madame Grandoni does, how the world views the
spectacle of a young unmarried man staying in the Princess's house on
terms of apparent social equality, without the benefit of a house-party:
'ladies' did not dress up and go for drives with their tradesmen, nor dine
with them of an evening. Hyacinth's happiness is intensified by an
awareness of the unreality of what is happening to him: 'a fear that
wrong movement of any sort would break the charm, cause the curtain
to fall on the play' (2. 27).

Reality on the other side of the curtain for Hyacinth is the work that
awaits him on Monday morning, and the fact that – as he explains to

Christina when she questions his need to leave – he has no money and only one suit. But for Christina 'the play' is real and her 'act' at Medley unfinished. Christina is one of the few of James's characters to appear in more than one novel: Madame Grandoni's reflections on her, in *Roderick Hudson*, sheds some light on Christina's behaviour here: 'she's an actress, but she believes in her part while she's playing it'; 'when the figure she makes to her own imagination, ceases to please or amuse her she has to do something to smarten it up and give it a more striking turn.'[34] Christina's search for a role (or a hat) may be compared to Hyacinth's, for like Hyacinth her origins are confused and she seems to be trying out several at once. Under a lady-like hat she may be entranced by Hyacinth's good breeding; under her socialist bonnet irritated by flaws in his working-class credentials; under a third she is the goddess in the painting which Rebecca West sees as an analogy for her relationship with Hyacinth – 'lying on a satin couch while a young man makes music for her at an organ; her eyes are softly intent, and the youth thinks she is suspended over the world in his music, but really she is brooding on the whiteness of his skin beneath his black beard'.[35] Mr Vetch, Hyacinth's father-figure, confronts the Princess with these contradictions: 'If you like him because he's one of the lower orders, how can you like him because he's a swell?' (2. 246) – a question which makes her very angry. Each of her personae is real to her while they last, and her belief in them is reflected in the perfection of her costumes. She has no very sinister designs; she is simply a class-tourist, needing to be constantly entertained, gratified and seduced.

On his return from his small Grand Tour of Europe, financed by a legacy from Pinnie, Hyacinth has problems in locating the Princess. In his absence she has decided her Woman's Mission is social reform, and finding that Hyacinth is insufficiently deprived and downtrodden – and boringly worshipful besides – she has moved on into what she sees as the more thrillingly authentic working-class orbit of the abrasive Paul Muniment. To effect this move she needs to shift scenery and change costume. In a show of solidarity with the huddled masses, she moves from Mayfair to lower-middle-class Madeira Crescent, where she receives Muniment in a desert of gimcrack furniture and ornaments, which he admires. Hyacinth has already noted crudities in Paul's taste, but Christina, having renounced fashionable society, and taken up what we would call 'radical chic', is more interested in the sexual charisma of power and ambition that emanates from Paul than in his aesthetic tastes. It is not that he appears before her, Keir Hardie-like,[36] in working clothes, for he too is in his 'Sunday toggery', but that whatever he chooses to wear – new gloves, new necktie, new hat – is crude and raw and has for Christina the smell of a bona fide East-Ender on the make. He in fact takes great care with his appearance and, when about to accompany the Princess on some subversive errand, he puts on a hat, 'a new one, the bravest he had ever possessed', his sister Rosy remarks, 'Well, you do look genteel!' (2. 288). Like Millicent's, his hat is a pledge of upward mobility, a token of future intentions.

Christina too prepares herself for this occasion and we note that she has not only changed her setting but also her style of dress. Waiting for Muniment, she stands before a glass 'arranging her bonnet ribbons' (2. 297). As we saw in the early encounter between Pinnie and Millicent, the bonnet by 1886 was on its way out. In her historical survey of English women's headdress and hairstyles, Georgine de Courtais makes no distinction between hats and bonnets after 1880, calling them both simply hats: bonnets had become tiny by 1890, she says, and 'tended more and more to be worn only by older women'.[37] So what is the Princess – whose whole career is founded on a successful appearance – doing in a bonnet?

From time to time in the history of costume an item of dress, while dropping out of contemporary fashion, takes on a second life as an element of uniform, or a symbolic part of a ritual, where it becomes fossilised and immune to change. This was beginning to happen to the bonnet in the 1880s. This bonnet is still with us in Salvation Army uniform, and that of nurses in some nineteenth century hospitals. The connection of the bonnet with good works grew out of its symbolic associations with feminine modesty, as the bonnet, unlike the hat, shielded the face and covered most of the wearer's hair. Even in its abbreviated 1880s form, it conferred on its wearer the aura of good character. A Newnham College student, Molly Thomas, when she went to be interviewed for her first teaching post in 1886, was lent a bonnet by her tutor to give her moral support and recalled that 'the strings of it were enough to check a tendency to laugh'.[38]

Social reform and 'good works' in London's East End were a fashionable topic in the England of the 1880s and 1890s. They feature, for example, in two novels by Mrs Humphry Ward: *Robert Elsmere* (1888) and *Marcella* (1894). James had corresponded with Mrs Ward in 1884, and became friendly with her in 1885 when she was busy with *Robert Elsmere* and he with *The Princess Casamassima*. According to her own memoirs they discussed literary matters and James, in his letters, shows a close interest in her novels. Charitable causes, we might say, had become as chic as Aesthetic Dress – in fact, the two often went together – and the adoption of causes by society *grandes dames*, such as Angela Burdett-Coutts and the Countess of Warwick, tended to turn the whole business into a modish pastime. Lady Charlotte, in *Robert Elsmere*, is advised to wear 'a dowdy dress and veil' for a visit to the East End, and she jokily promises to borrow an outfit from her housekeeper. The term 'East-Ending' is used by one of these modishly socialistic ladies, when Elsmere, the reformist minister, visits the bad but beautiful Madame de Netteville at her evening party. 'The latest?' comments a cynical guest; 'I suppose so, answers the lady; 'she is East-Ending for a change. We all do it nowadays.'[39]

The eponymous heroine of Mrs Ward's later novel, *Marcella*, starts as an enthusiastic but confused Fabian, interested in art as well as working-class deprivation. The acquisition of wealth, together with the shock of reality that comes from her involvement with a murder case, turns her to the nursing profession and London's East End. This is serious 'East-Ending' however, comparable to Elsmere's, and not a fashionable frivolity. We see her not only in her nurse's bonnet and cloak, but also in 'a little bunch of black lace that called itself a bonnet, with black strings tied demurely under the chin'.[40] The detail of the bonnet may seem almost frivolous, but it is a coded sign of female virtue, not fashion.

We might say, then, in Mrs Humphry Ward's words, that the Princess is 'East-Ending' and her bonnet is essential to her new identity. When Hyacinth sees her again after his return from Italy, it is in Paul Muniment's lodgings, sitting by his crippled sister Rosy, looking 'like a radiant angel dressed in a simple bonnet and mantle...she had made herself humble for her pious excursion; she had...almost the attitude of an hospital nurse; it was easy to see from the meagre line of her garments that she was tremendously in earnest' (2. 160). She is also performing for the benefit of another of Rosy's visitors, Lady Aurora Langrish, an ungainly aristocratic spinster whose diffidence hides a genuine philanthropy. Christina has rightly identified Lady Aurora as an appropriate model for her latest role.

After a glance 'which travelled in a flash from the topmost bow of [Lady Aurora's] large, misfitting hat to the crumpled points of her substantial shoes', Christina performs in her newest mode: 'I've *nothing* in the world – nothing but the clothes on my back!... there are no things in my house now.... Dear lady... I fear I must confess to you that my heart's not in bibelots. When thousands and tens of thousands haven't bread to put in their mouths I can dispense with tapestry and old china.' But, as Hyacinth reflects, 'though the lady in question could dispense with old china and tapestry, she could not dispense with a pair of immaculate gloves which fitted her like a charm' (2. 167–9). The question of her sincerity, however, ceases to trouble him: Christina's pose is not opposed to some genuine self, but is simply the latest among her many roles. Eager to emulate Lady Aurora, she decides the simplest way to assume the spinster's identity is to acquire her ramshackle wardrobe: 'she wished...to get her bonnets at the same shop, to care as little for the fit of her gloves' (2. 271). If only – Christina feels – she can get the costume right, the rest will follow.

Lady Aurora is the most consistently be-hatted figure in the novel, though of all the characters she has least to hide. When Hyacinth first meets her at the Muniment's she is 'crowned with a large, vague hat and a flowing umbrageous veil'. Although socially the grandest of the novel's characters, her clothes are in disrepair and look 'as if she had worn them a good deal in the rain' (1. 121, 127). She has actually very little money, but her shabby appearance is due more to indifference about herself in the face of the needs of others than it is to her pinched budget. Her hats are, therefore, not badges of fashion or occupation, nor theatrical disguises, but simply social necessities. The dilapidations of her appearance are nuances, within Balzac's 'vestignomie', that reveal a class in decline. Ironically, it is thus the aristocrat whose headgear is authentically working-class in function and meaning, a sign of self-respect and of social status that becomes particularly vital when that respect and position are under threat.

Christina's effusions only confuse Lady Aurora, whose hats and bonnets are much too out-of-date to be bought in a shop. By the 1880s Willet Cunnington records that the veils which had adorned every hat and bonnet in the 1870s were slowly passing out of favour and hats became tall rather than wide. Both Cunnington[41] and Stella Mary Newton also note that from about 1885 fashions reflected the decline of the British economy as well as moves toward social reform: 'wool "art" serge was more admirable than Lyons velvet and hand-thrown earthenware superior to Sèvres.'[42] In a grim, if inadvertent way, Lady Aurora's appearance is more genuinely in tune with the times than Christina's 'dull gown' and bonnet, which are symptomatic only of that self-regarding theatricality she so much wishes to escape.

Lady Aurora too is escaping: 'When one's one of eight daughters and there's very little money...and nothing to do but go out with three or four others in a mackintosh, one can easily go off one's head' (1, 251). Hyacinth responds to her shy kindness 'which took all sorts of equalities and communities for granted' (2. 190), but for the others Lady Aurora is a 'Lady': 'it is Belgrave Square that she brings to others...it is what they want from her.'[43] Lady Aurora shares Christina's affection for Hyacinth, but sadly, also, her passion for Paul Muniment. Class and gender positions are overturned here with a rough modernity, for Lady Aurora is the suppliant and Paul the aloof object of her adoration.

Muniment, however, is less interested in her yearning egalitarianism than in her snob value: to please him, therefore, 'she would try to cultivate the pleasures of her class if the brother and sister in Camberwell thought it right – try even to be a woman of fashion'. Hyacinth, calling on her for the last time, senses the poignancy of her performance as a lady. His final vision of her is in a 'light-coloured, crumpled-looking, faintly-rustling dress; her head was adorned with a languid plume, that flushed into little pink tips; in her hand she carried a pair of white gloves' (2. 356, 352). She is embarrassed by her own 'disguised and bedizened' appearance, an embarrassment which extends pinkly into her headdress. As Hyacinth had stood in the Mayfair house in his Sunday best, so Lady Auora stands in Belgravia in aristocratic plumage: the difference being that while a grubby apron would have been an accurate sign of Hyacinth's artisan status, his gentlemanly appearance had expressed his sense of self. Lady Aurora's appearance befits her rank but it is an imposed costume – it is not how she sees herself. Both vainly try to please those they love, but, as ideologues, Muniment and Christina are incapable of sustained affection, seeing in others not individual worth but class-types. Hyacinth knows she will fail to please, as he has failed, and, as tragedy queens tear at their hair in despair, he imagines 'the poor lady coming home and pulling off her feathers for evermore' (2. 356).

Lady Aurora cannot relinquish her headdress although it defines her class-status only, relegates her to the past and denies her an emotional reality. Christina can buy or borrow hats to trick out her current view of reality, but none of her headdresses are *her* 'for evermore' for she has no stable reality. Both women are attracted by the seemingly genuine revolutionary in Paul Muniment. But Muniment, biding his time, is *behind* the terrorist plot rather than an active participant; the plot itself fails because Hyacinth is finally incapable of exploiting his genteel demeanour to infiltrate a grand party and assassinate a duke. He shoots himself instead. Is there, then, amongst these characters a visibly successful revolutionary, someone whose subversive headgear breaks through the smug surface?

Millicent Henning, early in the novel, figures in Hyacinth's imagination as a triumphant figure, 'with a red cap of liberty on her head and her white throat bared so that she should be able to shout the louder the

Marseillaise of that hour' (1. 164). In Hyacinth's eyes, with his French
origins and revolutionary convictions, the glorious new hat, which so
crushed Pinnie, has metamorphosed into an emblem of revolution. His
repeated references to her robust beauty reinforce the connections with
Delacroix's figure of Liberty in his painting *Liberty Leading the People*,
who is both a Greek 'Nike' figure, and a sturdy Marianne of the Paris
streets. Millicent is also an emblem of those irreconcilable forces that
tear Hyacinth apart. If her physical beauty recalls one of those élitist
treasures that he now believes make the world 'less of a "bloody sell"
and life more of a lark' (2. 145), he also enjoys her irreverent attitude to
her social superiors, so different to his own. She is 'to her blunt,
expanded fingertips a daughter of London . . . a nymph of the wilderness
of Middlesex' (1, 61–2), one of his own class, in whose name he is
committed to destroy such treasures.

Both Christina and Millicent have figured as crowned goddesses in
Hyacinth's imagination. He falls in love with Christina and the world he
believes she represents, and remains in love even when he has recognised that metaphorically her diamonds are paste, her relation to the
'palaces and properties' of the past, fortuitous, and her interest in him
transient. Hyacinth's affection for Millicent is deeply rooted, but it is
constantly undercut by his contempt for the realities of her crude taste
and enthusiastic consumerism. He ignores the message of her splendid
hat as the token of contemporary success in the class-struggle, finding it
more palatable to translate it instead into the classical cap[44] of the
worker, in a painting which is a frankly romantic version of a revolutionary moment long passed. Millicent herself has 'no theories about
redeeming or uplifting the people' (1. 163); she simply scorns their
incapacity to lift themselves out of the dirt, as she has done. She
would agree with Balzac's contention that revolutions are as much a
battle between cloth and silk as they are between bayonets and barri-
cades.

Lionel Trilling's pioneering re-evaluation of *The Princess Casamassima*
foregrounded the authenticity of James's picture of the contemporary
political and social scene. Both Trilling and Edward Wagenknecht single
out James's sympathetic treatment of Millicent as a triumph 'because
she is so utterly unlike what anybody might expect from him'.[45] Trilling
reads Millicent's irritation with Hyacinth's manual labour as a demonstration that she herself 'does nothing less genteel than exhibit what
others have made'[46] and appropriately, James applies Balzac's 'vestignomie' as much to Millicent's hands as to her headgear. On her reappearance in Lomax Place, Pinnie notes that Millicent's hands were not

delicate: 'Her gloves covering her wrists insufficiently, showed the red-ness of those parts in the interstices of the numerous silver bracelets that encircled them' (1. 61) – a contrast to the subtle eroticism of Christina's white arm, shortly to be glimpsed by Hyacinth in the theatre. The coarsening effects of manual labour are shown almost as Millicent's genetic inheritance rather than as any actual consequence of working with her hands.

Millicent's place in the novel (and in Hyacinth's consciousness) is taken by Christina, and it is not until Christina loses interest in Hyacinth that Millicent reappears in his mind's eye, jangling her brace-lets. He recalls her fierce threats of revenge, when he had hinted at his own likely death, tossing her head 'as if it were surmounted by the plumes of a chieftainess', evoking shades of Pocohontas – another legendary heroine. His affection, however, is again undercut by the reality he cannot stomach: she is neither a goddess nor a heroic legend but 'a shopgirl overladen with bracelets of imitation silver' (2. 133).

As a fashion model Millicent embodies 'the look of the day'. This look is no longer that of the ethereal heroines of the mid-nineteenth century. Millicent's style is that of a mass-educated, mass-production society, a girl on whom every telegraphist, typist and shopgirl can realistically afford to model herself (see Figure 6). Despite the zeal of the Arts and Crafts Movement for improving the taste of working people like Milli-cent, what it in fact did was to reform the tastes of the upper-class intelligentsia, those who could afford its expensively designed, hand-made products – of which Hyacinth's exquisitely bound books are examples. Millicent's scorn for his craft as dirty drudgery is misplaced; the real problem is that it is a beautiful, unprofitable anachronism, which is why he loves it. As a shopgirl, she, on the other hand, success-fully adapts to a consumer society, laying vigorous hands on beer, buns and bracelets, unconstrained by the reverent idealism which prevents Hyacinth from ever realising his aesthetic longings.

James gives Hyacinth one last idyllic day with Millicent in Hyde Park, on the banks of the Serpentine, in a scene that creates a London version of the Impressionists' images of city-workers at leisure on the Seine. Appropriately, the version of class revolution that underlies the Impres-sionists' vision of Paris – in which Millicent could well have modelled for Renoir – is more robustly contemporary than that found in the wistful heroics of Delacroix's world. Having prepared herself for the outing to the Park, Millicent emerges from the house and 'instantly thrust her muff, a tight, fat, beribboned receptacle, at him, to be held while she adjusted her gloves to her large, vulgar hands' (2. 325). Lady

Figure 6   In a London department store. *The Girls' Own Book*, 1888.

Aurora's gloves had holes, Madame Grandoni's were too big, Christina's fitted to perfection but Millicent's gloves and muff, gestures towards gentility, cannot contain her powerful physicality. Sitting together in the Park, Millicent guesses that Hyacinth's 'trumpery Princess' has 'chucked' him, and she leans forward, 'her hands clasped in her lap and her multitudinous silver bracelets tumbled forward on her thick wrists. Her face, with its parted lips and eyes clouded to gentleness' (2. 335). Millicent's hands certainly take and consume, but they also give and comfort. As he tells the story of his betrayal, she lays her hand on his, takes it in her own, then rising, she grasps him and kisses him under a tree – a conclusion, one could say, to the Arcadian idyll begun at Medley. If Christina has been Keats's elusive Cynthia, then Millicent, in a public park, is the mortal Phoebe. Like Endymion, however, Hyacinth's quest is not to end here with a surrender to the consolations of physical immediacy; he seeks what he first saw in his vision of Christina: 'something antique and celebrated' (1. 207) – in short, the unattainable ideal.

Hyacinth can no longer see things in terms of class envy or conflict, for visual images and material objects have acquired other meanings for him. His adherence to the ideals of the past and his revulsion against 'conspicuous consumption' anticipate James's later dislike of '[t]he whole costly uptown demonstration'[47] of New York on his visit of 1905, and his consequent nostalgia for the virtues of an earlier America, which, in a short story of 1909, 'Crapy Cornelia', he embodies in a hat. James draws on the techniques of the new cinematograph, when he 'zooms' in on an old black hat as the catalyst for the choice the hero must make between the values of old and new America, and his switch from pictorial to cinematic analogies neatly pre-empts accusations of conservatism in a story that is otherwise deeply and – compared with *The Princess Casamassima* – simplistically conservative. Questions of social deprivation and privilege are not at stake here, however, as they are in the earlier novel; one finds instead the kind of 'Old/New Money' snobbery so often targeted in the novels of Edith Wharton. Indeed, Mrs Worthingham, the pretty widow of the story, is said to be modelled (unkindly) on Wharton.

The cultured middle-class White-Mason, poised to propose marriage to a wealthy New York widow, has been standing on the sunlit balcony of her smartly appointed apartment, pleasantly alive to the delights of her person, with 'her Dresden-china shoes and her flutter of wondrous befrilled contemporary skirts'. '[A]n incongruous object', however, suddenly interposes itself between himself and this bright prospect: it is 'a woman's head with a little sparsely feathered black hat, an ornament quite unlike those the women … were now "wearing", and that grew and grew, that came nearer and nearer, while it met his eyes, after the manner of images in the cinematograph.'[48] The hat belongs to Cornelia Rasch, a figure from the America of his youth. She and her rooms are dowdy with the memorabilia of their shared past: but she represents for White-Mason virtues lacking in glossy skyscraper New York to which he is now about to ally himself. He decides after all not to marry the widow: but neither does he marry the dull owner of the dull hat that had filled his vision, although he pledges some kind of allegiance to her. The story ends there, re-establishing 'finer' values but rather evading the issue of Cornelia's lack of personal charm for the sensuous hero, in a way that *The Princess Casamassima* does not. Political, aesthetic and erotic forces exert complex and fatal pressures upon Hyacinth's relations with two women which are left interestingly unresolved. The sudden jettisoning of Mrs Worthingham as a consequence of White-Mason's burst of nostalgia over an outmoded hat and some old photographs seems cruelly frivolous by contrast. The best one can hope is that Cornelia and White-Mason confine their anecdotage to one another.

The oppositional forces of Hyacinth's heredity constantly sabotage his attempt to create a self. His gentlemanly patrilineage is incompatible with that of his rebellious plebeian mother and this tension is exacerbated when, in his quest for his revolutionary roots in Paris, his allegiance to the 'palaces and properties' of a privileged past is paradoxically strengthened. James also makes it clear that this anarchist movement of the 1880s to which Hyacinth has fatally allied himself, is as much a thing of the past as a hierarchical aristocracy – fairly old-hat, one could say, and dedicated to class envy and destruction rather than social reform. The rather creaky melodrama of James's picture of the conspirators, of which commentators have often complained, may even be intentional: it certainly matches the mood evoked by the reference to the Delacroix painting. Schinkel, the arch-conspirator, is described as wearing a green coat, 'a garment of ceremony... impossible to procure in London or in any modern time. It was... of high antiquity, and had a tall stiff clumsy collar which came up to the wearer's ears' (2. 363): a style of the early nineteenth century, in fact. Schinkel's notion that taking pot shots at grandees will somehow bring about the millennium is as *démodé* as Cornelia's hat or Pinnie's cap. The plot only serves to bring home to Hyacinth the irreconcilability of his beliefs and the impossibility of his existence.

Millicent has held out her large red hands in vain to Hyacinth, to draw him out of this moribund past into her own seductive modernity. His inability to escape his environment, however, is not wholly predetermined, nor are his choices seriously limited by intellectual or material deprivation; on the contrary, the passionate nature of his mother and that of his 'supercivilised sire' have come together to produce in him an exceptionally responsive sensibility, which has been nurtured by a liberal upbringing. His commitment to revolution is as freely and intelligently given as is his appreciation of the art of the past. If he foresees his own violent end, no step he takes towards that end is inevitable. It is in his *created* self that his fate lies, and as we have seen, that self is unstable and fragmented, composed of incompatible allegiances in which he can find no ease. His hat first confuses those who see it; we next see it in his hand; thereafter the narrative ceases to record Hyacinth's sense of his own appearance and shifts instead into his consciousness of others: of Christina, Millicent, Paul, Sholto and Lady Aurora – but also of himself as seen by them. His final hat is an imaginary martyr's crown, which he superimposes on the 'crown' of social success that Millicent has imagined for him.

In a final search for a way out of this martyrdom, Hyacinth – accompanied by the Prince he once so alarmed – witnesses Christina's betrayal of him as she disappears into a darkened doorway with Paul. He then seeks out Lady Aurora, who, caged in Belgrave Square, is kind but powerless: then, recalling the affectionate reality of Millicent in the Park, Hyacinth walks through London to her shop, led on by this memory, like Orpheus by Eurydice. It is too late: she has moved on and beyond him. What he sees is her turned back, and 'the long, grand lines of her figure draped in the last new thing' (2. 423), her face towards Captain Sholto. Hyacinth is relegated to the shades.

Sholto has shadowed Hyacinth throughout the novel, as avatar and rival. Once Christina's lover, then her attendant pimp, he has now spotted a likelier future in Millicent. When Hyacinth had met him at the Muniment's, he had been struck by the 'ingenious cheapness' of Sholto's clothes 'to an effect coinciding... with poor Hyacinth's own' (1. 245). The details of this costume do not emerge until a subsequent encounter when Hyacinth notes Sholto's gentlemanly elegance in contrast to 'the pot-hat and shabby jacket' (1. 328) he had worn before. The pot-hat was an early lower-class version of the bowler hat; the mark, not of the worker but of a newly empowered member of that class, the foreman.[49]

Sholto does not pretend, however, to be either worker or foreman, for he shows himself to Hyacinth as equally at ease kitted out as a hunting, shooting gentleman on horseback – where the upper-class version of the bowler originated as a riding hat. He also appears as the man-about-town, where the bowler hat was soon to become a respectable alternative to the top hat. While Hyacinth envies Sholto's ability somehow always to look right, he is also puzzled by so often coming across him in unexpected places, comparing him to an inscrutable Mephistopheles. Sholto materialises before Hyacinth at key moments, in appropriate guises: like the sinister Sir Edmund Orme in James's eponymous ghost story, he is 'arrayed and anointed exactly as the occasion demanded'.[50]

None of the guises are the 'real' Sholto: alarmingly, there may be no one there – 'Sholto is only a collection of costumes'.[51] As Faust's Mephistopheles came for Christian souls, so Sholto comes for Hyacinth. He tells Hyacinth how, having once collected illuminated missals and ghost stories for Christina, he then 'began to collect little democrats. That's how I collected you' (2. 75). His guises are representations of possible personae (or hats) laid out for Hyacinth – to possess or be possessed by – the country gentleman, the man-about-town, the labour leader. Only Sholto's working-man's persona is clearly given a hat by James; as Michael Carter points out, '[the] pared back, generalised form of male headgear was a key element in embodying a number of positive meanings grouped around the new forms of male bourgeois work.'[52]

James could not have known how remarkably prescient was his focus on the 'pot' hat, the future headgear and symbol of the London businessman, a class to which the more astute members of the aristocracy, like Sholto, adapted themselves, in an alliance with the more ambitious of the city's lower classes. The middle-class male in a bowler could be a successful shopkeeper, or a threadbare bank-clerk precariously on the way up or down (E. M. Forster's Leonard Bast, for example, would have worn a bowler) or a dandy, or a gentleman – in each case the bowler represented respectability. But despite the hat's promise of upward mobility, gentility and even power, Hyacinth takes up none of these offered personae and the symbolic power of the bowler is resigned to Sholto – and possibly to Muniment. Claims on the affections of Christina and Millicent must also be resigned, and, having replaced Hyacinth in Millicent's life, Sholto looks straight through him, over her oblivious shoulder, as if he had already ceased to be. Ironically, the couple are replaying the relationship between Hyacinth's aristocratic father and his 'little milliner' mother; only here, as an employee of the department store, in one of the great institutions of twentieth-century culture, Millicent holds more of the cards.

Trilling noted the extent to which Hyacinth is seen as a child amongst parent-figures and here, having rejected one woman and been rejected by another, he regresses from the role of active adult male to that of the excluded child, face against the shop-window, watching 'the great scene of lust'.[53] Adopting Zola's image of the department store as the cathedral of the new consumer-culture, one might even see this scene as a sacrament, the celebration of an alliance between Sholto and Millicent; metaphorically they could be said to have exchanged hats rather than rings, Millicent having taken on the badge of ornamental uselessness and Sholto that of the successful worker. These are, however, performances of aspiration rather than actuality, since Millicent is the worker and Sholto the drone: 'the male hat became a sign of an egalitarian spirit, if not of an egalitarian reality.'[54]

Hyacinth has two further parent figures: Christina, in her *déclassé* 'East-Ending' bonnet, is paired with and then rejected by Paul in his 'genteel' new hat. The gentility of this hat (which is all we know of it) is symptomatic of his paradoxical wish simultaneously to emulate and destroy the properties of privilege: his conception of 'supreme social success'(2. 210) is a villa at Blackheath, an aspiration of Pooterdom. Muniment is an example of what Sean O'Faolain meant when he said that 'between England and Revolution there will always stand an army of bowler hats',[55] for we can be sure that Muniment will achieve his suburban villa without resort to pistols or the guillotine. For Hyacinth, the hero of this novel, there are no hats left, no way in which his dream-world (which is not in Blackheath), furnished with 'the conquests of learning and taste' (2. 145), can accommodate itself to class-envy, to the whole spiritually mean 'costly up-town demonstration'; no place where his ideas of beauty and social justice can be reconciled. If he is, as he had earlier described himself, 'to be every day and every hour an actor', a hero in his own drama, then he needs more 'panache', an identifying hat. In Samuel Beckett's play, *Waiting for Godot*, Lucky can only think (can only 'be', therefore) when he wears his bowler hat; when it is removed at the climax of his great speech, he collapses into silence and servility.

Hyacinth is not a convincing hero. If James is to symbolise the decay of *ante-bellum* American ideals with Cornelia Rasch's headgear, in his essay on 'The American Scene' (1905), he also deplores the contemporary American male's lack of instinct for hats; they had 'no sense of its "vital importance" in the manly aspect.'[56] Lacking a hat, therefore, Hyacinth lacks manhood, and James might even be accused of contributing our lack of confidence in him as a hero by repeatedly labelling him 'little'; this is particularly true in the Preface, where James – unconsciously perhaps – is recording the effect on himself of re-reading the novel. It also accounts for the childlike qualities noted by Trilling; though this then makes Trilling's categorisation of Hyacinth, as one of a line of pushy Young Men from the provinces, problematic. If he is 'to move from an obscure position into one of considerable eminence in Paris or London',[57] like Julien Sorel, Pip or Rastignac, he has to be determined on his share of the world's power and pleasure, to be a subversive undercurrent, a challenge to smugness; he must demand respect and all this literal and metaphorical doffing of his cap will not do.

Figure 7   Bowler hats, late nineteenth century.

Manners (of which dress is a part), are an indication, as Trilling says, of the direction of a man's soul; and 'in a shifting society great emphasis is put on appearance . . . status in a democratic society is presumed to come not with power but with the tokens of power'.[58] Dress is throughout a dream of alterity, of what one wants to be. Hyacinth as the sentient Jamesian hero on whom nothing is lost, is aware at the end that there is no future for the way he sees himself. At this final 'site of modernity', the department store, alternative selves *are* on offer, but it is Millicent, in her fantastic hat, who is the hero of the revolution, the one who points far into the future history of the working class, beyond Marxism to the late twentieth-century triumph of consumer capitalism. Hyacinth is self-excluded, self-effaced to the point of extinction. There is no place for the person he has become. The image of Millicent, his childhood's other self, together with Sholto, the recycled aristocrat, sends him back to the slums of his childhood and to annihilation. James's *Bildungsroman* has traced the development of his hero's *private* consciousness to the point which makes it impossible that he should adopt the bowler hat, standing as it does for an anonymous, standardised public identity (Figure 7). But he is then spared 'all the stale hells of modernity',[59] the twentieth century's *danse macabre*, which moves from the bowler-hatted Chaplin, a cog in the machine-production hell of *Modern Times*, to the Surrealist disembodied bowlers of René Magritte, to the denial of all progress, all movement, all time, in the purgatory of *Waiting for Godot*, inhabited by tramps in the last real bowler hats. From there the bowler hat enters the futuristic, horror world of Stanley Kubrick's *A Clockwork Orange*, on the heads of the 'droogs', conformists in a world of affectless violence.

7
'Muffled' and 'Uncovered' in *The Ambassadors*

Sensitive single males in Henry James's novels are well advised to avoid the beautifully dressed, mysterious women who attend Signor Gloriani's parties. The eponymous Roderick Hudson meets the fatal Christina Light, in 'vaporous white' through Gloriani, in Rome; Lambert Strether, of *The Ambassadors* has his New England preconceptions overturned around 1900 when he meets Marie de Vionnet at Gloriani's Paris garden party, in a black dress that isn't altogether black; and John Berridge, the novelist in the short story, 'The Velvet Glove', is enthralled by a 'Princess' in a dress of 'old gold' and pearls at Gloriani's – still throwing parties in Paris in 1910.

The potent garments those women wear, like those in *The Wings of the Dove* (published before but written after *The Ambassadors*) operate both as pictorial images and costumes for dramatic performances: socially and historically accurate, they perform as protean, multi-layered symbols, styles of dress which, as James wrote of the costume of eighteenth-century France, inspire 'both admiration and mistrust'.[1] Christina's exquisite white is appropriate to her age and status as a *jeune fille*, but it quickly becomes apparent from her behaviour that as a symbol of purity and innocence her dress is a cover, operating as a lure in the marriage market. The 'old gold' dress worn by John Berridge's 'Princess' – a colour made fashionable for evening wear by its compatibility with the new electric lighting – makes her for him, a goddess from antiquity. She is, in fact, better known under the pseudonym 'Amy Evans', the author of trashy romantic novels, whose fascinations have been turned upon Berridge to extract a preface from him for her next piece. In contrast to the tragedy that ensues from Roderick Hudson's passion for Christina Light – and indeed, the second tragedy that Christina, as the

Princess Casamassima, precipitates for Hyacinth Robinson (though here Gloriani's hands are clean) – Berridge's story ends in bathos, a consequence of the exalted fantasies he has woven round his vision of 'Amy Evans'. Lambert Strether, on the other hand, is rendered neither foolish nor tragic, despite more protracted deceits and deeper mysteries, which, in the person of Madame de Vionnet, are variously and very seductively clothed.

The encounters at Gloriani's with Christina and 'Amy Evans' to some extent serve to diminish the men concerned. Roderick Hudson's death is a tragedy but not a heroic one, and as we have seen in Chapter 6, even James found it difficult to speak of Hyacinth Robinson in anything other than diminutive terms. We receive his impressions of others but we also share his increasing loss of identity, to his detriment as a character. How, then, is the befooling of Lambert Strether, his uncovering of the deceits that have been practised upon him and his final understanding of what is, in truth, a really quite banal situation, capable of leaving him finally a more substantial and heroic figure than he was at the outset? He starts and ends the novel a bespectacled, middle-aged American widower of small means, with little to distinguish him beyond a lively taste in neckties. And he has frankly nothing much to look forward to on his final return to Woollett, Massachussetts.

Strether's first impression of Madame de Vionnet, in contrast to the raptures of Roderick Hudson and John Berridge over the women they encounter, is one of enigma rather than of dazzle: James, in his 'Project' of the novel, describes Strether as standing 'in a world of mystery'[2] in relation to Madame de Vionnet. But her effect on him can be measured by the fact that it is followed by one of the novel's key moments – Strether's exhortation to Little Bilham to 'live all you can', and not, like Strether himself, 'miss things out of stupidity'.[3] He has become aware of a lack: a lack of *what* is not yet clear, for this is not a summing-up of his experience of the events of the novel, but in fact an articulation of his sense, less than half-way through the novel, that his Woollett, Massachusetts-self is beginning to feel inadequate and impoverished, seen in the light of his unfolding experience of Paris.

What is it that he sees that changes him, that makes the difference? Dress, I believe, is a key element in his interpretation of what he sees, and in his change of vision. Dorothea Krook, as we have seen, points out in her study of this novel, that James's attention to dress is here unusually close. E. M. Forster, while also singling out dress for comment in his essay on the novel, actually *berates* James for constructing his characters 'on very stingy lines...[t]heir clothes will not take off'.[4] But

Forster is wrong here: on the contrary, they do just that – they take their clothes off. And, appropriately in this novel that is so very much concerned with sexual relations, what Strether in a sense sees – pictorially and dramatically – in two of the final scenes is 'undress'.[5]

I use the word 'undress' here in its eighteenth-century sense of being incompletely dressed, of wearing an intimate and informal style of dress rather than one intended for social occasions. Because we have now more or less elided distinctions between the formal and the informal in dress – except in relation to military uniform – we have lost this particular nuance to the meaning of 'undress'. What Strether sees is not an unclothed couple *in flagrante delictu*, as it were, or even an indecently clothed couple, but a couple who are clothed for each other's company rather than for the more public circumstances in which, by mischance, they find themselves. Strether's moral and aesthetic vision has by this point become sufficiently sophisticated to recognise the implications of what he sees, but he sees more and with a finer complexity of human sympathies than he would have been capable of in Woollett, where there are only two 'types', the male and the female, and only 'two or three' opinions on any given subject. The direction of his vision away from the blinkered perspectives of Woollett to that furthest point where he (like Chad) can only return to Woollett, changes him profoundly (unlike Chad) and is what grants him heroic and – since he must return – almost tragic status.

James, in his Preface, emphasises the centrality of Strether's 'process of vision . . . the precious moral of everything'; the process whose potential he had first seen in *The Portrait of a Lady*. This 'process' is one of an alternation between the pictorial and the dramatic, which James compares to his technique in *The Wings of the Dove* – 'parts that prepare for scenes, and parts that justify and crown the preparation' (xii). In costume terms what we have is 'dress seen' and 'dress enacted'. This kind of transformation can also take place within the mind, as in the final party scene in *The Wings of the Dove*, when Milly's previous black garments are transferred from Milly to Kate in Densher's imagination. The two principal structural elements of 'picture' and 'scene' are not alternatives, they cannot be neatly divided into the registration of interior thought, on the one hand, and the representation of characters in speech and action, on the other. The climactic idyll by the Seine in *The Ambassadors* owes much of its impact to its imperceptible shift in Strether's mind from a consciously pictorial, tranquil 'impression', to a scene of figures moving through a moment of high, if suppressed, dramatic tension.

Lambert Strether 'sees' Madame de Vionnet on six key occasions in *The Ambassadors* and notes certain details of her appearance. These form a part of his 'process of vision', his evolving consciousness of her, and constitute scenes which are increasingly replayed in his imagination. The reality of Marie de Vionnet, in other words, depends on the way Strether represents her to himself and also on how his own view of himself, of his past, has evolved. The moment by the river and Strether's meditation upon it culminate in a scene in which he recognises her poignant vulnerability – a vulnerability that is reflected in a dress whose resonances reach both forwards and backwards in time. What stands revealed by these scenes is the 'immorality' that should thrill the Woollett soul with anticipated scandal; but the education of Strether's sensibility – the 'civilising' of Strether – makes it instead a moment of recognition of a common humanity and of mutual loss.

The education of Frédéric Moreau, in Gustave Flaubert's *Sentimental Education* (1869), also begins on a boat-trip, where he catches sight of Madame Arnoux: 'It was like a vision.'[6] This vision is filled with the entrancing details of her costume, particularly her hat, and although Madame Arnoux herself, as the novel develops, proves to be nothing out of the ordinary for the reader, Frédéric is never the same again. Strether's education, the 'process' of his moral and aesthetic vision, begins as soon as he steps off the boat at Liverpool, although in this case it is the hero's consciousness, initially, of his *own* appearance, that provides a turning point: 'it is only because it begins with gloves, neckties, velvet ribbons and a lady of fashion,' as Philip Grover says, 'that it *can*, James would have us believe, later develop into the fuller discrimination of behavior and morals which forms the centre of the book'.[7] Because the 'adventure' of the novel is the journey of Strether's sense of *himself*, it must start with this personal 'sharper survey of the elements of Appearance' (20), rather than, for example, with his impression of Madame de Vionnet, his 'Madame Arnoux'.

His survey of himself, however, is provoked by an encounter with a 'lady of fashion' just the same, in the person of his compatriot, Maria Gostrey. A long-term resident of Europe, she impresses Strether with her 'expensive subdued suitability', and, pulling on 'a pair of singularly fresh soft and elastic light gloves', she stops him in his tracks with '[a] feeling for something, possibly forgotten, in the light overcoat he carried on his arm...something of which the sense would be quite disconnected from the sense of his past and which was literally beginning there and then' (20). Prompted by the elegance of Maria's ensemble, he begins to feel some inadequacy in his own person, in relation both to

/ A lady with parrot, Liébert,
Paris, *c.* 1875.

// The Hon. Caroline Lawley,
Camille Silvy, 1865.

III Victoria, Crown Princess of Germany, Mondel & Jacob, 1876.

IV Madame Réjanne in a tea-gown by Doucet, Anon., 1902.

V Lady Randolph Churchill, Van der Weyde, 1888.

VI Rosie Boote, later Marchioness of Headfort, Lafayette, 1901.

VII Afternoon dress by Paquin, Reutlinger, 1901.

VIII Dinner dress by Worth, Anon., 1910.

her and to his new European surroundings. Defining this as possibly a lack of the right hat or gloves he reassures himself that it is just this kind of defect that Europe and Maria Gostrey can put right. Whether there *is* in fact anything faulty about his appearance is irrelevant, for, as Richard Hocks points out, in this novel, James's leitmotif of the play between appearance and reality parallels William James's pragmatist belief that 'the apparent was not "inferior" to the real, since the apparent is after all, how the real comes to us in experience'.[8] In other words, if Strether *feels* his appearance is faulty then for him there *is* something lacking.

This 'thing' would be something fresh, and have nothing in common with his Woollett past; and yet, as Susan Griffin makes clear in her discussion of *The Ambassadors*, '[t]he past intrudes upon and organises the present': Strether is never free of his awareness of Woollett and of his own history which it represents. His perception 'shapes his world and his past ... [and] his understanding comes *as* he composes his visual picture'.[9] Strether's perception of his past is neither fixed nor entirely negative, but malleable and contributes to the education of his vision. It is worth noting here that James, in 1900, was also working on one of the novels he was never to finish, *The Sense of the Past*, and Strether's reference to the 'sense of his past' in the 'survey' of himself suggests that there might be connections between the two works. *The Sense of the Past* concerns a young American, Ralph Pendrel, who returns to an ancestral house in London at the turn of the twentieth century, where he encounters an 1820 portrait of himself. Ralph enters the past and finds in the pockets of his coat the vital props for his 'new' life. I shall be discussing this novel more extensively in Chapter 9, but one might note here in relation to Lambert Strether that Ralph, while in 1820, never loses a sense of his twentieth-century self, and, although James never found a way to get Ralph out of the past, his dual awareness of past and present is to be what saves him and sends him back to the present reality, according to James's notebooks. Returning to Lambert Strether, we should see him not as a quiescent receptor and reflector of impressions, but, as Griffin says, 'an active, interested self who survives by perceiving.'[10] A key detail we have of Strether's own appearance is that he wears spectacles.

Together with *The Wings of the Dove* and *The Golden Bowl*, *The Ambassadors* marks a return to James's international theme, but to an internationalism which is distinguished from the 'emphasised internationalism' of his earlier work, according to Philip Grover, by associating moral perceptions more closely with aesthetic ones: 'Morals are expressed in terms that are often aesthetic, and the moral sense is a developed aesthetic sense of discrimination'[11] – though one could say that the germs of this connection between a moral and an aesthetic sense were already there in *Daisy Miller*. The increased references to dress that we find in these last three novels are a part of that enhanced aesthetic perception that characterises James's return to his re-vision of the international theme. *The Sense of the Past*, in terms of dress references, is also one of the most solidly specific of James's novels and although it is rarely included among James's 'International' novels, in his 1900 sketch for the novel, he says he is 'rather taken' with the idea of Ralph as 'an "international ghost"'.[12] In the same year we find James, in a letter to Howells, mulling over Howells's request for 'a little "tale of terror" that should be also International'.[13] Strether, we might note, after thirty years' exposure to the moral and aesthetic standards of Woollett, is returning to Paris, as a kind of 'international ghost', to encounter a version of his younger self – Chad Newsome – and to measure the effect of Paris, and of quite other perceptions and discriminations than those of Woollett, upon Chad.

Before Strether meets Chad he has to be made aware of further wants of his own; not utilitarian necessities, but, faced by the London shops 'that were not as the shops of Woollett', he wants 'things that he shouldn't know what to do with... [that] make him want more wants' (37), so that finally 'lack' and 'desire', both connotations of the word 'want', become deliciously muddled for him. Deciding to give himself up to the enjoyment of the experience and allow 'a woman of fashion... [to float] him into society', Strether presents a contrast to the 'sacred rage' Waymarsh had felt, faced with the same consumer paradise and the same offer of help. Strether enjoys Maria's supervision of his purchase of a pair of gloves, 'the terms she made about it, the prohibition of neckties and other items till she should be able to guide him through Burlington Arcade', but then becomes aware that in the eyes of Waymarsh, and of Woollett, these '[m]ere discriminations about a pair of gloves' could represent 'the peril of apparent wantonness' (38). We see his actions and then his reflection upon, or revision of those actions – one in which he is conscious that he is not behaving like a proper American male, who would, like Mr Ruck or Mr Miller, leave such matters to his womenfolk. Moreover his hedonistic indulgence in such frivolous European occupations looks like a betrayal of his ambassadorial role as representative of the New England ethos.

Having witnessed Strether and Maria shopping or window-shopping all morning, Waymarsh bolts into a passing jeweller's shop. When Maria wonders at this, Strether explains that Waymarsh '"can't stand it." "But can't stand what?" "Anything. Europe." "Then how will that jeweller's help him?"' asks Maria, worrying that Waymarsh will be overcharged. Waymarsh, like Strether, is aware of some personal lack. Unlike Strether, however, he does not 'survey' himself or his past for the cause of this unease, but instead becomes bewildered and enraged. He knows there is something of value to be had here, but as values for him are essentially financial, all that he can do is 'buy' in furious protest at the culture he will not give the time or effort to understand. 'He has struck for freedom', says Strether, freedom, that is, from a sense of his own inadequacy, and exerted the only power he has, that of money, to appropriate as much of Europe as he can presently lay his hands upon.

Waymarsh's frenzied shopping, like that of the Rucks of 'The Pension Beaurepas', has the effect, sartorially, of emphasising his Americanness rather than of 'making him over' in European fashion, as had happened to Daisy Miller. We see him later rather startlingly dressed in white for the summer, with 'a straw hat such as his friend hadn't yet seen in Paris', which made him resemble 'a Southern planter of the great days' (268). Along with all its other associations (see Chapters 3 and 4), white seems to be a colour James returns to when he wants to suggest Americanness: Jim Pocock in Paris exhibits a 'constant preference . . . for white hats' (213); in *The Wings of the Dove*, Milly's white dress at her final great party reminds Densher of her national origins. Waymarsh is inescapably American: in *The Ambassadors*, Miss Barrace, another American long-term resident of Paris, finds Waymarsh an endearingly antique 'type': 'the grand old American' of her father's generation. She refers to him as 'Sitting Bull', and describes further visitations of the 'sacred rage' to Strether, in which Waymarsh has attempted to swamp her with presents. Waymarsh's moral sensitivities, so affronted by Strether's shopping for gloves with Maria, seem blind to the indelicacy of plying a maiden lady with unsolicited gifts. He has simply succeeded in parting with a great many dollars and gained nothing but an exacerbated sense of national solidarity and the amused mockery of Miss Barrace. What Strether has acquired, on the other hand, is not so much a hat or a pair of gloves in the course of his shopping, but an aesthetic education in the pleasures of discrimination, the registering of new impressions about himself, and a leisurely browse with a 'woman of fashion' over the field of choice in matters of personal adornment; all of these constitute civilised occupations that are neither 'wanton' nor unimportant.

Frédéric Moreau's education leaves him, at the end of Flaubert's novel, almost as much of an adolescent in relation to women as at the beginning; and in many ways Hyacinth Robinson could be said to have regressed into childhood by the time he puts a pistol to his head. Strether's initiation into 'shopping' is a kind of preliminary lesson before the more adult experience of his evening in London with Maria, but his response to both experiences 'resembles that of an uninitiated young man still under the maternal wing'[14] as Carren Kaston puts it. To judge from his enraptured state, his rendezvous with Maria Gostrey might almost be his first intimate experience with a woman, though throughout the evening he recalls similar occasions from his past featuring Mrs Newsome. For the reader there is also, surely, at the back of Mrs Newsome, the figure of Strether's dead young wife. Something has clearly been absent from these earlier moments that has left Strether now in such a naive state of ecstasy that he is hard put to 'supply' enough 'names' (41), as he says, to characterise his evening in London.

In this, the first of the novel's several pleasurable and celebratory meals, Strether dines *à deux* with Maria, 'over a small table on which the lighted candles had rose-coloured shades.... He had been to the theatre, even to the opera ... with Mrs Newsome ... but there had been no little confronted dinner, no pink lights, no whiff of vague sweetness, as a preliminary.' Wondering *why* such pleasurable civilities had been missing, he notices that Maria's dress – or that small part of it visible across the table – was 'cut-down' 'in respect to shoulders and bosom, in a manner quite other than Mrs Newsome's, and [she] wore round her throat a broad red velvet band with an antique jewel ... attached to it in the front' (42). Strether's impression of Maria is of a general scented rosiness rather than of any specific style of dress; in that he registers that the dress is 'cut-down', one could say that he observes an *absence* of dress (therefore an exposure of pink bosom), rather than a presence. This is not just an incidence of 'late-blossoming lust' (in John Betjeman's phrase), but, we may note, Strether's observation of a distinctive aspect of women's evening dress around 1900.

European fashions changed radically after 1897, according to Willett Cunnington, Paris regaining its fashion lead. Colours became softer and less dramatic than during the first half of the decade, but in evening dress the most dramatic development was the exposure of the bosom: 'The Victorian décolletée is reaching such a pitch,' according to a commentator of 1899, 'that the bodice hangs on the shoulders by a miracle.'[15] In Sargent's double portrait of Ena and Betty Wertheimer, of 1901, the dresses – particularly that of Ena – demonstrate this astonishing defiance of gravity in a 'provocative display of physical allure'.[16] The Wertheimer sisters are wearing full formal evening dress, which would be even more 'cut-down' than, for example, the dinner dress that Maria would be likely to be wearing. Her dress would have to see her through dinner and the theatre, so could not be too perilously poised on the outer reaches of decency. Charles Dana Gibson's *The Education of Mr. Pip*, a pictorial narrative of an American family touring Europe in 1899, provides an illustration of an expatriate American dinner-party in Paris, in which the foreground figure is that of a highly décolletée young woman whose unadorned charms are placed on the table before the company like an especially delectable dish. Near her sits a more mature and ampler lady who has added a velvet band around her throat to break up the not always flattering effect of expanses of older flesh.[17] One could imagine Maria's appearance as a combination of these two figures (Figure 8).

Figure 8   'In the American Colony'. Charles Dana Gibson, *The Eduction of Mr. Pip*. 1899.

Maria's very physical presence calls up pictures from the past for
Strether: the 'rueful' recollection of Mrs Newsome, whose dress, however, 'was never in any degree "cut-down", and [who] never wore round
her throat a broad red velvet band'; she wore instead 'at operatic hours, a
black silk dress – very handsome, he knew it was "handsome" – and an
ornament that his memory was able further to identify as a ruche' (42,
43). 'Handsome', though often used in literary English to denote good-
looking women, has masculine connotations and thus cuts out any
suggestion of erotic femininity: what Strether retrospectively 'rues' is
that Mrs Newsome's dress in contrast to Maria's, appears to him now to
have been cut unromantically (and unaesthetically) high. He is regret-
ting, in fact, an excess of dress and the omission in his past of those
appeals to the senses he is now enjoying. Paradoxically, it is the absent
Mrs Newsome who presents the more sharply described image here,
although Maria's has the more dramatic effect. As if to underline the
over-buttoned up impression of this recollection of Mrs Newsome,
James puts her, as he had put the Ruck women, in black silk – the
American fall-back position in respectable female dress. The handsomeness of the black silk suggests a measure of its quantity, quality and cost,
rather than its enhancement of womanly charms – a contrast to Maria's
feminine sensuousness.

Susan Griffin interprets Strether's concentration on Maria's arms,
shoulders and bosom as his evasion of her sexuality, a sign that the
past, embodied in the memory of Mrs Newsome's puritanical modes,
still has a hold on Strether's perceptions.[18] I would suggest, however,
that Strether's impression of Maria – all pink, warm and perfumed – is an
intimate and erotically charged image of what he can actually see of her
across the table; it was, after all, precisely this suggestive contrast
between a comprehensively swathed lower body and an almost wholly
exposed torso that the fashions of the *fin de siècle* aimed at: a contrast
effectively exploited, for example, in the graphic art of Aubrey Beards-
ley. 'The fact is,' writes Max O'Rell, a satirist and journalist, in 1901,
'that it is practically impossible for you to say what it is that the women
wear around a dinner-table. Women dress for breakfast and undress for
dinner.'[19] The voyeuristic narrator of *The Sacred Fount* – also of 1901 –
pondering appearances at a country-house party, remarks how '[w]e
were all so fine and formal, and the ladies in particular at once so little
and so much clothed, so beflounced yet so denuded'.[20] The power of
Mrs Newsome's black-robed figure, looming across the perspectives of
time and space, is irretrievably diminished, and her dress rendered
démodé in contrast to Maria's sensuous redefinition for Strether of what

it means to be a 'lady'. A lady can be somewhat undressed and decidedly seductive – another heady mixture, in fact, of 'lacks and desires' – and still be a lady.

In deciding to exclude Mrs Newsome from any part in the novel's chronological events, James places her instead in a spatial relation to those events. Mrs Newsome, in America and envisaged from Europe, can thus tower threateningly or shrink impotently, advancing or receding according to the state of Strether's mind. Most Victorian literature narrates 'aperspectivally', according to F. K. Stanzel's *Theory of Narrative*: that is, 'the orientation [of objects or persons to one another] remains undetermined, and it will be undertaken by every reader on the basis of his individual imagination if at all....A tendency towards perspectivism, however, is first noticeable in the novels of Flaubert and Henry James.'[21] Strether, James's 'pre-eminent' mirror 'of miraculous silver',[22] is above all, therefore, a mind engaged in constant perspectival reflections. Sharing a candlelit table with Maria in Europe, Strether is conscious of Mrs Newsome's claims on him from across the Atlantic. In this perspective scheme he finds himself placed between the two women who 'complicate' his vision with their 'ramifications' of effect: 'What was it but an uncontrolled perception that his friend's velvet band somehow added, in her appearance, to the value of every other item.... What, certainly, had a man conscious of a man's work in the world to do with red velvet bands?' He likes the velvet band absurdly much, but, feeling there is some unmanly, un-American activity about such sentiments, cannot say so; it becomes for him 'a starting point for fresh backward, fresh forward, fresh lateral flights' (42) and in particular it focuses his mind's-eye on the recollection of Mrs Newsome's very high-cut neckwear, her 'ruche'.

The ruche was a version of the velvet band; it was, however, the closure, the finishing touch to a complete ankle-to-chin garment, as opposed to the band, which was a separate – and in Maria's case, somewhat distant – accessory to the dress. The band draws attention both to its attached jewel and to the erotic zone between itself and the dress. Both styles reflected the fashion for a 'high neck accent', a vogue which originated in the swan-necked Queen Alexandra's taste for choker necklaces and high-necked dresses and blouses. In 1903 it was reported that in London 'instead of wearing pearls or diamonds around the neck, some of the smartest women were wearing a very narrow band of black velvet from which hung the most beautiful pearls and diamonds'.[23] Willett Cunnington records that with evening dress in 1898 '[a] pearl dog-collar or a velvet band with diamond clasp, or band of quilled muslin [was] worn around the neck', as well as 'Medici collars'[24] – the two latter styles approximating the Elizabethan 'ruche'.

The association of 'queenliness' with these forms of neckwear weaves its 'ramifications' into the complexity of the evening's impressions on Strether. In one of his 'backward flights' he recalls telling Mrs Newsome that 'her ruff and other matters' made her look like Queen Elizabeth (see Figure 9). The consequence of his remark – 'as "free" a remark as he had ever made to her' – was that the lady wore her 'frills' more often. Now, *tête-à-tête* with Maria, these associations not only seem 'imperfectly romantic' but, more damagingly for Mrs Newsome, 'vaguely pathetic'. That the simile, at the time, should have seemed daringly 'free' in Woollett, and one 'that no gentleman of his age . . . could ever to a lady of Mrs Newsome's [age] . . . have embarked on' (43) is sad enough, but

Figure 9   A ruche, 1895.

worse is the fact that the ruche now seems to him quite *unattractive*. It represents, as Maud Ellman says, 'her strangulating certainties, as opposed to the red ribbon around Miss Gostrey's neck, which represents the principle of difference, insofar as it transforms "the value of every other item" of her dress'.[25]

It is at this point that Strether begins his cumulative portrait of Mrs Newsome, related to Maria during the course of the novel. In this 'portrait of a lady' the initial symbol of the stiff ruff is first associated with the 'fixed intensity' (250) of Mrs Newsome's imagined gaze at his back, and then later, and more disparagingly, its strangulating qualities are contained in his description of her as being 'packed as tight as she'll hold' (300) and thus incapable of admitting surprises. The elaborately emblematic portraits of Elizabeth I, deliberately dehumanised reminders of a queen's political power, colour our image of the absent ruffled Mrs Newsome – and not to her advantage, when set against the charms of Maria's 'trinket' in its intimate, déshabillé setting.

The comparison of Mrs Newsome with Queen Elizabeth, and her contrast to Maria, leads Strether into further royal associations: 'It came over him...that Miss Gostrey looked perhaps like Mary Stuart' (43). Painted images of the rival queens would naturally feature similar collars, but images of Mary Stuart invariably evoke legends of her beauty, her love-life and the romantic if tragic circumstances of her death. Such associations bode well for neither woman: Maria's affections will be sacrificed, but the Virgin Queen will also remain remote, a personification of the repudiation of desire. The red band around Maria's neck is lent a new, even macabre significance from its association with the beheading of Mary Stuart – most velvet bands recorded in the fashion notes around 1900 are, after all, black. James's choice of red, while lending itself to the general warmth of tone of this occasion, has further dark connotations when we reach a later moment of intimacy with another 'Mary', Marie de Vionnet, Maria's replacement in Strether's Parisian adventure. On his final evening with Marie de Vionnet he is reminded of Madame Roland on the eve of execution – and the reader may make a 'backward flight' to the novel's earlier reference to a tragic execution. Knowing James's attention to the importance of the 'representative trifle' he will certainly have been aware that, during the Reign of Terror, in a moment of sardonic humour, the chic Parisian accessory was a red neck ribbon. The multiplication of forms of Maria's name – Mary and Marie – might well bring to mind, at the end, a fourth, Marie Antoinette. All these 'Marys' present ultra-feminine but doomed appeals against the powers of moral or political disapproval.

The walls of Woollett's moral absolutism are breached at the start of the novel by the supper with Maria, and the image of Mrs Newsome is damaged by Strether's recognition that there is something unattractive, even pathetic about it. '[A] change had been set in motion in his Woollett soul,' as Dorothea Krook notes; '[f]or the first time in his life, the aesthetic has found entrance to it.'[26] Once awakened, Strether's aesthetic discrimination, in relation to dress, extends itself over the rest of the evening. In the theatre Strether registers a second, less appealing instance of 'décolleté' in 'a great stripped handsome red-haired lady' in the seat beside him, and on the stage he observes 'a bad woman in a yellow frock who made a pleasant weak good-looking young man in perpetual evening dress do the most dreadful things' (44). While moralistic and reductive Woollett attitudes here begin to reassert themselves, they are undermined by the ironic tone with which Strether registers the banality of the piece. At the turn of the century, yellow – as we saw in 'The Velvet Glove' – was the fashionable colour for evening frocks, and the 'bad' women in late century melodramas, like Mrs Erlynne, for example, in Oscar Wilde's *Lady Windermere's Fan*, were always dressed in the latest styles.

The stage picture causes Strether, in a 'forward' and 'backward flight', to associate the events of the play with his mission to rescue Chad from the 'bad' woman in Paris, and as he falls back into the Woollett view of things, he dismisses the unknown woman associated with Chad as 'base, venal – out of the streets'. Strether's trite rhetoric expands to compare this lurid image of 'fallen' womanhood with Mrs Newsome's 'admirable life' which Chad has 'darkened', but he is suddenly pulled up short by Maria's mischievous line: 'And is wonderful...for her age?' (45). Disquieted by the recollection of his recently damaged perception of the lady, he at first rejects such a description, then contradicts himself, and then lamely denies that he was referring to Mrs Newsome's personal appearance anyway. Maria is one of James's most skilful *ficelles*, and in the dialogue that follows the scene in the theatre she draws out the history of Strether's relationship with Mrs Newsome. Memories of Woollett and impressions of Europe battle it out in his account, which ends in laughter when Maria concludes that Mrs Newsome must be 'a *moral* swell', who does her hair beautifully; 'it's tremendously neat – a real reproach' (52). Strether's complicit laughter is, in effect, the first sign of his surrender of the values of Woollett to those of Europe.

Maria Gostrey, as Dorothea Krook unflatteringly says, is 'a colossal red herring as to the leading lady in the Strether drama of consciousness'.[27] But Strether must encounter Chad before meeting Madame de Vionnet (a Scarlet Woman rather than a Red Herring), who is responsible for any changes to Chad. Although Strether registers 'a phenomenon of change so complete that his imagination ... felt itself ... without margin or allowance' (90) when he meets Chad, we are told almost nothing of what constitutes this astonishing change, other than that he has become a great deal more civilised. There is little to be gleaned from Chad's grey-streaked hair and his 'crush' hat other than that Chad has aged quickly and is a theatre-goer. The staged nature of his entrance into Strether's box is significant, however, as is the earlier impression Strether has had of the façade of Chad's Paris house, which, in contrast to the lack of information he gives us about Chad's person, Strether carefully notes as 'admirably built', discreetly ornamented, the complexion of the stone 'a cold fair grey, warmed and polished a little by life' (69). The handsome if ambiguous mask of warmth, chill, discretion and polish is one worth bearing in mind in relation to Chad's subsequent perform-ances.

The question of Chad's transformation is, as Dorothea Krook says, the 'one great pocket of ambiguity' in *The Ambassadors*, and of key import-ance in Strether's 'process of vision'. Without reliable, independent confirmation of his sense of a change in Chad, Strether has no case for abandoning his original mission, for pleading with Mrs Newsome to let Chad stay in Paris, or for pleading with Chad to remain with Marie de Vionnet, the author of his supposed transformation. As Krook demon-strates, there is in fact no such confirmation available, and Strether, like the governess in *The Turn of the Screw*, 'can choose only on the basis of something other than the evidence ... choose only by an act of faith – "blind" faith ... in the validity and integrity of [his] own vision of things'.[28] This does not invalidate Strether's perception; it simply leaves us with the possibility of more than one interpretation of the data, and it forces Strether into a more acute awareness of the 'process of his vision' – the possibility that, as Chad himself says, Strether has 'rather too much' imagination – and his sense that this process may prove to be a lonely and confusing business.

Chad's presentation of himself to Strether in the theatre is a prelimin-ary to his 'staging' of Strether's first encounter with Madame de Vionnet in Gloriani's garden. Mrs Newsome as Gloriana, sends Strether, her knight, to the rescue and so we might expect him to meet the enchant-ress in a garden, Gloriani's 'Bower of Bliss'. Anticipating an older woman, a *femme du monde*, he is disconcerted first by her 'air of youth' (although she has a grown daughter) and by her dress. In keeping with her role as seductress, she is in black, 'but in black that struck him as

light and transparent . . . her hat not extravagant; he had only perhaps a
sense of the clink, beneath her fine black sleeves, of more gold bracelets
and bangles than he had ever seen a lady wear'. His expectations receive
a drop: 'There was somehow not quite a wealth in her; and a wealth was
all that, in his simplicity, he had definitely prefigured' (128). Having
envisaged a sumptuous Ingres 'odalisque', perhaps, or a luxuriously set-
up 'Dame aux Camellias', Strether is confused by finding Marie de
Vionnet 'meagre' – lacking something, somehow. And yet whatever is
lacking, it is neither the appearance of respectability nor social status, as
is evident from her demeanour at the party. If she is that alarming
phenomenon, the *femme du monde*, then 'Mrs. Newsome herself was as
much of one' (129).

Strether has constantly to revise his definition of 'a lady'. Mrs Newsome's stern handsomeness has given way to Maria Gostrey's warm
voluptuousness, and expecting perhaps further developments in this
direction, he is faced instead with something unfamiliar in the United
States – pared-down Parisian chic, 'the aesthetic of absent things',[29] that
was surfacing in Paris under the auspices of fashion designers such as
Paquin and Poiret, in the early 1900s. Willett Cunnington, recording the
chief features of fashion changes at the turn of the century, notes 'the
widespread use of transparent over-dresses' together with 'a growing
taste for monochrome colouring, or at least cloudy evasive tones
which blend into a whole, [leaving] nothing to distract the eye from
the sinuous lines': citing, for example, an 'Afternoon Dress of embroidered net over black taffeta'.[30] In contrast to the sharply corseted outlines
and colour contrasts of English and American styles before 1897, materials were soft and clinging, favouring silky crepons, shot silks and
chiffons. Masculine alarms occasioned by the bicycling New Woman
in her 'tailor-made' had produced 'an apparent swing-back to the ultra-
feminine in fashion':[31] it was not, however, a return to the voluminous
drapes of the 1880s, where dresses seemed to be assembled out of
disparate bits, but to something approaching the single serpentine
sweep of the Empire style. 'Never in the history of female attire' –
enthuses Max O'Rell – 'have women dressed so exquisitely as they do
in this year of grace 1901. No more bustle, no more outrageous sleeves
. . . the figure is gracefully accentuated . . . without any exaggeration . . .
draped in beautiful limp materials of soft, delicate hues.'[32] Paul Poiret's
even simpler and more dramatic versions of this style a couple of years
later expressed his belief that 'the inherent mystery and charm of a
woman should be evoked by suggestion and understatement'.[33] Anne
Hollander convincingly attributes this fashion change to the increasing

dominance of photography as the central visual authority: elegant female dress became 'aesthetically simplified, totally visible and comprehensible in one instant of the camera's flash'.[34] In a Paris filled with echoes of the *ancien régime*, the loosely draped silhouette of Paquin is for Madame de Vionnet a perfect expression of identity. She has found the self-expression through clothes that Isabel Archer had so strenuously denied was possible.

Her identity is however ambiguous. The black of her dress, in contrast to the impregnable opacity of Mrs Newsome's respectable black, is light and transparent (Plate VI), her eyes are strange and her hat 'not extravagant'. The fashionable hat in turn-of-the century Europe had reached some sort of apogee in size and exuberance, 'with some twenty to thirty million dead birds imported into this country [Britain] annually to supply the demands of murderous millinery'.[35] Strether could well have been expecting to see headgear like Mamie Pocock's when, stepping off the train in Paris, she adjusts 'the immense bows of her hat' (210). A temptress *not* sporting the latest line in millinery is departing from the melodramatic stereotype that he has come to confront. The black over-dress does, however, cover another layer; and beneath her transparent sleeves he hears rather than sees such a multiplicity of gold bangles as would seem to contradict his initial impression of meagreness and modesty.

Jeanne de Vionnet at Gloriani's garden party 'in a white dress and a softly plumed white hat', is a counterweight to her mother's enigmatic light/dark appearance, and as an unambiguous example of the *jeune fille* she provides Marie de Vionnet – as Pansy had provided Gilbert Osmond – with the credentials needed to gain the trust of the American innocent abroad. For Strether, Jeanne figures briefly as an acceptable reason for Chad's 'attachment' to Paris – and certainly a 'virtuous' one – but he is soon disabused of this happy if conventional idea by Little Bilham. After Marie de Vionnet announces that she and Chad are 'marrying' Jeanne to a young man 'found' for her by Chad, Jeanne fades from the picture. This somewhat arbitrary disposal of the girl disturbs Strether's democratic assumptions about a woman's right of choice in marriage. It should forewarn him of Chad's ruthlessness in relation to women, as well as raise the question of what lies beneath Marie de Vionnet's 'cover' of irreproachable motherhood.

Having caught Strether's imagination at the garden party, Marie deepens the effect by inviting Strether to her old Paris apartment, where he sees her against a background redolent of 'some prosperity of the First Empire, some Napoleonic glamour', but which is nevertheless of 'supreme respectability' (145, 146). Strether's surrender is completed at Chad's dinner party where she overwhelms him with an irresistible combination of effects. She enters at a little distance from Strether and, in a glance that takes her in from shoulders to feet and then returns to her head to review the whole effect, he registers fluid surfaces, broken tones of green and grey, watery gleams of submerged jewels and beautiful naked shoulders rising out of a cloud of foam:

> Her bare shoulders and arms were white and beautiful: the materials of her dress, a mixture, as he supposed of silk and crepe, were of a silvery grey so artfully composed as to give an impression of warm splendour; and round her neck she wore a collar of large old emeralds, the green note of which was more dimly repeated, at other points of her apparel, in embroidery, in enamel, in satin, in substances and textures vaguely rich. Her head, extremely fair and exquisitely festal, was like a happy fancy, a notion of the antique.... He could have compared her to a goddess still partly engaged in a morning cloud, or to sea-nymph waist-high in the summer surge. (160)

James records with a precision surpassed only by the lyricism with which he does it, the heart-stopping beauty of this woman, as well as the fashion means by which she achieves her effect. Dorothea Krook remarks on the unusual attention James gives to this dress; there is, she says, 'a delicacy of relish in the details ... one can only surmise the artistic reasons ... her exquisite taste, her consummate sense of *comme il faut* in the matter of dress as in everything sensuous.'[36] While agreeing with Krook, I would go further in finding this passage both an example of James's skill in using dress as an intrinsic element in his narrative and symbolic structure, and a demonstration of his close observation of contemporary modes. The 'wealth' that Strether had expected to find in his 'bad woman' is here, not in a display of conspicuous consumption of clothing and jewels, but rather in a plenitude of ravishing, understated and suggestive effects.

By 1900 dresses for the evening aspired to the condition of underwear, for underwear itself had become more luxurious and more important. The new conception in dress, according to Cunnington, was that it 'should be fluffy and frilly, undulating in movement with ripples of soft foam appearing at the feet, colours harmonizing with each other, surfaces broken with flimsy trimmings and revealing submerged depths of tone', to create the illusion of women as 'beings composed of stuff less solid than flesh and blood': the woman of fashion, Cunnington remarks, 'seemed to have plunged up to the knees in an enormous meringue'.[37] Soft pastels were fashionable: 'pale colours with a vivid touch at the neck... One colour and material over another'. Evening dress is 'décolleté... vaguely "Empire" in shape'; and among examples described, Cunnington records a 'dress of lettuce-green satin veiled with a pale-grey mousseline de soie embroidered in silver and jet and jewelled with large turquoises'[38] – almost a replica, in fact, of Marie de Vionnet's gown.

Marie de Vionnet at Chad's party is not 'muffled', as she had been earlier in her black over-dress, but 'uncovered' and in her element. Evoking for Strether 'a cornucopia of images drawn from antiquity, mythology, poetry and painting'[39] she might be Undine, or Raphael's Galatea, triumphantly riding the foam. Balzac believes that '[d]ressed in a peignoir or decked out for a ball, a woman is completely different. Two women, in fact.'[40] Although the peignoir and evening dress have, by the end of the century, moved closer together, Marie de Vionnet, 'dressed for a great occasion' rather than the boudoir, reveals new aspects of herself for Strether: 'like Cleopatra in the play, indeed various and multifold. She had aspects, characters, days, nights.... She was an obscure person, a muffled person one day, and a showy person, an uncovered person the next. He thought of Madame de Vionnet to-night as showy and uncovered' (160–1). Like Cleopatra on the Nile, Marie de Vionnet's element is water, a linked metaphor of fluidity and change which runs through the entire narrative, from the moment Strether steps off the boat at Liverpool to the epiphanic 'Lambinet' river-scene. If she is a naiad from antiquity, she is Odysseus's siren too; but the contemporaneity of her appearance suggests a version of the siren – the demonic mermaid of Victorian art and literature, identified by Nina Auerbach as one in whose 'mysterious hybrid nature... humanity is only an appearance'.[41] Beauty, in such images, rises out of depths of ambiguity and danger: the swathing and obscuring of Marie de Vionnet below the waist is not a denial of her sexuality, any more than is the mermaid's swishing tail, for the shifting, undulating movements of her silks and chiffons are pointers to and an enhancement of her sexual mystery and power. The magnificent shoulders that emerge from that suggestive haze are those of a goddess of antiquity, a mermaid 'older than the rocks on which she sits', and of the living woman of fashion of 1900.

Strether's awareness of the aesthetic and erotic charm of bared shoulders began with Maria Gostrey. Significantly we hear of Maria's departure from Paris and her refusal to see Marie de Vionnet from Marie herself at the party, when she asks Strether of Maria's whereabouts. The underlying implications of her question make him feel uneasily that he has become a 'question between women' (161). In Strether's perspectival gaze, Marie's shoulders now supersede Maria's as Maria's had replaced Mrs Newsome's black silk ones. A function of dress has always been to direct the eyes towards the erotic zone of the moment. The hysteria occasioned by Sargent's portrait of *Madame X* in her slipping shoulder-strap, makes it clear that shoulders were very exciting at the end of the nineteenth century; and in George Moore's novel, *A Drama in Muslin*, first published in 1886 and revised in 1915, we find perhaps the ultimate vision of 'shoulders'. The scene is the 'Drawing-Room' at Dublin Castle, where the debutantes are being presented to the Lord-Lieutenant:

> Shoulders were there of all tints and shapes. Indeed, it was like a vast rosary, alive with white, pink, and cream-coloured flowers: of Maré-chal Niels, Souvenir de Malmaisons, Mademoiselle Eugène Verdiers, Aimée Vibert Scandens. Sweetly turned, adolescent shoulders, blush white, smooth and even as the petals of a Marquise Mortemarle; the strong, commonly turned shoulders, abundant and free as the fresh rosy pink of the Anna Alinuff; the drooping white shoulders, full of falling contours as a pale Madame Lacharme....[42]

The description continues for several more lines, but the extract sufficiently demonstrates the febrile eroticism of Moore's vision of female shoulders. It might be instructive to recollect for a moment another dress description of 1886 – that of Lesbia's seduction outfit in Mary Braddon's *Phantom Fortune*, which we have already seen in Chapter 3. Both descriptions aim at an effect of sensuality and both could be accused of excess. But where we get an instantly forgettable and un-focused catalogue of fashion jargon from Braddon, the impact of Moore's image is overwhelming – and has indeed been criticised for its extravagance – although he in fact gives no dress details at all. The heady, suffocating luxuriance of elaborately dressed female forms is conveyed by the vista of naked shoulders and the outrageous extension of the old analogy of girls with roses – less a fashion than a gardening catalogue. That no one would be likely to be familiar with all the species of roses named simply adds to the extravagance of Moore's effects. As influenced by the French novel as James, Moore sets the scene 'perspec-tivally': in the crush of a room packed with girls in white formal dresses, the narrator as participant can be aware only of a sea of pink and white flesh – the dresses beneath will be scarcely visible. The excess of the description is visually accurate, but is also a reflection of the inherent absurdity of such formal occasions. In Jamesian terms, Moore has described these things 'only in so far as they bear upon the action',[43] and if the description breaks up the narrative, as does Strether's vision of Madame de Vionnet, then it does so because, like James, Moore wishes to fix the perspective and focus the reader's attention at this point.

Strether's senses are ravished by Marie de Vionnet and 'her bare shoulders', but, as his Woollett self rallies, he reflects that the 'formula' used for his seduction has been 'rough'. Irritation follows unease: he dislikes first Marie de Vionnet's questions about Maria, and even more those about Jeanne's feelings for Chad. It is only when she brings the conversation back to herself and her relation to him, in promising not to question Jeanne further – ' "Anything, everything you ask", she smiled' (163) – that Strether knows himself to be in thrall to her again. The extent to which he is enthralled can be measured by his subsequent eulogy of Madame de Vionnet to Little Bilham, in which he concludes that a relationship with such a woman 'can't be vulgar or coarse', a sentiment with which Little Bilham agrees. The connotations of 'vulgar or coarse' for these two are, of course, crucially different: Strether, deny-ing that the relationship is 'vulgar or coarse', refers to the absence of a sexual element, the Europeanised Little Bilham seems to have in mind something closer to the French concept of an *amitié*; a reciprocal rela-tionship between two people (of whatever sex), which need not be sexual but which certainly does not exclude that possibility. Strether expands on his exalted idea of the relationship between Chad and Marie to Little Bilham, who does not disillusion him, concluding that, with so wonderful a relationship, Chad and Madame de Vionnet should 'face the future together!' (169).

In his infamous dismissal of the novel, F. R. Leavis accused James of not making clear what it was that Paris meant to Strether, and of asking us to take the symbol 'too much at the glamorous face-value'.[44] But as Joseph Warren Beach replied, the final valuation of the meaning of his experience for Strether is not superficial and must undergo 'a long course of "visions and revisions"'.[45] At Chad's party we see in Marie de Vionnet the 'glamorous face' of Paris, but Strether's valuation of this 'glamour' is confused, one of 'flights and drops', in which he finally manages to yoke the Woollett morality of his past to his newly awakened aesthetic (or even sexual) sensibility by affirming his belief in the 'virtue' of the attachment. Marie de Vionnet, however, perhaps aware of Strether's need to be assured of her good faith, contrives their next meeting in Notre Dame where, now 'muffled' rather than 'uncovered', she wears a 'revised' version of the transparent black over-dress under which now 'a dull wine colour seemed to gleam faintly through the black' and she has a 'slightly thicker veil'. Her appearance, 'romantic far beyond what she could have guessed' (175, 176), is both modest and richly pleasing, with just a suggestion of the ecclesiastical; but when the couple move from the cathedral setting to the waterside-restaurant for lunch, where the dress is seen instead against the light summery colour notes of a straw-coloured Chablis and a tomato omel-ette, Marie's appearance suddenly takes on all the joyous allure of Renoir's celebrations of Paris café life, and the dress's red glints against black suggest seduction rather than religion. The meanings of Marie de Vionnet's dress-signs are endlessly elusive: is her black the 'dramatic' and 'dangerous' variety, of Anne Hollander's categories of black dress, or is it the respectable and 'sober'[46] version? As Nicola Bradbury says, these riddles, like the central riddle of the 'virtuous attachment', 'are not simply ambiguous and ironic: they rise beyond the construction of an 'either–or' meaning, just as Strether's understanding is to do.'[47]

Strether has to face a new assault on his senses when ambassadorial reinforcements arrive from Woollett, in the shape of the Pococks. Sarah looks 'fairly hectic' when Strether enters the Pocock's hotel sitting-room, for Madame de Vionnet is already there with over-solicitous offers of help with shopping: 'She struck him as dressed, as arranged, as pre-pared infinitely to conciliate' (220). Her choices in dress have hitherto been calculated to meet each occasion, not as chameleon-like camou-flage, but rather to *create* the occasion, to suggest an effect. To meet Sarah Pocock she has chosen the same 'discreet and delicate dress' in which she met Strether in Notre Dame: 'It seemed to speak – perhaps a little prematurely or too finely – of the sense in which she would help Mrs Pocock with the shops' (221). Sarah Pocock is not open to sugges-tions. As she signally fails to see any change in Chad, so she fails to register Marie's elegant notes of seemly black (she speaks of Marie as not even 'an apology of a decent woman'), and resists any idea that she is not competent to deal with Paris shops. In the face of the confident crudities of Woollett, Marie's discretions, subtleties and solicitations are not only wasted but miscalculated; they are read simply as wanton wiles.

The interview is a disaster. Sarah's dislike of Marie is as conspicuous as the dress she wears later at Chad's party, where, 'dressed in the splend-our of crimson', she affects Strether 'as the sound of a fall through a skylight' (258). Massive, crimson, loud and abusive, Sarah has all the seduction and fashion sense of the Red Queen in *Alice*. Strether's per-spective again takes in Woollett, in the person of Sarah who stands for

that darker Queen, Mrs Newsome; between them and Strether is Marie
de Vionnet, for once mistakenly dressed. What he sees, however, does
not return him to the Woollett fold, but rather strengthens his allegiance to Marie. Where her superlative elegance at the earlier evening
party had an equivocal effect on him, now her inability to charm, to
make any sort of impression on Sarah other than a repeatedly worsening
one, endears her to him, revealing her as humanly and hopelessly at a
loss, but nevertheless brave in pursuing the interview to its awful end.
She no longer presents that flawless vision of other-worldly beauty:
though her dress may still be as fashionably 'muffled' as ever, she has
in fact 'uncovered' for Strether the first hints of vulnerability and uncertainty.

Facing Woollett again, Strether's awareness of Mrs Newsome intensi-
fies, with the difference that he now measures the distance between
them. He has wanted her to share in the education of his consciousness,
and he now realises that expansions of her New England horizons were
never a part of Mrs. Newsome's plan. She 'hasn't budged an inch', he
says to Maria: he was 'booked by her vision' to find 'horrors', but now
that his ways of seeing have developed in so different a direction she has
repudiated him (299, 300). But if Woollett has 'thrown him over', so it
seems has Paris, for Chad and Marie de Vionnet have left town. Strether,
suddenly freed from all ties, and feeling perhaps that this European
adventure is nearing its end, does the Parisian – rather than the tourist
– thing and takes the suburban train into the countryside. It is here,
famously, that the process of his vision culminates in an epiphany in
which the visual and the dramatic, the aesthetic and the moral are
suffused into one intense point.

During this 'rambling day' Strether reflects on his relation with Marie
de Vionnet, finally arriving at a riverside inn, as perfect in the summer
evening light, in the rightness of its colours and effects, as Marie de
Vionnet had seemed in her 'old high salon'. The 'spell of the picture' is
that it was 'more than anything else a scene and a stage'; but stages are
platforms for action, unlike pictures. As Strether waits for supper, his
attention is caught by a movement and a colour on the river: visually it
was 'exactly the right thing – a boat . . . containing a man who held the
paddles and a lady, at the stern, with a pink parasol . . . the young man in
shirt-sleeves, the young woman easy and fair' (309). The 'fine pink
point', which catches Strether's eye, shifts literally and metaphorically
from the pictorial 'right thing' to being, in one small sharp concealing/
revealing motion of the parasol, a dramatic disturbance of the picture.
Its very pinkness makes it the 'wrong thing' since it draws Strether's eye

to Chad as 'the coatless hero' and Marie de Vionnet as the owner of the parasol. They meet with exclamations of pleased surprise, and the evening that follows is convivial enough over supper at the Cheval Blanc, with Marie de Vionnet chattering compulsively in French. As they all three take the train back to Paris, Marie's chatter falters into fatigued silence while Chad is mute.

Strether's 'real experience' is to come, as James says in one of the rare authorial interventions in this novel, when, in his hotel room that night, he reviews the day's events. What he makes out is that 'there had been simply a *lie* in the charming affair' and Marie de Vionnet's feverish manner had been a 'performance' (313). How to put one's finger on the lie? If, as she has said, she and Chad had intended only a day's excursion out of Paris, returning like Strether by train at nightfall, it was evident 'that she hadn't started out for the day dressed and hatted and shod, and even, for that matter, pink parasol'd... From what did the drop in her assurance proceed as the tension increased... but from her consciousness of not presenting, as night closed in, with not so much as a shawl to wrap her round, an appearance that matched her story? She had admitted that she was cold.'[48] She and Chad are quite 'uncovered'; they are in 'undress' on the train. That is, they are not literally indecent but dressed for the privacies of a shared life rather than for the publicities of suburban trains and sociable suppers. James *does* show a 'bedroom scene' and they *do* take their clothes off – or to be precise, they *have* taken them off and they had intended to take them off again – for the picture in Strether's mind's eye is of '[h]er shawl and Chad's overcoat and her other garments, and his, those they had each worn the day before... at the place, best known to themselves... at which they had been spending the twenty-four hours, to which they had fully meant to return that evening' (314). It is thus not the sexual act as such that we see, but the intimacies of a country-inn bedroom scattered with discarded garments, and waiting, like a stage for the performers to return.

As Strether contemplates his befooling and 'the quantity of make-believe involved', together with his drastically revised image of the 'virtuous attachment', he feels surprisingly unresentful of their deception but instead touched by the revelation of the depth and mutuality of that attachment. He has been self-deceived: 'he had dressed the possibility in vagueness, as a little girl might have dressed her doll', he has 'muffled' what was apparent to all but him, with the moral blinkers of Woollett. What he has uncovered, he believes, is indeed a 'wonderful' and enviable relationship, of a kind that he himself has never had, and may now never have. This is his lack, and 'it made him feel lonely and

cold' (315), colder and certainly lonelier than Chad and Marie de Vionnet on the evening train. The 'undressing' of Marie and Chad has
revealed to him his own condition as poor 'unaccommodated man'
with scant lendings. The 'lie' upon which the evening has been conducted, he concludes, was not wrong but a tribute to their good taste in
allowing his impoverished version of their situation to prevail. What has
now changed for Strether are the very criteria by which he determines
what is 'right'. He has not abandoned the moral seriousness inculcated
by his past, but recognises that the precepts of Woollett are inadequate.
The criteria by which he now judges, to which the 'process of his vision'
has led him, are embodied for him in the distinction, the discrimination, the 'virtue' of the person of Marie de Vionnet.

What of Chad? He leaves explanations to Madame de Vionnet, and
Strether receives a request to visit her that evening. As he passes the time
until his appointment, Woollett instincts briefly surface to make him
wonder why he feels no need to punish the sinners. He is, he sees, mixed
up with their 'typical tale of Paris ... they were no worse than he, and he
no worse than they': his lack of an urge to occupy the moral high
ground measures the distance he has travelled from Woollett, though
at the back of his mind he worries that somebody must pay 'something
somewhere and somehow', but that Marie de Vionnet will find a way –
in her great goodness – 'to make the deception right' (317, 320).

The summer night threatens thunder, and because of the heat
there are only a few candles lit in Marie de Vionnet's apartment. As he
moves through the old rooms, their tapestries swaying in the draught
from open windows, he hears the sounds of the Paris streets, and in a
leap back of one hundred years – like that of Ralph Pendrel in *The Sense
of the Past* – he imagines himself on the eve of the Revolution: 'the
sounds had come in, the omens ... the smell of revolution, the smell
of the public temper – or perhaps simply the smell of blood'. If he has no
urge for retribution himself, there is blood in the air nevertheless.
The city, the house and the woman have so acted upon Strether's
senses that what colours his vision is not the New England past of
prohibitions but the no less grim Paris of revolution, and when Marie
de Vionnet enters she is absorbed into that context. She is dressed 'as for
thunderous times ... in the simplest coolest white, of a character so old
fashioned ... that Madame Roland must on the scaffold have worn
something like it. The effect was enhanced by a small black fichu
or scarf, of crape or gauze, disposed quaintly round her bosom and
now completing as by a mystic touch the pathetic, the noble analogy'
(319).

Marie de Vionnet's style of dress has so far been modelled on the sinuous lines of 1900 that mark the change from the styles of the early 1890s. Here, however, she is either reverting to historic dress – which is how Strether sees it – or anticipating the more pronounced 'empire' line of Paul Poiret's designs, which first appeared around 1904.[49] The detailing and style of Paul Iribe's drawing of 1908 of a Poiret dress contains conscious references to the early 1800s. James, I believe, wants his image to convey equally a sense of the historical and the avant-garde. In *The Wings of the Dove*, the fantasy-image of Milly and Kate dressed in 'antique' costume of Maeterlinck's dramas, suggests the aesthetic tastes of the 1890s, but could also be read as anticipating the later 'folk-art' style of the Ballets Russes. Fanny Assingham's idiosyncratic 'Oriental' garments in *The Golden Bowl* go even further in this direction. Turning again to *The Sense of the Past*, we find Ralph Pendrel exclaiming, at his first sight of Nan (the girl he falls in love with in 1820), 'Why she's modern, modern!'[50] She is, of course, in the high Empire-style of *circa* 1810, but Ralph, with his eyes of 1900–10, finds her wholly 'modern'. Both images can be held by the mind – a subtlety of narrative levels that the silent film approached in its technique of montage, but could never quite achieve as the novel does.

Marie is now in pure white with a black fichu over her beautiful shoulders. This white is obviously not that of a *jeune fille*, though the appeal to connotations of purity stands. Madame Roland wore white to her execution; Marie Antoinette was reduced to a simple shift on the scaffold. As Balzac said, the Revolution was a debate between silk and cloth as well as about politics, and to avoid the guillotine, extreme caution had to be exercised in dress. Correct revolutionary dress, like early twentieth-century dress, emulated 'déshabillé': 'Les femmes sont représentées en "chemise" avec un simple fichu voilant la poitrine.'[51] Portrait painters, such as David, according to Aileen Ribeiro, reflected 'in their economy of detail and bare essentials the political and social tensions of the period . . . it would have been rash, especially during the Terror, to hint at an *ancien-régime* luxury in dress.'[52] Marie's dress could be seen to reflect the cautions and terrors of a possible victim; but victim of whom or what? In colouring and style it is the simplest dress statement she has made: 'Her passion simplifies and abases her,'[53] James says – and though her erotic shoulders are soberly covered, we might say that Strether sees her fully revealed. If he sees a sacrificial victim, we may recollect the many Jamesian victims in white: Daisy Miller, Pansy Osmond, Isabel before her marriage, Milly in her final great moment. For Nanda Brookenham and Little Aggie of *The Awkward Age*, the correlation of whiteness with sacrifice is made clear: they are 'lambs with the great shambles of life in their future...and the far-borne scent, in the flowery fields, of blood'.[54] The turn of the screw in *The Ambassadors* is that if Marie is a victim, she is also a deceiver and an adventuress. Deception and adulterous love here take on the colours of innocence and nobility.

As becomes evident in Strether's last conversation with Chad, Marie is to be sacrificed. Chad, it seems, will return to America, seduced by the new 'art' of advertising: 'It's an art like another, and infinite like all the arts,' he enthuses. No wonder Strether feels 'a little faint' (341). It is a betrayal not only of Marie and all that she represents – all indeed that Strether has come to value – but also of Strether's belief in Chad's great metamorphosis, which now amounts to no more than polish on a stone façade. One could say the values of the past, of the *ancien régime*, are to be sacrificed to the new democracy of the market-system – but it is more than that. It is the betrayal of moral values and continuities that are not specific to a time or place. The meanings of Marie's final dress – her last shift – are thus over-determined: she is in 'undress', although she is modestly covered; the dress is historical and ultra-modern; it is a statement of innocence and a confession of culpability; it is the dress of youth and of death. The dress contains both closure and futurity, as well as evoking Strether's whole experience of Paris. 'Uncovered' as they now are to each other, they experience a moment of mutual revelation, a recognition of a common humanity that is the essence of falling in love, while at the same time they know it is a loss and an ending.

Her tears are in part for the loss of Chad and of youth, but more deeply they express a longing to be as sublime as Strether had believed her to be. The values of Woollett, that American sense of duty to others, is what Marie invokes when she turns on her self in disgust – '[w]hat it comes to is that it's not, that it's never, any happiness at all, to *take*. The only safe thing is to give.' Despairing and conscious of imminent betrayal she none the less berates herself for having 'upset everything in your mind...your sense of...all the decencies and possibilities': 'Where *is* your "home" moreover now...?' (323). She is right, of course; he stands to lose what little he had in Woollett, and his state of mind is irretrievably altered. But the sublimity of her effect on him now is stronger even than when she appeared to him a goddess, and whatever he has lost in Woollett, the gain represented by his 'process of vision' – in which Woollett has its place – is immeasurable. What gives Strether stature is that this outcome, despite its denials, is a positive one: to be right is '[n]ot, out of the whole affair to have got anything for myself'

(346). Marie de Vionnet has addressed herself – and dressed herself – according to 'some conception of him... to some element in him of which he has himself been unconscious'.[55] Seeing her clearly, her appearance resonant with all her own and her city's past, and yet unmistakably modern, he sees how he is seen. He has lacked this view of himself; the view that bears witness to old as well as new sensibilities: 'Through a synthesis,' Daniel Vogel says, 'Strether's limited Massachusetts propriety has evolved into a higher order of rightness.'[56] Looking down the perspectives of the past, Strether, an international ghost, visits what might have been, had things been other than they are – 'Ah but you have *had* me!' (326) he tells her. As old Mr Touchett remarked of Ralph's renunciation of love for Isabel, 'Things are always different from what they might be.'[57]

8
Depravities of Decoration in *The Golden Bowl*

The brief Edwardian period opened exuberantly on a new century; but with the shadows of World War I gathering at its close, it has lent itself to wistful images of long garden parties and Indian summers: a commentator on Edwardian portraiture calls it 'a period in which wealthy socialites enjoyed unparalleled luxury, and were bathed in the sunlight of an eternal summer',[1] the social historian, Hebe Dorsey refers to the belle epoque as 'the last act of an operetta whose actors did not know the end was in sight'.[2] In keeping with this general air of *carpe diem*, Edwardian fashions were both outrageously extravagant and touchingly fragile: 'Summer muslin dresses printed or painted, with immense chiffon fichus, huge frothy parasols, tea-gowns with long "angel sleeves" of chiffon, evening confections quivering with chiffon and lace – in such a guise the fashions of the 1900s floated serenely towards the Niagara of 1914.'[3] James Laver considered it 'probably the last period in history when the fortunate thought they could give pleasure to others by displaying their good fortune before them' and he composed an ode to its memory, visualising

> The men, frock-coated, tall and proud,
> The women in a silken cloud.[4]

James's last great novels fall within this period, but it is *The Golden Bowl* which most justifies the term 'Edwardian', not only because of its English setting, and its suggestion of the adulterous country-house parties so much associated with 'Edward the Caresser' (as James called him), but also because of the extravagance of its images of display and of dress. It has been said of Edwardian women's dress that 'though

sumptuous, [they] were seldom showy...[m]uch of the extravagance...lay beneath the surface.'[5] Something similar could be said of
James's novel, whose images in fact conceal almost *more* than they display. They present us with 'a certain indirect and oblique view',[6] as
James says, of the action. Corrupting as well as redemptive, commercial
as well as aesthetic, the images of *The Golden Bowl* contain truths that are
also falsities and there is no one view of events which has more validity
than another: as Phyllis van Slyck says, 'neither an ethical nor an
aesthetic stance in this novel guarantees such a truth.'[7]

Marie de Vionnet's image in her 'Directoire' dress, seen by Strether at
the conclusion of *The Ambassadors* against the *ancien régime* ambiance of
her Parisian house, operates as a last revelatory statement about her fears
for the future and her regrets about the past. As Prince Amerigo walks
down the 'high modernity' of London's Bond Street, at the start of *The
Golden Bowl*, he too considers his future prospects as well as his past.
Amerigo, although a 'Modern Roman', is conscious of a family history
of popes and potentates, to whom once 'the world paid tribute'. The
objects he gazes at in the shop windows, 'in silver and gold, in the forms
to which precious stones contribute...were as tumbled together, as if in
the insolence of Empire, they had been the loot of far-off victories' (1. 3).
As the scion of empires and victories even further off, his material substance has long gone – he cannot afford the luxuries he views – but as his
name suggests, he also represents a merchant-adventurer tradition that
had once filled the coffers of the Old World with gold from the New. At
the end of the 'Season', when London society was hunting and shooting
in Scotland, Amerigo embarks on the very Edwardian venture of marriage to a 'Dollar Princess', Maggie Verver. Whether he emerges as the
hunter or the hunted, the looter or the loot, is never quite settled.

Walking along the busy street, reviewing the six months of his 'pursuit', his attention is distracted by 'the possibilities in faces shaded, as
they passed him on the pavement, by huge beribboned hats, or more
delicately tinted still under the tense silk of parasols' (4). He has just
finalised the legal arrangements for his marriage, so the question of
'possibilities' under hats rings a little oddly. Amerigo's attitude to
women is, however, fairly simple: it is 'more or less to make love to
them' (22), and there are, he reflects, at this stage in his career, more he
has made love to than not. The mystery of hidden faces is a recurring
theme in the novel, here lent reality by current fashions. According to
Cunnington, the Perfect Lady, having adopted for day-wear a simple
two-piece costume, 'insists the more upon sex in the *chapeau*'[8] – the kind
of hat worn by Mamie Pocock as she steps off the train in *The Ambas-*

sadors (see Figure 10). Camille Clifford, the much-photographed 'Gibson Girl' of the period, is always seen in gigantic hats, tipped well forward, which provide a balancing accent to the proportions of her tight-hipped, sweeping skirts. In order not to hide her face she holds her chin very high.

By contrast, when Amerigo recalls his conversation with Maggie at the conclusion of the afternoon's business, he remembers 'how extraordinarily *clear*... she had looked in her prettiness'. They had been discussing Maggie's father, Adam, when Amerigo had remarked that whereas he now knows the Ververs well, they know only his recorded history not his private self. Maggie's friendly clarity prompts her to explain to Amerigo how his historical lustre fits into Adam's plans for his greatart collection: 'You're a rarity, an object of beauty, an object of price....

Figure 10   A lady's hat, 1900.

You're what they call a *morceau de musée'* (1. 9, 10, 12). If Amerigo is charmingly amusing about his role as a collector's piece: 'I have the great sign of it... that I cost a lot of money' (1. 12, 14) – he is also aware of his commodification. Such clarity in laying out his future status to her fiancé, either betokens great confidence or great stupidity on Maggie's part.

His fate 'practically... sealed', Amerigo is on his way to Fanny Assingham, the woman who has 'made' the Prince's marriage – one of James's most entertaining expatriate American matrons. Despite Amerigo's sense of the providential nature of his marriage – debts settled, palaces mended and future assured – he worries about what will be required of him by an American billionaire. What value is he expected to give? What is he to do? Or is he simply to 'be' inertly, as in a museum? Of the central characters, the Prince is the most conspicuously on show, and yet, beyond his dark blue eyes and general air of striking handsomeness, we never learn how he looks. Images of Renaissance art and architecture are invoked, warriors and rulers of the past – but never the twentieth-century aspect of the Italian man-about-town. What we do learn from the first page is of his immediate aesthetic response to things and people. Because Amerigo is to a large extent the reflecting consciousness of Book 1, we only hear of his effect on others. Thus he is told that to Adam Verver he is an object of beauty, antiquity and great rarity. Maggie's perspective, however, controls Book 2, and for her Amerigo has an overwhelming physical and psychological charisma. His glamour is conveyed by its effect on Maggie rather than by any material details, but we might well ask if it is for these qualities that he has been 'got'?

Amerigo turns to Fanny in Book 1 to be soothed. Although she is a part of his past, someone who *does* know him, she is one of the few women to whom he has not made love. She is more of a fairy godmother than a mother-figure. Herself without material wealth, she has produced the Verver billions for the Prince, as she will do later for Charlotte Stant. One of the paradoxes of the novel is that it is Fanny, the least wealthy, least sexually available character who presents the most opulent appearance. We do not see Fanny through Amerigo's eyes, but through those of an imaginary photographer, or an observer of a *tableau vivant*. Foreshadowing the novel's last view of Amerigo and Charlotte together, Fanny and Amerigo are surveyed at a distance for their effect. Fanny, the spectator considers, might be said to gratify one's sense of a modern 'type' rather than the 'modern sense of beauty'.

Fanny does not at all resemble the tall, elegant Gibson Girl – the Charlotte Stant 'type' – capable of vigorous independent activity in the fields of sport, tourism and flirtation. However, her 'crisp black hair made waves so fine and numerous' that it conforms to 'the fashion of the hour [more] than she desired'. This abundance characterises Fanny's looks in general: 'Her richness of hue, her generous nose ... these things, with an added amplitude of person on which middle-age had set its seal, seemed to present her insistently as a daughter of the South, or still more of the East, a creature formed by hammocks and divans, fed upon sherbets and waited upon by slaves.' Her quite frugal life is, in fact, led mainly in the interests of others; and, though she would have preferred to adopt a less showy style, she has chosen to play up her 'flagrant appearance': 'She wore yellow and purple because she thought it better, as she said ... to look like the Queen of Sheba than like a *revendeuse*; she put pearls in her hair and crimson and gold in her tea-gown for the same reason: it was her theory that nature itself had overdressed her and that her only course was to drown ... the overdressing' (1. 33, 34). Rather than risk vulgarity by forcing her plump, colourful person into the pale sinuosities of the day, she settles for a style which reads like the antithesis of the Gibson Girl's rather hoydenish ways; neither does it conform to the soft, pastel *frou-frou* of the Edwardian beauty. Far from depicting her as unfashionable, however, James gives Fanny a style whose elements had been around on the fashion margins for some time, and shows her anticipating a look which a few years later was to become *the* 'fashion of the hour'.

   Appropriate to her role as fairy godmother, or a djiin from the lamp, Fanny's appearance is exotically oriental and her colour preferences *outré*. Her choice of dress, however, is in a tradition of reformist styles begun in the previous century. A photograph of the novelist, Beatrice Harraden, in 1903, shows her in a loose gown, or 'djibbah', a garment borrowed from Egypt.[9] The oriental had been an alternative minority fashion since the 1860s, a part of the Aesthetic, 'greenery-yallery' vogue, associated with Liberty's Oriental Emporium. This style was not one favoured by James, as we see from his description of the dreary garments of Mark Ambient's sister in 'The Author of *Beltraffio*' of 1884. Orientalism in the arts was moving, however, from the stage of 'japonaiserie' – that is, the introduction of oriental objects or motifs into western clothing, interiors and paintings for purely decorative ends – to that of 'Japonisme' – a more serious attempt to translate the underlying principles of an oriental aesthetic into western forms. A pink satin robe of 1900 from Liberty's is high-waisted in Empire fashion, but asymmetrically cut across the front in a way that is Japanese in inspiration. The flat cut sleeves and the rich floral embroidery are also orientalising.[10] The robe represents a real break with contemporary modes although it still plays light-heartedly with a mix of styles. In 1904 Paul Poiret produced his revolutionary 'Confucius' coat in lacquer red, with sleeves and body merged in one waistless, head-to-toe sweep of silk, Chinese motifs appliquéed on the front and sleeves, and a front-fastening in Chinese style.[11] Two further events in the art world established these dramatic colours and simple shapes as a ruling aesthetic. First, the impact of the barbaric palette of *Les Fauves*, seen at the 1905 exhibition in Paris, rendered fashionable pastels insipid; then in 1908, the audacious designs and colours of the Ballets Russes exploded onto the European art scene, sounding the death-knell of paler Edwardian taste.

Léon Bakst's designs for the Ballets Russes' 'Schéhérazade' of 1909 let loose 'a whole debased and bastardized spirit of Orientalism.... Society women gave *tableaux vivants* dressed as Eastern slaves'.[12] Analogies with Fanny's costume are admittedly anachronistic, but there is an interesting economic slant to the comparison. The sumptuous effects created by the Ballets Russes costumes were actually achieved quite cheaply, using canvas, felt, string, appliquéed and painted ornament. Fanny's choice of dress is dictated as much by the impossible cost of keeping up with the style of her social circle as it is by her generous physique. It's all a performance, a bit of a fake, but it's an honest fake: as the narrator concludes, '[w]ith her false indolence . . . her false leisure, her false pearls and palms and courts and fountains, she was a person for whom life was multitudinous detail' (1. 35).

Fanny's exotic, magic aspects connect her with the novel's other magician, the polyglot 'antiquario' in Bloomsbury. The golden bowl starts from his hands and ends in hers. Her voluptuous, Queen-of-Sheba surface, like the gilding on the bowl, looks costly, but no one claims it is gold, and so it is not a fake. And yet the bowl contains a flaw; but if no one sees the flaw, does it matter? Fanny lies; but if no one calls her bluff – does it matter?

The fantastic, somewhat bogus quality of her appearance reflects another aspect of her character: she busies herself with fantasies about the lives of others in a way which, however well-intentioned, invites catastrophe. As Carren Kaston says: 'It is not only that Fanny's scenarios have little to do with the "reality" of the novel, but that they introduce an irresponsible superfluity of plot'[13] – like Schéhérazade, she tells stories and plays with fire. The colours associated with Fanny are the colours with which Poiret shocked everyone – '[t]here were orange and lemon crêpes de Chine which they would not have dared to imagine'.[14] Fanny has a 'lemon-coloured mantle' and an 'amber train', in which there are gleams of ruby, garnet and topaz (1. 364, 399), colours of fire. The mystery of hidden aspects has been suggested at the opening of the novel, and it is Fanny who 'knows' enough about the relationship of Amerigo and Charlotte Stant to throw light on Maggie's desperate uncertainties in Book 2. But she doesn't know everything, so, rather than risk destroying the marriages she promoted, she chooses to obscure matters with a 'saving lie'. Fanny comments on the novel's events, but as Adré Marshall notes, they are 'insights of dubious viability'. Compared with the 'illumination of wisdom' afforded by Ralph Touchett in *The Portrait of a Lady*, Fanny, 'though often astute, is something more like an *ignis fatuus* than a guiding light.'[15]

Fanny, having produced Maggie and her millions for Amerigo, now throws a time-bomb in his path by producing Charlotte Stant, whom Amerigo knew before his engagement. The extent of his 'knowledge' is itself an unknown, but to judge from Amerigo's internalised impression of her, it is intimate. James had posited an imaginary photographer as his focaliser at the beginning of this scene; the consequent description of Fanny reads like a 'studio' pose against a backcloth. In contrast, the impact of Charlotte on Amerigo is much closer to that of the snapshot 'Kodak factor' which James initially resisted on grounds of its 'universal inclusion and rampant vulgarization'.[16] As James warmed to Impressionism, so too he found merits in 'camera vision' – even in cinematic vision, as we saw in the short story, 'Crapy Cornelia'. Anne Hollander points out that camera vision 'eventually became the ultimate reference for everyone's sense of visual truth'; as a consequence fashions of this period adapted themselves to the 'Kodak factor', and by 1910, overall unity, 'compactness of design', 'the blur of chic'[17] had become the desired fashion effect.

When Charlotte enters, Amerigo's immediate impression is of 'a tall strong girl who wore for him at first exactly the air of her adventurous situation, a reference in her person, in motion and gesture, in free vivid yet altogether happy indications of dress, from the becoming compactness of her hat to the shade of tan of her shoes, to winds and waves and custom houses, to far countries and long journeys, the knowledge of how and where and the habit, founded on experience, of not being afraid' (1. 45). The sentence is long and relatively unpunctuated, requiring the reader to take it all in one 'breath', so to speak. Charlotte's hat is probably a brimless toque, a more practical alternative to the wide-brimmed, burdened hats of the Bond Street ladies. A photograph of the dancer, Topsy Sinden in 1906, shows her not only in a toque but also a boa[18] – an accessory Charlotte later acquires. The winds of freedom and fearlessness that Charlotte brings with her strike Amerigo forcibly, since he has just had his future decided with a sense of a 'crunched key in the strongest lock' (1. 5). She refreshes him with her elegant and 'amusing' taste and prompts his recognition that they share the same contemporary world. No museums here.

Amerigo's instant empathy with Charlotte is reinforced by his second, more intimate re-view of her. Her hair, the shade of a 'tawny autumn leaf', gives her 'the sylvan head of a huntress':

> He saw the sleeves of her jacket drawn to her wrists, but he made out the free arms within them to be of the completely rounded, the polished slimness that Florentine sculptors...had loved. ... He knew above all the extraordinary fineness of her flexible waist, the stem of an expanded flower, which gave her a likeness also to some long loose silk purse, well filled with gold pieces, but having been passed empty through a finger-ring that held it together. It was as if, before she turned to him, he had weighed the whole thing in his open palm and even heard the chink of metal. (1. 47)

The association of Charlotte with the goddess, Diana, makes her, like Amerigo, a hunter. It also evokes images of the nude goddesses of classical and Renaissance art, a line of thought pursued by Amerigo as he not only surveys her dress but retraces the body within. (He 'knew' her 'flexible waist'...) He is in effect caressing her undressed form, but slips through a combination of metaphor and simile into appreciation of her *dressed* elegance, so that there is as much of the aesthetic as of the erotic in a gaze that finally settles on the crudities of economics, 'the chink of metal'.

Money is not all the image suggests. In her discussion of the draped nude in European art, Hollander observes that '[t]he sensuous pleasure taken by the hairless human body in the sliding touch of fabric is conjured by any image of draped flesh...[d]rapery near or on the nude figure...makes it easier to take. It ensures both a high level of sensuous pleasure and a lower quotient of disturbing, crude eroticism.'[19] Amerigo, on the eve of his marriage, cannot afford much erotic disturbance, but his sensuous appreciation of Charlotte's outward appearance together with his deeper 'knowledge' (biblically speaking) of her, ensures that when Fanny is called away, he does not – as propriety indicated – pick up his hat and go.

Amerigo's impression of Charlotte's appearance is embodied in the sinuous, pouched concave/convex effect of contemporary styles (Plate

VII), the effect precisely of a loose silk purse girdled by a narrow ring that James invokes: 'the floppy pouching of blouse or bodice by day, and the lace valance protecting the décolletage in the evening, composed a refined denial of anatomical facts. The whole spirit of Edwardian design was... to combine suggestion with concealment.'[20] There is a contradiction in Amerigo's image of the costume, however: the silk purse is filled with gold, but to go through the ring it must be almost empty. The convexity of the Edwardian bodice suggested an improbably large 'monobosom', but the extreme concavity of the waist below contradicted this: in fact, these anatomical disparities were achieved by padding and corsetry. The narrow ring and slender form successfully disguise the imperfections of natural shapes, and yet the linked connotations (of 'purse', 'gold pieces', 'ring', 'open palm' and 'chink of metal') do finally confront us with vulgar economic realities. Charlotte has 'chic' but has she cash?

Fanny's exotic, theatrical robes functioned as cheerful camouflage for the realities of her budget and her embonpoint, but Charlotte is different: she dissimulates for her life: she 'always dressed her act up... she muffled and disguised and arranged it... her doom was also to arrange appearances... the only thing was to know what appearance could best be produced and best be preserved' (1. 50). Like Edith Wharton's Lily Bart, Charlotte has arrived at a crisis: marital possibilities are diminishing along with her finances. We do not know how close Charlotte is to Lily's critical thirtieth year – only that she is some years senior to Maggie. But for someone whose career as perennial guest depends on a smart appearance – 'Ladies on a four-day visit to a country house could not wear the same dress twice and so would have required at least twelve to sixteen complete ensembles'[21] – time is running out. 'If I were shabby,' Lily Bart says, 'no one would have me: a woman is asked out as much for her clothes as for herself. The clothes are the background, the frame, if you like: they don't make the success, but they are a part of it. Who wants a dingy woman?'[22] Every public appearance must be calculated. Fanny's colours are rich and bold, the only riches she can afford. We are not given Charlotte's colours other than the tawniness of her hair and shoes; between lies a silky, suggestive 'blur of chic'. The appearance of money is given without its reality. At Fanny's, Charlotte 'arranges' another 'hour' with Amerigo, in which they find but do not buy the golden bowl for Maggie. It is the 'hour' that leads to her subsequent liaison with Amerigo, as well as being the catalyst for its final dissolution.

The narrative of Book 1 of *The Golden Bowl*, as its title 'The Prince' suggests, is given mainly from Amerigo's perspective. It does, however, move between other narrative viewpoints: Fanny's and notably Adam Verver's. What Adam Verver 'knows' will become of increasing concern in Book 2, where we are denied his perspective, and information about him is filtered through Maggie's partisan consciousness. But in Book 1, as Adam's eyes dwell pleasantly on Amerigo, his latest 'representative precious object', we move into a 'narrated monologue' – to use Dorrit Cohn's term – in which Adam reflects on the journey his aesthetic taste has taken to its present, and, he believes, infallible state. The moment of recognition of his talent as a collector – a genius 'not far below the great producers and creators' – had come on a trip to Europe with ten-year-old Maggie, just after his wife's death. He refers to this overnight miracle in vague terms – 'something' in him has made him 'somehow' equal with the 'great seers'. Instead of defining this epiphanic moment, as one might expect, he recollects an earlier time when he had been without this 'intelligence', and wonders '*why* he had been what he had, why he had failed and fallen short' (1. 141), even when financially he was already successful.

These 'years of darkness' that he recalls are characterised for him by his honeymoon trip to Europe with a young wife, when he had 'bought almost wholly for the frail fluttered creature at his side, who had her fancies . . . of the Rue de la Paix, the costly authenticities of dressmakers and jewelers. Her flutter – pale disconcerted ghost as she actually was, a broken white flower tied round, almost grotesquely for his present sense, with a huge satin "bow" of the Boulevard – her flutter had been mainly that of ribbons, frills and fine fabrics; all funny pathetic evidence . . . of the bewilderments overtaking them as a bridal pair' (1. 142). If Maggie is now in her early twenties, this honeymoon must have taken place around 1880, one of the most frilled and ribboned moments of the nineteenth century. In contrast to the fluid lines of Edwardian modes, subtly enhanced by lace, the fashions of the 1880s might well have struck the eye of 1904 as 'grotesque' even 'pathetic', although the epithets seem unduly harsh. In general it takes about thirty years for a fashion to move from looking out-of-date, to looking absurd, before it becomes interestingly historical.

That Adam should assign the years of his aesthetic 'darkness' to the harmless, if confused enthusiasms of his young American bride before the heady excitements of Paris fashions in 1880, casts a worrying light on the connections between his emotional and aesthetic sensibilities. He implies that the lack of taste was hers: 'they had loved each other so that his own intelligence...had temporarily paid for it. The futilities, the enormities, the depravities of decoration and ingenuity that before his sense was unsealed she had made him think lovely!' And he wonders, chillingly, whether the splendours of his connoisseurship could have bloomed quite so distinctively, had her early death not providentially released him to 'rifle the Golden Isles' and to go on, unimpeded by the distractions of marital affection, to scale 'his vertiginous Peak' of 'Taste' (1. 141, 143). Adam, thus, does not regret the early death of his young wife, but her bad taste (as it now seems to him), which, in his then love for her, had prevented the operation of his own rare potential.

What role do the affections play now in Adam's life? We are told that Maggie is his single affectionate tie. Otherwise his ruling passion is the vision of his museum in American City. It will be 'a house from whose open doors and windows, open to grateful, to thirsty millions, the higher, the highest knowledge would shine out to bless the land'. Moreover, it will be 'a monument to the religion he wished to propagate...the passion for perfection at any price' (1. 145–6). James, as R.B.J. Wilson remarks, 'does not blush to show us many things, but his judgment of them is a nicer question.'[23] What James shows us here, surely, is the mind of a monomaniac. The ruthless energy that has allowed Adam Verver to retire, a billionaire at forty-seven, is now directed at this messianic project of redeeming a continent from the aesthetic 'darkness' in which he believes he himself once foundered. To this end he has set himself up in Eaton Square in London, and at Fawns, a country house, which Adeline Tintner has identified as based on the Rothschild's 'château', Waddesdon,[24] a house James knew well. The collecting habits of the Rothschilds, from the evidence at Waddesdon, certainly matched the scale of collecting suggested by Adam Verver. Some 'economies' of truth in the attribution of works of art were practised by European experts and entrepreneurs such as Bernard Berenson, only too eager to act as agents for the like of Verver, who only cared 'that a work of art of price should "look like" the master to whom it might perhaps be deceitfully attributed'. Otherwise, James says, 'he had ceased...to know any matter of the rest of life by its looks' (1. 147). In other words, Adam's 'passion for perfection' does not involve a passion for learning or authenticity, but is concerned with impressive resemblances and attributions to Old Masters; furthermore, his aesthetic sense (unlike Lambert Strether's) applies to few other areas of his life, and, most revealingly for the purposes of my analysis here, not at all to his own appearance.

When we move to Fawns, some years after Maggie's marriage, father and daughter meet to discuss the problem of the unwelcome pursuit of

Adam by one of their house guests. Since he has been deprived of her guardianship by her marriage, Maggie says he now needs the protection of marriage himself, and suggests their good friend, Charlotte Stant. Maggie's suggestion comes directly after a passage describing her own reduction to a 'passive pulp' before Amerigo's heartbreaking handsomeness. We are then faced with Adam – 'a small spare slightly stale personage, deprived of the general prerogative of presence'. Adam's lack of presence and his 'neat colourless face' reduce him almost to nullity in public. And it is a self-effacement that extends to his clothes, which have been 'adopted once for all as with a sort of sumptuary scruple. He wore every day of the year, whatever the occasion, the same little black "cutaway" coat, of the fashion of his younger time; he wore the same cool-looking trousers, chequered in black and white ... a white-dotted blue satin neck-tie; and over his concave little stomach, quaintly indifferent to climates and seasons, a white duck waistcoat' (1. 169, 170, 171). According to Dorothea Krook, James's most passionate interest was the difference 'the possession of it [money and power] makes to the quality and conduct of life', and what happens to James's millionaires and heiresses 'is exemplary and instructive'.[25] What, then, does this man choose to wear – the richest of all James's tourists, a man able to indulge the wildest dreams of Kate Croy, or even Gilbert Osmond? Exactly the same coat, trousers, waistcoat and tie every day of his life. This is conspicuous consumption of a high perversity and conjures up surreal visions of wardrobes of cloned suits and ties. Judith Woolf calls him 'Andrew Carnegie played by Charlie Chaplin',[26] an observation made pertinent by Chaplin's unchanging appearance in every film. At the age of forty-seven – eight years younger than Lambert Strether, who had a morning's fun choosing gloves – Adam Verver's sartorial imagination is closed for business, his self-acclaimed aesthetic sensibilities reduced here to monotony, and his taste virtually fossilised.

Moreover, the fashion stratum in which he preserves himself is that of his 'younger time', the time in which the first Mrs Verver's regrettable taste flourished – or at any rate fluttered. The 'cutaway' morning coat became fashionable in the early 1880s, replacing the frock coat. This coat could either be part of a matching suit, or a dark jacket over lighter or patterned trousers. White waistcoats were often, though not invariably, associated with summer. A photograph of a young MP, James Lowther, in 1880, shows him in a dark cutaway, checked trousers and a white waistcoat.[27] But by 1904 the fashionable man was wearing a three-piece lounge suit, or even a sports jacket; frock coats were formal wear, and the morning coat for conservative town and business wear. Following King

Figure 11   'Mr. A. Merger Hogg at his country home'. Charles Dana Gibson, *The Weaker Sex*, 1903.

Edward's lead, tweed suits or Norfolk jackets were *de rigueur* in the country. The incongruity of Adam's costume is highlighted by Charles Dana Gibson's caricature of 1903, of a 'Mr. A. Merger Hogg', in which a desiccated American business man, in a cutaway suit, white waistcoat and necktie, stands in the park of a grandiose mansion, dictating to a typist (see Figure 11). Adam's clothes are appropriate only to daytime in the City. No wonder he needs someone – as Maggie puts it – to 'do the social', since the resolute fixity of his appearance effectively isolates him from society .

Adam and Maggie agree that Charlotte will make them 'grander'. Charlotte's social expertise at Fawns first removes unwanted guests and then so pleases Adam that he invites her to accompany him to Brighton on a 'shopping' expedition for a set of priceless oriental tiles. In Brighton Adam, made amorous by his conquest of the tiles – 'oh so tenderly unmuffled and revealed' (1. 215) – proposes to Charlotte, explaining that he wishes to put Maggie's mind at rest over her 'abandonment' of him on her marriage. Having examined the proposition, and warned him that she too has a high price, Charlotte provisionally accepts. A few days later the pair are in Paris awaiting Maggie's and Amerigo's response to their news and we see that Adam has paid an initial instalment on Charlotte's cost. They are in the hotel court, when Charlotte, rising from her chair, looks about 'for a feather boa that she had laid down. . . . He saw her boa on the arm of the chair . . . and after he had fetched it, raising it to make its charming softness brush his face – for it was a wondrous product of Paris, purchased under his direct auspices the day before – he held it there a minute before giving it up' (237). The boa was to 1904 what the bow was to 1880 – if rather more expensive: 'Nothing is so characteristic of the period', according to James Laver, 'as the feather boa. . . . The best feather boas were made entirely of ostrich plumes, and were very full behind the head and very long, sometimes costing as much as ten guineas.'[28] Adam betrays a susceptibility to the sensuous delights of feminine adornment, despite his earlier indictment of 'depravities of decoration'; but the tenderness of his gesture – that might better have been offered to Charlotte – is confined to the costly article. The boa has, however, another function in veiling Charlotte's reaction to a telegram she has just received from Amerigo, and which would compromise her if seen by Adam. She throws the boa over her shoulder, turning from Adam to the telegram, the boa hiding her face. Having studied the telegram's message, she looks up, saying, 'I'll give you what you ask' (239), an acceptance of marriage that sounds remarkably like the closing of a business deal.

We return to Charlotte several years later, now married, and seen ascending a grand staircase at a 'great official party'. She has exacted further payment: 'For a couple of years now she had known as never before what it was to look "well" – to look, that is, as well as she had always felt... that in certain conditions she might.' We see the scene from Charlotte's perspective, and this is the first of several occasions when she sees or is seen from above or below. She feels herself 'in truth crowned... the unsurpassed diamonds that her head so happily carried, the other jewels, the other perfections of aspect and arrangement that made her personal scheme a success, the *proved* private theory that materials to work with had been all she required and that there were none too precious for her to understand and use'(1. 245–6). Other than her trophy jewels we are not told what she wears, for we are within what James elsewhere called that 'most personal shell of all, the significant dress of the individual'.[29] She is conscious that her 'dire accessibility to pleasure'[30] in personal adornment, her quest for sumptuary perfection has been met; details are immaterial. Surveying the crowd, she is aware only of the 'sweep of train and glitter of star and clink of sword' (1. 246) – the lights, colours and sounds of the great occasion seem subsumed into her own person. But the moment of pleasure is also a crisis, for although she represents the Verver billions, Veblen-fashion, she is in fact without Adam, and the object of 'queer reflexions' from London faces. Unhusbanded, in 'her high tiara, her folded fan, her indifferent unattended eminence', she appears either superior to the conventions or in violation of them, so that when Amerigo returns to her side – Maggie having gone home to Adam – she keeps him by her, a public display of the bizarre Verver viewpoint that 'thinks more on the whole of fathers than of husbands'(1. 257). The demonstration has also been for the benefit of the Assinghams, and when Fanny – panicking at the implications of what she sees – tries to gauge the meaning of this unusual pairing of wife and son-in-law, Charlotte replies that she must 'act as [the situation] demands of me'(1. 261), implying that she must pretend as well as perform.

Pretence, however, is a demanding business. Later, alone in Portland Place, hoping to find Maggie (who is with Adam), Amerigo looks from the window down into the rainy street, and sees Charlotte in 'a shabby four-wheeler and a waterproof' (1. 295). Her feint of calling on Maggie is dropped when they are alone. 'What else, my dear, what in the world else can we do?' Amerigo watches her drying her shoes at the fire, and takes in the 'odd eloquence – the positive picturesqueness... of a dull dress and a black Bowdlerised hat that seemed to make a point of insisting on their time of life and their moral intention, the hat's and the frock's own, as well as the irony of indifference to them practically playing in her so handsome rain-freshened face.' What is the wife of a billionaire, only lately seen queening it at a grand party, doing in a hired cab, a raincoat, a dull dress and a sexless hat? Amerigo begins to read her performance (even the hat is a 'Bowdlerised' text) which is both a pretence (of modest means) and a declaration of truth (her abiding passion). Her appearance brings their past back to him, superimposing it on the present, 'as in a long embrace of arms and lips', effectively draining their present situation of any reality. Like Merton Densher, Charlotte believes they can be 'as they were' before their prosperity: 'It makes me feel as I used to – when I could do as I liked'. The import of 'the conscious humility of her toneless dress' (1. 299) may seem ana-logous to Jane Eyre's resumption of her shabby frock after Rochester's adulterous proposal, but is in fact the reverse.

The main features of Charlotte's married life emerge in the dialogue that follows. She is nominally mistress of her house, but her physical presence is overlooked and immaterial to its family life, which is essen-tially that of Adam, Maggie and the 'principino'. We see a sociable, sensual woman beset by boredom and loneliness; the child that might have made the difference has been denied her – as she makes clear – by Adam's impotence. Charlotte's initiative in coming to Portland Place is an appeal to Amerigo, couched in the language of a dress of earlier days. He is seduced not by eroticised elegance, but by its opposite – a dull image which evokes a past more alive than the present. If the Verver pair find their parent/child relationship more real than their married one, then are the lovers not safe, free and justified in resuming an equally real relationship? Their pact to protect the 'sweet simplicity' of the Ververs, is ironically sealed with one of the most mutually passionate embraces in James's fiction.

In his essay on 'The Future of the Novel' (1899), James deplores the Anglo-American novel for its mistrust of anything 'but the most guarded treatment of the great relation between men and women'.[31] We do not follow Amerigo and Charlotte into bedroom details, but the avowed mutual desire of their traitorous kiss makes inevitable a consummation of their adultery, one that will be 'arranged' at Matcham and concluded in Gloucester. If it is 'indirect and oblique' in its presentation, it is also, as James claims in his Preface, the 'very straightest and closest' to that relation in intention: 'You shall have everything' (1. 363), Charlotte says to her lover.

This message first has somehow to be communicated to Amerigo – that passive precious object – and, as before, Charlotte speaks through her clothes. At the end of a weekend at Matcham, Amerigo waits for her on the terrace. The pair have remained at Matcham to spread 'some ampler drapery' over Lady Castledean's dalliance with Mr Blint, so they themselves are freed for the day. Amerigo, gazing at the view and musing on the 'relation between a given appearance and a taken meaning', looks up to see Charlotte at a window: 'He had been immediately struck with her wearing a hat and jacket – which conduced to her appearance of readiness not so much to join him, with a beautiful uncovered head and a parasol . . . as to take with him some larger step altogether'(1. 354, 355–6). 'The larger step' has been on his mind too, but the practicalities of taking it have eluded him. Charlotte's 'given appearance' signals her intention of spending their day elsewhere; the alternative – hatless and parasolled – would have been to patrol Matcham, covering Lady Castledean's own 'larger steps'. Charlotte's talent is to 'arrange' appearances, not only to look elegant but also to allow meanings to be 'taken'; and while the beauties of the English scenery may elude Amerigo, the semiotics of dress and sexual relations do not. We are not now dealing with clothes as fashion but as language: 'something in the very poise of her hat, the colour of her necktie' tells him 'he could count on her'. Sex has returned to her 'chapeau': looking at one another, the physical distance between them vanishes and their eye meet instead across an imaginary loving-cup. Day turns to a night of amorous encounter – 'it only wants a moon, a mandolin and a little danger', Amerigo jokes – and to complete the picture, Charlotte throws him a white rose. As Fanny's 'orientalism' has been a jokey 'dressing-up' of more sober realities, so the lovers' parody of a romantic cliché constitutes an agreement to proceed to adultery. With Charlotte dressed to go, the natural conclusion to this scene will take place elsewhere, under the cover of sightseeing in Gloucester.

In his preface to the novel, James claims that Maggie is shown 'first through . . . her husband's exhibitory visions of her' (viii). However, having once registered Maggie's clarity and prettiness, she hardly seems to figure thereafter in Amerigo's consciousness. Adam reflects briefly on her resemblance to an unspecified piece of classical statuary, ' "generalised" in its grace'; but also recalls her being described as 'prim', like nun. Maggie's appearance in Book 1, therefore, is almost drab and ahistorical – 'lost in an alien age'. Her hair alone is specifically noted as 'very straight and flat over her temples, in the constant manner of her mother' (1. 187–8). In contrast to the abundance of Edwardian coiffures, those of the 1880s and 1890s were close to the head, with a fringe, 'plain or consisting of small curls . . . low on the forehead'.[32] Only a resolute disregard for fashion or profound piety could have convinced such a young woman to dress her hair in the style of a dead mother. If Adam is locked into his 'younger time', then Maggie is there too, a strange amalgam of wife and child.

The Assinghams worry about the Ververs. No more so than on the evening of their return from Matcham, ahead of Amerigo and Charlotte. Fanny begins by swearing to the innocence of the latter pair: 'There's nothing,' she says to the Colonel, just after we have heard Charlotte promise to give Amerigo everything. She ends by admitting that while she doesn't want to be wrong, she has imagined horrors. What has prompted her sense of something 'wrong' is a break in Maggie's routine, a routine that is itself abnormal. Maggie has driven Fanny 'home', before herself going 'home'. The question arises as to what constitutes 'home' for Maggie, since she breaks her routine by returning to wait for Amerigo in Portland Place, which is in fact her home. Fanny knows that Amerigo will expect her to be, as always, at Eaton Square, with Adam – her home in all but name. '"She has everything there"' Fanny explains to her husband, '"she has clothes."... "Oh you mean a change?" "Twenty changes if you like... [s]he dresses really... as much for her father – and she always did – as for her husband"' (1. 373). Home is where the wardrobe is.

What has prompted Maggie's break with routine? Nothing really beyond an ache to see Amerigo, and an instinct of unease; an instinct, however, which is elaborated into the rococo complexity of the pagoda image that opens Book 2. Maggie now becomes the central reflecting consciousness of the novel. We do not yet know how Maggie looks, and we will, in fact, *never* know – but we do learn what it is to occupy her 'personal shell'. We have moved from dress as a performance – Fanny's Queen of Sheba act – to dress as language – Charlotte's messages to Amerigo. Now, as Maggie becomes conscious of 'appearances', we have dress 'inhabited'. The social success of Amerigo and Charlotte – arch-arrangers of appearance – has risen in Maggie's life, like an exquisite tower, and the Verver pair have up to now basked in its reflected glory; the 'social' thing was, after all, what the other two had been 'got' in to do. Suddenly, on the day that Amerigo is due to return from Matcham, Maggie ceases 'to take comfort in the sight of it'; some part of her life has been allowed to lapse, like the steps of her 'once-loved dancing'. 'She would go to balls again', she decides, 'take out of the deep receptacles in which she had laid them away the various ornaments congruous with the greater occasions' (2. 11). Maggie's urge to disinter her talents and her unused jewels for the social stage, is both a question of dressing herself anew *and* of taking an active part in a narrative that, although it is her own, seems somehow to have slipped into other hands. Her realisation that this most natural image of a wife waiting for a husband will seem to Amerigo an aberration, prompts Maggie to 'dress' the occasion up.

She does not want to look as if she has 'waited and waited', so she places herself with a book by the fire, in 'her newest frock, worn for the first time, sticking out, all round her, quite stiff and grand; even a little too stiff and too grand for a familiar and domestic frock, yet marked none the less this time, she ventured to hope, by incontestable intrinsic merit' (2. 12). How could *any* dress have 'incontestable' or 'intrinsic' merit? The adjectives seem grossly out of place until we recollect that the function of clothes here is to communicate intention. The frock is *new*, incontestably new, and marks a new step for Maggie. Maggie's change of dress is comparable to Mrs Bulstrode's change of clothes at the end of *Middlemarch*: the 'little acts which might seem mere folly to an onlooker', but were 'her way of expressing to all spectators' that 'she had begun a new life'.[33] All the same, in contrast to Amerigo's first sight of Charlotte – silkily seductive, breathing adventure and described in an unpunctuated rush – Maggie's survey of herself is not confident, it contains hesitations, qualifications and is spotted with commas. The dress may be new, but the words that her free indirect discourse suggests she has used to herself about the dress – 'stiff', 'grand' and 'sticking out' – are not those of someone 'au fait' with fashion. They are the jerky phrases of an inarticulate child; the way one imagines Catherine Sloper might have seen *her* awful red dress.[34] Maggie is half-aware that her formality is rather much for supper at home, but like Catherine, she hopes the 'merit' of the dress can compensate for any deficiencies. She controls her nervous desire to pace the floor, although she knows that the 'rustle' and the 'hang' of the dress will make her feel 'still more beautifully bedecked'. As she sits pretending to read, she surveys 'the front of her gown, which was in a manner a refuge, a beguilement' (2. 13). The sense of being perfectly dressed, as a lady is reported to have said to Emerson, 'gives a feeling of inward tranquillity which religion is powerless to bestow'.[35] But tranquillity in this dress eludes Maggie, despite its 'incontestable' grandeur.

Maggie is disquieted by the question of whether or not the dress 'would at last really satisfy Charlotte. She had ever been, in respect to her clothes, rather timorous and uncertain; for the last year... she had lived in the light of Charlotte's possible and rather inscrutable judgment of them. Charlotte's own were simply the most charming and interesting any woman had ever put on.' What Maggie sees above all that makes her nervous is the bodice of her dress. The Edwardian bust was massive, swelling out like a pouter pigeon, enhanced by padding and ornament, especially lace. The description of a bodice of 1905 in *The Queen* magazine is lyrical over 'a scheme of tender pink chiffon, gold, spangled net and fine appliqué lace lightly diamanté'.[36] Adam has described Maggie as 'slight', and if she is indifferent to modes in hair, it is unlikely she will have the savoir-faire to deal with the imperatives of the fashionable bosom.[37] Aware of Charlotte's stylishness, Maggie feels 'the impossibility of copying her companion' or of discovering what Charlotte really thinks of her 'under any supposedly ingenious personal experiment. She had always been lovely about the step-daughter's material braveries... but there had ever fitfully danced at the back of Maggie's head the suspicion that these expressions were mercies, not judgments' (2. 13–14). She guesses that Charlotte considers her hopeless by any serious standards of dress, even ridiculous.

Speculating on Charlotte's possible reaction to the dress, Maggie thinks that this time her appearance may surprise Charlotte as being 'a little less out of the true note than usual' (2. 14). This seems unlikely: among many examples and descriptions of Edwardian dress I cannot find a single example of a dress that is stiff and sticks out. The description, in fact, is the antithesis of the vertical, flowing Edwardian look, of silks, chiffons and crêpe-de-chines. Maggie would not have bought her dress 'off the peg': like Catherine Sloper, she would have supervised its creation. She does indeed look different, though perhaps not exactly in the way she had intended.

Maggie's 'inward scene' is sharply interrupted by the 'outward' on Amerigo's entry. She is later to remember his expression when he sees her: he looks '*visibly* uncertain' and embarrassed, her appearance so startles him that for a moment she half expects him to ask ' "What in the world are you 'up to'?' ... It had made for him some difference that she couldn't measure, this meeting him at home and alone.' Although he says nothing, she believes him 'to have been harbouring the impression of something unusually prepared and pointed in her attitude and array' (2. 16–17). If her dress is not only markedly formal for an evening at home, but also unstylish, or overdone – how then is he to react? By 'smiling and smiling' and taking her in his arms he does the right thing, for she cannot in fact explain her actions other than in terms of her need for him, but nevertheless, the moment of his uncertainty is burnt on her memory.

For the moment, Amerigo meets her disquiet with the reassurance of his embrace, but her sense of being 'handled' grows from here. She takes up the social life she has neglected, begins to 'dance' again, but instead of being a participant, she feels excluded: like some costly 'dressed doll', handed about, or a circus artiste, vulgarly exposed 'in short spangled skirts', capering and posturing to order, in 'her expected, her imposed character'. She knows Charlotte and Amerigo are watching her, but she does not know why: 'Her grasp of appearances was...out of proportion to her view of causes; but it came to her...that if she could only get the facts of appearance straight...the reasons lurking behind them... wouldn't perhaps be able to help showing' (2. 51, 71, 52). An *appearance* of family loyalty is presented to Maggie and Adam, as they return home from a walk in the park, when they look up and see Charlotte, in Maggie's place beside Amerigo on the balcony of Portland Place: 'he bareheaded, she divested of her jacket...but crowned with a brilliant brave hat...which Maggie immediately "spotted" as new, as insuperably original, as worn...for the first time; all evidently to watch for the return of the absent, to be there to take them over again' (2. 98–9). They greet the Ververs affectionately, like faithful retainers to returning royalty; but they themselves strike the pair below as 'truly superior beings'. By removing her jacket, Charlotte has made herself 'at home' in Maggie's home, and her usurpation, signalled in the crowning perfection of her hat, overwhelms Maggie.

However acute Maggie's suspicions become, she is trapped by lack of knowledge, by the need to protect Adam, and by love – for whom, she refuses to say. Believing that Fanny holds the key, she speaks to her of her helplessness, her torment, her 'miracles of arrangement' (2. 110). But Fanny too is trapped, by knowing too much and too little to set Maggie's mind at rest, although she sees her friend approaching some sort of crisis. Events briefly unfold from Fanny's perspective, and, on a summons to Portland Place, she realises immediately she enters the room that the crisis has arrived. 'The Princess was completely dressed... showing a deck cleared...for action.' Maggie, in 'the large clear room' where everything is in place, looks out of place: 'for the first time in her life rather "bedizened." Was it that she had put on too many things, overcharged herself with jewels, wore in particular more of them than usual, and bigger ones, in her hair?' The 'fluttered' ghost of Maggie's mother in Paris is evoked by the effect Maggie's appearance has on Fanny: 'nothing more pathetic could be imagined than the refuge and disguise her agitation had instinctively asked of the arts of dress, multiplied to extravagance, almost to incoherence.' Maggie, with her clarity and her 'small still passion for order and symmetry', is trying to mount a challenge to Charlotte's seductive command of the language of dress, but has fallen instead into extravagance and inarticulacy. Her attempts to bolster her own confidence by over-embellishment, arming herself with defence-works of dress and jewellery, signal an entry into the game at which Charlotte is not only an old hand, but also sets the rules. Maggie is not only likely to lose, but her endeavours to reinvent herself in defiance of her natural simplicity and clarity, the inheritance of 'dusting and polishing New England grandmothers', (2. 152) is a violation of identity. The impression she gives Fanny is of a bedizened but frozen religious icon, capable of miracles perhaps, but not action.

In some ways this is an accurate impression, for Maggie's radical realignment of the two marriages is accomplished invisibly and silently. The first 'miracle' is the presence in the room of the golden bowl holding the knowledge of Amerigo's and Charlotte's past. Fanny smashes it; but once the meaning behind the bowl is 'taken' its 'given appearance' becomes secondary. Maggie's dilemma now is that by exposing to Amerigo her knowledge of the 'fault' in the bowl, she not only risks losing him but also risks destroying Adam, who 'never in his life proposed to himself to have failed'. If she is to restore order, she must also retain appearances and accept that – as Fanny says – '[t]here are many things we shall never know' (2. 175). When Amerigo enters, therefore, she turns away to avoid any show of his guilt – she does not need the appearance, now she has the meaning. She bends down before Amerigo to pick up the pieces: 'Bedizened and jewelled, in her rustling finery, she paid, with humility of attitude, this prompt tribute to order' (2. 182). This single gesture holds the key to her final victory. Her finery, however unstylish, is a reminder to Amerigo on which side his bread is buttered; her obeisance, on the other hand, is a reassurance that the degradation of a confession will not be exacted. She will proceed in silence, and apparent humility, winning him back from Charlotte, and the game of 'dress' will be consonant with that restraint. She will meet Charlotte now in the guise of her old self: simple, humble, unsuspecting Maggie. This course of action will have the advantage that she will have 'to falsify nothing'; she need only be 'consistently simple and straight' (2. 186). By playing herself, Maggie has changed the rules, since Charlotte's 'game' is based wholly on the play of appearance. Maggie's is a double-bluff, she is herself, but she *has* changed: she can thus make a work of fiction of their joint lives.

Charlotte soon realises that control has slipped into other hands. Positions are reversed and she needs to know why. At Fawns, as Maggie stands outside the brightly lit windows watching a game of cards within, Charlotte breaks away from the group, and comes out of her 'cage' into the night to confront Maggie. Charlotte pauses, and Maggie moves towards her, seized with a fear comparable to that of Milly Theale before the prowling Kate Croy. Maggie's terror, described in terms of lurid violence, arises from her awareness of Charlotte's desperation as well as of her own risk. They exchange commonplaces on the threat of storm, and Maggie with a gesture as banal as their remarks, offers Charlotte her shawl (2. 243). The gesture is not, however, banal when we consider the objects involved. Shawls have been used by James before: they were deployed by Eugenia Münster in *The Europeans*, to beguile as well as to evade, and also to a lesser extent by Catherine Sloper, as a kind of ironic tribute to her aunt's talent for embellishment – these novels, however, are set in the 1840s and 1850s. When the bustle arrived in the 1880s shawls disappeared, as they interfered with the vertical line of the dress. Mantles or jackets replaced the shawl, and shawls were *not* worn again except by the elderly and the indigent. Boas, lace, gauze stoles and scarves covered the shoulders of the early 1900s.

No wonder, then, that Charlotte rejects the offer; if Maggie were less ignorant of dress, the offer might almost be an insult. Particularly when we see that Charlotte, having entered the house, is magnificent in evening dress; 'dragging her rich train . . . she rose there beautiful and free'. Maggie, on the other hand, 'had kept the shawl . . . and clutching it tight in her nervousness, drew it round her as if huddling in it for shelter, covering herself with it for humility. She looked out as from under an improvised hood – the sole headgear of some poor woman at somebody's proud door'(2. 247) – a *tableau vivant*, as it were, of Humility pleading with Pride. This is, of course, the reverse of the situation, though much still hangs on Maggie's answer to Charlotte's question – 'Have you any grounds of complaint of me?' Maggie now knows not to play by rules dictated by others, so she answers Charlotte with a question of her own: 'What makes you want to ask it?' Charlotte, unable to admit to the reason, describes the impression she has had of a change in Maggie's 'manner'. This plays into Maggie's hands: Charlotte has been mistaken, she says, in that she has received a false impression – Maggie's 'manner' has not changed. Charlotte is thus no wiser, but neither does Maggie absolve Charlotte of wrongdoing – 'I accuse you – I accuse you of nothing' (2. 247–8, 250). Now knowing that Amerigo must have lied to Charlotte, she swears to her own lie, allowing the shawl to fall from her shoulders, in a gesture of openness – a gesture that also lets the cover of humility drop. Charlotte, in view of the others, kisses her.

It is crucial for Maggie's purposes that the appearance of Charlotte's superiority is maintained. Publicity is required, Maggie feels, 'to crown her own abasement'. Charlotte must be seen to be perfect because '[Adam] wasn't a failure, and could never be' (2. 278, 274). This infallibility can only be assured at the cost of severing his relationship with herself, so Maggie manoeuvres him into suggesting that the time has come for Charlotte and himself to return to American City. As he does so Maggie surveys 'her perfect little father' adoringly – as though for the last time – his essential characteristic for her being his marvellous youthfulness. Not an aspect noted by anyone else, it has to be said: the Assinghams remark on his premature elderliness, and see him as inconceivably funny, possibly stupid too (1. 393, 2.135).

Many of the speeches in this novel are imagined, appearing, as Elizabeth Ermarth observes, 'at their mental origin only';[38] and in the days that follow her public embrace of Charlotte, Maggie imagines passages between Amerigo and Charlotte in which she senses the 'beatitude' of her own growing triumph. Passages between Charlotte and Adam are unimaginable for Maggie, but their resonance may be sought in Adam's appearance who, in 'a straw hat, a white waistcoat and a blue necktie' (2. 283) remains unchanged. The one addition to his outfit, discerned in Maggie's imagination, is the silken rope by which he now leads Charlotte around Fawns, and which will eventually take her to 'the awful place over there' (2. 288) in America. Maggie's pity for Charlotte grows, and mentally she pleads with Adam for mercy. The 'inveteracy' of Adam's outward aspects, his 'inattackable' ivory surface leads Maggie to wonder about 'the unfathomable heart folded in the constant freshness of the white waistcoat' (2. 305) – into which the prehensile thumbs that hold the silken noose are hooked. Maggie, no more than Charlotte, or indeed anyone else, can fathom Adam. Close to the end, when Fanny probes the extent of the Ververs' knowledge, she says, '[y]ou know how he feels' – not naming names: Maggie says twice, 'I know nothing' (2. 305) – echoing her 'I accuse you of nothing'. Names are not to be named, knowledge is not to be articulated, bluff is not to be called, flaws are not to be seen, if Maggie is to succeed in the 'business of cultivating continuity' (2. 80). 'If I knew,' she says, 'I should die' (2. 305). The very violence of her language is a measure of the disharmonies and the abysses that threaten the gilded surface. The realignment of relationships that 'creates a world for others to live in' – Maggie's fictional work of art – however smoothly resurfaced, must exclude Charlotte from its real intimacies, for she has 'proved herself by nature disqualified for participation'.[39] In her new self-confidence Maggie's awareness of her own 'shell' diminishes, although her awareness of Charlotte's grows – there is, as she says, 'an awful mixture in things'. Charlotte's mantle of pride is the necessary obverse to Maggie's lying shawl of humility, but is as thinly stretched over a fissile surface as gilt on the bowl. James, as Leo Bersani says, 'proposes a kind of sincerity absolutely divorced from truth'.[40]

At Fawns Maggie looks down into the summer glare of the garden at noon, and to her surprise sees 'a moving spot, a clear green sunshade in the act of descending a flight of steps'. From directly above only the top of the parasol can be seen, but as the figure moves away from the house Maggie 'recognised the white dress and the particular motion of this adventurer' (2. 306–7). Now in the hatless and parasolled state that she had evaded at Matcham, Charlotte – adventurer no more – flees the house into an illusion of freedom, bound as she is by her silken rope. The prohibitive imaginary line drawn by Gilbert Osmond for Pansy in his garden, operates here too. Maggie looks down on Charlotte, as Charlotte has once looked down on Maggie, and Maggie's awareness that '[t]he relation today had turned itself round' becomes acute as she follows Charlotte into the garden. Her pursuit of the white dress down shaded avenues not only brings to mind Charlotte's own earlier pursuit of Maggie onto the terrace at Fawns, but the governess's pursuit of Jessel, and even Spencer Brydon's ambiguous hunt of his *alter ego* in 'The Jolly Corner'. Charlotte's reaction to being cornered answers to Maggie's own sense of herself as a 'wild west' gunman. What she in fact points at Charlotte is the first volume of a book, to replace the second one, that Charlotte has taken in error. Charlotte's terror – that Maggie will confess to her lie – is evident in her appearance: 'she bristled with the signs of her extremity... unveiled and all but unashamed, they were tragic.... Pride indeed had the next moment become the mantle caught up for protection and perversity; she flung it round her as a denial of any loss of her freedom', and Maggie wonders, with disguised sadomasochism 'if there weren't some supreme abjection with which she might be inspired' (2. 312–13). Her 'charity' lies in allowing Charlotte to save face 'while having to know that she is being so allowed', so that, as Sallie Sears points out, 'she can continue to pretend that her final vengeance... is an act of compassion.'[41] Charlotte's white dress and green parasol may suggest youth and freshness, even a simplicity that should appeal to Maggie's renewed austerities. But white is also the colour of sacrifice, and she makes a last brave stand with her perversion of the facts – that Maggie's opposition to her marriage has failed and the move to America is Charlotte's idea, and is a beginning not an end.

Maggie bows her head, conceding 'failure'; and giving Charlotte Volume 1 in place of Volume 2, directs her, in effect, to begin anew.

Strether sees Marie de Vionnet for the last time in a white dress that recalls Madame Roland on the eve of execution, and as Maggie plans to give the ex-lovers one last meeting before parting, she thinks of 'how noble captives in the French Revolution . . . used to make a feast or a high discourse of their last poor resources' (2. 341). We know Chad will be Marie de Vionnet's doom, but Maggie does not speculate on Charlotte's executioner. The correlation between Charlotte's fate and Maggie's actions is unseen, for she and her father have 'so shuffled away every link between consequence and cause that the intention remained . . . subject to varieties of interpretation' (2. 345). Even for Amerigo the saving lie of Charlotte's supremacy must hold; and to this end Maggie allows herself one sharp crack of the whip over him, when he proposes to correct Charlotte's view that Maggie is a fool: 'Aren't you rather forgetting who she is?' Charlotte is Mrs Verver and thus 'incomparable'; Charlotte is 'great', Charlotte is 'beautiful, beautiful', Maggie reiterates, and therefore 'It's success, father.' If Maggie – whom Adam trusts implicitly – says so, then it is so: 'The shade of the official, in [Charlotte's] beauty and security, never for a moment dropped; it was a cool high refuge, the deep arched recess of some coloured and gilded image' (2. 356, 357). Charlotte has joined Amerigo in the museum 'as high expressions of the kind of human furniture required aesthetically by such a scene . . . [a] contribution to the triumph of selection'. Adam and Maggie view the pair at a distance, like the imaginary photographer of Chapter 2, and complacently conclude that they have 'got some good things' (2. 360) – as ugly a phrase as James could bring himself to pen.

What, Maggie asks herself has she done all this for? To be alone with Amerigo, she decides. The fear that he may think a confession is owed occurs to her as he returns from his leave-taking, for in her mind's eye he comes holding a money-bag, as though in payment for sins. We may remember that the first seductive image of Charlotte was of a silk purse that promised and denied wealth, the purse, perhaps, that Maggie now 'sees'. The linked connotations around these two images of money contribute a material context to the human sacrifice we have witnessed: the sacrifice of Charlotte to Maggie, whose 'execution' has been tastefully veiled by Charlotte's own 'mastery of the greater style' (2. 368). Charlotte is gone and Amerigo says he now only 'sees' Maggie, but we don't know what he sees – this beautiful male product of a culture so long identified with the visual arts. We know it is not the blur of chic, the triumphs and seductions of dress he has known in Charlotte. These attributes are now the property of a small, stale monomaniac in American City. All he sees is Maggie, and, having achieved her ends by rejecting 'material braveries' in favour of shawls of humility, it is horribly possible that she, like her father, will now begin to dress according to some 'sumptuary scruple', and spend her billions filling wardrobes with identically dull dresses. When James's American Princess finally 'strikes back',[42] with what Daniel Fogel refers to as her 'horrifyingly informed and organized innocence',[43] when she recognises and wrestles with the evil she believes has come to sit at her table, and abides by her notions of high decorum, we cannot be sure that the results will not be terrible. The story she makes of it is incontestably 'subject to varieties of interpretation'.

9
New Fashioned Ghosts

When Maggie Verver goes to her chest to recover the ornaments she needs for her struggle with Charlotte, James is returning to an image he had created forty years earlier. In a story of 1868, 'A Romance of Certain Old Clothes', a pair of eighteenth-century American sisters battle to the death and beyond for the favours of a young Englishman, using the weapons of dress. The clothes they fight with are 'buried' in an old chest. Maggie's chest and its contents remain vague – neither exactly real nor exactly symbolic, but in the early story the chest and clothes are realised in some detail.

In this concluding chapter I want to look at some of James's ghost stories and concentrate on the surprisingly significant role that dress plays in the description of ghosts. James's ghost stories are very often concerned with the possession of one character by another, and such a process is confirmed not just by interior feelings but also by appearance. Dress thus contributes to a confusion of identity or a usurpation of identity in a series of narratives considered here, starting with 'A Romance of Certain Old Clothes' and ending with the unfinished novel, *The Sense of the Past*.

If James's stories of the ghostly could be said to figure at the far end of the scale between Realism and Romance, we might then ask how works such as *The Turn of the Screw* and 'The Jolly Corner' combine their realistic substance with their romantic effects, since the essence of a ghost's effect is presumably the uncanniness and other-worldliness of its appearance. The introduction to *The Oxford Book of Ghost Stories* defines ghosts as the 'returning dead... traditionally at home in mists and shadows...and we do not expect them before twilight...their actions...rather than those of the living must be the central theme; and most of all, each ghost...must unquestionably be dead.'[1] Despite the fact that he produced some of the genre's most disturbing apparitions, James's ghosts consistently resist such criteria, and are described in terms that are not at all shadowy or other-worldly. His ghosts are dressed, and their costume exhibits a quite worldly specificity of detail.

When asked by the Deerfield Summer School to comment on 'materialism' in the novel, James wondered what they meant by 'materializing tendencies'. 'There are no tendencies worth anything,' he wrote, 'but to see the actual or the imaginative, which is just as visible, and to paint it.'[2] This letter of 1884 lies between the four early ghost tales and the twelve later ones – a fallow period for Jamesian spectres, in fact – though, as Martha Banta has argued and James's letter suggests, as his fiction comes increasingly to focus on presentation of the consciousness, so the borderline between what is seen and unseen, the actual or the psychic, is correspondingly difficult to draw. There is a ghost for Isabel Archer as there is for Merton Densher, and the narrator of *The Sacred Fount* is no less haunted than the governess at Bly. Banta suggests that as 'James came to annex several worlds to the consciousness – the worlds of immediate social being and of ghostly encounters in the past and present – he also pressed forward certain experiments in narrative strategy for their encompassment.'[3] His ghosts start as literal and externalised in 'A Romance of Certain Old Clothes', for example, but become progressively metaphorical and subjective, and finally, in *The Sense of the Past*, disruptive – even destructive – of the narrating and reflecting consciousness. Seen with different kinds of specificity of dress, these ghosts seem to usurp or complicate the narrator's role, and in paying attention to these spectral clothes, we find that they illuminate James's narrative methods in a surprisingly clear way.

We might say that ghosts, clothes and rivalry form part of a complex of interests for James. The many covertly antagonistic relationships between women in his major novels are prefigured in the rivalry of the two New England sisters of 'A Romance of Certain Old Clothes', Viola and Perdita,[4] over the Englishman, Arthur Lloyd. Their wooing of him is at first conducted in a minor key of 'ribbons and top-knots';[5] it is not until Arthur declares a preference for Perdita that costume begins to be deployed in a more sinister way. Wishing Perdita long life and many children, Viola forces on her sister 'a bit of lace of her own' (250), and sets in motion the substitution of herself for Perdita.

Dress is a central interest of both sisters. But for Viola, defeated in courtship and gripped by her 'inordinate love of dress' (250) – foreshadowing Kate Croy's 'dire accessibility' to personal ornament – the wedding preparations are painful to watch. When she sees a blue and silver brocade sent to Perdita by Lloyd, a material better suited to her own majestic fairness than to Perdita's slight, dark looks, she rouses herself from misery to hold the material against herself before the mirror. The two have already played out preliminary rivalries in front of a mirror, but now the game becomes more serious. The mirror, as Anne Hollander says, 'has always had a very bad reputation ... because of the very power it seems to have of generating, not just reflecting, an image inside its depths'.[6] Viola makes 'a dazzling picture', and Perdita – in sympathy or malice – remarks that it is a pity the brocade is not for her. Viola now takes over the work of Perdita's trousseau and 'innumerable yards of lustrous silks and satins, of muslins and velvets and laces passed through her cunning hands' (251–2). That cunning, James leads us to suppose, works into Perdita's gowns something more than stitches, motivated as it is by a fierce desire for possession.

A year later Perdita lies dying in child-bed, tormented by the fear that Viola will replace her as Lloyd's wife. She consoles herself with the idea that Viola cares more for 'finery and jewels' than she does for Lloyd (who is in truth a dull dog), forgetting that one way to acquire the clothes would be to acquire the man. Perdita makes her husband vow that her great wardrobe shall be 'sacredly kept' for their child. In an image which combines entombment with that of a Sleeping Beauty, she visualises her dresses, in particular a carnation satin, 'quietly waiting', locked in the iron-bound chest, 'keeping their colours in the sweet-scented darkness' (256). Viola, however, wastes no time supplanting the dead Perdita in both her husband's and child's affections; but the couple do not prosper, and Viola feels that her talent for dress is unfulfilled. Her triumph over Perdita will not be complete until she has 'the great wardrobe', and she broods over the chest in which her sister's 'relics' lie imprisoned. Lloyd is blackmailed into giving her the keys and shortly afterwards he finds her in the attic, kneeling before the 'treasure of stuffs and jewels' dead, with 'the marks of ten hideous wounds' (262) on her face.

We have no way of knowing what it is that Viola encounters, since James in these early tales has not yet developed his narrative method of the 'reflecting consciousness'. Perdita's ghost explodes unexpectedly upon us, and as T. J. Lustig complains in his book on James's ghosts, it 'ruptures the fabric of the text ... with more violence than sense'.[7] Reviewing a novel by Mary Braddon in 1865, James maintained that 'a good ghost story must be connected at a hundred points with the common objects of life',[8] and he may have felt that the colours and textures of the story's dress notations provided those anchors to reality. His avoidance, even at this early date, of structural details that might date the clothes or make them realisable indicates a wariness over how best to represent the past, avoiding the cheap effects by which 'a passable historic *pastiche*'⁹ was often obtained. As late as 1901, when James was working on *The Sense of the Past*, he wrote of these difficulties to Sarah Orme Jewett in relation to her own historical novel: 'You may multiply the little facts that can be got from pictures & documents, relics & prints, as much as you like – the *real* thing is almost impossible to do.'¹⁰ For the purposes of the rather simple plot of 'A Romance of Certain Old Clothes' the fabrics had to be able to assume a shape and force in the imagination which might be diminished if they were simply to become matters of bodice, sleeve and petticoat. No credible connection, however, is made between the fatal and particularised disfiguring of Viola's face at the end, and the story's swathe of gorgeous fabrics.¹¹ Elizabeth Bowen, in her unashamed retelling of James's tale, 'Hand in Glove', puts her finger, as it were, on the plot's weak spot: she makes the coveted articles of clothing a collection of delectable gloves.

Although Viola is not a ghost she is in fact the more alarming of the two sisters and her maleficent powers are implicit early in the story, first as she stitches the trousseau and then when she appropriates Perdita's wedding veil. Perdita tries to retrieve it but draws back from Viola in instinctive fear. In a later tale, 'The Ghostly Rental' of 1875, the narrator actually does tear the veil from a seeming phantom, a black-clad lady haunting an abandoned house. As it happens she is not a ghost at all, but as the narrator reflects, 'a sham ghost that one accepted might do as much execution as a real ghost':¹² the paralysing *effect* of an apparition is what really counts. Discussing the distinctions between romantic and realistic treatments of a subject in the Preface to *The American*, James observes that it is a question of 'perceived effect, effect after the fact'.¹³ It is in this uncertain area of effects that James's later apparitions emerge: they are seen with varying degrees of detail, and begin to usurp and complicate the narrator/reflector's role – a development latent in 'The Ghostly Rental' but clearly present in 1891 in 'Sir Edmund Orme'.

Sir Edmund Orme is central to my argument here, as James's first fully visualised and dramatised apparition. We see Orme placed in relation to three main characters: to the woman who once jilted him, Mrs Marden, he is a visible, vengeful spectre; to the narrator, he is an increasingly sympathetic and very physical presence; but to Mrs Marden's daughter, Charlotte, courted by the narrator, he is an unseen threat. The context of Orme's ghostly appearances is the cheerful ordinariness of mid-century Brighton, where the narrator first sees Orme, 'a pale young man in black',¹⁴ in church, just after he has decided to propose to Charlotte.

The narrator simply registers Orme as another young man, like himself, sitting by Charlotte, and kindly lends him a prayer-book.

After he has learned from Mrs Marden that Orme is actually a ghost, encounters with the spectre leave the narrator with the impression of 'a splendid presence'; very well dressed in full mourning, if a little old-fashioned (865). Orme apppears in broad daylight and as far as the narrator is concerned is a normal and friendly presence – the effect 'of the strange and sinister embroidered on the very type of the normal and easy'[15] that James wrote of wanting to create for this tale. Mrs Marden, on the other hand, lives in mortal terror of Orme. We learn much of Orme's and of her past, but, curiously, nothing of the narrator; neither his name, history, nor family. Because the narrator is our reflecting consciousness it is easy to overlook the fact that he is a blank and that the progressively substantial figure of Orme's ghost has insinuated itself on the empty space of the story, as the narrator's alter ego. While we learn nothing of the narrator's appearance, he speaks of his own grow-ing admiration for Orme: he feels Orme to be 'a fact' – positive, indi-vidual and respectable, someone who had 'the perfect propriety of his position' and was 'always arrayed and anointed, and carried himself ever, in each particular, exactly as the occasion demanded' (874). Char-lotte finally sees Orme at a party, in evening dress like every one else, including – we assume – the narrator. It is when she accepts the narra-tor's offer of marriage here that the ghost leaves Charlotte and closes in on Mrs Marden, who then dies of sheer fright.

Orme, according to Mrs Marden, had latterly only been seen in con-junction with Charlotte and the narrator. Mrs Marden is sure that if Charlotte rejects the narrator (as she herself had rejected Orme), she will be harmed. Not only, therefore, does the identifiable and material Orme 'possess' the anonymous, invisible narrator in order to play out an improved version of the past, but we begin to feel that the narrator's rather bullying courtship of the girl parallels Orme's own past pursuit and present terrorization of Mrs Marden. In fact, the narrator's admira-tion for the beautiful mother grows at the expense of the girl, who has 'a kind of rosy blankness'; and he establishes with the mother 'silent reciprocities' (871) of communication, very different from the rather rocky progress of his understanding with Charlotte. The marriage, one feels, is not promising; moreover we know from the framing device at the start of the tale that Charlotte will die within the year. The death of Mrs Marden is thus not only an act of ghostly revenge on Orme's part, the removal of a rival to Charlotte, but a sinister parallel and portent which returns us to the start of the narrative circle.

The scarcely 'happy' ending of 'Sir Edmund Orme' prefigures the demonic conclusion of *The Turn of the Screw*, a tale which has been the subject of so much critical debate that one sympathises with Martha Banta's temptation 'to drive right past the front gates of Bly'. But as Banta also says, it is 'the style and the structuring of the experience undergone by its participants'[16] rather than the existence or non-existence of the ghosts that is crucial to the narrative; and as the governess's experience and description of the ghosts' clothes are a part of that structuring, Bly is worth a detour.

The links between the presentation of the ghosts in *The Turn of the Screw* and the published proceedings in the 1890s of the Society for Psychical Research – which James certainly read – have been fully explored by Peter Beidler. The Society's ghosts, unlike the transparent wraiths and headless horsemen of legend, were sartorially 'a boring lot'.[17] Female ghosts were reported as favouring unremarkable black dresses; males, like females, wore the standard dress of whatever years of the nineteenth -century they belonged to, in which class and occupation were often identifiable. James's depiction of Miss Jessel and Peter Quint owes much to these reports, despite James's disclaimer in his preface to *The Turn of the Screw* that '[r]ecorded and attested ghosts are ... so little expressive, as little dramatic, above all as little continuous and conscious and responsive, as is consistent with their taking the trouble – and an immense trouble they find it, we gather – to appear at all.'[18] James wanted to invest these mundane spectres with the 'old sacred terror' (xv); their dull purposelessness, however, was inadequate to his own 'excursion into chaos' (xviii).

For the reader to 'think the evil' (xxi) as James required, he or she would have to enter into the relation between the ghost and the narrator/protagonist, to sense as well as to question the reality of these appearances. In order to think the evil and sense the terror in a way that was consonant with a real aesthetic purpose and not just a sensational one, it was necessary not only to see what the reflecting consciousness sees, but to *see* the reflector 'seeing'. The invisibility of the narrator in 'Sir Edmund Orme' meant that James sacrificed the reader's awareness of the process of the narrator's possession by Orme. The debate, however, over the reliability of the governess's descriptions of the ghosts in *The Turn of the Screw* shows how successfully James explored this problem seven years later. Readers have always been able to 'think the evil' in this tale for themselves.

One of the central objections to dismissing the governess in *The Turn of the Screw* as a hallucinating hysteric is that the housekeeper, Mrs

Grose, recognises the dead valet, Quint, from the governess's description of him. The bar to accepting her accounts of the ghosts unreservedly is that her several versions of the scenes with the ghosts do not tally. While certain dress details are recounted with the clarity of a realist novel, the most vivid accounts are of subjective and unverifiable *effects*. We see the governess 'seeing', and we see that her perceptions and prejudices about social class, sexual mores, professional and maternal rivalry over the children colour her judgement and her descriptions. The whole business of description, the legacy of the realist tradition as represented by George Eliot and Balzac, is thus thrown into doubt by the unresolved status of the governess's visions.

The specific details we are given of dress, I should emphasize, are very few. But these details are telling and they allow the consciousness which registers them within the ghost story to construct competing, if dislo-cated, versions of the real. While declaring that what she sees on the tower of Bly is 'as definite as a picture in a frame', the governess records only Quint's hatlessness – a sign that he belongs to the house – but her subsequent spoken *impression* of the figure prompts Mrs Grose's recogni-tion of him. These details are speculative: he is not 'a gentleman', for although smart, his clothes 'are not his own' (190–1). At this, Mrs Grose adds the detail of a stolen waistcoat, one that might have led the governess to mistake Quint for his master, although she doesn't say so. By mid-century the growing ubiquity of the dark cloth suit meant that '[c]olour and pattern in male dress were now largely concentrated on the waistcoat',[19] marking a class distinction, as well as making it a conspicu-ous item of dress. The uncle and Quint are the same 'type': lady-killers in fancy waistcoats, and Miles, the 'type' in the making, '[t]urned out for Sunday by his uncle's tailor, who had had a free hand and a notion of pretty waistcoats' (248). It is in this finery that Miles makes queasily flirtatious remarks to the governess.

In the case of the appearances of Miss Jessel by the lake, it is the hat, or more accurately the absence of the hat (for the female a sign either of disaster or loss of respectability) that characterises the link between Jessel, the governess and Flora. When the governess first sees Jessel she describes her simply as 'an apparition'. For Mrs Grose she expands this to a figure of 'unmistakable horror and evil: a woman in black, pale and dreadful'. Adding 'stroke to stroke', she asserts the woman was '[i]n mourning – rather poor, almost shabby... wonderfully handsome. But infamous' (203, 206). Black dress, as we have seen in earlier chapters, contains contradictory meanings – respectability and mourning, but also seduction and sexuality. Governesses in art and fiction were often in black and usually downtrodden, but, like Lady Audley, they could also be sexual opportunists. The governess's leap from the former to the latter category – from respectability to infamy – is partly conditioned by current iconography, but perhaps also by her own jealousy over the children and her illicit yearnings for the uncle.

Jessel appears three times in a black dress, the third time usurping the governess's place in the schoolroom. The final sighting, with Flora and Mrs Grose by the lake, however, focuses on their mutually hatless state. Failing to find Flora in her room, the governess decides she has gone outside to Jessel: Mrs Grose is shocked – ' "Without a hat?" I naturally also looked volumes. "Isn't that woman always without one?" ' – the first time she has mentioned this. The governess makes for the door and again shocks Mrs Grose: 'You go with nothing on?' to which the governess replies, 'What do I care when the child has nothing?' Hatlessness has now expanded metaphorically to a general and dangerous nudity, an idea so foregrounded that Flora's first words when they find her are 'Why where are your things?' to which the governess answers 'Where yours are, my dear!' (271, 272, 277) The circuit of exposed, hatless females is completed with the arrival of Jessel and concludes with Flora's rejection of the governess and her descent into the foul language that shocks Mrs Grose. The governess sees Flora's fury as the result of an imputation upon 'her respectability' (285), although in a very Jamesian muddle over possessive adjectives, the 'respectability' could be Jessel's or Flora's. The governess knows her own reputation will be at stake when Flora meets her uncle.

The term *alter ego* was introduced by William James in his writings on psychology in the 1890s, and we find Henry James using the term for the apparition that is the other self of the protagonist of the tale 'The Jolly Corner' of 1908, Spencer Brydon. After years of exile, Brydon has returned to a modern and commercialised New York which – seeing himself as a man of culture and imagination – he detests. The one detail we have of his personal appearance early in the story, a monocle, suggests a refusal to see fully. In New York he is surprised to find in himself the 'lively stir... of a capacity for business'[20] and this discovery draws him to one of the houses he owns in the city, the Jolly Corner, in search of the man of business he might have become, had he stayed in America.

He begins to prowl about the house, encouraged by Alice Staverton, his link with the past, who claims to have seen Brydon's other self in a dream. He chooses to search at night, as if in a dream, in a house lit only by the street-lamps from outside. Brydon is not the narrator, but in a literal way he is a 'reflecting consciousness', for through the darkness he catches gleams of his own appearance: he sees 'the steel point of his stick' on the black and white marble floor, and, 'in the light of fairly hunting on tiptoe, the points of his evening shoes' (456). His imagination begins to colour the hunt with nightmare qualities in which he becomes conscious of how his own eyes, 'large, shining and yellow' must alarm his 'poor hard-pressed alter ego' (458). His awareness of himself in relation to the ghost, which he has virtually wished into existence, then begins to alter – he feels he is being followed, 'he was kept in sight, while remaining himself...sightless' (460). Is he the pursuer or the pursued? Has the man of business overtaken – or been taken over by – the man of imagination? Believing he has closed the door on his pursuer he begins to leave, only to find the front door blocked by 'a spectral yet human man of his own substance'. The man's face is buried in his hands but otherwise 'every fact of him' is 'hard and acute... his queer actuality of evening dress, of dangling double eye-glass, of gleaming silk lappet and white linen, of pearl button and gold watch-guard and polished shoe' (475). These actualities that shine out of the darkness are traditionally 'ghostly' in their fragmentary glitter, but they are also credible as the details of evening dress that would indeed be visible in light from the street. What Brydon sees is also, of course, a mirror-image of himself in evening dress – except that the ghost has a *double* eye-glass and a mutilated hand. The ghost's appearance is Brydon's own – *almost*. The horror in a ghost story, as Elizabeth Bowen suggests, 'lies in happenings that are just, *just* out of true'.[21]

Brydon faints at this sight and comes to 'himself' the next morning, pillowed in Alice Staverton's lap. That the prolonged and intensely dramatic struggle against 'the apparitions of the self'[22] should simply have a 'happy ending' in a woman's lap is, as Martha Banta suggests, unsettling. The demonic terrors of *The Turn of the Screw* and of James's own nightmare of the Galerie d'Apollon, on which 'The Jolly Corner' is based, cannot be resolved by the love of a good woman. Indeed, *The Turn of the Screw* could be read as the antithesis of that classic dénouement. The 'romance' is not *that* kind of romance but has to do with the shifting ambiguities between actuality and consciousness. Brydon has sought a romantic *frisson* in an old house: ironically, he finds real horror in his own dual personality, represented by the absolute contemporaneity of the ghost. In allowing Brydon to 'faint' and then be rescued by his 'true love', James uses an avoidance strategy more often employed by Mrs Radcliffe's susceptible heroines.

In *The Sense of the Past* the complexity of this 'self-hauntedness', the play between actuality and consciousness, can lock James into problems which seem inescapable, even for him. James began the novel in 1900, revised it in 1914, but it lay unfinished at his death in 1916. In it Ralph Pendrel, an American in London in 1900, faces his own image in a portrait of a century before. He can either reject that other self or make the unimaginable imaginative leap and enter the past. It is on the transaction between Ralph and his painted past self, and a discrepancy in dress, that the unresolved plot of the novel hangs.

When Ralph first encounters the portrait of the young man he notes enough detail to date the costume to around 1820. Actualities such as a dark green coat, high collar, grey gloves and beaver hat provoke in Ralph the desire to see more, as does the man's strangely backward-glancing face, latent with life and movement, 'as if he had turned it *within* the picture'.[23] James, in his preface to *The American*, spoke of the ability of the romancer insidiously to cut the cable that tethers the balloon of experience to mundane reality: it is at this second encounter that James cuts his cable. As Ralph enters the room he realises that the thing he had thought of had taken place: 'Somebody was in the room... the young man, brown-haired, pale, erect with the high-collared dark-blue coat... presented him the face... [which] confounded him as his own' (87, 88). Ralph neither faints nor rejects his alter ego, but willingly enters the past. As he does so we might note that the coat in the first encounter with the portrait was green, in the second, blue. James wrote and rewrote *The Sense of the Past* over sixteen years and as both references to the coat are contained in the 1900 section, he would have re-read it in 1914. It is impossible to say what he might finally have made of his draft, but it seems reasonable to suggest that the anomaly in dress was not an oversight, and was to play a part in the effort, recorded in James's notebook, to rescue Ralph from a situation both he and the ghosts come to find intolerable.

On his arrival in the past Ralph finds he is engaged to his cousin, Molly. He again notes those details that allow us to date her dress to around 1820 – sprigged muslin with sleeves short enough to display a good deal of arm and shoulder; and these arms embrace Ralph in a disturbingly fleshly way, for a ghost. Ralph, on the evidence of his unchallenged welcome into the past, decides that, while in 1900 he had been considered 'overdressed for New York' (145), his appearance here among the ghosts is acceptable. Interestingly, the years between 1800 and 1820 are those in which male dress first took its modern form; so a frock-coated male of 1900 could have passed in 1820. The ghostly starts to complicate the narrative method, in that Ralph is conscious of both his nineteenth- *and* twentieth-century selves as well as of the way the ghosts are experiencing *him*. His own growing unease runs parallel to, and is indeed fed *by*, his awareness of the ghosts' mounting alarm in relation to him. It is impossible to dismiss anyone in this circle of uneasily communicating consciousnesses as more or less real than any other. Who is the ghost here?

The crisis comes when Ralph meets Molly's younger sister, Nan, and falls in love with her. Nan's dress, unlike the other clothes seen by Ralph in 1820, is rendered simply by its effect on him: 'Why she's modern, modern!' (280). Falling in love with Nan's modernity clarifies for Ralph the urgency of his real ties to the twentieth-century. Ralph's paradox is that what he loves in Nan compels him to leave her to return to his twentieth-century American fiancée, Aurora Coyne. As if to exacerbate the paradox, Aurora is likened to 'an Italian princess of the cinquecen-to ... [with] low square dresses, crude and multiplied jewels' (8), a description which evokes the anachronistic elements of *fin de siècle*, Aesthetic Dress. This rather heavily decorated fashion presented a sharp contrast to the light, high-waisted Empire style which replaced it (Plate VIII), just before the outbreak of the First World War. Nan, in her dress of 1820, is the modern girl, not Aurora of 1900 (see Figures 12 and 13).

We know from James's notes of 1910 that 'the climax of the romantic hocus-pocus' (336), as he put it, was that Nan should discover Ralph's bizarre secret but love him enough to help him escape. But how? The key, for James, was 'whether the portrait *in* the house in 1910, is done from Ralph in 1820 ... or accounted for as coming into existence after-wards' (342). The portrait is the escape route. But if the first green-coated 'Ralph' is actually himself, painted during his visit to the past of 1820, then the second blue-coated man is his ancestor – or vice versa. We would want to know the colour of the coat in the portrait *after* Ralph's return; and especially the colour of Ralph's own coat. We would also like to know just through whose eyes have we been seeing all this? Has that 'possession' of another being – the theme common to all these stories – finally come about right under our noses?

Although James freed his romantic balloon dramatically from reality in *The Sense of the Past*, the dress worn in this spectral world is perhaps the most realistically – and most unnervingly – detailed in James's work, the last demonstration of James's delight in a 'palpable imaginable *visitable* past'[24] and a radical challenge to our assumptions about the realist novel. Actualities are filtered through consciousness, and con-sciousness is capable of alarming jumps and dislocations, as well as odd accommodations. What we have seen in these stories is a growing – and sometimes a defeating – complexity. James does not opt for some static

Figure 12   Three gowns by Paul Poiret, 1908.

Figure 13   Full dress. *The Ladies' Monthly Museum*, 1804.

point between realism and Romance: what we see developing in his treatment of ghostly dress is what he described in the preface to *The American*, as the writer's commitment 'in both directions...by some need of performing his whole possible revolution'.[25] How was the revolution to be performed here? James never found the way back, and Ralph remains trapped in the 1820s.

*   *   *

Ralph Pendrel's limbo could be James's own, for he never found a way out of the novel. James, like Pendrel, longed to enter the 'palpable, proveable world' of the past, to pursue and possess characters as physical facts not just as decoratively displayed collections of historically verifiable bits and pieces. Like Balzac, he relished the sense 'of another explored, assumed, assimilated identity – enjoyed it as the hand enjoys the glove when the glove ideally fits'.[26] The unease of Maggie in her new dress in Book 2 of *The Golden Bowl*, Ralph Pendrel's awareness of both selves, could be seen as versions of this hand in the glove: dress inhabited and felt, rather than dress externally described.

The packed descriptions of Balzac's fictional world had earlier been James's 'delight', but also his 'despair' – they combine the problem of avoiding banality while still providing 'solidity of specification'. James's frequent irritation at Anthony Trollope's habit of reminding readers that his stories were make-believe, arose from James's sense that, while Trollope's world was also densely detailed, his 'little slaps at credulity' were a 'terrible crime', for 'it is impossible to imagine what a novelist takes himself to be unless he regard himself as a historian and his narrative as a history'.[27] Taking James's recurring metaphor of 'the house of fiction' for the novelist's art, Trollope might be accused of building novels in bad faith, where details are a kind of inessential narrative stucco work. James spoke of his own 'technical rigour', of piling 'brick upon brick', 'scrupulously fitted together and packed in. It is an effect of detail of the minutest'; but sound, for the ground below stretches 'at every point to the base of the walls'.[28] Even the earliest of his dress notations in which colours, embellishments and accessories are foregrounded, prove, when tested, to be solid structural supports, aspects of the social circumstances, personal life and development of a character that cannot be removed without damage to the whole. For James, as for Roland Barthes, the described fragment of dress has a deeper value than a bow-by-bow account: 'if it tells us of a rose on a dress, it is because the rose is worth as much as the dress.'[29]

We have seen how, with *The Portrait of a Lady*, James moves further into the individual consciousness, how costume becomes a more complex form of communication, a debate not only with others but with the self. Barthes sees dress as 'an argument' with 'a powerful semantic value', not only to be seen, but to be *read*: 'it communicate[s] ideas, information, or sentiments'.[30] James's achievement is to have developed this 'argument' in dress into one in which the visionary and poetic plays an increasing role, but in which, paradoxically, the actual and historical facts of dress are simultaneously sharpened and increased. Hyacinth Robinson's conversion to past ideals is fatal, but his images of Christina, Lady Aurora and even earthy Millicent, embodied in real and imagined headgear, extract poetry from the unheroic fashions of modern life – the task Baudelaire set for the artist of the nineteenth century. The strangely shifting dress metaphors of *Wings of the Dove* mark Merton Densher's emotional shifts, as well as the shifts between nations and cities; Lambert Strether's 'uncovering' of Marie de Vionnet to a final simplicity is also a revelation of himself, of how he has been seen. These are moments of high psychological drama. These dramas of consciousness can also enter the occult, with the desire to 'possess' another being – to step, literally, into their shoes. Sir Edmund Orme, Ralph Pendrel and even Maggie Verver must emulate their author and inhabit the 'habited, featured, colored, articulated form of life'[31] they desire to control.

Some years ago at a literary conference in Europe, I mentioned to a fellow Jamesian that I was starting on the project that lies behind this book – an exploration of dress in James's novels. She exploded with disbelief and roared with laughter, saying that there *was* surely no dress in James's work, or if there was it was surely of no consequence. I hope that I have shown that this is a mistaken view of James. There is dress in his novels, and it has a function. I do not wish to claim that dress is the figure in James's carpet, the key to all his mysteries, but I think that to test such details, to trace their functions within a single work, or across the *oeuvre*, is to reveal not only their integral, structural qualities, it is to demonstrate development in James's symbolic and narrative patterns.

Even when not directly represented in the narrative, clothes are an indispensable and working part of a character's consciousness: '[Dress] must renounce every egotism,' says Roland Barthes, 'every excess of good intentions; it must pass unnoticed in itself yet it must also exist.'[32] Henry James's art of dress may perhaps have passed unnoticed, but it exists; it is not insistent, it is not described when it has no bearing on the action; indeed, its very absence may be significant – why do we not know how Amerigo dresses? What does he *see* in Maggie? But take dress away and you remove Catherine Sloper's sad articulacy, Isabel Archer's resistance to her fate, Marie de Vionnet's understated but heart-stopping beauty, and the trap that Charlotte Stant sets for herself with her genius for 'appearances'. The habits of dress in a novel should be like the habits of thought: to be right they must seem natural, even unnoticed. But right or wrong, dress affects the way people see themselves, the way they feel about and communicate with others. Those feelings and communications are by no means fortuitous or frivolous, as James well understood. Milly Theale's unsuccessful appearance is, as Elizabeth Bowen might have said of her, 'more than a pity; it is a pathological document.'[33] Georges Perec denied that fashion speaks 'of caprice, of spontaneity, fantasy, invention, frivolity'. 'Fashion,' he says, 'is entirely on the side of violence, the violence of conformity... the violence of the social consensus and the contempt it conceals within it.'[34] James on the whole prefers to locate violence offstage; but it is there, even if it 'goes on irreconcilably, subversively, beneath the vast smug surface'.[35] Dress, in all its manifestations – as fashion, seduction, history, language, theatre, painting, politics, nationalism and even demonic possession – is a vital brick in Henry James's House of Fiction. In dress the subterranean, the complex and even the violence of human relations is revealed, and it is a subject which therefore, I believe, repays our attention.

Notes

Chapter 1

1 Elizabeth Bowen, 'Dress', in *Collected Impressions* (New York: Alfred Knopf, 1950) pp. 111, 112.
2 Dorothea Krook, *Henry James's The Ambassadors: A Critical Study* (New York: AMS Press, 1996) p. 58.
3 Michael Irwin, *Picturing in the 19th Century Novel* (London: George Allen, 1979) p. 91.
4 Kimberley Reynolds and Nicola Humble, *Victorian Heroines* (New York: New York University Press, 1993).
5 Anne Hollander, *Seeing Through Clothes* (Berkeley: University of California Press, 1993) pp. 424, 430–2.
6 Honoré de Balzac, 'Traité de la Vie Elégante', in *Oeuvres Diverses* (Paris: Louis Conard, 1938) p. 162 (my translation).
7 Franco Moretti, *The Way of the World* (London: Verso, 1987) p. 144.
8 Philippe Perrot, *Fashioning the Bourgeoisie* (Princeton: Princeton University Press, 1994) p. 3.
9 Martha Banta, 'The Excluded Seven', in *Henry James's New York Edition*, ed. David McWhirter (Stanford: Stanford University Press, 1995) p. 256.
10 Simon Nowell-Smith, *The Lesson of the Master* (Oxford: Oxford University Press, 1985) footnote, p. 120.
11 F. W. Dupee, *Henry James: Autobiography* (London: W. H. Allen, 1956) p. 52.
12 Dupee, p. 337.
13 Isaiah, iii, 16–24.
14 Aileen Ribeiro, *The Art of Dress* (Newhaven & London: Yale University Press, 1995) p. 3.
15 Jean-Christophe Agnew, 'The Consuming Vision of Henry James', in *The Culture of Consumption*, eds. R. W. Fox and T. J. Jackson Lears (New York: Pantheon Books, 1983) p. 72.
16 Fred Kaplan, *Henry James: The Imagination of Genius* (New York: William Morrow, 1992) p. 467.
17 Dupee, p. 24.
18 Dupee, pp. 158, 159.
19 Dupee, p. 161.
20 Dupee, p. 161.
21 Nowell-Smith, p. 29.
22 Henry James, *The Awkward Age*, New York edition, 1909 (Fairfield: Augustus M. Kelley, 1976) p. 78.
23 Adeline Tintner, *Henry James and the Lust of the Eyes* (Baton Rouge: Louisiana State University Press, 1993) p. 125.
24 Nowell-Smith, p. 58.
25 Edith Wharton, *A Backward Glance* (London: Century, 1987) p. 175.

26 J. L. Sweeney, ed., *The Painter's Eye* (Madison: University of Wisconsin Press, 1989) p. 261.
27 Viola Hopkins Winner, *Henry James and the Visual Arts* (Charlottesville: University of Virginia Press, 1970) p. 68.
28 Sweeney, p. 112.
29 Sweeney, p. 84.
30 Sweeney, pp. 228, 222–3.
31 Hollander, p. 431.
32 Peter Rawlings, ed., *Henry James: Essays on Art and Drama* (Aldershot: Scolar Press, 1996) pp. 353, 491.
33 Rawlings, p. 406.
34 Henry James, *Literary Criticism: American and English Writers* (New York: The Library of America, 1984) pp. 606, 608.
35 James, *American and English Writers*, pp. 744, 745.
36 James, *American and English Writers*, p. 497.
37 James, *American and English Writers*, p. 404.
38 James, *American and English Writers*, pp. 462, 471.
39 Henry James, *Literary Criticism: French Writers, Other European Writers etc.* (New York: Library of America 1984) p. 67.
40 James, *Literary Criticism: French Writers*, p. 97.
41 James, *Literary Criticism: French Writers*, p. 126.
42 James, *Literary Criticism: French Writers*, p. 148.
43 Henry James, *The Golden Bowl*, New York edition, 1909 (Fairfield: Augustus M. Kelley, 1976) pp. xiv, xxi.

Chapter 2

1 Peter Brooks, *The Melodramatic Imagination* (New Haven & London: Harvard University Press, 1995) p. 5.
2 Honoré de Balzac, *Lost Illusions* (Harmondsworth: Penguin Books, 1971) p. 165.
3 Charles Dickens, *American Notes* (Oxford: Oxford University Press, 1957) p. 81.
4 *The Habits of Good Society: A Handbook for Ladies and Gentlemen* (London: James Hogg & Sons, 1859) p. 162. This book was published in New York, by Carleton, in 1869, according to Karen Halttunen.
5 Louisa Tuthill, *The Young Lady's Home* (Philadelphia: Lindsay & Blakiston, 1848) p. 264.
6 Lois Banner, *American Beauty* (New York: Alfred A. Knopf, 1983) p. 23.
7 Henry James, *Lady Barbarina etc.*, New York edition, 1908 (Fairfield: Augustus M. Kelley, 1976), p. 317.
8 Charlotte Stewart, 'The American Girl in Fiction', *Woman's World*, ed. Oscar Wilde (London: Cassell & Co., 1889) pp.101, 102.
9 Ian F. Bell, 'Displays of the Female: Formula and Flirtation in "Daisy Miller"', ed. N.H. Reeve, *Henry James: The Shorter Fiction* (London: Macmillan, 1997) p. 25.

10   Henry James, *Daisy Miller & An International Episode* (New York: Harper and Bros., 1892) p. 11. All further quotations are from this edition and cited in parentheses in the text.

11   Sweeney, p. 140 n., and Winner, pp. 87, 88.

12   Sweeney, pp. 140, 141.

13   Brian McFarlane, *Novel to Film* (Oxford: Clarendon Press, 1996) p. 161.

14   Hollander, p. 424.

15   Stewart, p. 102.

16   Henry James, 'Americans Abroad', ed. Maqbol Aziz, vol. 3, *The Tales of Henry James* (Oxford: Oxford University Press, 1984) pp. 520–21.

17   Banner, p. 169.

18   Mrs John Sherwood, *Manners and Social Usages* (New York: Harper & Bros., 1884) p. 8.

19   *Henry James Letters*, ed. Leon Edel, Vol. II (Cambridge, Mass.: Harvard University Press, 1975) pp. 303, 304. Mrs Lynn Linton had attacked a type of modern young Englishwoman as extravagant, immoral and unmannerly in an article in the *Saturday Review* of 1868.

20   Lionel Trilling, *The Liberal Imagination* (New York: Garden City, 1950) p. 200.

21   Henry James, 'Speech of American Women', in *Henry James on Culture*, ed. P. A. Walker (Lincoln: University of Nebraska Press, 1999) p. 72.

22   Henry James, 'Manners of American Women', in *Henry James on Culture*, p. 99.

23   Balzac, *Œuvres Diverses*, p. 184.

24   Henry James, *Lady Barbarina etc.*, New York edition, 1908 (Fairfield: Augustus M. Kelley, 1976) p. 412. All further quotations are from the reprint edition and cited in parentheses in the text.

25   C. Willett Cunnington, *English Women's Clothing in the Nineteenth Century* (London: Faber and Faber, 1938) p. 255.

26   C. W. Cunnington, *The Perfect Lady* (London: Max Parrish, 1948) p. 50.

27   William Dean Howells, *A Hazard of New Fortunes*, ed. Tony Tanner (Oxford: Oxford University Press, 1965) p. 443.

28   Hebe Dorsey, *Age of Opulence* (New York: Harry N. Abrams, 1986) pp. 126–7.

29   Huybertie Pruyn Hamlin, *An Albany Girlhood*, ed. Alice P. Kennedy (New York: Washington Park Press, 1990) p. 185.

30   'By a Lady', *Woman: her Dignity and Sphere*, (New York: The American Tract Company, 1870) p. 227.

31   Miss Oakey, *Beauty in Dress* (New York: Harper & Brothers, 1881) p. 56.

32   Oakey, p. 169.

33   The comic potential of the Rucks, as well as their latent sinister aspects, was recast in 1984 by Anita Brookner in her novel *Hotel du Lac*, set in a Swiss hotel, in which an English mother and daughter, having already bled their male to death, are now shopping across Europe on the proceeds.

34   Leon Edel, ed., *Letters of Henry James*, vol. 1 (Cambridge, Mass.: Harvard University Press, 1980) p. 347.

35   Ian F. Bell, p. 22.

36   Henry James, *Literary Criticism*, vol. 1, p. 23.

37   Henry James, *Literary Criticism*, vol. 1, p. 24.

38   J. C. Agnew, p. 82.

39   Henry James, *English Hours* (London: William Heinemann, 1905) p. 7.

40 Three years later, in 1882, James took up the question of Aurora Church's fate in 'The Point of View', a story written as a collection of letters recording a range of disparate experiences of America. The opening and closing letters are from Aurora. We learn that the European hunt for a 'gros bonnet' has failed and that Mrs Church has now invested in seven trunks of clothes for an assault on the cities of America's eastern seaboard. In Aurora's final letter, we learn that the dresses have counted for nothing – 'they all have better ones' – that Americans curiously expect to marry for love, which she doesn't; and that now the Churches are going to stake everything on a sortie into the American West to bag a pioneer – a sort of matrimonial Gold Rush. The Rucks, we hear, have simply disappeared.

41 Ian F. Bell, p. 30.

Chapter 3

1 Henry James, *Washington Square* (Harmondsworth: Penguin Classics, 1986) p. 38. All further quotations are from this edition and cited in parentheses in the text.

2 Alison Adburgham, *Shops and Shopping* (London: Allen & Unwin, 1981) p. 91.

3 Henry James, *The Europeans* (Harmondsworth: Penguin Classics, 1984) p. 33. All further references are to this edition and cited in parentheses in the text.

4 If James had a 'bad jacket' moment with Thackeray, as a child, then the seven-year-old Alice James had an even worse 'crinoline' moment when Thackeray 'suddenly laid his hand on her little flounced person and exclaimed with ludicrous horror: 'Crinoline? – I was suspecting it! So young and so depraved!' James, *Autobiography*, p. 52.

5 The Habits of Good Society, p. 182.

6 Elizabeth Hardwick, *Sight-Readings* (New York: Random House, 1998) p. 32.

7 Balzac, *Œuvres Diverses*, p. 158 (my translation).

8 Charles I. White, *Mission and Duties of Young Women* (translated from the French of Charles Sainte-Foi) (Baltimore: Kelly, Hedian & Piet, 1860), pp.107, 108.

9 Ian Bell, *Washington Square: Styles of Money* (New York: Twayne Publishers, 1993) p. 6.

10 Karen Halttunen, *Confidence Men and Painted Women: A Study of Middle-Class Culture in America, 1830–1870* (New Haven: Yale University Press, 1982) p. 174.

11 Tuthill, p. 101.

12 James at one point puts Catherine in her twenty-first year and shortly after makes her twenty-two. As a compromise I have made her twenty-one.

13 Banner, p. 18.

14 Cunnington, *English Women's Clothing*, p. 134.

15 Oakey, pp. 49, 164.

16 John F. Casson, *Politeness and Civility: Manners in 19th Century Urban America* (New York: Hill and Wang, 1990) p. 130.

17 Cunnington, *English Women's Clothing*, p. 131.

18 Oakey, p. 43.

19 Sherwood, p. 307.

20 Oakey, p. 169. See also Sherwood, p. 114
21 Richard Poirier, *The Comic Sense of Henry James* (London: Chatto & Windus, 1960) p. 166.
22 William Wyler's 1949 movie version of the novel, *The Heiress*, adds a good deal of non-Jamesian content to Ralph Richardson's (Dr Sloper) dialogue in order to bring out the contrast between Catherine and her dead mother.
23 Richard Poirier, p. 172.
24 Cunnington, *The Perfect Lady*, p. 20.
25 Banner, p. 21.
26 Cunnington, *English Women's Clothing*, p. 175.
27 Aileen Ribeiro, *Ingres in Fashion* (New Haven & London: Yale University Press, 1999) p. 188.
28 Mary Mc Carthy, ' "The Heiress": A Dramatisation', in *Washington Square and The Portrait of a Lady*, ed. Alan Shelston (London: Macmillan Press Casebook Series, 1984) pp. 43, 44.
29 W.D. Howells, *A Modern Instance* (Harmondsworth: Penguin Books, 1977) p. 417.
30 James, *Literary Criticism*, Vol. I, p. 609.
31 Balzac, *Eugénie Grandet*, transl. M.A. Crawford (Harmondsworth: Penguin Books, 1985) p.92. All further quotations are from this edition and are cited in parentheses in the text.
32 Honoré de Balzac, *Eugénie Grandet* (Paris: Flammarion, 1964) pp. 77, 78.
33 Balzac, *Œuvres Diverses*, p. 185 (my translation).

Chapter 4

1 Hyppolite Taine, *Notes on England* (London: Thames and Hudson, 1970) pp. 20, 46.
2 Anthony Mazzela, reviewing a home video version of the production for *The Henry James Review* (vol. 14, no. 2, 1993) felt that the production had somehow mislaid its central character: 'We watch Isabel Archer, but we do not see her' (p. 181).
3 Henry James, *The Complete Notebooks*, eds. Leon Edel and Lyall Powers (Oxford: Oxford University. Press, 1987) p. 13.
4 Dale M. Bauer, 'Jane Campion's Symbolic *Portrait*', in *The Henry James Review* (Spring 1997) p. 194.
5 Diane F. Sadoff, ' "Intimate Disarray": The Henry James Movies', in *The Henry James Review* (Fall 1998) p. 290.
6 Karen Michele Chandler, 'Agency and Social Restraint in Jane Campion's *The Portrait of a Lady*', in *The Henry James Review* (Spring 1997), p. 193.
7 Hollander, p. 376.
8 Brooks, p. 18.
9 Adeline Tintner, ' "In the Dusky, Crowded, Heterogeneous Back-shop of the Mind: The Iconography of *The Portrait of a Lady*', in *The Henry James Review* (Winter–Spring 1986) p. 146.
10 The Gothic, melodramatic qualities of the novel have been noted by Jacques Barzun, Dorothea Krook and more recently by Peter Brooks and Joseph Wiesenfarth.

11   Adeline Tintner's contribution to the *Henry James Review*'s special issue on *The Portrait of a Lady*, in 1986, drew attention to the way James revised his iconography for the 1908 edition. Among these revisions she believes that James included references to a current fad for collecting antique dress. She gives as an example Countess Gemini's memory of her mother 'wearing a Roman scarf thrown over a pair of bare shoulders'. James added in 1908 'timorously bared of their tight black velvet' and the phrase '(oh the old clothes!)' Tintner concludes that '[t]he last words make the difference in the later description of the costume of the 1820s'(155). James's use of dress is, however, more accurate than this. Long scarves or stoles, often decorated with classical motifs, were worn from the Empire period until mid-century when they were replaced by the cashmere shawl. Tight-sleeved black velvet, however, is more descriptive of the fashions of *c.*1840 than 1820 – a decade when sleeves ballooned and fabrics were light in both weight and colour. The subsequent reference to 'the American Corinne's' glossy ringlets reinforce the 1840 date, as does the novel's own chronology. Mme de Staël's Corinne operated as a model of independence for clever nineteenth-century women: in the early 1840s, Emerson described Margaret Fuller as the 'Yankee Corinne'. Though Mme de Stael's Corinne was a free-spirited figure of the Empire period, her Jamesian American successor is described as speaking 'softly and vaguely', sighing a great deal and 'not at all enterprising' (2. 228). She is, in fact, the American version of the Sentimental Woman of the 1840s; described by Karen Halttunen as an admirer of Republicanism, but 'less active than at any period in the century... absorbed in acquiring the art of expressing emotions by graceful attitudes rather than by movement' (Cunnington, *Englishwomen*, qtd. in Halttunen, p. 79). Working back from 1876 as the approximate date of Countess Gemini's remark, her childhood is unlikely to have taken place much before 1840. James may be reflecting a 1908 craze for antiques but he is also being as accurate about dress of the 1840s as he is in *The Europeans* and *Washington Square*.

12   Henry James, *The Portrait of a Lady*, New York edition, 1908 (Fairfield: Augustus M. Kelley, 1976) pp. 1, 16. All further quotations are from the reprint edition and are cited in parentheses in the text.

13   Hollander, p. 369.

14   Hollander, p. 377.

15   Henry James, *The Tales of Henry James*, Vol. I, ed. Maqbool Aziz (Oxford: Oxford University Press, 1973) p. 190.

16   Hollander, p. 376.

17   Balzac, *Œuvres Diverses*, p. 161.

18   Dorothea Krook, *The Ordeal of Consciousness* (Cambridge: Cambridge University Press, 1967) p. 23.

19   Tintner, p. 155.

20   *The Habits of Good Society*, p. 182.

21   Judith Woolf, *Henry James: The Major Novels* (Cambridge: Cambridge University Press, 1991) p. 47.

22   Joseph Wiesenfarth, *Gothic Manners and the Classic English Novel* (Madison: Wisconsin University Press, 1988) p. 138.

23   Ellen Moers, *The Dandy* (London: Secker & Warburg, 1960) pp. 34, 35.

24   Balzac, pp. 161, 163, 177.

25 Hollander, p. 377.
26 Lois Banner, *American Beauty* (New York: Alfred Knopf, 1983) p. 198.
27 Oakey, p. 11.
28 Margaret Oliphant, *Phoebe Junior* (London: Penguin Books and Virago, 1989) pp. 19, 20.
29 Cunnington, *The Perfect Lady* p. 44.
30 Cunnington, *Englishwomen's Clothing* p. 300.
31 John Harvey, *Men in Black* (London: Reaktion, 1995) p. 10.
32 Harvey, p. 14.
33 Philippe Perrot, p. 183.
34 Adeline Tintner sees Isabel's 'Plutonian richness' of costume here as foreshadowing her return to Osmond's house of darkness, and links it to Ralph's remark on his reluctance 'to be snatched away like Proserpine...to the Plutonian shades' ('The Iconography of *The Portrait of a Lady*', p. 155).
35 Agnew, p. 86.
36 The 'cuirass' bodice, fashionable in the late 1870s, did indeed – as Penelope Byrde notes – 'have the appearance of a piece of armour...The bodice was well boned on the inside to ensure a perfectly straight, smooth line' (Byrde, p. 72).
37 Banner, p. 171.
38 Henry James, *The Painter's Eye*, ed. J.L. Sweeney (Madison: Wisconsin University Press, 1989) pp. 142–3.
39 Henry James, *Hawthorne* (London: Macmillan, 1879) p. 42.
40 Mary Braddon, *Phantom Fortune* (London: Maxwell, 1884) p. 256.
41 Henry James, *Literary Criticism*, Vol. 1, p. 495.
42 Agnew, p. 85.
43 Krook, *Ordeal of Consciousness*, p. 51.
44 John Ruskin, 'Of Queens' Gardens', in *Sesame and Lilies* (London: Collins Press, n.d.) p. 119.
45 I. A. Richards, *Principles of Literary Criticism* (London: Routledge, 1964) p. 49.

Chapter 5

1 Henry James, *The Wings of the Dove*, New York edition, 1908 (Fairfield: Augustus M. Kelley, 1976) pp. 148, 147. All further quotations are from the reprint edition and cited in parentheses in the text.
2 'A Member of the Aristocracy', *Manners and Rules of Good Society* (London: Frederick Warne, 1892) p. 222.
3 Viscountess Florence Harberton, 'Mourning Clothes and Customs', *Woman's World* (August 1889) pp. 418–21.
4 Byrde, p. 159. Byrde also records an entry in a woman's magazine of 1890 suggesting that scent-bottles, purses and even bookmarks should be in mourning colours.
5 Joan Severa, *Dressed for the Photographer: Ordinary Americans & Fashion, 1840–1900* (Kent, Ohio: Kent State University Press, 1995) p. 467.
6 James, *The Real Thing* (London: Macmillan, 1893) pp. 268, 269.
7 James, *The Spoils of Poynton etc.*, New York edition, 1908 (Fairfield: Augustus M. Kelley, 1976) pp. 465–6.

8   Banner, pp. 163, 164.
9   Howells, *A Hazard of New Fortunes*, p. xii.
10 Banner, p. 176.
11 Hollander, p. 377.
12 Cunnington, *The Perfect Lady*, p. 64.
13 Viola Hopkins Winner, *Henry James and the Visual Arts* (Charlottesville, University Press of Virginia, 1970), p. 83. The identification of Lord Mark's Bronzino with the Panciatichi portrait was first made by Miriam Allott, 'The Bronzino Portrait in *The Wings of the Dove*', *Modern Language Notes*, 68 (1953), pp. 23–5. Adeline Tintner has, however, also pointed out that there was a Bronzino female portrait at Baron Rothschild's country house, Waddesdon, a house that James was familiar with.
14 Tony Tanner, *Henry James and the Art of Nonfiction* (Athens and London: University of Georgia Press, 1995) p. 13.
15 Judith Woolf, *The Major Novels of Henry James* (Cambridge: Cambridge University Press, 1991), pp. 113–14.
16 Edith Wharton, *The House of Mirth* (Harmondsworth: Penguin Books, 1985) p. 134.
17 As Judith Funston points out, James's association of his own art with portraiture was not unqualified: if his 1890 essay on Daumier praises the artist, it is more guarded about his art – 'Art is an embalmer... it prolongs, it preserves, it consecrates, it raises from the dead' (Sweeney, p. 238). The point is developed by Funston in 'James's Portrait of the Artist as a Liar', *Studies in Short Fiction* 28 (1989) pp. 431–8.
18 John Harvey, *Men in Black* (London: Reaktion Books, 1995), p. 43.
19 Cunnington, *The Perfect Lady*, p. 69.
20 Cunnington, *The Perfect Lady*, pp. 61, 64.
21 Brooks, p. 5.
22 Eliza Lynn Linton, 'In Sickness', *The Girl of the Period and Other Essays* (London: Richard Bentley, 1883) p. 211.
23 Mrs J. E. Panton, *Within Four Walls* (London: The Gentlewoman, 1893) pp. 165, 171.
24 Quoted in Aileen Ribeiro, *Dress and Morality* (London: Batsford, 1986) p. 148.
25 Sherwood, pp. 132, 129.
26 Sherwood, p. 131.
27 Frederick Crews, *The Tragedy of Manners* (Connecticut: Archon Books, 1971), p. 72.
28 Maurice Maeterlinck, *Théâtre*, I (Paris: Bibliothèque Charpentier, 1925) p. 210.
29 Adeline Tintner, *The Museum World of Henry James* (Ann Arbor, Michigan: UMI Research Press, 1986) p. 140.
30 Byrde, p. 171.
31 Henry James, *An International Episode and Other Stories*, ed. Gorley Putt (Harmondsworth: Penguin, 1985) pp. 13, 16, 19, 28, 29.
32 Fred Kaplan, p. 467.
33 The confusion possible between ghosts and girls in white provided the dramatic opening to Wilkie Collins' novel *The Woman in White*. John Harvey develops this point in Chapter 6 of his book, *Men in Black*.
34 Tanner, *Nonfiction*, p. 10.

35   Sweeney, pp. 256–7.
36   James, *Autobiography*, p. 544.
37   Lyndall Gordon, *A Private Life of Henry James* (London: Chatto & Windus, 1998) p. 1.
38   Henry James, *Complete Notebooks*, p. 106.
39   John Berger, *Ways of Seeing* (London: BBC and Penguin Books, 1980) p. 46.
40   Eugenia Münster, 'actress', adventuress and prototype for Kate, begins and ends her role in *The Europeans* (1878) also in front of a mirror.
41   Hollander, p. 393.
42   Henry James, *The Critical Muse*, ed. Roger Gard (Harmondsworth: Penguin Books, 1987), p. 195.

Chapter 6

1   Henry James, *The Princess Casamassima*, New York edition, 1908 (Fairfield: Augustus M. Kelley, 1976) 1, p. xxii. All further quotations are from the reprint edition and cited in parentheses in the text.
2   Mark Selzer, 'Surveillance in *The Princess Casamassima*' in *Henry James: A Collection of Critical Essays*, ed. Ruth Bernard Yeazell (New Jersey: Prentice Hall, 1994) p. 100.
3   Fred Miller Robinson, *The Man in the Bowler Hat* (Chapel Hill: University of North Carolina Press, 1993) p. 16.
4   Richard Heath, 'Politics in Dress', in *Woman's World*, ed. Oscar Wilde (London: Cassell & Co. 1889) pp. 399, 400.
5   Michael Carter, *Putting a Face on Things* (Sydney: Power Publications, 1997) pp. 111–12.
6   The hat makes one of its last significant appearances in literature in the novels and plays of Samuel Beckett.
7   Gwen Raverat, *Period Piece* (London: Faber & Faber, 1952) p. 259.
8   Balzac, *Œuvres Diverses*, pp. 180, 181 (my translation).
9   See, for example, Richard Sheridan's *The School for Scandal*, Act IV.
10 Mike Fischer, 'The Jamesian Revolution in *The Princess Casamasssima*', *The Henry James Review* 9, ii (1988) p. 94. Fischer believes that Hyacinth consciously 'swaddles that past in disguises in order to "cover...up" his character.'
11 Philip Sicker, *Love and the Quest for Identity* (New Jersey: Princeton University Press, 1980) p. 66.
12 Stella Mary Newton, *Health, Art and Reason* (London: John Murray, 1974) Plate 45. The Vicar of St Jude's Church, Whitechapel arranged exhibitions of paintings in the church schoolhouse in 1881 and 1882, for the benefit of the largely working-class population of the area.
13 Sarah Levitt, *Fashion in Photographs, 1880–1900* (London: Batsford/National Portrait Gallery, 1991) p. 128.
14 Although the terms 'hat' and 'bonnet' are often interchangeable, the bonnet is distinguished from the hat by being tied under the chin with ribbons. The bonnet was also worn further back on the head and until the 1880s, when it became small and heavily decorated, its brim usually curved around the face.

15 Cunnington, *The Perfect Lady*, p. 54.
16 Cunnington, *Feminine Attitudes in the 19th Century* (London: Heinemann, 1935) p. 267.
17 Alison Adburgham, *Shops and Shopping* (London: Allen and Unwin, 1981) pp. 106–7. Adburgham comments on these old ladies' memories – 'What magic is there in millinery that makes it immortal? Hats must possess some poetic quality that the romantic heart . . . remembers.'
18 Eugen Weber, *France, Fin de Siècle* (Cambridge, Mass.: Belknap Press, 1986) p. 81.
19 Bill Lancaster, *The Department Store* (London: Leicester University Press, 1995) p. 64. The other two institutions of display were the museum and the exhibition. In Emile Zola's *Au Bonheur du Dames* the visual effects contrived by a Paris department store inspire in its customers an almost religious ecstasy.
20 Carter, p. 142.
21 Joel H. Kaplan and Sheila Stowell, *Theatre and Fashion* (Cambridge: Cambridge University Press, 1994), p. 1.
22 Nowell-Smith, p. 188.
23 Henry James, *Collected Travel Writings* (New York: The Library of America, 1984) p. 492.
24 Kenneth Graham, *Henry James: A Literary Life* (London: Macmillan, 1995) p. 32.
25 Charles Anderson, *Person, Place, and Thing in Henry James's Novels* (Durham, N. Carolina: Duke University Press, 1977) pp. 154–60. Adeline Tintner, *The Museum World of Henry James*, pp. 75–6, 131.
26 John Keats, *The Major Works*, ed. Elizabeth Cook (Oxford: Oxford University Press, 1990) pp. 75, 76.
27 Ian Jack, *Keats and the Mirror of Art* (Oxford: Clarendon Press, 1967) p. 146.
28 Marie Simon, *Fashion in Art* (London: Zwemmer, 1995) pp. 84, 85.
29 Levitt, p. 75.
30 Cunnington, *English Women's Clothing*, p. 359.
31 Newton, p. 147.
32 Hyacinth asks Paul Muniment, a committed socialist, to visit the Princess. Advising him to buy gloves for his work-stained hands, Hyacinth then changes his mind and adds: 'No, you oughtn't to do that. She wants to see dirty hands' (1. 230). Muniment shrewdly remarks that Christina is making a game of Hyacinth.
33 Philip Grover, *Henry James and the French Novel* (New York: Barnes & Noble, 1973) p. 64.
34 Henry James, *Roderick Hudson*, New York edition (Fairfield: Augustus M. Kelley, 1976) pp. 196, 369.
35 Rebecca West, *Henry James* (London: Nisbet & Co., 1916) p. 77.
36 As one of the first British working-class MPs, Keir Hardie entered Parliament in 1892 wearing a cap and a rough tweed suit. However, as Stella Mary Newton and Sarah Levitt both point out, this outfit has more to do with 'reformed' dress than working-class dress.
37 Georgine de Courtois, *Women's Headdress and Hairstyles in England from A.D. 600 to the Present Day* (London: Batsford, 1986) p. 136.
38 Levitt, p. 60.

39   Mrs Humphry Ward, *Robert Ellesmere* (Oxford: Oxford University Press, 1987) p. 503.
40   Mrs Humphry Ward, *Marcella* (London: Virago Press, 1984) p. 398.
41   'It was noticeable during these years that economy was striking the perfect lady very hard.' Cunnington, *The Perfect Lady*, p. 53.
42   Newton, p. 131.
43   Elizabeth Allen, *A Woman's Place in Henry James* (London: Macmillan, 1984) p. 97.
44   The figure of Liberty, in Delacroix's *Liberty Leading the People*, is wearing the Phrygian cap, emblem of the worker and traveller in the representational arts of ancient Greece and Rome.
45   Edward Wagenknecht, *Eve and Henry James* (Oklahoma: Oklahoma University Press, 1978) p. 61.
46   Lionel Trilling, *The Liberal Imagination* (New York: Garden City, 1950) p. 89.
47   Henry James, *Collected Travel Writings*, p. 486.
48   Henry James, *The Finer Grain* (London: Methuen, 1910) pp. 194, 197.
49   Sarah Levitt quotes an Edwardian memoir of the Salford slums: 'for men with any claim at all to standing, the bowler, or "Billy Pot" was compulsory wear. Only the lower types wore caps' (Levitt, p. 128). Fred Miller Robinson, in his history of the bowler hat, makes it clear that the bowler arrived at its twentieth-century eminence from both upper and lower-class sources, and that the hat continued to cross class boundaries throughout its history. It was both protective and progressive – gentlemanly country wear, which like so much sports wear transferred to city fashion; protective industrial wear, which quickly became the sign of the successful, upwardly-mobile worker, and adopted as well by those who wished to display their modernity and their democratic credentials: 'the bowler hat is a sign of modern times ... the times of the emerging and expanding modern middle classes' (Miller Robinson, p. 4). The 'pot' hat features regularly in the novels of George Gissing of working- and lower middle-class life in the 1880s and 1890s.
50   Henry James, *The Ghostly Tales*, ed. Leon Edel (New Brunswick: Rutgers University Press, 1948) p. 167.
51   Michael Ginsberg, *Economies of Change* (Stanford: Stanford University Press, 1996) p. 178
52   Carter, p. 113.
53   Trilling, p. 76.
54   Carter, p. 113.
55   Quoted in Miller Robinson, p. 167.
56   James, *Collected Travel Writings*, p. 505.
57   Trilling, p. 62.
58   Trilling, p. 210.
59   Miller Robinson, pp. 45–6.

Chapter 7

1   Henry James, *Literary Criticism: French Writers etc.*, p. 652.
2   Henry James, 'Project of a Novel', in *The Ambassadors*, ed. S.P. Rosenbaum (New York: W.W. Norton, 1994) p. 386.

3 Henry James, *The Ambassadors*, ed. S.P. Rosenbaum (New York: W.W. Norton, 1994) p. 132. All further quotations are from this edition and are cited in parentheses in the text.

4 E.M. Forster, 'Pattern in *The Ambassadors*', in Henry James, *The Ambassadors*, ed. S.P. Rosenbaum (New York: W.W. Norton, 1994), p. 427.

5 I use the substantive 'undress' as it was commonly used in the seventeenth and eighteenth centuries to describe informal female dress, according to the Oxford English Dictionary. It seems to have been at first interchangeable with 'dishabillé' or 'déshabillé', which then replaced 'undress' in the nineteenth century and was still being used in this sense in the mid-twentieth century.

6 Gustave Flaubert, *Sentimental Education*, trans. by Robert Baldick (Harmondsworth: Penguin Books, 1964) p. 18.

7 Philip Grover, p. 153.

8 Richard A. Hocks, *The Ambassadors: Consciousness, Culture, Poetry* (New York: Twayne Publishers, 1997) pp. 81–2.

9 Susan Griffin, *The Historical Eye* (Boston: Northeastern University Press, 1991) pp. 47, 54, 44.

10 Griffin, p. 43.

11 Grover, p. 163.

12 James, *Notebooks*, p. 189.

13 Philip Horne, ed., *Henry James: A Life in Letters* (London: Penguin Press, 1999) pp. 339–43.

14 Carren Kaston, *Imagination and Desire* (New Jersey: Rutgers University Press, 1984) pp. 91, 93.

15 Cunnington, *English Women's Clothing*, p. 413.

16 Elaine Kilmurray and Richard Ormond, eds., *John Singer Sargent* (London: Tate Gallery Publishing, 1998) p. 157.

17 *The Gibson Girl and her America*, selected by E.V. Gillon Jr (New York: Dover Publications, 1969) p. 40.

18 Griffin, pp. 48, 49.

19 Max O'Rell, *Her Royal Highness Woman* (London: Chatto and Windus, 1902) p. 86.

20 Henry James, *The Sacred Fount* (London: Methuen & Co., 1901) p. 199.

21 F. K. Stanzel, *A Theory of Narrative*, trans. by Charlotte Goedsche (Cambridge: Cambridge University Press, 1984) p. 122.

22 Henry James, *The Princess Casamassima*, p. xvi.

23 Hebe Dorsey, p. 128.

24 Cunnington, *English Women's Clothing*, pp. 410, 414.

25 Maud Ellman, "The Intimate Difference" in Henry James, *The Ambassadors* (New York: W. W. Norton & Company, 1994) pp. 506–7.

26 Krook, *The Ambassadors*, p. 11.

27 Krook, *The Ambassadors*, p. 11.

28 Krook, *The Ambassadors*, pp. 114, 115.

29 Martha Banta, "The Excluded Seven", p. 356.

30 Cunnington, *English Women's Clothing*, p. 408.

31 Cunnington, *English Women's Clothing*, p. 402.

32 O'Rell, p. 85.

33 Quoted in Banta, 'The Excluded Seven', p. 257.

34 Hollander, *Seeing Through Clothes*, p. 328.
35 Quoted in Cunnington, *The Perfect Lady*, p. 62.
36 Krook, *The Ambassadors*, p. 59. Unhappily at this point there is either a major typographical error on the part of the publisher, AMS, or an overlooked hiatus in Krook's manuscript, which was unfinished at her death, for the lines that follow make no sense.
37 Cunnington, *English Women's Clothing*, pp. 402, 403.
38 Cunnington, *English Women's Clothing*, pp. 411, 413.
39 Krook, *Henry James's 'The Ambassadors'*, p. 58.
40 Balzac, 'Traité de la Vie Elégante', p. 168 (my translation).
41 Nina Auerbach, *Woman and the Demon* (Cambridge, Mass.: Harvard University Press, 1982) p. 96.
42 George Moore, *A Drama in Muslin* (Gerrards Cross: Colin Smythe, 1981) pp. 172–3.
43 James, *Literary Criticism: American and English Writers*, p. 608.
44 F. R. Leavis, *The Great Tradition* ([1948] Harmondsworth: Penguin Books, 1974.) p. 186.
45 Joseph Warren Beach, *The Method of Henry James*, Introduction, p. xlviii (Philadelphia: Albert Saifer, 1954). Quoted in Henry James, *The Ambassadors* (New York: W. W. Norton, 1994), p. 440.
46 Hollander, pp. 369, 377.
47 Nicola Bradbury, *Henry James: The Later Novels* (Oxford: Clarendon Press, 1979) p. 42.
48 Marie would, anyway, be unlikely to have brought a shawl. Shawls, except for the working class, had gone out of fashion (see Chapter 8). She would have had a jacket, a stole or possibly a boa. James is using the word in the general sense of a shoulder covering, I imagine.
49 An unpublished thesis by Dorothy Behling, 'French Couturiers and Artist/Illustrators: 1900 to 1925', notes 'a definite trend towards an empire silhouette' in the years between 1902 and 1908. Quoted in Valerie Steele, *Paris Fashion: A Cultural History* (New York: Oxford University Press, 1988) p. 223.
50 Henry James, *The Sense of the Past* New York edition, 1909 (Fairfield: Augustus M.Kelley, 1976), p. 280.
51 J. Tulard, *Les Salons de Peinture de la Révolution française* (Paris, 1989) p. 47, quoted in Aileen Ribeiro, *The Art of Dress* (London: Yale University Press, 1995) p. 89.
52 Aileen Ribeiro, *The Art of Dress*, pp. 89, 90.
53 Henry James, 'Project of a Novel', p. 399.
54 Henry James, *The Awkward Age*, p. 239.
55 Henry James, 'Project of a Novel', pp. 386–7.
56 Daniel Mark Fogel, *Henry James and the Structure of the Romantic Imagination* (Baton Rouge: Louisiana State University Press, 1981) p. 3.
57 Henry James, *The Portrait of a Lady*, 1, p. 258.

Chapter 8

1 Kenneth McConkey, *Edwardian Portraits* (Woodbridge, Suffolk: The Antique Collectors' Club, 1987) p. 15.

2 Hebe Dorsey, p. 6.
3 Cunnington, *The Perfect Lady*, p. 65.
4 James Laver, *Edwardian Promenade* (London: Edward Hulton, 1958) pp. 4, 5.
5 Alison Gernsheim, *Victorian and Edwardian Fashion: A Photographic Survey* (New York: Dover Publications, 1981) p. 85.
6 Henry James, *The Golden Bowl*, New York edition, 1908 (New Jersey: Augustus M. Kelley, 1971) p. v. All further quotations are from the reprint edition and cited in parentheses in the text.
7 Phyllis van Slyck, '"An innate preference for the represented subject": Portraiture and Knowledge in *The Golden Bowl*', *Henry James Review*, 15 (1994) p. 186.
8 Cunnington, *The Perfect Lady*, p. 64.
9 Katrina Rolley, *Fashion in Photographs: 1900–1920* (London: Batsford, 1992) p. 28.
10 Stephen Calloway, ed., *The House of Liberty* (London: Thames and Hudson, 1992) p. 73.
11 Poiret's Chinese coat, as well as later versions by Worth, Paquin, Fortuny and the Callot Soeurs were on display at an exhibition at the Museum of Textiles, Kyoto, Japan, June, 1994
12 Laver, *Edwardian Promenade*, p. 156.
13 Carren Kaston, *Imagination and Desire in the Novels of Henry James* (New Jersey: Rutgers University Press, 1984) p. 157.
14 Paul Poiret, *My First Fifty Years*, quoted in *Four Hundred Years of Fashion*, ed. Natalie Rothstein (London: V. & A. Publications, 1999) p. 82.
15 Adré Marshall, *The Turn of the Mind* (London: Associated University Presses, 1998) p. 154.
16 Peter Rawlings, 'Henry James and the Kodak Factor', in *Henry James: Essays on Art and Drama*, ed. Peter Rawlings (Aldershot: Scolar Press, 1996) p. 12.
17 Hollander, pp. 328, 333, 330.
18 Rolley, p. 50, pl. 42.
19 Hollander, pp. 184, 185.
20 C. Willett Cunnington, quoted in Laver, *Edwardian Promenade* (London: Edward Hutton, 1958) pp. 147–8.
21 Jane Ashelford, *The Art of Dress* (London: The National Trust, 1996) p. 242.
22 Wharton, *The House of Mirth*, p. 12.
23 R. B. J. Wilson, *Henry James's Ultimate Narrative* (St. Lucia, Australia: University of Queensland Press, 1981) p. 129.
24 Tintner, *The Museum World of Henry James*, pp. 212–19.
25 Krook, *The Ordeal of Consciousness*, pp. 12, 13.
26 Woolf, p. 136.
27 Levitt, p. 18, pl. 6.
28 James Laver, *Taste and Fashion* (London: Harrap, 1937) p. 103.
29 James, *Literary Criticism: French Writers*, p. 148.
30 Kate Croy's description of herself in *The Wings of the Dove*, 1, p. 28.
31 James, *Essays on Literature*, p. 107.
32 de Courtais, p. 134.
33 George Eliot, *Middlemarch* (London: Blackwood & Sons, 1874) Chapter 74.
34 Maggie's unease in her dress would have been understood by Gwen Raverat, who as a child found all the fashions from 1890 to 1914 'preposterous,

hideous and uncomfortable. . . . Except for the most small-waisted, naturally dumb-bell-shaped females, the ladies never seemed at ease'. Corsets in particular drove her to stubborn rebellion. Gwen Raverat, *Period Piece* (London: Faber and Faber, 1952) pp. 255, 258.

35 Quoted in Quentin Bell, *On Human Finery* (London: Hogarth Press, 1976), p. 19.
36 Laver, *Edwardian Promenade*, pp. 149–50.
37 Martha Banta also senses that Maggie is somewhat under- endowed. Martha Banta, *Henry James and the Occult* (Bloomington: Indiana University Press, 1972) p. 85.
38 Elizabeth Deeds Ermarth, *Realism and Consensus in the English Novel* (New Jersey: Princeton University Press, 1983) p. 264.
39 Ermarth, pp. 266, 265.
40 Leo Bersani, *A Future for Astyanax* (London: Marion Boyars, 1978) p. 147.
41 Sallie Sears, *The Negative Imagination* (Ithaca: Cornell University Press, 1963) p. 221.
42 Sears, p. 192.
43 Fogel, p. 3.

Chapter 9

1 M. Cox and R. A. Gilbert, eds., *The Oxford Book of Ghost Stories* (Oxford: Oxford University Press, 1986) pp. xv, ix.
2 James, *Literary Criticism*, Vol. 1, p. 93.
3 Martha Banta, *Henry James and the Occult* (Blomington: Indiana University Press, 1972), p. 168.
4 James altered Viola's name to Rosalind in his revision of 1885. These two Shakespearean heroines share cross-dressing habits and take the lead in the courtship.
5 Henry James, *Complete Stories, 1864–1874* (New York: Library of America, 1999) p. 247. All further quotations are from this edition and cited in parentheses in the text.
6 Hollander, pp. 391–2.
7 T. J. Lustig, *Henry James and the Ghostly* (Cambridge: Cambridge University Press, 1994) p. 55.
8 Henry James, *Literary Criticism*, Vol. 1, p. 742.
9 Henry James, *Literary Criticism*, Vol. 1, p. 679.
10 Quoted in Philip Horne, *Henry James: A Life in Letters*, p. 360.
11 James may here be remembering the shock effects of Prosper Mérimée's story 'The Venus of L'Ille', which he translated at the age of eighteen. In this story of the rivalry between an ancient Roman bronze Venus and a young, nineteenth-century bride, the bridegroom is found dead with the marks of a metal body upon him. James returned to Mérimée's story again in 'The Last of the Valerii'.
12 Henry James, *Complete Stories, 1874–1884* (New York: Library of America, 1999) p. 181.
13 Henry James, *The American*, p. xiv.

14 Henry James, *Complete Stories: 1884–1891* (New York: Library of America, 1999) p. 859. All further quotations are from this edition and cited in parentheses in the text.
15 Henry James, *The Altar of the Dead etc.*, New York edition, 1909 (Fairfield: Augustus M. Kelley, 1976) p. xxiv.
16 Banta, p. 114.
17 Peter Beidler, *Ghosts, Demons and Henry James* (Columbia: University of Missouri Press, 1989) p. 114.
18 Henry James, *The Aspern Papers etc.*, New York edition, 1909 (Fairfield: Augustus M. Kelley, 1976), p. xix. All further quotations are from this edition and cited in parentheses in the text.
19 Byrde, p. 97.
20 Henry James, *The Altar of the Dead etc.*, p. 438. All further quotations are from the reprint edition and cited in parentheses in the text.
21 Quoted in Cox and Gilbert, p. x.
22 Banta, p. 151.
23 Henry James, *The Sense of the Past*, New York edition, 1909 (Fairfield: Augustus M.Kelley, 1976) p. 73. All further quotations are from the reprint edition and cited in parentheses in the text.
24 Henry James, *The Aspern Papers etc.*, p. x.
25 Henry James, *The American*, p. xv.
26 Henry James, *Literary Criticism*, Vol. 2, p. 132
27 Henry James, *Literary Criticism*, Vol. 1, p. 1343.
28 Henry James, *Literary Criticism*, Vol. 1, pp. 1080, 1083.
29 Roland Barthes, *The Fashion System*, trans. M. Ward and R. Howard (New York: Hill, 1983) p. 5.
30 Barthes, 'The Diseases of Costume', in *Critical Essays* (Evanston: Northwestern University Press, 1979) p. 46.
31 Henry James, *Literary Criticism*, Vol. 2, p. 132.
32 Roland Barthes, 'The Diseases of Costume', p. 42
33 Bowen, *Collected Impressions*, p. 112.
34 Georges Perec, *Species of Spaces and Other Pieces* (London: Penguin Books, 1997) p. 156.
35 Henry James, *Princess Casamassima*, 1, p. xxii.

Bibliography

Adburgham, Alison, *Shops and Shopping* (London: Allen & Unwin, 1981).

—— *Shopping in Style* (London: Thames and Hudson, 1979).

Allen, Elizabeth, *A Woman's Place in Henry James* (London: Macmillan, 1984).

Anderson, Charles, *Person, Place, and Thing in Henry James's Novels* (Durham, N. C.: Duke University Press, 1977).

Ashelford, Jane, *The Art of Dress* (London: The National Trust, 1996).

Auerbach, Nina, *Woman and the Demon* (Cambridge: Harvard University Press, 1982).

Balzac, Honoré de, 'Traité de la Vie Elégante', in *Oeuvres Diverses* (Paris: Louis Conard, 1938).

—— *Lost Illusions* (Harmondsworth: Penguin Books, 1971).

—— *Eugénie Grandet*, transl. M.A. Crawford (Harmondsworth: Penguin Books, 1985).

—— *Eugénie Grandet* (Paris: Flammarion, 1964).

Banner, Lois, *American Beauty* (New York: Alfred A. Knopf, 1983).

Banta, Martha, *Henry James and the Occult* (Bloomington: Indiana University Press, 1972).

Barthes, Roland, *The Fashion System* [1967] (New York: Hill, 1983).

—— *Critical Essays* (Evanston: Northwestern University Press, 1979).

Beidler, Peter, *Ghosts, Demons and Henry James* (Columbia: University of Missouri Press, 1989).

Bell, Ian, *Washington Square: Styles of Money* (New York: Twayne Publishers, 1993).

Bell, Millicent, *Meaning in Henry James* (Cambridge, Mass.: Harvard University Press, 1991).

Bell, Quentin, *On Human Finery* (London: Hogarth Press, 1976).

Berger, John, *Ways of Seeing* (London: BBC & Penguin Books, 1980).

Bersani, Leo, *A Future for Astyanax* (London: Marion Boyars, 1978).

Bowen, Elizabeth, *Collected Impressions* (New York: Alfred Knopf, 1950).

Bradbury, Nicola, *Henry James: The Later Novels* (Oxford: Clarendon Press, 1979).

Braddon, Mary, *Phantom Fortune* (London: Maxwell, 1884).

Brooks, Peter, *The Melodramatic Imagination* (New Haven & London: Harvard University Press, 1995).

Calloway, Stephen ed., *The House of Liberty* (London: Thames and Hudson, 1992).

Carlyle, Thomas, *Sartor Resartus* (Oxford: Clarendon Press, 1913).

Carter, Michael, *Putting a Face on Things* (Sydney: Power Publications, 1997).

Casson, John F., *Politeness and Civility: Manners in 19th Century Urban America* (New York: Hill and Wang, 1990).

Chatman, Seymour, *The Later Style of Henry James* (New York: Barnes and Noble, 1972).

Courtais, Georgine de, *Women's Headdress and Hairstyles in England from A.D. 600 to the Present Day* (London: Batsford, 1986).

Cox, M. and Gilbert, R. A. eds., *The Oxford Book of Ghost Stories* (Oxford: Oxford University Press, 1986).

Crews, Frederick, *The Tragedy of Manners* (Connecticut: Archon Books, 1971).

Cunnington, C. Willett, *English Women's Clothing in the Nineteenth Century* (London: Faber and Faber, 1938).

—— *The Perfect Lady* (London: Max Parrish & Co. Ltd., 1948).

—— *Feminine Attitudes in the 19th Century* (London: Heinemann, 1935).

Dickens, Charles, *American Notes* (Oxford: Oxford University Press, 1957).

Dorsey, Hebe, *Age of Opulence* (New York: Harry N. Abrams,1986).

Dupee, F.W., *Henry James: Autobiography* (London: W.H. Allen, 1956).

Eliot, George, *Middlemarch* (London: Blackwood & Sons, 1874).

Edel, Leon, ed., *Henry James Letters* (Cambridge, Mass.: Harvard University Press, 1975).

—— *The Life of Henry James*, 2 vols. (Harmondsworth: Penguin Books, 1977).

Ermarth, Elizabeth Deeds, *Realism and Consensus in the English Novel* (New Jersey: Princeton University Press, 1983).

Flaubert, Gustave, *Sentimental Education*, trans. by Robert Baldick (Harmondsworth: Penguin Books, 1964).

Fogel, Daniel Mark, *Henry James and the Structure of the Romantic Imagination* (Baton Rouge: Louisiana State University Press, 1981).

Fox, R.W. and Lears, T.J. Jackson, eds., *The Culture of Consumption* (New York: Pantheon Books, 1983).

Freedman, Jonathan, *Professions of Taste* (Stanford: Stanford University Press, 1990).

Gernsheim, Alison, *Victorian and Edwardian Fashion: A Photographic Survey* (New York: Dover Publications, 1981).

Gillon, E.V. Jr., *The Gibson Girl and her America* (New York: Dover Publications, 1969).

Ginsberg, Michael, *Economies of Change* (Stanford: Stanford University Press, 1996).

Gordon, Lyndall, *A Private Life of Henry James* (London: Chatto & Windus, 1998).

Graham, Kenneth, *Henry James: A Literary Life* (London: Macmillan, 1995).

Griffin, Susan, *The Historical Eye* (Boston: Northeastern University Press, 1991).

Grover, Philip, *Henry James and the French Novel* (New York: Barnes & Noble, 1973).

Habegger, Alfred, *Henry James and the 'Woman Business'* (Cambridge: Cambridge University Press, 1988).

The Habits of Good Society: A Handbook for Ladies and Gentlemen (London: James Hogg & Sons, 1859).

Halttunen, Karen, *Confidence Men and Painted Women: A Study of Middle-Class Culture in America, 1830–1870* (New Haven: Yale University Press, 1982).

Hamlin, Huybertie Pruyn, ed., Alice P. Kennedy, *An Albany Girlhood* (New York: Washington Park Press, 1990).

Hardwick, Elizabeth, *Sight-Readings* (New York: Random House, 1998).

Harvey, John , *Men in Black* (London: Reaktion, 1995).

Hocks, Richard A., *The Ambassadors: Consciousness, Culture, Poetry* (New York: Twayne Publishers, 1997).

Holland, Lawrence, *The Expense of Vision* (Princeton: Princeton University Press, 1964).

Hollander, Anne, *Seeing Through Clothes* (Berkeley: University of California Press, 1993).
—— *Sex and Suits* (New York: Kodansha, 1994).
Horne, Philip, ed., *Henry James: A Life in Letters* (London: Penguin Press, 1999).
Howells, William Dean, *A Hazard of New Fortunes* (Oxford: Oxford University Press, 1965).
—— *A Modern Instance* (Harmondsworth: Penguin Books, 1977).
Irwin, Michael, *Picturing in the 19th Century Novel* (London: George Allen, 1979).
Jack, Ian, *Keats and the Mirror of Art* (Oxford: Clarendon Press, 1967).
James, Henry, *The Altar of the Dead etc.*, New York edition, 1909 (Fairfield: Augustus M. Kelley, 1976).
—— *The Ambassadors*, ed. S.P. Rosenbaum (New York: W.W. Norton, 1994).
—— *The American*, New York edition, 1908 (New Jersey: Augustus Kelley, 1976).
—— *The Aspern Papers etc.*, New York edition, 1909 (Fairfield: Augustus M. Kelley, 1976).
—— *The Awkward Age*, New York edition, 1909 (Fairfield: Augustus M. Kelley, 1976).
—— *Lady Barbarina etc.*, New York edition, 1908 (Fairfield: Augustus M. Kelley, 1976).
—— *Collected Travel Writings* (New York: Library of America, 1984).
—— *The Complete Notebooks*, eds. Leon Edel and Lyall Powers (Oxford: Oxford University Press, 1987).
—— *Complete Stories, 1864–1874* (New York: Library of America, 1999).
—— *Complete Stories, 1874–1884* (New York: Library of America, 1999).
—— *Complete Stories: 1884–1891* (New York: Library of America, 1999).
—— *Complete Stories: 1892–1898* (New York: Library of America, 1996)
—— *Complete Stories: 1898–1910* (New York: Library of America, 1996)
—— *The Critical Muse* (Harmondsworth: Penguin Books, 1987).
—— *Daisy Miller & An International Episode* (New York: Harper & Bros., 1892).
—— *English Hours* (London: William Heinemann, 1905).
—— *The Europeans* (Harmondsworth: Penguin Classics, 1984).
—— *The Finer Grain* (London: Methuen, 1910).
—— *The Ghostly Tales*, ed. Leon Edel (New Brunswick: Rutgers University Press, 1948).
—— *The Golden Bowl*, New York edition, 1909 (Fairfield: Augustus M. Kelley, 1976).
—— *Hawthorne* (London: Macmillan, 1879).
—— *An International Episode and Other Stories* (Harmondsworth: Penguin, 1985).
—— *Letters*, Vols. I–IV, ed. Leon Edel (Cambridge, Mass.: Harvard University Press, 1980).
—— *Literary Criticism: American and English Writers* (New York: Library of America, 1984).
—— *Literary Criticism: French Writers, Other European Writers* (New York: Library of America, 1984).
—— *The Portrait of a Lady*, New York edition, 1908 (Fairfield: Augustus M. Kelley, 1976).
—— *The Princess Casamassima*, New York edition, 1908 (Fairfield: Augustus M. Kelley, 1976).
—— *The Real Thing* (London: Macmillan, 1893).
—— *Roderick Hudson*, New York edition (Fairfield: Augustus M. Kelley, 1976).

—— *The Sacred Fount* (London: Methuen & Co., 1901).

—— *The Sense of the Past*, New York edition, 1909 (Fairfield: Augustus M. Kelley, 1976).

—— *The Spoils of Poynton etc.*, New York edition, 1908 (Fairfield: Augustus M. Kelley, 1976).

—— *The Tales of Henry James* (Oxford: Oxford University Press, 1984).

—— *Washington Square* (Harmondsworth: Penguin Classics, 1986).

—— *What Maisie Knew*, New York edition, 1908 (Fairfield: Augustus M. Kelley, 1979).

—— *The Wings of the Dove*, New York edition, 1908 (Fairfield: Augustus M. Kelley, 1976).

Kaplan, Fred, *Henry James: The Imagination of Genius* (New York: William Morrow, 1992).

Kaplan, Joel H. and Stowell, Sheila, *Theatre and Fashion* (Cambridge: Cambridge University Press, 1994).

Kaston, Carren, *Imagination and Desire* (New Jersey: Rutgers University Press, 1984).

Kilmurray, Elaine and Ormond, Richard, eds., *John Singer Sargent* (London: Tate Gallery Publishing, 1998).

Krook, Dorothea, *Henry James's The Ambassadors: A Critical Study* (New York: AMS Press, 1996).

—— *The Ordeal of Consciousness* (Cambridge: Cambridge University Press, 1967).

'A Lady', *Woman: her Dignity and Sphere* (New York: The American Tract Company, 1870).

Lancaster, Bill, *The Department Store* (London: Leicester University Press, 1995).

Laver, James, *Edwardian Promenade* (London: Edward Hulton, 1958).

—— *Taste and Fashion* (London: Harrap, 1937).

Leavis, F. R., *The Great Tradition* (Harmondsworth: Penguin Books, 1974).

Levitt, Sarah, *Fashion in Photographs, 1880–1900* (London: Batsford/ National Portrait Gallery, 1991).

Linton, Eliza Lynn, *The Girl of the Period and Other Essays* (London: Richard Bentley, 1883).

Lustig, T.J., *Henry James and the Ghostly* (Cambridge: Cambridge University Press, 1994).

Maeterlinck, Maurice, *Théâtre*, I (Paris: Bibliothèque Charpentier, 1925).

McConkey, Kenneth, *Edwardian Portraits* (Woodbridge, Suffolk: The Antique Collectors' Club, 1987).

McWhirter, David, ed., *Henry James's New York Edition* (Stanford: Stanford University Press, 1995).

Marshall, Adré, *The Turn of the Mind* (London: Associated University Presses, 1998).

Matthiesson, F.O., *Henry James: the Major Phase* (New York: Oxford University Press, 1963).

'A Member of the Aristocracy', *Manners and Rules of Good Society* (London: Frederick Warne, 1892).

Moers, Ellen, *The Dandy* (London: Secker & Warburg, 1960).

Moore, George, *A Drama in Muslin* (Gerrards Cross: Colin Smythe, 1981).

Moretti, Franco, *The Way of the World* (London: Verso, 1987).

Newton, Stella Mary, *Health, Art and Reason* (London: John Murray, 1974).

Nowell-Smith, Simon *The Lesson of the Master* (Oxford: Oxford University Press 1985).

Miss Oakey, *Beauty in Dress* (New York: Harper & Bros., 1881).

Oliphant, Margaret, *Phoebe Junior* (London: Penguin Books and Virago Press, 1989).

O'Rell, Max, *Her Royal Highness Woman* (London: Chatto and Windus, 1902).

Panton, Mrs. J.E., *Within Four Walls* (London: The Gentlewoman, 1893).

Perec, Georges, *Species of Spaces and Other Pieces* (Harmondsworth: Penguin Books, 1997).

Perrot, Philippe, *Fashioning the Bourgeoisie* (Princeton: Princeton University Press, 1994).

Poirier, Richard, *The Comic Sense of Henry James* (London: Chatto & Windus, 1960).

Powers, Lyall, '*The Portrait of a Lady': Maiden, Woman and Heroine* (Boston: Twayne, 1991).

Raverat, Gwen, *Period Piece* (London: Faber & Faber, 1952).

Rawlings, Peter, ed., *Henry James: Essays on Art and Drama.* (Aldershot: Scolar Press, 1996).

Reeve, N.H., ed., *Henry James: The Shorter Fiction* (London: Macmillan, 1997).

Reynolds, Kimberley and Humble, Nicola, *Victorian Heroines* (New York: New York University Press, 1993).

Ribeiro, Aileen, *The Art of Dress* (New Haven: Yale University Press, 1995).

—— *Ingres in Fashion* (New Haven: Yale University Press, 1999).

Richards, I. A., *Principles of Literary Criticism* (London: Routledge, 1964).

Robinson, Fred Miller, *The Man in the Bowler Hat* (Chapel Hill: University of North Carolina Press, 1993).

Rolley, Katrina, *Fashion in Photographs: 1900–1920* (London: Batsford, 1992).

Rothstein, Natalie, ed., *Four Hundred Years of Fashion* (London: V. & A. Publications, 1999).

Ruskin, John, *Sesame and Lilies* [1865, 1871] (London: Collins Press, n.d.).

Sears, Sallie, *The Negative Imagination* (Ithaca: Cornell University Press, 1963)

Severa, Joan, *Dressed for the Photographer: Ordinary Americans & Fashion, 1840–1900* (Kent, Ohio: Kent State University Press, 1995).

Shelston, Alan, ed., *Washington Square and The Portrait of a Lady* (London: Macmillan Press Casebook Series, 1984).

Sherwood, Mrs John, *Manners and Social Usages* (New York: Harper & Brothers, 1884).

Sicker, Philip, *Love and the Quest for Identity* (New Jersey: Princeton University Press, 1980).

Simon, Marie, *Fashion in Art* (London: Zwemmer, 1995).

Stanzel, F. K., *A Theory of Narrative* , trans. by Charlotte Goedsche (Cambridge: Cambridge University Press, 1984).

Steele, Valerie, *Paris Fashion: A Cultural History* (New York: Oxford University Press, 1988).

Sweeney, J. L. ed., *The Painter's Eye* (Madison: University of Wisconsin Press, 1989).

Taine, Hyppolite, *Notes on England* (London: Thames and Hudson, 1970).

Tanner, Tony, *Henry James and the Art of Nonfiction* (Athens and London: University of Georgia Press, 1995).

—— *Henry James: the Writer and his Work* (Amherst: University of Massachusets Press, 1985).

Tintner, Adeline, *Henry James and the Lust of the Eyes* (Baton Rouge: Louisiana State University Press, 1993).

—— *The Museum World of Henry James* (Ann Arbor, Michigan: UMI Research Press, 1986).

Trilling, Lionel, *The Liberal Imagination* (New York: Garden City, 1950).

Tuthill, Louisa, *The Young Lady's Home* (Philadelphia: Lindsay & Blakiston, 1848).

Veblen, Thorstein, *The Theory of the Leisure Class* (Harmondsworth: Penguin Books, 1967).

Veeder, William, *Henry James: the Lessons of the Master* (Chicago: University of Chicago Press, 1975).

Wagenknecht, Edward, *Eve and Henry James* (Oklahoma: Oklahoma University Press, 1978).

Walker, P. A., ed., *Henry James on Culture* (Lincoln: University of Nebraska Press, 1999).

Ward, J.A., *The Imagination of Disaster: Evil in the Fiction of Henry James* (Lincoln: University of Nebraska Press, 1961).

Ward, Mrs Humphry, *Marcella* (London: Virago Press, 1984).

—— *Robert Ellesmere* (Oxford: Oxford University Press, 1987).

Weber, Eugen, *France, Fin de Siècle* (Cambridge, Mass: Belknap Press, 1986).

West, Rebecca, *Henry James* (London: Nisbet & Co., 1916).

Wharton, Edith, *A Backward Glance* (London: Century, 1987).

—— *The House of Mirth* (Harmondsworth: Penguin Books, 1985).

White, Charles I., *Mission and Duties of Young Women*: translated from the French of Charles Sainte-Foi (Baltimore: Kelly, Hedian & Piet, 1860).

Wiesenfarth, Joseph, *Gothic Manners and the Classic English Novel* (Madison: Wisconsin University Press, 1988).

Wilson, R.B.J., *Henry James's Ultimate Narrative* (St. Lucia, Australia: University of Queensland Press, 1981).

Winner, Viola Hopkins, *Henry James and the Visual Arts* (Charlottesville: University Press of Virginia, 1970).

Woolf, Judith, *Henry James: The Major Novels* (Cambridge: Cambridge University Press, 1991).

Yeazell, Ruth Bernard, ed., *Henry James: A Collection of Critical Essays* (New Jersey: Prentice Hall, 1994).

Index

Shopgirls, 106
Shopping, 120, 121, 122
  Americaness of, 121
  recreational, 27
  Rucks as symbolic of, 22
Shoulders, naked, 133–4
Sicker, Philip, 93
Sidgwick, Henry, 7
Silence, 39
Silk, 162
  black, 22, 23
Sinden, Topsy, 149
'Sir Edmund Orme', *see under* James, Henry
Small Boy and Others, A, see under James, Henry
Snobbery, 16, 25, 54, 70, 108
Sobriety, 23
Social manners, 32
Social reform, 100
Spectatorship, 90
'Spoils of Poynton, The', *see under* James, Henry
Stanzel, F.K., *Theory of Narrative*, 125
Stern, Madame, portrait as goddess Diana, 97
'Story of a Masterpiece, The', *see under* James, Henry
'Story of a Year, The', *see under* James, Henry

Taine, Hyppolite, 45
Tanner, Tony, 71, 74, 83
Taste, 35, 153
Temple, Minny, 47, 85, 86
Thackeray, William, and the 'buttons' incident, 3
Tiaras, 157
Tintner, Adeline, 2, 47, 51, 82, 153
Tissot James, 9, 39, 45, 63
  'The Deck of H.M.S. Calcutta', 17
  portrait of Miss Lloyd, 17
Tournure, 17, 20
  dual meaning of, 20
'Travelling Companions, The', *see under* James, Henry
Trilling Lionel, 19, 105, 111, 112–13
Trollope, Anthony, 183

Turn of the Screw, The, see under James, Henry
Tuthill, Louisa, *The Young Lady's Home*, 15, 33; *see also* advice manuals
'Two Faces, The', *see under* James, Henry

Underwear, 132
Undress, 117, 138, 139

van Slyck, Phyllis, 144
Veblen, Thorstein, 15, 55
Veils, veiling, 88, 103, 173
Velásquez, Diego, portraiture, 9
Velvet, 55
  band, 122, 123, 125, 127
  black, 56
  use of in *The Portrait of a Lady*, 54
'Velvet Glove, The', *see under* James, Henry
Vestignomie (Balzac's theory of dress), 21, 41, 42, 50, 55, 92, 94, 103
Vogel, Daniel, 142
Vulgarity, 16, 17, 25, 32, 135, 147
  avoidance of, 31
  nouveau riche, 32
Vulnerability, 76

Wagenknecht, Edward, 105
Walpole, Hugh, 7–8
Ward, Mrs Humphry
  Marcella, 101, 102
  Robert Elsmere, 101, 102
Warwick, Countess of, 102
Washington Square, see under James, Henry
Watts, G. F., portrait of Mrs Percy Wyndham, 63
Wealth, social markers of, 43
Weatherproofing, 60
Wells, H. G., 7, 96
West, Rebecca, 100
Wharton, Edith, 7
  A Backward Glance, 8
  The Age of Innocence, 30
  The House of Mirth, 75
What Maisie Knew, see under James, Henry